CALL ME
MADAME ALICE

K.W. GARLICK

Call Me Madame Alice
by
K.W. Garlick

First Stillwater River Publications Edition

ISBN-10: 0-997-87786-3
ISBN-13: 978-0-997-87786-1

Library of Congress Control Number: 2016957358

1 2 3 4 5 6 7 8 9 10
Written by K.W. Garlick
Published by Stillwater River Publications, Glocester, RI, USA.

Although inspired by some actual individuals and events, this is a work of fiction. The views and opinions expressed in this book are solely those of the author and do not necessarily reflect the views and opinions of the publisher.

DEDICATION

To my wife JoAnne

and my two sons Shelby and Travis

ACKNOWLEDGEMENTS

I would like to thank the following friends for their support and encouragement. Joe Bains, Jerry Cutter, Lany Cutter, Lorie Brown, Gene Rinker, Shelby Garlick, Travis Garlick, Nick Howard, Allison Dixon, and David Palmer

Sarah

AUGUST, 1918

It was no longer theory. It had become fact – it was suddenly crystal clear. Sarah Dianne Shepard was now confident that she had finally solved the mystery.

She had just finished reading the Tarot cards for the Diamond twins. They had surprised her with their unannounced visit. She had heard their girlish laughter and squealy voices as they capered up her walkway and on to her front porch. She hadn't been quick enough to hide from their prying eyes as they peered through her front door like two children in a game of hide and seek. Regina and RoAnne Diamond were the last patrons Sarah wanted to see on this day.

Her spirit had been shallow and without energy all day and Sarah knew the tragedy lurking in her past was once again tugging at her life force as it had for the last six years. Sarah struggled daily to rediscover her passion for life again. It had been like a fragile plant growing on a rocky hillside, getting too little sunlight and too little nourishment but struggling to survive. And now there was a bud with the promise of a blossom. Sarah had begun to peel away the layers of sadness and loneliness that the demise of that doomed ship had brought to her life. Over 1,500 souls were taken suddenly to an early and watery grave in that catastrophe, and though she was not a passenger on that fated voyage it had nevertheless reached out across the leagues and the years and tried to include her as another one of its victims. But through some miracle or turn of luck, or perhaps simply through her own simple inner mettle, she had begun to rekindle her life force. It had given Sarah hope, and hope can heal.

But today there had been a step back and Sarah's spirit was low. It had nudged her in the morning and raised her from a peaceful slumber. It was as if she was being punished for yesterday's cheerfulness. *You wake me from a restful night for this,* she challenged the unseen bearer of this dark mood. *Haven't I already suffered long enough? Go back to your dark world, send me your opposite sister, the one that stands in the mirror and smiles at me, the friend that offers me confidence and optimism.*

"Madame Alice, please read our cards again," one of the twins shouted through the door. Sarah could not tell them apart. This was their third visit and their previous callings had found her in this same gloomy temperament. How was that so? She slid the deadbolt back and opened her door to her naïve clients.

"Please come in, young ladies, you certainly are persistent in your efforts to secure the outcome you want. The cards can only tell us so much." She was met with the twins' nervous laughter, the girls in their innocence and enthusiasm not registering her dark mood. Her brow furrowed blackly and a glint of steel crept into her voice. "Twice now I have read them and each time they have foretold the same thing. You will have quite ordinary lives. Why is that so hard for you to accept?"

"You may even come to see it as a blessing," she finished enigmatically.

The twins seemed stunned with Madame Alice's frankness. But their girlish verve could not keep them discomposed for long. "Just one more time!" they pleaded like children who could not get enough rides on their father's shoulders Except they were not children. The Diamond twins were born under the sign of Aries and had turned twenty-one this past April. They were not the most attractive young women, their faces were round with protruding eyes, broad noses and pouting lips. Their complexion was olive, and their long dark brown hair was pulled back with barrettes.

Madame Alice had wondered why the twins did not use makeup. It could only help.

Perhaps it was this homely keenness that softened her. "Of course, why not?" she said, and the twins jumped with glee and hugged each other like teenage girls that had just been asked to the high school dance.

"Let's have a seat," Madame Alice offered, and they settled into the table that was just a few steps away, round and unadorned, where the cards already lay wrapped in their protective swatch of silk, the better to guard them against physic disturbances. The reading mimicked the previous ones: she chose the Celtic Cross layout, a simple spread, she thought, for simple girls. For the Court Card – the card that represents the questioner, if only perfunctorily – she chose the Page of Pentacles. It suited their dark hair and dark complexions, their naïve persistence.

After a few peremptory shuffles she had the twins both cut the deck into three piles, their hands bunched together as if they were playing with a Ouija board. This was not strictly necessary, but the girls had insisted upon it from the outset. As they placed the cards into separate piles she intoned the words of command that began every reading: "Now you must think very hard about an important question you desire to be answered."

This always set the girls to giggling once more; they were no doubt wondering about their future husbands, how many children they would have, the cut of their wedding dresses. Madame Alice smiled indulgently; frivolous things certainly, but not without their own value.

3

And then the reading proceeded much as it had before. The Cover Card was the Ace of Cups, a powerful card that represented the abundance of beauty and pleasure, joy and love, that was the girls' present environment. The Cross Card – another Cup, the Five – showed that the only thing working against them was their childish desire for *everything* to be completely ideal. Madame Alice cautioned them against letting the perfect become the enemy of the good. The Nine of Cups was Beneath them and the Six of Cups Behind, representing the comforting surroundings they had enjoyed throughout their lives and the idyllic childhood they had experienced that was just beginning to wan. The reading thus far showed only that one suit, the Cups that stand for emotional and financial fulfillment, and their abundance only reinforced the happy (if rather dull) future the twins had in store. As she turned the Crown Card, which gave a glimpse of their lives in the long term, she was not surprised to find the Ten of Cups: a young couple with their arms around each other, two children dancing with glee, a bright rainbow arcing over the whole joyful scene. It foretold of romance and fertility, marriage and children, lasting happiness, contentment, love. It provided instant comfort to the twins and they giggled and squeezed each other's hands; apparently it had been an issue of concern for them. Again their lives were to be quite common: boring but satisfying, plagued only by those fleeting annoyances that are forgotten quickly

All Tarot decks contain seventy-eight cards; fifty-six make up the Minor Arcana; ancient but of less import, they resemble regular playing cards but instead of hearts, clubs, spades and diamonds their suits are composed of cups, swords, wands and pentacles. There is also an extra court card – the page – and the knight replaces the jack. The twenty-two cards that remain are called the Major Arcana, and draw their mysterious symbolism from a variety of sources: The Zodiac, the Kabbalah, the occult knowledge of the ancient Egyptians. Their presence in a reading carries more weight than the Minor Arcana; an abundance of them almost guarantees whatever future they point to will almost certainly come to pass.

Only ten cards are used for the spread Madame Alice had chosen for the twins, the Celtic Cross. The first six paint a broad picture of the present, the sixth card itself a culmination of the previous five that forms the shadowy outline of things to come.

As Madame Alice was about to place this card down her heart stopped. It was happening again. She was stunned and could not let go of the card. This was the third time in a row that it had revealed itself in the sixth position. It was The Devil. It spoke of terrible suffering, bondage of the soul, deceit, uncertainty, torture, death. Her hand suddenly felt cold and lifeless, as if it belonged in a coffin, and she sat there frozen in fear, her eyes locked with the eyes of the bearded figure where it perched on its shaggy goat's legs, its black wings splayed, its horns pointed wickedly downward, in its hand a chain that snaked through an iron ring and terminated around the necks of two naked figures, a man and a woman.

"Are you all right Madame Alice? You look like you have seen a ghost, you do not look well. Is there something bad in the cards?" The twins nervously asked.

"I am all right," The card still hovered in her hand over the table. She did not want to put it down, did not want to continue the reading. This was no longer the future of the twins in front of her that was being divined. This was something much more sinister, and it had happened before. As if some invading will had dashed aside her focus on the girls and went straight for her own destiny like a terrier after a rat. She did not want to see, did not want to know, but as she watched her hand, unbidden, placed the card in its position and returned to the deck for the next.

The last four cards of the Celtic Cross form a staff situated to the right of the first five, which form a cross. The next in the spread, the seventh of ten, reveals the deepest, darkest fears of the Querent. She watched her hand turn the card. It was, as it had been before, the Fool, but upside down, *reversed,* as the nomenclature had it. This shifted the meaning to the polar opposite of what it would be had the card been in its upright position. Normally the youthful lad, with his traveling stick and his little dog nipping at his heels, represented not folly and foolishness but birth and rebirth, a new journey, a clean slate, and a willingness to meet new challenges. Reversed, the card was far more calamitous; it warned of indiscretion and thoughtless action, of faulty choices and incorrect assumptions that could lead one into a world of trouble. Or worse. She knew deep down that this is what she feared the most: to be wrong. To dredge up old feelings and uncover old secrets that were nothing more than smoke, and in the process destroy not only the life she had built – no, rebuilt – for herself, but for all those who were touched by the long tentacles of past tragedies.

And so it played out as it had before, her hand laying cards and returning to the deck as if controlled by another. The eighth card again The Hermit, also reversed, revealing what those around her thought, that she was possessed of a great immaturity, an inability to let the past lie. And here again, the ninth card, Justice, the figure with its regal crown and long, upright sword; what she longed for most in the world. More than ease and comfort. Until finally the tenth and final card, the ultimate portent of the future. And once more that terrible card, the looming Tower struck by a jagged bolt of lightning, its apex aflame, the fiery bodies falling to earth. Here the augury was more than clear: Catastrophe. Conflict. The overthrowing of old ways of life. Earthquakes and storms and shipwrecks.

Why had these ominous cards surfaced three readings in succession, always in the same order, always in the same position? The Devil did not belong in this interpretation of these cards. Three readings in a row and each time she had told Regina and RoAnne that their lives were to be of a common existence, the initial layout speaking only of a satisfying if mundane existence, only to have those last four cards negate the whole analysis. It was if the cards had foretold of the twin's unexceptional lives, then canted wildly and spoke of some other destiny, one more fraught with consequence, as if they would discover the Fountain of Youth or stumble on to the location of the Holy Grail. Only worse. It made no sense. It was obvious the card was not meant for them. Madame Alice collected all the cards and returned them to the deck, trying hard to conceal the quiver in her hands and arms.

"Young ladies we are finished," she said. "As I have said before, you will both have quite conventional lives; that is not all that disappointing, I can assure you of that." They seemed a little frustrated but accepting as she walked them to the door and wished them well.

She returned to the table and stared at the deck of cards again, hoping for some insight, and knowing but not fully accepting that the final cards were meant for her all along, and what's more – that they were somehow connected to the *Titanic* and the tragedy it had brought into her life. Madame Alice saw herself on a path that led nowhere, but every path has a destination. The *Titanic*, the Tower, and the Diamond twins; where was the common thread?

She began to think about the twins and how remarkable their likeness was. She had looked for the subtlest differences in them, but could find none. Twins can easily trick the unsuspecting, but if they chose so they could also deceive for the purpose of a more malicious deed. Sarah wondered how that thought had surfaced, and then there was that shocking moment of instant clarity. It all fell into place. My God, they had deliberately sunk the *Titanic!* No not the *Titanic*, but another vessel. A ship so similar as to be indistinguishable. A twin. The bastards!

* * *

She sat there for a long time, trying to fathom the impact of her revelation. She finally raised herself from her chair and ventured into the kitchen. Her insides turned as she prepared herself an early evening tea with honey. Typically, there would have been a meal with her tea, but now she had no appetite. Her disturbing moment of transparency had destroyed that.

Taking her delicate china cup in her hands, no longer shaking now, she settled into her favorite rocker on the rear deck of her little cottage in Portsmouth, Rhode Island. It faced west and out over Narragansett Bay and except for overcast days, the view from her rocker was always relaxing and welcomed. Tonight it was just the thing she would need. The remnants of a stunning August sunset were giving way to twilight, and sailboats with their spinnakers filled by a southerly summer wind were being coaxed along on a sea of brilliant oranges, pinks and yellows. The thought of boats once more brought her back to the *Titanic* and the act of devious trickery involved in its sinking. It was the epiphany that Sarah had sought for so long.

She began to reflect on how she had finally arrived at this critical point. It had taken six long years to put all the pieces together. Her inquiry into the tragedy of the *Titanic* had been passionate, methodical – and had become her obsession. She was also driven by her developing suspicion that something very malevolent was buried within her conclusion, something very dark and disturbing. The more Sarah examined the disaster the more certain she became that it was not the series of tragic events as told by company officials, government authorities, or reported by journalists. Like Regina and RoAnne Diamond switching classrooms or hoodwinking the babysitter, they had deceived everyone – and now Sarah had finally seen through their deception.   She knew she would have to examine it even more deeply. There had to have been a cover-up of huge proportions, and yet no one had suspected a thing. How far the cover up reached was anyone's guess, but it had to be extensive. Sarah had advanced her theories as to why and who might be involved in the appalling deed and ensuing cover-up, but they would only be theories until she could find validation from an insider, someone who shared the dark secret.

That someone, she was sure, would be Jacob Sweeney.

It was her unique gift that told Sarah he would be the only one that would break away from that dark inner circle and confirm what she knew to be the truth. Sarah had the ability to envision what others could only imagine and to sense what few could distinguish. She was clairvoyant. She had seen Jacob in many of the newspaper and magazine photos she had collected. He was always removed from the subject of the picture, hovering on the fringe, a reluctant participant, but always there. A short, stocky man with thick bushy eyebrows, he was completely bald, lending to his countenance a lopsided quality: more hair on his face than on his head. His dress was plain, more like the common man, always in his open-collared shirt, woolen jacket, and baggy pants. It was all quality attire, but it seemed out of place with all those around him in their fine, tailored three-piece suits.

His name had been mentioned in the hearings and he was brought in to testify at these same hearings in the United States and in Great Britain. She had read his testimony; it had all seemed very rehearsed. His answers were short, mechanical, and never very revealing. It was obvious to her that his answers were meant to be guarded. Sarah had wondered why he had never been cross-examined. He should have been. But again they had all been fooled, no need to grill the man if he had nothing to hide. Sarah's conclusion and suspicions had told her that this deceiving inner circle that must be using Jacob Sweeney as a tool had much to hide, and her gift kept pushing her towards him. He was indeed the man that would have the answers that Sarah desperately sought.

Sarah knew that Jacob lived in Belfast, but she would need to ask her father for his assistance in locating him further. Her father had moved his family to the United States in the 1890s, but still had strong political and economic connections in England and Ireland. Her older brother, Frederick Jr., still lived in England. Sarah had shared a great deal of her investigation with her brother, and he was also acutely aware of her special gift. In the past he had experienced its reach first hand and offered to help his sister. With this startling new insight, she would have to enlist his help once again. She knew they were treading on very dangerous ground and would need to be cautious.

She looked again out over the bay, feeling both afraid of this new knowledge and empowered by it. The sun was going down and the ships had all but disappeared. She rocked silently, her insides all turmoil, as the waning sun turned the bay into a sparkling black mirror.

Delilah

OCTOBER, 1938

Any sense of family I had was gone, destroyed by wind and water. How this terrible tragedy was brought upon us is well documented. We have seen all the pictures, viewed all the statistics, read all the articles, and learned where the mistakes were made. But what no one offers is the why; why are these natural disasters allowed to happen? Who creates them? They leave only death and debris in their wake, and the victims that are left to put their lives back together. Where is our God that is supposed to protect us? Why has He forsaken us?

I have searched every day for these answers, but I know there are none. It is all part of some larger, divine plan. That's supposed to comfort us.

10

What is not documented, however, are the hundreds of heartbreaking accounts that defined the real human suffering of that tragic event. My story is just one of those hundreds. It is a narrative of a very close and very loving family suddenly ripped apart and left to live in a world of strange and frightening events. My mother says it is a living hell. My mother is right.

* * *

My name is Delilah Ann Miller. I am seventeen and the oldest of four siblings. My father said I entered the world with thick, wavy dark hair and that I immediately cast a spell over him. He said he had experienced all the emotions that come with the birth of one's first child. In the beginning there was much anticipation and excitement. Then there was the physical and emotional exhaustion.

My father had vowed that he would be there during the delivery. It was only because he knew the doctor that he was allowed in. He was good friends with the doctor's son; in fact, they had gone through the Naval Academy together and later attended each other's weddings as the best man.

My mother had also insisted that my father be there. She cared little about contemporary medical wisdom, which held that the presence of any man save the doctor would be such a breach of decorum as to give the delivering woman cause for hysterics. But how could it possibly be anything but calming for her to have my father there by her side?

There were moments towards the end of the delivery when complications arose. My father was asked to leave the room. These complications turned out to be minor and insignificant, but in that moment of time that brief reflection on the potential and sudden loss of his beautiful bride and their first child was a numbing terror to my young father. But things turned out well in the end, and he was allowed to return to the delivery room in time to hold my mother's hand and witness my arrival. Tears streamed down his face. He was immediately filled with overwhelming relief and joy. He said it was

11

a day that made him feel as strong and invincible as Samson. On that day, as he has told me a thousand times since, I became his little Delilah. He had the Biblical story a little mixed up, but since my mother loved both the name and the emotional connection my father had attached to it, Delilah it stayed.

The strange and frightening events that have come to plague me to the core began not long after that terrible storm in September. It was about eighteen months after we had moved into our new home in Jamestown, Rhode Island. My father, a career naval officer, had been transferred to his new assignment at the Naval War College in Newport, Rhode Island. There was uneasy news coming out of Europe. A tyrant in Germany was threatening the peace and stability in Eastern Europe and our country was beginning to prepare for what many thought was inevitable, though the majority of people were opposed to any kind of American involvement. It had only been a brief twenty years since the end of The Great War. The country had suffered. It was supposed to be the war to end all wars. But things were in play and the Navy was moving personnel and ships.

The Navy had offered military housing in the Newport area, but my father had opted for a beautiful Victorian on the Beavertail section of Jamestown, Rhode Island. A rugged ferry provided regular, dependable service to the island, and there was abundant access to the many launches that the Navy maintained at the base. The Navy also provided compensation to those officers who opted out of military housing, and so my father, Captain Jeffrey W. Miller, took me, my mother Katherine, my sister Stephanie, my fraternal twin brothers Corey and Thomas, and Claudia, a trusted and longtime servant, and moved us to the shoreline. My father called the new house our "painted lady." It was the spring of 1937.

* * *

The movers were doing their thing under the scrutiny of my mother. My father took me by the arm and said we should take a brief walk around our new home and yard. We were bundled up in our heavy woolen P-coats, as the bay waters that surrounded our property still held onto winter's chill. We stood back from the front door so that we could take in all of the house's grandeur; it was visual and welcoming. I knew my father was pleased with our lucky find.

"You know Delilah," he mused, "your mother and I had looked at several houses in Newport, and some others here on Jamestown, but when I saw this place I knew immediately this would be our home. Your mother felt about the same way. Shall I give you a little background on Victorian architecture and how it is applied here?"

"Do I have a choice?"

"Not at all," he said with a grin.

My father began his tour. "Delilah," he said, "understand that the Victorians were not the most practical in their house designs. But what they lacked in practicality, they more than compensated for in presentation. Because back then it was all about the look, the pizzazz." He lifted his arms in an expansive gesture. "Take a good look at this home. This is pure Victorian. It's all about the detail. The first floor exterior is all yellow clapboard. The second floor exterior is all red-painted cedar shingles. Look at the broad white trim that separates the two floors..."

He stopped briefly. "You should be taking notes," he joked.

"I am my father's daughter; I don't need to take notes." My father laughed.

He continued: "You see that green stripe that surrounds the second floor of the house? If you take a closer look, you'll see that it is actually made up of three very small rows of pointed shingles," and he pointed up at the house with the index finger on the end of his long arm. With his cap and P-coat on he could have been a statue of a midshipmen pointing the way through a dense fog.

"That is a lot of work for such an intricate detail! The foundation lattice that surrounds the house is also painted this same color green. All the white trim and gingerbread is impressive. This is pure glitz! This must have been quite a task to construct, and even more of an ordeal to maintain the paint over the years. But labor was cheap back then," he said, casting an eye at the movers.

I felt like I was on a field trip for a class titled "Victorian and Late Nineteenth Century American Architecture." I wanted to tell my father that it was time for the outdoor lecture to end. I was sixteen and a junior in high school – Victorian structural design was not a priority. But I knew he was truly enamored of the architecture of our new home and that he felt it was his obligation to pass these insights on to his daughter. But my father was right. It was a beautiful home.

"Your mother and I will have to see what it will take to make this our permanent home. It is hard to say what the Navy has in store for us, but I would love to put down some roots here." He turned and looked out over the bay. "I suppose we'll see," he said.

The interior of the house was just as striking. There were three large bedrooms upstairs with a large common bath. Each bedroom had its own hand sink with running water. There was also a large master bedroom with its own powder room. The previous owner had gone to great lengths to install the most up-to-date plumbing, electrical wiring and fixtures. The first floor had an additional bedroom, a bathroom, and a large living room with broad windows that faced south. These windows gave us a panoramic view of the opening to Narragansett Bay, and no doubt would offer many sunlit days, even in the throes of winter. There was also a large kitchen with an adjacent pantry, a formal dining room, a study that would soon be inventoried with numerous books and reference materials. Both of my parents were avid readers and strongly believed that their children should have access to as much literature and resources as were available.

There was also a small office that my father quickly settled into. The dining room and living room had large Tiffany chandeliers. All the door and window trim were fluted oak with beautiful rosettes. Large double doors offered entrance to our home. They were also made of solid oak and were ornately hand crafted. Each door had a clear glass window that was outlined with red, yellow and green stained glass, the same color scheme as the exterior of the house. There was a small receiving area just inside these doors. A wide staircase with ornate maple newel posts and balusters led to the second floor. There was a landing at midpoint were my mother tried to keep fresh flowers on a small end table. The upper sash on all the windows in the house were trimmed with the same colored stained glass inserts as the front door. It looked so beautiful at night, with the lights on; our house, warm and inviting.

We would never have suspected that this gentle and stately home would be tormented by bizarre and frightening events that would have a deeply disturbing impact on our family. They began not long after tragedy had struck our home on that September morning and they have become an unpredictable and terrifying part of our daily existence. They did not, however, start that way.

That first episode occurred in our carriage house. The carriage house is an ornate building located about 150 feet down the hill from our home and was painted the same soft yellow as the house. It had recently been rebuilt. It also had abundant white trim and gingerbread with matching green lattices, four stalls, two holding pens, and storage rooms for livestock supplies. Time had moved on and the gasoline engine had long since replaced the need for horse power. The carriage house was no longer serving its original purpose, but it had been well maintained and was vital to the character of our property. I did, however, keep my ten-year-old chestnut mare Grace there. Grace was such a simple pleasure to ride here in Jamestown. The weathered and empty trails that snake throughout our neighborhood were our hideaway all that spring.

I had been there one early spring afternoon, tending to Grace, feeding and grooming her – or, as my mother would say, doing her "feeds and needs." I thought I saw a shadow move quickly past me and then out the barn doors. I immediately sensed a small vibration under my feet. Maybe it was something Grace was doing. But Grace was just standing there, ears back, content with the brushing I was giving her. The vibration grew in intensity and the harness and tackle on the stall post began to shake. Then it suddenly stopped. I looked around to find the source of the vibration. Grace's ears had cocked forward; something had alerted her too. But there was nothing to indicate where the vibration had come from and nothing remained of the shadow. The weather was perfect. I waited a bit and then moved on. I thought very little of it at the time.

The carriage house also has a special room for me: a room in the loft that ran the entire length of the building. It was a wide open area with broad double-hung windows on each end. One window faced east, out to the mouth of Narragansett Bay and Rhode Island Sound. The other window faced our house. The loft also has a ladder that led to the middle of the roof peak, where a decorative cupola had been installed over a large roof vent. Sometimes on hot days we would open the vent and it would pull in the cool summer breezes from all corners of the barn.

The loft became my little sanctuary. I loved the smells there: hay and horse and oiled leather tack. There was a small staircase to the left of the barn door with a landing at midpoint that led up to the loft. Most summer days I would open the old double-hung windows on either end. They were stiff and did not move up and down easily, probably from the lack of use and fifty years' worth of paint layers, but there was always a breeze. My mother and father put in some secondhand furniture along with a comfortable full-size bed. I also gave it my personal touch with soft fluffy pink curtains, family pictures, and secondhand paintings. The abundant daisies, black-eyed Susans, and daffodils that grew all around our home always seemed to find their way into my special room, whether in a vase or a Mason jar.

The previous owners had also left an old vanity in the loft. It was still in very good condition and its ornate mirror swiveled on shiny brass dials. I would spend countless hours sitting in front of the vanity trying to tame my dark curls. I always wished I was prettier. I thought I was very plain and much too tall. My mother was always pointing out that I was slouching. I can remember being in church or out shopping with her and inevitably there would be the cries of "Delilah please stand tall!" or "Delilah! Straighten yourself! Be proud of the height that you got from your father. Besides, five-foot-eight is not that distracting for a young lady as beautiful as you." She meant

16

well, but I was never quite able to believe these words. My mother and grandparents tell me I have my father's looks, for better or worse, and his height and mannerisms too, although I don't think I will ever be as organized as he is, nor do I wish to be. It borders on obsessive. He is a committed Navy man and he is so striking in his uniform. I love the way the junior officers and enlisted men salute him whenever we visit the Naval base. I know I will always be his special little girl.

Sometimes, on warm summer evenings, I would spend the night up in the loft. The musty barn smell of the carriage house would lull me to sleep.

I also kept my diary in this room. It was a gift, from my Aunt Meg, and I had no trouble finding things to write about. It was the part of the day that I looked forward to most. I could retreat into my own little world and reflect on the day. I often wrote about my parents, their loving nature and occasional gentle chidings. I do not always agree with them, but I believe that they always have my best interest at heart.

I also wrote about my younger sister, Stephanie. Stephanie is fourteen and the redhead of the family. Every family of good English and Irish heritage seems to have one. She has an abundance of freckles to accent her blushing cheeks and is thin and wiry, all arms and legs; my father calls her his "little spider." Stephanie is also the artist of the family, and it puzzles my mother and father, as there seems to be no artistic creativity anywhere in their ancestry. She sometimes paints with oils, but her real enjoyment is the simple craft of pencil and paper. She can pick up her pad and an assortment of pencils and be off in search of her next rendition. She has a collection of scenes from all over the island. Sometimes she will leave her most recent portfolio on the kitchen table for our review, as she is not shy about sharing them with her family. Often we would sit at the table and admire my sister's work. My mother would call up to Steph's room and ask her to come down.

"It's time to talk about these wonderful sketches," she would say, which meant it was time to reinforce her efforts to get my sister to start working with her colors. Stephanie knew why she was being called to the kitchen. It had happened before.

"Oh my heavens!" my mother would exclaim. "Steph, these drawings are wonderful! But I don't think you do these beautiful scenes the integrity they deserve. You should bring them to life with color!"

"I like them just the way they are, Mother. Why don't you like them?"

"Sweetheart, I never said that I didn't like them! They are absolutely beautiful! I just wonder what a little color would do to the depth of your sketches. Learning how to mix your oils is an art, too."

But Steph loved the simplicity of raw graphite and blank white paper. Maybe when she was older she would tackle the concept of color, but for now she saw no need to complicate her art.

I especially loved to write about my delightful fraternal twin brothers. I can remember so vividly the day my mother and father came home from the hospital with them. We were still living in Philadelphia and I was in the fourth grade at the Carver Elementary School. Corey had a thick head of platinum blond hair and Thomas was as bald as a peach, but they both had the bluest blueberry eyes that I had ever seen. I decided that very day that educating Corey and Thomas James – T.J. as we all liked to call him – would become my mission in life. I would teach my little brothers about horses, baseball, girls, protect them from the hard lessons, but most of all just shower them with love and kisses. My sister Stephanie adored her little brothers too, but I don't think she had the mothering instinct that I seemed to possess.

My senses were abruptly alive, the skin on my arms and at the back of my neck instinctively prickled with the stab of a thousand tiny needles. I was lying on my bed in the loft and I was suddenly aware that I was no longer alone, although my eyes told me to discount that perception. I could not, there was something or someone pressing in on me, a familiar feeling or intuition, like walking into my living room in the dark of night and knowing where my father's big leather recliner was. I did not need to see it to avoid it. I simply knew it was there.

The room began to vibrate ever so slightly. Three murky shadows suddenly emerged from the wall and floated before me. They appeared to struggle against their two-dimensional constraints, seeking the freedom of an earthly, three-dimensional world. The vibrations suddenly diminished and the dark shadows vanished as quickly as they had appeared. My insides turned and my heart raced with this foreign experience. It was some weeks after the terrible events of that day in September. I tried to tell myself that it was a case of frayed nerves, that I was still dealing with this new reality. It worked for a while. But only a while.

Then again in my bedroom, a few days later, the same vibration, the same three shadows, this time stationary on the far wall. But now there was also a humming sound and then, as before, the shadows quickly vanished and the shaking abruptly stopped. I was frozen with fear. I needed to share these episodes with my father. He would probably have a simple explanation. At least I hoped he would.

I found him in his office seated at his big desk, busy with paperwork, probably Navy related. He was always so organized and obsessed with detail. "A place for everything and everything in its place," or "The devil is in the details." Good grief, how many times had I heard those expressions?

It was midday and his office was filled with bright sunlight. I waited at the door. Normally I would have respected his privacy, but today I needed answers. He must have sensed this, because he motioned me in right away. I knew I would have to wait while he collected all his paperwork, stored it in the right folder, and then placed it correctly in the filing cabinet. It was almost painful to watch, he went about it so slowly and methodically. He made some quick notations on a small pad, mumbled something to himself, and looked up at me.

"What's on your mind?" His voice was warm but concerned. "You look like you have seen a ghost and have the weight of the world on your shoulders. I know my daughter well enough to know when something is bothering her."

19

"I think I have seen a ghost or two," I began hesitantly, and told my father about the episodes. I described the troubling vibrations and the haunting shadows and humming noise and where they had occurred. He listened to me intently, a serious expression on his face. He seemed a little mystified, but if he had any explanation he did not offer it. In the end he dismissed them, but not harshly.

"I am not sure what they are all about, Delilah. I wouldn't worry about them. If it happens again we will talk more then, but I don't think it will." I hoped he was right.

My optimism in my father's confidence was ruined several weeks later on a Saturday night. He was in the living room and I was at the kitchen table with T.J., educating him on the intricacies of Chinese checkers, when the vibrations began. Even T.J. sensed them. He stopped and looked at me, seeking an explanation, and then a single shadow appeared on the wall. It moved along towards us and then, as before, it was over in a moment – vanished, with no trace of its origin. Suddenly the hair on T.J.'s head moved as if by a puff of wind. His eyes widened in terror and he trembled in fear.

"Daddy!" I screamed and immediately clutched T.J. in my arms and ran to my father's side in the living room. He was sitting in his big leather recliner reading and was startled by my scream. He focused intently on me as I stumbled over my words, trying to explain what had just happened. T.J. could only nod and tremble with a child's fear.

"Let's have a look," he said calmly.

"Daddy, please, don't go in the kitchen," I begged. "Something is in there. It touched T.J."

"Oh, I'm sure it was nothing. Maybe a breeze through the window. More than it really is," he said. It was one of my father's favorite expressions.

We walked back into the kitchen and the stillness of the empty room was all that greeted us.

"Oh Daddy, I'm sure there was something here. It wasn't just a breeze, there was shaking and an unnatural shadow!"

"Honestly, I think you may have been a little sleepy. You were up early today and you had a very active day." My mother had

had an especially chaotic day, she had experienced some early morning nightmares and her screaming had dragged us all out of a very deep sleep. The rest of the day was spent dealing with my mother drifting between nightmares and restless naps.

"No, no, no, Daddy," I pleaded.

"Delilah, please, look around the room," my father said. "What am I supposed to see? What do you see? What should I do? More than it really is," he said again. He leaned over and whispered in my ear. "You're also beginning to scare T.J. even more." Then he straightened up and announced it was time to go to bed. "I will put T.J. down. You should hit the sack too. We were all up early this morning and it's been a trying day. Come on now, Delilah. Lead the way. Say goodnight to your mother on your way. Goodnight, sweetheart."

I walked up the stairs and stopped at my mother's room. Her door was open and I looked in. The room was dimly lit by a small nightlight next to her bed and I could only see the outline of her frail body under the linen. She was sleeping, probably sedated, and her breathing was slow and shallow. She had moved herself out of my father's room not long after the tragic events and had settled into her own separate room. She was spending more and more time there. My father was deeply hurt when she left his bed; he said that my mother now shared a room with a tormented soul.

It was sad to see what my mother had become. She had been such a beautiful and vibrant woman. She and my father had a storybook romance, the kind that seemed to exist only in fairy tales and I had heard them speak of it many times over the years.

* * *

They had met in Philadelphia, Pennsylvania. My dad had graduated from the Naval Academy in Annapolis a year earlier and had been assigned to the Naval shipyard in Philadelphia. My father's good friend Stan Morrison, another ensign from the academy, had been pestering him for several weeks about attending the Devon

Horse Show in the Bryn Mawr Township. It was one of several affluent towns along what they called the Main Line, a Pennsylvania railroad line that ran from Philadelphia northwest out to Villanova. The Devon Horse Show was the largest outdoor horse show in America. Stan had been several times in his youth and ridden in some of the equestrian events. It was not far from his home in Trenton, New Jersey, and had become a regular family outing. Stan had only fond memories.

The show added a county fair to the event in 1914 and it had now expanded to a weekend event. The organizers of the affair had decided to donate a portion of the proceeds to the Bryn Mawr Hospital, which helped to bring the community together for a worthy cause. My father was not an admirer of horse flesh but had given into Stan's incessant pleadings to go to this equestrian spectacle.

The two young ensigns in their dress whites did their best to mingle with society. Charles Hires, patriarch of the Hires Root Beer empire, was a key contributor and an active participant in this worthy event. He could be seen bustling about, glad-handing both men and women, dressed in an all-white three piece suit. Women wore their best lace gloves and their finest sunhats. Men too wore their finest vested suits and choicest fedoras. My father made the remark that it was certainly a sophisticated crowd, but Stan corrected him: "cosmopolitan would be the better adjective. Cosmopolitan means culture and breeding; sophistication implies jaded indulgence." My father thought that Stan was taking himself a little too seriously and told him so. They both had a good laugh.

There was an area of the county fair called Easy Street. It was there a culinary cornucopia of entrées, sandwiches, desserts, and drinks were sold to visitors. The two ensigns purchased their hefty sandwiches, corned beef and sauerkraut, and took their seats at one of the few empty tables. Already seated next to them was the young debutante Katherine Ann Parker – my mother – and some of her friends. They had volunteered to help with the fair's refreshments and had taken a brief respite to sample some of the creative appetizers.

My father said he was instantly smitten with my mother's beauty; he was suddenly hypnotized and not capable of speech. A quick poke in his ribs from Stan broke the trance.

"Easy Jeffrey," said Stan. "You're starting to drool. Cool it down a bit or you'll scare her off."

My father tried his best to heed his friend's advice. This beautiful woman with the raven hair and green eyes had abruptly stolen his heart. He nodded his head and said hello, and she returned it with a warm and inviting smile. Katherine was equally as smitten by this tall, handsome ensign.

"Hello, Navy," she said with a teasing grin.

"I was hoping my herringbone suit wouldn't give me away. I wanted to blend in with all the other riffraff," ensign Miller replied.

"No, I am afraid your disguise didn't work. You're all 'anchors away' from where I sit." They both laughed.

"My name is Jeffrey, and this my good friend, Stan. Would you mind if we joined you ladies for lunch?"

Her friends quickly searched each other's body language and facial expressions for the right collective response. Katherine, however, never took her eyes off Jeffrey.

"I think that would be nice. Please join us, Navy."

The ladies made room at their table for the two ensigns and, although there was some group dialogue in the beginning, it quickly turned into a conversation between Stan and the two other young ladies. Jeffrey and Katherine had instantly become absorbed in their own little world. They saw or heard no one else.

It was soon time for the girls to return to their volunteer work. My father asked if he could call on Katherine next Sunday and she thought it would be wonderful if he did.

Call on my mother he did, that following Sunday. He greeted her parents and then walked her to Fairmount Park to mingle with the other lovers. They were soon holdings hands as their day seemed to race by. Jeffrey stole a kiss from my mother near the end of their outing, although my mother would later say that it was hardly a theft; she had been wishing for it all day.

23

From then on they spent every possible moment together, riding the trails that crisscrossed the Parker estate, spending evenings in the parlor, or out with friends. They desired to be husband and wife as quickly as possible. They saw no need to place restrictions on their love affair.

My mother and father were married at Christ's Church in Philadelphia on April 29, 1917, almost a year after they met at the horse show and county fair. It was an intimate setting and the wedding party was small. Stan Morrison, my father's good friend, was the best man, and my Aunt Meg was the maid of honor. My father and mother felt that that was more than enough. The wedding reception, however, was a huge, gala event, held at the grand ballroom at the Admiral's Inn in Philadelphia, with hundreds of friends and family attending. Stan gave a touching and hilarious toast to the new couple. Katherine had her tearful dance with her father. Everyone had a memorable time.

My father spent a great deal of time with Katherine's family during the months leading up to the wedding. They were an established and affluent family from Chestnut Hill, a wealthy suburb of Philadelphia. The Parkers did their best to welcome Ensign Miller to his new family and he quickly became an accepted and welcomed quest in the Parker household. My mother's parents were intrigued by this young Navy man. Her father admired his focus and drive. He saw a committed naval officer, a good provider, and a loving husband from a wealthy, established family in the Stamford, Connecticut area. Her mother loved his raw good looks, his inviting personality, and likewise saw the deep love he had for her daughter. She knew the Navy would eventually take her daughter away from her. The military was very adept at splitting families apart, and Katherine would travel with her husband wherever the Navy sent him.

However, the real pleasant surprise for Jeffrey at the Parker home was meeting and getting to know Katherine's younger sister, Margret. They were exactly one year apart in age. Katherine's father always joked, "What are the odds of having two daughters born on the same day exactly one year apart? Odds have nothing to do with it, it was all hard work. Fun, but hard!" He would twitch his eyes and give my grandmother a devilish grin. My grandmother would blush and tell my grandfather to be careful what he said. He would laugh out loud.

My father said he quickly learned that his sister-in law had a deep, joyous passion for life. It was just one long, blissful journey for her, and she was going to capture every single moment that she could.

Meg had an attraction about her. She had the same raven hair as all the Parker women, but Meg chose to keep it much shorter than her mother or Katherine. She also shied away from makeup; "too much maintenance," as she would say. It was also clear that Meg had no time for commitments. Or simply chose not to have any. She left a trail of broken hearts as evidence, though she was never mean-spirited or selfish about it. She often said she ended her relationships early just to avoid any hurt feelings or misunderstandings: She simply did not want the "complications," as she saw them, that come with intimate relationships with men.

Katherine and her parents did not understand it. They may have had their suspicions (as I would find out later), and it may have frustrated her mother, but in time everyone accepted it. I can remember sitting at the kitchen table and asking my mother and father why Aunt Meg had never married and rarely seemed to have any boyfriends. It was just so puzzling to me. I thought she was absolutely stunning and felt her personality was magnetic. My parents looked awkwardly at each other and I thought it odd. My mother stumbled over her words.

"I'm not real sure how much your Aunt Meg really likes men, if at all," she said.

This I found even more perplexing. I turned to my father.

"Why wouldn't she like men?"

My father looked pained, as if he had eaten something disagreeable. He turned to my mother for the answer.

"Sometimes things don't always turn out the way you think they should. Sometimes people choose a different path. You will understand later on, but this is enough for now," she finished gently.

I was even more confused.

Aunt Meg loved her older sister and they were extremely close. She was so very happy for her sister and was intuitively convinced that Katherine and Jeff were perfect for each other. She could see that Jeffrey loved her sister dearly, and for that reason she would be able to tolerate sharing her sister with this new man. But who would she confide in now that her special sister had a new best friend? Her only option was to make it clear to Katherine and Jeffrey that they weren't losing a sister, they would only be gaining a lifelong pest. It would just be a part of her love affair with life to stay as close as possible to this loving couple and to be that special aunt to the children they were sure to have.

The next few weeks were uneventful and allowed me to move past the incident in the living room. T.J. had bounced back and was almost unaware that the event had even happened. I spent many of the next several days up in my room in the carriage house writing in my diary. I had decided not to include the scary event with T.J. Diaries were supposed to be for happy thoughts mostly. I did record some sad thoughts or events, like my grandmother's stroke and the death of my cat Bandit, but certainly not these disturbing ones.

Sometimes I would read my diary and relive the special events. Like the day Aunt Meg had given me my diary.

My parents had rented a house for the month of July on the shoreline in Point Pleasant, New Jersey. It was something we had done for several summers and it was always so much fun. My mother's and father's families would visit at different times, and there were always so many things to do. The whole family had spent the week swimming, beach combing, and shopping at all the little tourist traps. Aunt Meg had become a permanent fixture in our family by then and everyone just loved having her around.

It was our last night in the cottage. We were leaving the next morning. We had packed most of our belongings, and my father's Dodge Touring Car sat in the drive way with luggage already secured to its roof. Aunt Meg and I decided to take one last walk on the beach. The sun was fading and it was the end of a glorious day.

Aunt Meg stopped me on the beach and said, "I have something for you." She handed me a small package neatly wrapped with plain brown paper and a bright yellow ribbon and bow. Aunt Meg was always buying little knickknacks for her nieces and nephews. She loved spoiling us.

We stood on the beach facing each other. We were both barefoot and standing in ankle-deep surf. A soft onshore breeze was gently blowing our hair.

I was a little surprised and quickly unwrapped the package. Inside was a royal blue diary with gold bond and gilded edges.

"Every teenage girl should have a diary," she said. "I know it doesn't seem like much, but if you are faithful to it and write in it just about every day, it will become the most precious thing that you will ever possess. Write about your mother and father, Stephanie, about the twins, your boyfriends, your future husband, and your future children. Heck, even write about your crazy Aunt Meg! But just write."

I was deeply moved by this special gift and the charge that came with it. It seemed very important, grown-up even. "I promise I will write every day. This is so thoughtful, Aunt Meg." I hugged her.

"But there is a special message with this diary that I want to tell you now. You know how much I love you all, and you know how close I am to your mother. You need to know that I am and will always be there for you no matter what kind of trouble you are in and no matter where you might be. I will find you, and if I need to I will bring you home. Do you understand this? I am here for you. I will find you. You know I have crazy magical powers!" she said and laughed. I laughed too. She had no magical powers, but I loved her.

This memory, and others, are perhaps the only things that sustain me now. I cherish them and secret them away as I once did with that royal blue diary. That we were once a happy family living our happy lives seems impossible now, but the fact remains, encased in my memory like a precious flower under glass. I can only hope that we may someday return to that state. I ask for it, in the night, when I am alone in my bed.

Jacob

APRIL, 1919

Sarah's father's associates located Jacob quite easily and the information was passed along to her brother. However, confronting Jacob Sweeney and prying into a very sensitive subject would be challenging. Her brother anguished over how to best approach Jacob and finally decided on the direct route. He would simply travel to Jacob's home and knock on his door; no sense in reaching out for an opportunity to talk, there would never be any reciprocation. Surprise would be his most effective tactic.

The logistics in getting to Belfast were involved: It would take two long days of navigating the English Channel and the Irish Sea before docking in Belfast. But Frederick Jr. had a business associate that lived in that same area and had made the journey to

Belfast several times before. He was accustomed to long days at sea and the rollicking weather that sometimes accompanied them. Luckily, both days and nights were uneventful, and the ship docked gently in the harbor on the third sunrise.

When Frederick Jr. arrived his business associate had a motor car and driver waiting for him. They drove directly to Jacob's home. It was a late Sunday afternoon in the waning days of April and the meadows had turned green. Tulips, daffodils, forsythia, and lilacs were in bloom everywhere. Frederick's mother had always said that the vibrant colors that arrive with spring are the rewards for a bland and empty winter. Jacob's residence was a modest Georgian-style home with impressive landscaping. They parked their car alongside shoulder high hedges growing alongside a solid-looking stone wall. Frederick instructed the driver to wait at the vehicle; he would be back shortly. He followed the hedges to an imposing, hand-crafted iron gate fashioned between stately stone and mortared columns. The gate had just been freshly painted a glossy black and had been left open to dry.

Frederick Jr. carefully stepped around the gate and walked briskly up the cobblestone path to the front door. He used the large brass knocker to make his presence known. He was surprised to see Jacob Sweeney answer the door himself. There was no mistaking him, although he seemed shorter and slighter than the pictures and description his sister had forwarded to him. Sarah had told him he was in his early sixties, but he seemed older. His head was round and his thick jaw seemed to disappear into his even wider neck. He held a large cigar in his left hand and the end of it was soggy and well worn. His hands and his teeth were stained with nicotine and tobacco. It was obvious he enjoyed his cigars and had done so for many years.

"Mr. Sweeney, my name is Frederick Shepard Jr.," he said as he extended his hand. Jacob reluctantly extended his, but made sure their shake was quick and without substance.

"How did you get through the gate?" Jacob replied.

"I think the gate was left open to dry, it smelled of fresh paint."

"Probably so," said Jacob, his stare and summation of Frederick was becoming more critical by the second.

"Look, Mr. Sweeney, I will try to make this quick." Frederick Jr. told him the purpose of his visit, about his sister's unique and potent gift and her tragic connection with the *Titanic,* as diplomatically as he could. There was no way to sugarcoat it.

"I know this must sound completely absurd and must border on insanity to you, but I can assure you that my sister did not arrive at this point without a great deal of research and reflection. Please let her meet with you. She would need to travel from the U.S. Surely you don't think she would entertain such a long journey if she was not convinced of its worth. I know that she can better explain this crusade of hers. She is convinced it will lighten the burden you have carried for so long. Please give her that opportunity."

Jacob immediately became angry by this unannounced visit and this stranger's accusations. His face turned red and his broad chest seemed to expand even more; despite being in his older years, he was still an intimidating man.

"Mr. Shepard," he all but shouted, "I have heard all this bullshit before! It was an awful tragedy and it touched a lot of people's lives, but all this talk of conspiracies and cover-ups is just moronic. Do you offer any proof? And don't tell me more about your sister's special gift of clairvoyance. I don't place much value in that kind of crap."

"Let me explain a little bit more—" Frederick began.

"No, I don't think so. I strongly suggest you leave my property before I have you thrown out on your ass."

Frederick Jr. knew he would need to complete his script as quickly as possible. His time with Jacob had run its course and polite patience would be fleeting.

"Mr. Sweeney, I can offer no proof. I know only that my sister desperately wants to share her gift with you, something you place no value on. But if you listened to her, perhaps you would be more accepting of such rare abilities. She had a wonderful marriage destroyed and suffered far reaching consequences because of this same tragedy. It is what drove her to solve a mystery that only a very few people know of."

Jacob seemed a little moved that Sarah had been drawn into this tragedy, too. He softened his demeanor ever so slightly.

"I am sorry for your sister; as I said, this catastrophe touched many people's lives. However, the tragedy is not my fault and I am done talking to a complete stranger about it. Time to move on, Freddy."

Jacob reached in behind the front door and extracted a billy club with a worn leather strap and a number of dents and scratches on it. It was clear that it had been used before. Nothing more needed to be said; Frederick immediately tipped his hat and returned to his car.

Later that night, in his Belfast hotel room, Frederick Jr. thought about his visit with Jacob. He had accomplished very little and he owed his sister more than that. Should he make one more effort to reach out to Jacob? There had been some dialogue and it had never become too heated; and although he could not be sure of it, he felt he had struck a chord with Jacob. Frederick convinced himself to make another attempt to connect with Jacob. He would return the following Sunday. In the meantime, he had business he could conduct in the Belfast area.

He returned to Jacob's home on Sunday at the same time as the week before. The iron gate was closed and locked. Frederick's gaze traveled down the walkway and came to a stop at the front door. He was thinking about his next move – or if there should even be a next move – when the front door opened and Jacob emerged. He walked slowly down the cobblestone path. His slow gait and slumped posture told Frederick there would be a disappointing summary.

Jacob reached the iron gate but did not open it. They faced each other through the open bars.

Frederick extended his hand through the gate. "Hello Mr. Sweeney," he said. Jacob ignored it.

"Mr. Shepard, I was hoping you would not return, but I also knew you would. You must certainly have a special relationship with your sister to risk so much, because although you may not know it, you are indeed risking a great deal. Please go home, let this sad

31

tragedy rest in peace. If you pursue this any further you will not like the outcome."

He quickly turned and was up the walkway and in his front door in brief seconds. Conversation was no longer an option.

* * *

"Jacob, my people tell me you have had a visitor, and they also tell me he was not a welcome guest." Cheswick had surprised him early on a Saturday morning. Cheswick loved surprises. It always tipped the scale in his favor and put the unsuspecting at a disadvantage. Now he stood in Jacob's drawing room, probing with his pointed questions.

"Apparently you had to persuade this visitor to leave your premises on his last visit. You should tell me about this intruder. He seems to be persistent in his efforts to meet with you. One can only wonder what might be the purpose of these unannounced and uninvited visits."

Jacob despised Dudley Cheswick, always had. He had been an unwelcomed shadow for almost eight years. Powerful men had secured his services to keep a well-guarded secret just that, and now he had invited himself into Jacob's home, asking questions he knew Jacob would have answers for.

He could remember his first meeting with him in his office in the shipyard. Most of Jacob's time was spent in the yard; his responsibilities were best served interacting with the tradesmen and that meant he was rarely in his office. He returned there at the end of one typically long and hectic day to find a stranger sitting contentedly behind his desk.

"Mr. Sweeney, I have taken the liberty of making myself comfortable in your office. I hope you don't mind, but you will soon discover that I take a lot of liberties with a lot of things." He raised himself slowly from Jacob's chair and approached him with a challenging stare. He was shorter than Jacob, with cold, piercing dark eyes and a thin mustache that seemed evil. He was a thin, almost frail man. Jacob wanted to squash him like the cockroach he was.

"Jacob, my name is Dudley Cheswick," he said as he extended his small, bony hand. As much as Jacob did not want to shake it, his instincts told him he should. Cheswick's grip was lifeless and served no purpose. These were hands that were never meant to convey strength, but he knew he had just shaken hands with the Devil.

"Mr. Cheswick, maybe you can tell me a little about yourself? I am at a complete loss as to who you are and why you're sitting at *my* desk in *my* office."

Cheswick pouted his lips and shook his head disapprovingly at this inquiry. "Jacob, no need for the hostility. I am simply doing my job. You will learn over time, I do it exceptionally well. You were told not so long ago to orchestrate a very dark undertaking, and you and others were told to maintain a level of secrecy about those actions. I am here to remind any and all of those instructions and do whatever I think is necessary to secure that secret. I am not here to be your friend; it is important that you always bear that in mind."

It had come down to this: a little weasel of a man had been hired by some powerful men to maintain their cloak of conspiracy. Dudley Cheswick would always be around the next corner, hiding in the shadows, spreading fear as a tool to intimidate and relishing every moment of it. He would be like the devil on Jacob's shoulder. And where was the angel? Jacob, as of late, had begun to doubt there was one.

Why do they not simply kill me? he thought. *That is the cliché the old salts throw around: dead men tell no tales. Why attach this minder to me? And for how long? How long until it has become sufficiently forgotten? Five years? Ten? Will he haunt me, like a ghost, reminding me of my past wickedness until I am a ghost myself?*

These were questions without answers. No way to know how long this grim *thing* of a man would be dogging Jacob's heels. And no way to know if – or *when* – those shadowy and powerful men in charge of things behind the scenes might order his death. Jacob, never a churchgoing man, nonetheless found himself thinking suddenly of a biblical passage that seemed to rise up to the surface of his mind out of nowhere.

No one knoweth the hour.

He turned to Cheswick.

"I suppose you had better sit down."

* * *

Back in the present, though again in his drawing room, Cheswick was regarding him with a faint smile that turned the corners of his pallid lips.

"So, who is this uninvited guest and why is he here? It is a rather simple question, Jacob, is it not?"

Cheswick had made himself comfortable on the sofa. He had removed his Brixton cap and placed it on the cushion next to him; his right hand drummed an annoying beat on the end table. He really was a tiny, unimpressive man and he seemed lost in the girth of the large couch.

"Come on Jacob, I don't want to be here anymore than you want me here."

Jacob knew he would tell Cheswick most of what he wanted to know, but he was damned if he would tell him everything. *Just enough to get him of my back*, he thought. True, he had chased Frederick Shepard Jr. from his property, but Jacob sensed he was a decent man and was sincere in his efforts to help his sister. Pestering Jacob about dark deeds that he had participated in was something he did not need, but he wished the younger Frederick no harm. Jacob decided he would try to minimize the potential damage that was in his future, should he return.

"Dudley, the man that has called on me twice is named Frederick Shepard. I don't know where he lives. I know almost nothing about him. We did not get into the particulars. He was indeed asking questions about the *Titanic*, but made no mention of why he was so interested in the tragedy. Our exchanges never allowed that to happen. I kept them brief and off the topic. You have my permission to follow up with him and ask these same questions, but I don't think you ever need my permission for anything you do, do you?"

"No, that's true." Cheswick sat there as if in thought for several moments and then said, "I suppose I will be leaving now." He had to almost struggled to remove himself from the large sofa. "I hope you have told me everything about this Frederick Shepard. I will investigate Mr. Shepard and I will have my people watch for his return, if he is so naive." He returned his cap to his oily salt and pepper scalp.

"Good day, Mr. Sweeney. No need to walk me to the door, I will see myself out."

As he watched Cheswick exit the drawing room, mincing along on the balls of his feet like a bad actor, Jacob wondered what would happen to his overcurious visitor. He had tried to warn him of the consequences that lie ahead if he pursued the dangerous path he was on. He could hardly be blamed for what might happen to the lad, be it violent or otherwise. Jacob hoped for a peaceful outcome.

Jacob

APRIL, 1919

Frederick had business commitments in Belfast that would tie him up for the whole of the next week. It seemed to move at a snail's pace. He had wired his sister in Rhode Island that the visits with Jacob had not been productive, but the he would try one last time on the day his steamer was scheduled to return to England.

"Sir, apparently there is a Frederick Shepard Jr. visiting our Mr. Sweeney and he seems to be asking rather pointed questions about the *Titanic*."

Dudley Cheswick sat in a poorly lit room in a rundown boarding house in Belfast. The curtains had been closed and the gentleman he spoke to had immersed himself in the shadows of the room. He had a dark, wide-brimmed hat tipped low on his brow; Cheswick could see very little of his face. All of their meetings were like this. Dark rooms with very specific instructions given, some with very dire consequences.

"What can you tell me about him?" came a voice from the dark corner of the room.

"As I said, his name is Frederick Shepard, Jr. He is from Nottingham, England, and operates a moderately sized but profitable lace mill there. His father immigrated to the states about twenty years ago with his family. Shepard chose to purchase his father's lace mill and remain in the U.K. His father is now well connected in New York City and knows some very powerful men. I'm not so sure how strong his ties in England and Ireland are anymore, though. How do you want to proceed?"

There was silence in the room for a while. Finally, the voice responded. "We need to remove this bloodhound from the trail, but we need to be careful how we do that. We don't want to ruffle the feathers of a big bird in New York. Continue to watch Sweeney's house; if this prying fool returns, then send a message. Dirty the suit he is wearing, make sure he understands the message, but if he has an accomplice or if his driver returns with him, then they should be the target of the very clear message you have been hired to deliver."

"How clear do you want it to be?"

The reply was immediate and forceful. "Cheswick, as goddamn crystal clear as it needs to be. Once we define an assignment, when have I ever placed any restrictions on what you do?"

* * *

Frederick and his driver saw the two men standing at the front gate when they arrived in their motor car. "Not the friendliest looking blokes, Mr. Shepard," his driver remarked. "I'd keep a wide berth around them."

"I will heed your advice, but let's hope they have nothing to do with my visit. Please wait here."

He was wrong. The two men approached him as soon as he exited the vehicle; when they asked for the reason of his visit, he told them. The smaller of the two men gave a slight nod and his counterpart suddenly punched Jacob in the face. His nose was immediately broken and he was knocked to the ground. Both men were quickly on him and began to viciously kick him in the ribs. Suddenly they stopped. They picked Frederick up and dragged him back to his car, forcefully placing him in the front seat. Another man had appeared out of nowhere and was holding his driver at knifepoint.

The smaller of the men leaned into the vehicle so that he was only inches from Frederick's bloodied nose. "Now, my good friend, do you understand that this is more than just a warning, it's a bloody promise? If you ever bother Mr. Sweeney again you will permanently lose the use of your legs. Or worse. Do you understand me, my good friend?"

Frederick nodded his head.

The obvious leader of this group of thugs turned to the largest man in their collection. "Stanley, make sure Mr. Shepard of Nottingham has a clear understanding of what I just told him." The big man reached in and with a powerful grip twisted Frederick's already broken nose several times. He screamed in agony as blood poured onto his white Oxford shirt and Windsor-knotted tie.

"Okay Stanley, that should do it. I think our friend here has retained the more important elements of our conversation. Wouldn't you agree, Mr. Shepard?"

Frederick could only nod his head again.

"That's what I was hoping you'd say. And by the way, you should get your friend to a hospital rather quickly, he seems to be bleeding quite badly." He tipped his hat, and with that the three street thugs walked back briskly to the gate, disappearing behind the hedges.

Frederick had not even noticed that his driver had been stabbed. The man had not uttered a word. He was holding his left side with both hands; bright red blood had soaked through his white shirt and was spilling through his desperate grip. Frederick quickly realized that this man he barely knew was dying. He jumped out of the motor car and, despite the pain of his fractured ribs and bloodied nose, quickly moved around to the driver's side, pushed his driver over to the opposite side, jumped in, and started the auto, driving in a complete panic to the nearest police station. It was the only public building he knew how to get to.

Policemen at the station scrambled to do what they could: a doctor was quickly summoned. But Frederick's new friend was already dead when he arrived. Many of these policemen knew death when they saw it. An investigation was immediately set in motion and the crime scene was examined. Jacob's possible involvement was also reviewed. In the end the investigation went nowhere: there were no witnesses, no one matching Frederick's description could be located, and Jacob Sweeney was cleared of any connection or wrongdoing. Frederick was horrified and saddened by the whole event.

Frederick knew his obligation to his sister had run its course. These men or someone else had done their homework. They knew who he was and where he was from and they had indiscriminately murdered a man for no other reason than to send a message; apparently the beating he sustained was not sufficient enough. This was as far as he dared go with his probing. It had become incredibly dangerous. He telegraphed his sister to let her know that things had turned quite ugly.

* * *

Sarah was appalled by the death of the poor man and by the beating sustained by her brother. She persecuted herself for not anticipating this reaction. Jacob Sweeney or some other powerfully connected people were pushing back. Sarah thought it would be the latter; Jacob was still the soft underbelly of the beast. She knew a different approach would be needed. Too much was at risk to continue on this way.

She made one last attempt on her own to appeal to Jacob's humanity. She wrote him a revealing letter about herself and what she had concluded through all her diligence and her special gift. She appealed to his inner spirit and moral compass. She hoped it might resonate with him; he had been forced to compromise his integrity by men who would sell their own mother's soul with little forethought or regret.

Mr. Sweeney, she wrote, *I am appalled by the senseless murder of this poor, innocent man who knew nothing of the tragedy that I have pursued, and also by the horrible beating my brother suffered. Why did it have to escalate to this horrible level? But I sense you are as equally appalled by these despicable actions as I. You must carry a heavy burden because of the* Titanic, *but it should not be your liability. And yet there are those that are forcing you to carry it for them. I too carry the weight of that tragedy, but for a different reason, and it pulls on my spirit daily. Please give me the opportunity to talk with you. I know we could be of great comfort to each other.*

Sarah vowed that whatever he confided in her she would take to her grave. It would be their secret and for their healing only. There was so much she wanted to tell him. She hoped that someday he might trust her. But Sarah heard nothing from Jacob Sweeney.

Delilah

NOVEMBER, 1938

The loss of my sister Stephanie, my brother Corey, and Aunt Meg had deeply hurt. It left me feeling empty and so dreadfully sad. They were my family, but they were also my closest friends and confidants. There was no longer any energy in my home; a lifeless quietness now existed there, and the walls and their contents suffered in silence from the forced, painful, sudden subtraction of life. There is something about a family that helps separate a house from a home. The unguarded and sometimes brutally honest dialogue, the hurt feelings healed by siblings more concerned with healing and forgiving than anything else. Running up the stairs and down the halls, opening and closing doors, flushing toilets and running water. *How was your day?* Laughing and crying, whistling and singing, teasing and loving, when suddenly removed, strips a home of its character, makes its existence pointless.

I missed my family terribly, and writing about them in my diary was the only thing that helped me cope with their loss; that, and time.

I was lying on my bed in the loft of the carriage house doing exactly that; our sadness and my mother's deep depression had already filled too many pages. My mother was devastated on the inside. Her family had always defined who she was, and the loss of her children and her sister had torn away her identity. The few times she may have looked into a mirror she would have seen only a lifeless stranger asking, *why do you stare at me?*

My mother's sadness and emptiness were profound. It had begun to attack her spirit. She was lifeless and not capable of defending herself. Her depression had secured itself to her and was slowly killing her. I wanted so much to help, but like the image in the mirror, she no longer recognized me either. It was painful.

My writing for that day was complete and I was in a rare moment where nothing pulled at me. I was not happy, but I was not sad. I knew it would not linger. Then suddenly the shadow of the unseen visitor appeared on the near wall. The vibrations began again and my glass of lemonade on my father's sea chest began to quiver. The hair on my neck stood on end. Two more shadows appeared and all three seemed to gather around me.

For the first time they appeared to take on human form. My bed began to shake, pictures and paintings dropped from the walls, shattering their frames and glass. I held my breath, trying to control my fear, and then the same soft breeze that had moved T.J.'s hair now gently moved my own and caressed my cheek. I quickly looked at the vanity mirror in my room, expecting to see the shadows of these unwanted beings, but there was nothing there save my own terrified image. Then the mirror shattered into a thousand pieces.

It was instinctive: I screamed and lurched from my bed, scramble down the stairs, and ran from the carriage house in absolute terror. I was in the entry way of our house before I knew it. I climbed the stairs to my mother's room two at a time and burst through the door. She was sleeping again and Claudia, who saw to most of my mother's needs, was with her. My sudden entrance into the room startled her; she just looked at me with a piercing cold stare. It was clear that she was upset with me for potentially interrupting my mother's nap, although there was little chance of that, not with the medication she was taking to keep her stable. I then ran to my father's room, but when I got there I remembered that he and T.J. had taken the ferry to Newport and would be gone all day. I ran to my room and threw myself on the bed. The mumbling noise, which now sounded like muffled, indiscernible voices, had followed me into the room.

A single shadow appeared on the bedroom wall. It moved towards me with outstretched hand and an accusing finger. I covered my eyes and screamed again. The vibrations and muted voices suddenly stopped as if commanded; what followed was only absolute silence, just like the other times. I wrapped myself in my quilt and lie there for what seemed like hours. I finally fell asleep and dreamed of my father and mother, my sister and brothers, Aunt Meg, and happier times.

✳ ✳ ✳

It was around this same time that my mother, with the help of Claudia, began to seek out spiritual help. My father was grudgingly supportive in the beginning. He felt it might help ease my mother's pain. We had all suffered from the events of that awful day in September, but my mother was overwhelmed by them and had quickly fallen into a deep depression. My father, T.J., and I had somehow persevered, gathered what remained of our family, and struggled forward. My father's love and his will to hold his clan together had assured us there would be a healing process, although it would at times be difficult to gauge.

Father had tried so many times to reach inside my mother and find just the smallest spark. Maybe with all his love he could slowly rekindle it, but my mother only withdrew more. My own pleadings to my mother were either met with a wall of silence or a startled look of shock. It was if she was saying, *How dare you, with all that I have lost?*

The Episcopal minister of Saint Mathew's in Jamestown began to call on my mother. We had begun attending his parish shortly after our arrival in Jamestown and had quickly become accepted members of the congregation. My parents had come to like Reverend Chard and his flock. The Reverend was a short, stocky man of French Canadian descent. He had long since lost most of his hair and, when not in church administering to his pastoral duties, he was usually seen in his cherished scarlet French beret. It kept him warm in the winter and the sun off his unprotected head in the summer. He had grown up in Lac-Delage, a small town about fifteen miles northwest of Quebec City, and still had a slight French Canadian accent. He had been an accomplished youth hockey player and had been recruited by several semi-professional hockey clubs, but knew his true passion was to take God's plan to the world.

Reverend Chard began to visit my mother on Sunday afternoons, not long after tragedy had struck our family. He would arrive at three o'clock and Claudia would greet him at the door, taking his coat and cherished beret. My father and I made a point of not being in the living room during these visits; it was just too painful to participate in my mother's agony. His attempts to get her to rejoin the church were met with indifference.

"Katherine, I did not see you in church this morning. We missed your fine voice. You should visit us next Sunday. You are always welcomed in God's home."

"That's nice," was all my mother could mumble.

"I don't think Mrs. Miller is ready for that type of activity, Father Chard," Claudia interjected.

"She needs the love and support of her parish, it can only help."

"I'm not sure...," my mother whispered

"Trust me, Father, it would not help," Claudia pronounced.

"Maybe so. Well anyway, how are you Katherine?" And then my mother would begin to cry, which would rapidly escalate to uncontrollable sobbing, all the time asking the Reverend why this had happened to her. He struggled for answers but never found them. He implored her to turn to her faith, to understand that with time and God's help she could heal these deep wounds. In all his years of serving the church he said he had never met such a tortured and undeserving soul.

After a while my mother's crying and the questions with no answers would end. She would then quickly retreat into her world of silence and isolation. The Reverend would tenderly try to engage my mother in conversation, but she was not capable of it. Father Chard felt so inadequate: one of his lambs was drowning in a sea of grief and isolation and he was like a shepherd that could not swim nor had a branch to extend into the vortex that was sucking his lamb down into the darkness. He was a man of great patience and moral fiber, but all his visits ended with him leaving our house frustrated and emotionally drained. The Reverend would leave promptly at four o'clock and my father would always see him to the door and thank him for his visit. He was usually too tired and saddened to respond. Occasionally he would turn to my father and hold his arms out to the side, shrug in frustration, and then leave.

Over the next few months, Reverend Chard's visits became less frequent. I believe he began to acknowledge that my mother's tortured soul was beyond his expertise. He told Claudia that he believed what my mother needed most was time, but my mother had also begun to talk with Reverend Chard about reaching out to her lost loved ones in ways that were not accepted by him or the Church. My mother wanted to reach across the barrier that separates the living from the dead. It saddened him, and he approached Claudia about this new direction.

"Telling Mrs. Miller that she might communicate with her deceased loved ones is something I cannot be a part of, and I believe you do a big disservice to this poor, troubled woman. I would think her health and stability would be your primary concerns. Séances, mystic chants, and a crystal ball tell me just the opposite: you are manipulating a very fragile woman."

Claudia became angry and defensive. "I am no gypsy, I have no crystal ball, and who gives you the right to sit in judgment? You have visited with us for over two months of Sundays and what has your approach or faith accomplished for Katherine? You of Christ's ministries are so pious and unaccepting of anything different or foreign. I believe in my Haitian elements and I will use them in any way that might help this troubled family. That is my intent, and you need to accept that whether you like it or not."

"God have mercy on you, Claudia St. Louis. You are traveling down a path with the Devil."

"No, I am not. And where did your path lead us? I am done, thank you for your visits." She handed him his coat and beret and Reverend William H. Chard left our home without saying a word. Claudia watched until his car was out of sight.

"Katherine, the Reverend is a good man, but he is too suspicious and too eager to unfairly label people. We shall begin a new approach, and we will connect with our loved ones in the other world. You must trust me, Katherine."

"If you think so," my mother muttered.

Reverend Chard's visits had given my father just the slightest hope for my mother, and he was saddened when he no longer called on Sundays. Claudia had compromised my mother's recovery and my father was angry with her.

Claudia had always been a paradox to my father. She had been with our family for several years, and before that she had worked in my grandparents' home in Chestnut Hill. My mother had lobbied for Claudia's assistance about two years after I was born. Servants had been a way of life for my mother, but my father was uncomfortable with them. They were an unnecessary cost, and he felt his privacy was always being intruded upon. He did admit later, after the twins were born, that he was glad to have Claudia around.

Claudia St. Louis was born in Port-au-Prince, Haiti. She was the niece of a trusted woman that used to work for my mother's parents. She had immigrated to America with her mother when she was ten years old.

Her mother had been only fifteen years old when she gave birth to Claudia. It had been a difficult delivery, and the complications had resulted in her mother never having any children

46

after that. Her mother and father, despite their youth and forced marriage, were very much in love. She was devastated when her young husband of four years, a fisherman by trade, disappeared at sea one day. He had been putting in long days working the reefs around the island. There are over a thousand miles of pristine coral reefs around Haiti and Miguel had been diving very successfully for the sea sponges that proliferated all along these coral reefs. He had also been fortunate in netting many of the abundant reef squids that seemed to be attracted to the sponges. Miguel knew he had to fish these areas quickly and as efficiently as he could. Once word got out that he was on to something other fisherman would swarm to the area. There was already speculation that Miguel was on to something big; there had been too many days in a row when he had traded his abundant catch for a healthy sum of money.

Miguel had confided to his young wife that the fishing was very good, but he was exhausted. He was typically home around noon time; these last ten days he had returned home around 5 p.m. His pockets were full with the profits of his continuous diving, but he was famished and dog-tired. Maria would have his evening meal prepared and he would inhale it like a man caring little about taste and more about survival. He would spend a brief few minutes with his beautiful little girl, kissing her and gently stroking her chestnut curls with hands that were scraped, cut and blistered from the long hours of digging among the coral. Miguel would fall asleep with her in his arms with Maria pleading in the background not to go to the reefs the next day. He slept like the dead, only to rise at sunrise the next day and start all over again. The rejuvenating energy of his youth, and only that, allowed him to attack each new day.

His small wooden skiff was found still anchored near the reef he had been working. There was no sign of Miguel. There had been an intensive search by friends and family and much speculation that he had drowned or fallen victim to the black-tip sharks that were always in the area. Other fisherman knew the area, and they knew where the currents might take a body. They expanded their exploration each day and, after four days of searching and praying, they finally abandoned their efforts. His body was never recovered.

It was ironic that, while close friends and relatives hunted for Miguel, others now fished this same area. To them it made no sense not to take advantage of Miguel's lucky and plentiful find. It was a bitter reality for Maria, and she told the wives of these same men that they would not be welcomed when the community came together to mourn Miguel's passing. Their hypocrisy would not be tolerated. She would need this inner strength if she and her baby daughter were to survive.

Maria struggled to make ends meet as a single mother in Haiti. She and her little girl had begun attending Saint-Louis du Nord, the local Catholic parish, soon after Claudia was born. Maria had never been receptive to what the Church offered her on a personal level, but she clearly understood what its education might offer her child.

Claudia was exposed there to the heavy hand of the Catholic Church and its version of schooling for the first ten years of her life in Haiti. It deeply defined who Claudia would become later in life. Her mother also exposed her to the prominent black magic subculture that was deeply entrenched in all of Haiti. Maria was deeply connected to her Haitian roots and was going to make sure that her daughter would always be connected to her Haitian heritage – black magic included.

It took six years for Claudia's mother to save enough money to allow her to leave Haiti. She sometimes worked the most degrading jobs for the most minimal wages. She purchased passage for her and her daughter on a freighter that was bound for Philadelphia. Maria sought out the only family she had left, an older and only sister who had immigrated to America years before and had been living in Philadelphia ever since.

Claudia and her mother were soon settled in the west section of Philadelphia. Her aunt's family welcomed their new arrivals with opened arms, and it made their assimilation that much easier. Claudia and her mother quickly attached themselves to the local Catholic parish of Saint Joesph's. Unlike her mother, Claudia enjoyed the sense of family that their parish offered and applauded the structure and discipline of a parochial school, as she had in Haiti.

"I don't know how you became so organized," Maria would exclaim. "It didn't come from your father. He saw no purpose in structure. He was such a free spirit; that is why I loved him so much."

But at night her mother and her aunt would always bring her back to her Haitian roots, sharing with her the mystic tradition of Haitian black magic and voodoo. Claudia's mother and aunt were raised in a home where voodoo and black magic had a strong presence. Their father was a *houngan*, a Creole word the means fortune teller, caster of spells or curses, and sometimes healer of the sick. Their father's knowledge of herbs and potions and their perceived healing powers made him a popular and sometimes a feared member of the community. There rarely was a day when there wasn't someone at their home seeking spiritual guidance or having spells cast on those that had brought injustice or misfortune into their lives. It was an environment that exposed Claudia's mother and her aunt to the dark side of Haitian traditions. They quickly became aware of how crippling and controlling the fear of the unknown could be. Their father was a master of controlling people's lives with this island voodoo and black magic. He saw it as his task in life. Their mother thought he was too controlling with his knowledge. She saw no need to introduce more fear and uncertainty into people's lives. There already was enough of that on this island of crippling poverty.

Claudia, with her aunt's recommendation, began to do small cleaning and babysitting jobs at the Parker home. She worked hard and quickly became a trusted young girl among the work staff and family. She soon became the teenage nanny to my mother and Aunt Meg, and from that point she became a fixture in my mother's family. She developed a very close relationship with my mother and Aunt Meg, and welcomed the opportunity to join our family in their move to Rhode Island. She was not always the most loving nanny, but she was dedicated and fiercely loyal to my mother.

Claudia was a deeply religious woman, but she also sought spiritual guidance through astrology, Tarot cards, and the paranormal, which sometimes involved reaching out to deceased loved ones. Her Haitian environment of voodoo and black magic no doubt had contributed to this. My mother and father thought this should create some inner conflict for Claudia. How could Claudia, with her Catholic education and her close attachment to her parish, be so involved with the dark side of her Haitian culture? Claudia saw no conflict at all. She was Catholic, but she was also Haitian. It was as simple as that. My mother and father were amused by her conflicting interests and found it zany and entertaining at times.

Claudia had done astrological charts on me, my sister, and the twins when they were born. She had read the Tarot cards numerous times for my family when we had lived in Philadelphia. It was usually on a Sunday afternoon. We would sit at the kitchen table and wait our turn while Claudia read the cards. My father would always find something to do when Claudia took them out. He knew we enjoyed our psychic get-togethers, but wanted no part of it. "Typical male," Aunt Meg would say. My mother and Aunt Meg would try to put their own cosmic spin on how Claudia interpreted what the cards were saying. We would laugh, and Claudia would always take it in stride, but sometimes she would end the sessions by telling my mother and Aunt Meg that the cards told her that a very long separation would enter their lives someday. They were to be separated by a great distance, and only after a very long struggle would they finally be together. Aunt Meg would only laugh and say that could never happen. She would never stray too far from this family. Claudia would shake her finger and walk off. She was very passionate about it. It was this passion that had made it very difficult for Claudia to accept the fact that she had not foreseen the horrible events that unfolded on that terrible day in September.

Jacob

MAY, 1921

"Mr. Shepard, there is a Mr. Jacob Sweeney here to see you," said the butler. "He has apologized several times for this sudden, unexpected visit and hopes you will see him. He is not a well looking man, sir."

Frederick Jr. was seated at his dining table and was just finishing a late lunch.

"Mr. Jacob Sweeney?" he questioned.

"Yes, Mr. Shepard, and as I said, he looks quite sickly. I might be concerned that he has something contagious."

"Thank you Martin, please show him into my office. I will be there shortly. Oh, and please bring in some tea for us."

A man that several years ago had set three hoodlums upon him to murder his driver and to beat him in order to intimidate him had somehow re-entered his world and now was about to enter his home. It made no sense, and yet he knew why Jacob was here. His sister had predicted it. Sarah had foreseen Jacob's path to redemption before Jacob himself had visualized it. This would be a challenging reunion for both men.

Frederick found Jacob in his office and was immediately stunned by his physical appearance. He had lost a lot of weight, his once thick neck and broad chest were gone, and his clothes hung loosely with little disclosure of the man within. His eyes were sunken and his complexion was pallid. Like drops of water on a hot skillet, all of Frederick's anger and bitterness quickly evaporated. This man before him was no longer his enemy; all Frederick could feel was compassion and pity.

Jacob struggled to his feet, "Mr. Shepard, thank you for allowing me into your home. You could have easily turned me away and you would have been justified to do so. Please believe me, I knew nothing beforehand about the killing of your driver and the beating you received. I did tell someone who you were and that's all I told them. If you remember, that's all you divulged to me, that and your sister's obsession with the *Titanic,* and I told them nothing of that. I told the ring leader that I believed you were a good man and that I had discouraged you from ever returning again. He assured me that no harm would come to you, but some powerful men thought otherwise and orchestrated that whole despicable act. I was horrified by it. I would never have participated in or condoned such a heinous turn. That is simply not the cut of my cloth. "You are of deep character and a better man than I shall ever be."

Jacob extended a cold and skeletal hand to Frederick and it felt fragile and exposed. Not long ago that same hand had securely gripped a menacing billy club that had convinced Frederick to quickly end his conversation and re-think his strategy.

"I suppose I could have done that, but I can see that holding grudges or seeking vengeance now will do nothing for either one of us. I can only see you are not a well man and I am sorry for that."

"I have lung cancer, Mr. Shepard. Forty years of cigars and those same years in the shipyard, breathing welder's smoke, insulation, and toxic fumes have taken their toll. I do not have long to live, maybe six months if God sees it so, although he owes me nothing."

"Please, call me Frederick. My God, how did you make it here? I would think you would have stayed at home in Belfast."

"I have a motorcar and driver outside waiting for me. My doctors in Belfast insisted that I seek out the staff at Saint Stephen's hospital in west London. They were convinced that it was where I would receive the finest care and have the best chance of escaping my death sentence. I now know there is little hope of that, and they have told me so, but they can provide the heavy medication that can ease my discomfort. I now live in a small cottage, also in west London. I have an old friend that will help me through these last few months of my life."

"That sounds like a very dear friend."

A lot had happened to Jacob since their meeting three years ago. His wife had suddenly passed away from influenza in 1919. He retired from the shipyard in 1920. His two daughters had immigrated to Boston with their husbands shortly after their mother's death. It was not a sudden move. Both their husbands had been approached by a major shipbuilder in Quincy, Massachusetts, and had been offered lofty positions. The twenty years of experience at the Harland & Wolff shipyard secured by their father-in-law had paid dividends. He told Frederick of standing at a lonely pier on a frigid morning in February and waving goodbye to his family. There had been last minute hugs, tears and I-love-yous. He would never see his children and grandchildren again.

Jacob had kept his poor health a secret. His two daughters and their families had a new and better life waiting for them in the United States. Denying them that opportunity would serve no purpose. There was nothing they could have done for him. His cancer was just too aggressive.

Now he was alone and dying.

"Frederick, I shall come to the point: you visited me three years ago and told me of your sister Sarah and her unique gift. You also told me of her sad connection with the *Titanic*, a ship that now has me in its death grip. I was so wrong with the way I had you treated that day, I torture myself incessantly over my actions. I hope you can forgive me for those terrible deeds, I know I will never absolve myself of them. Your sister also wrote me a letter shortly after your visits and, because my ego would not allow for an outsider to question my actions even though I have been challenging them from the very day I became involved with *Titanic's* undoing, I foolishly threw the letter away. Her letter resonated with me and I now know that I must relieve myself of the burden she knew I carried. I do not want to face my God without trying to cleanse my soul."

"What do you want me to do?" Frederick asked.

Jacob had begun to cry and his hands were trembling when he spoke.

"Again, you are man of good character. I need to reach out to your sister and pray that she will make a long journey so that I might share a terrible secret with her."

"I will send her a telegram immediately, but don't forget, Jacob, I do this for her also."

"We all know that we will be venturing into very perilous terrain. There are very powerful people involved here. This is something I will share only with Sarah. It's important for her to clearly understand that."

Frederick quickly sent his sister a telegram: *Jacob Sweeney arrived at my door this a.m.— needs to share his affliction—has cancer—suggest you secure passage a.s.a.p.*

* * *

Jacob now wanted to share his secret; in fact, he needed to share it. Sarah had hoped it might come down to this. In the end it would be his need to share this terrible burden that would prevail. But it had to be on his terms, and he held all the cards. He was dying. This added even more leverage and urgency. Sarah would have to go to him. He would only talk to her directly, and only from the security of his own home. It was what he demanded. He had been deeply involved in a despicable act. He hadn't perpetrated it. Some very powerful men had done that and these men would go to any lengths to protect their secret.

Sarah was now bound for England. She had quickly arranged travel on the first passenger liner out of Boston. Her father's connection once again proved to be invaluable. The accommodations were minimal but enough. She had to share a cabin with two sisters who were returning to England to spend time with family. They had immigrated to the States many years ago, married, and raised their families. They hadn't been home to England in twenty-eight years. They were looking forward to their return and were a little emotional. Their father had passed away and they had lost two of their brothers in the War. They had brought many pictures of their children and grandchildren and were so eager to share them with their mother, who was in her early eighties, still healthy and sharp; she had even helped with financing their trip. It would be a wonderful, unforgettable reunion.

This was all part of a delicate journey for Sarah. She hoped she could right a terrible wrong, although the justice she sought would never be the product of any court of law. There would never be a rendered verdict, no decision in favor of the plaintiff, and any retribution would be fleeting. Knowing the truth would be enough for Sarah. She knew this was the right path for her and she would follow it to its end.

Delilah

SEPTEMBER, 1938

A magnificent full moon had given closure to an especially hot day and an equally blistering summer. It was the first day of fall, September 21, 1938, and it would become the most tragic day of my life and for so many other people.

It is difficult for me to relive the events of that day because they are still very raw. They are, however, still crystal clear in my memory.

We had expected Aunt Meg to arrive for the Labor Day weekend and the end of our summer vacation, but a change in her travel plans had delayed her arrival by just over two weeks. The whole family was disappointed. We had all been looking forward to her visit; it had been almost a year since her last. Aunt Meg would be staying with us for the next couple of months. She had always wanted to experience New England in the fall. She even had her black

56

gelding, Buck, transported up to Jamestown several days before her arrival. Buck and Grace had been stable mates in Chestnut Hill.

She finally arrived on Thursday, the twenty-first while I was in school. I couldn't wait to get home. Everyone was excited to have Aunt Meg in the house.

Aunt Meg and I rode on the beach that night, and at one point we dismounted and strolled through the surf with our horses in tow. We had a lot of catching up to do.

"So tell me, is Michael Coleman still the dreamboat he was last year, or have you moved on to some other young man? You know you have to tell me everything." She was always teasing me about the boys I had crushes on. She insisted I share these intimate details with her – how else could she offer any special guidance?

"Oh, he turned out to be a real jerk. Decided Karen Anderson, the ditsy cheerleader, was more his style. Her middle name is not lightning and that says a lot about him."

"Well my dear, just keep looking and keep your standards high. Now, have you done any writing in your diary?"

"All the time! But enough about of me, tell me about your trip to Paris." I always wanted to hear about her travels.

"It was marvelous! I went to visit Napoleon's tomb at the Dome des Invalides. It's all about the French military, but impressive. And so many wonderful restaurants! Though there is a lot of uneasiness with all of Hitler's aggressive rhetoric and deeds. It's very unnerving to the French."

It had been a crystal-clear evening with a dazzling full moon. It was a night that I would always remember. I would only realize just how special it was less than twenty-four hours later.

My mother allowed us to stay home from school the next day. We were just too excited with Aunt Meg in the house. My mother felt that school would be a waste of time. "Let's call it a mini family vacation," she said.

The next morning Aunt Meg and I decided to go riding again. We made our way to the beach. It was such a short distance from the house. The water looked inviting, and since we were dressed in shorts and light blouses, we decided to take a swim. It might be a little uncomfortable on the ride home, since leather and water don't always mix, but we didn't care. Aunt Meg and I were amazed how warm the water was, certainly a lot warmer than it had been just the night before. The sky had a strange orange glow to it.

After our quick swim we made our way back to the house. The skies had darkened a little and it looked like rain. My father had gone to work at the Naval base in Newport. The wind picked up a little, a steady rain began to fall, and everyone retreated to the house. My mother and Aunt Meg had gone to the living room with Stephanie and the twins. Claudia was in the process of making an apple pie. We had several apple trees in the yard and it had been a bumper crop that summer. I went to my bedroom to change into dry clothes and to write in my diary about our ride and swim. Within a couple of hours the wind had steadily increased in intensity and the rain was pelting my window. I looked out at the bay and saw a sea of turmoil. I was becoming concerned, and went downstairs to the living room to see if my mother and Claudia shared my worry.

National Weather Bureau, Washington, D.C.

SEPTEMBER 20, 1938

The headline of the *New York Times* read, "Britain and France Tell Czechs to Accept Adolf Hitler's Terms or Face Potential Loss of Whole Country." The day was September 20, 1938. Hidden away in the back pages of this same newspaper was a small article that read, "Severe tropical storm which gave concern to residents of Florida's east coast is making a wide northward arc and is apparently heading out to sea." The passage of time would prove just how perceptive Britain and France's concerns were and how costly Hitler's terms were to be. History would also reveal regrettably how faulty their weather forecast was regarding that tropical storm.

On September nineteenth the Jacksonville office of the U.S. Weather Bureau issued a hurricane warning for Florida's upper east coast. The residents and authorities of Jacksonville had endured a Labor Day storm three years earlier and began to make broad preparation for this one. Fortunately, the storm turned north and everyone in that area of concern let out a deep breath. The bureau then issued warnings for the Carolina coast and transferred authority to the bureau's headquarters in Washington D.C.

At 9:00 a.m. on September twenty-first the bureau in Washington D.C. issued a northeast storm warning for the expansive area from Block Island, Rhode Island north to Eastport, Maine and west to Atlantic, New Jersey. In reality, the storm's center was further south and the weather bureau had greatly underestimated its intensity.

Twenty-eight-year-old rookie meteorologist Charlie Pierce had just recently been assigned to the Washington, D.C. office and this was to be his first hurricane season. Tropical depressions form off the coast of west Africa and begin their wandering path eastward. Most of these depressions never approach a dangerous size or strength, but some do, and predicting their path and intensity is a demanding task. Tens of millions of people, as well as all the busy shipping lanes in the vast Atlantic Ocean, hang on every statement issued by the D.C. weather bureau. Young Mr. Pierce welcomed the challenges of his first hurricane season; in fact, he relished it. But today had been a long and frustrating day.

"Hey Bernie, come take a look at this." Charlie had all his maps and weather data spread out all over his reference table. Three big pendant lights hung from the ceiling; they were always on, even on the most sun filled days.

"What's up, Charlie?"

Bernie Thompkins shuffled over to Charlie's table, He was average height, average weight, had short dark hair with just a bit of gray at his temples, wore a short-sleeved white dress shirt with a dark, nondescript tie, a pocket protector, and black rimmed glasses; Bernie could have been a Norman Rockwell interpretation of a government meteorologist.

60

"I'm worried about this storm that just got passed up to us from our Florida office. This one could get real ugly. Right now it's about three hundred miles south of Hatteras." He pointed to the maps. "It's still small, but very intense."

"Yeah, Charlie, I've been listening to feedback from shipping in that area. Couple of freighters and a coastal barge getting bounced around pretty good, but nothing really remarkable. I wouldn't be too concerned with it. Looks like the Gulf Stream will drag it further east into the colder Atlantic waters. That thing will be a foggy morning in London in about a week."

"I'm not so sure about that, Bernie." Charlie pointed to his maps again. "See these two high pressure systems, one to the northwest and this huge one to the northeast, which appears to have stalled? I think this unremarkable storm, as you say, is going to get squeezed between these two systems and ride this narrow furrow right up into Long Island and New England."

Bernie thought for a bit then took a step back from the table, put the back of his right hand on his hip, and scratched the crown of his head with his other hand.

"I don't know, Charlie, you're describing a scenario that is extremely rare. I don't know how you can be so sure of this. I've been here twelve years and I've never seen anything like what you're predicting. You better run this by Mitchell, but I don't know how receptive he's going to be. We already had a discussion about this one and everyone was in agreement, this wasn't worth the brain matter. Maybe a small craft warning at the most."

"You had a meeting! How come nobody told me?"

"Charlie, you've only been here six months. I think you need to earn your stripes."

"How fucking snobbish is that! Where is Mitchell?"

"In his office. You better hurry, he's on his way home and it's been a long day."

Charlie Pierce hurried down the corridor, past the empty offices. The fourth floor of the government building was very still; everyone had punched out and gone home. *Sort of like the calm before the storm*, Charlie thought to himself, and then he heard Charlie Mitchell's voice sounding like he was on the phone.

Charles 'Charlie' Mitchell was the respected and celebrated chief meteorologist of the D.C. office. He had been promoted to that position twenty-three years ago and had gotten lazy, as young Charlie Pierce saw it, resting on his laurels.

Mitchell said "See you in a bit" and hung up the phone. "My wife," he said to his young understudy. "What's on your mind? A little late for you to be hanging around."

"Ah, Mr. Mitchell, I want to talk to you about this storm just south of Hatteras. I am very concerned about it."

"Enough of the Mr. Mitchell crap, Charlie will do. One Charlie to another. We took a look at that thing this afternoon, it's an intense little thing all right, I'll grant you that, but it's already made its typical swing almost due east. It will quickly fall apart once it gets over colder water."

"Charlie, I'm not so convinced as you are. Please hear me out."

"I can't do that right now. We have dinner plans with Congressman Sanders and his wife and I am already running late."

"Please, here me out, I've got some new information that begs for analysis."

"Can't do it, but have all your ducks lined up for tomorrow morning. I'll get our team organized for a late morning conference, you'll have the floor, but be ready." He left the room, briefcase in hand, and hustled down the corridor. *Fuck your ducks* Charlie said to himself. *Tomorrow morning may be too late.*

They met the next morning at 10:30 a.m. in the conference room; Charlie Mitchell had outlined the purpose of the meeting with his two advisors earlier. The conference room was already stifling from the heat and humidity that had settled into the D.C. area overnight. All four of the windows were open, and two ceiling fans and a big pedestal fan in the rear corner of the room fought a losing battle against an entrenched opponent. Charlie Mitchell and his two consultants sat at the conference table with open shirts and loosened ties. Mitchell sat at the back facing the blackboard. He took a handkerchief from his hip pocket, cleaned his dark framed glasses, and then wiped the sweat from his brow and round bald head. His suspenders seemed to pull on his large torso like they were holding back the tide. Pierce wondered if anyone could look more uncomfortable; he knew this would be a brief discussion.

"Okay Charlie, we're all ears," said Mitchell. "Let's hear your concerns."

Charlie Pierce had taped his broad map to the blackboard and had an additional one on the conference table. He was bone tired, had slept very little that night, and had not bothered to shave that morning. He wore the same white shirt and tie as yesterday. *Good thing this is not a job interview,* he thought to himself. He took a long pull on his coffee.

"Gentlemen, I think we need to re-think this one."

He began his analysis of the data. He had been tracking the storm since the Florida office had handed it off to their bureau. Charlie again explained how he anticipated the squeeze play between the two stationary high pressure systems.

"This won't be the predictable early fall hurricane that everyone thinks it will be. Some of you think that the storm has already made an eastward turn. I don't think it has. In fact, I am convinced of that."

Bernie Thompkins had been drumming his fingers on the conference table. He didn't like this young upstart, didn't like his cockiness, and wanted to make points with his boss. He saw his opportunity.

"Charlie, how the hell would you know that?"

Pierce instantly focused on Bernie, thought to himself, *you kiss-ass prick.*

"Bernie, how the fuck do you know it *has* turned east?"

Charlie Mitchell jumped in. "Okay everybody, calm down. Pierce, finish what you got to say and then we'll make a decision."

Pierce continued. "We had a record breaking summer, the Gulf Stream has not been this warm as far back as our records go. There are two stationary high pressure systems over the northeast and mid-Atlantic, with just a sliver of space between them, and that sliver is directly over the toasty Gulf Stream. I expect this storm to ride right up that trough and it will suck up every bit of energy from that warm water. We also have a full moon and an autumn equinox tossing in its two cents. I anticipate this to blossom into something evil. It will have sustained winds of at least a hundred and twenty-five miles an hour and it will be traveling fast, probably around thirty-five miles an hour. My calculations have this monster slamming into Long Island and Rhode Island Sound with a minimum twenty-five-foot storm surge. We need to warn a lot of people."

Bernie Thompkins was itching to score points again; he had been looking at his watch and pulling at his tie during all of Pierce's presentation.

"Well Pierce, why don't we just tell everybody to get on the freaking ark with all the other animals?"

"You really are an incompetent fool, Bernie," Pierce shot back.

Bernie and Bill Campbell, the other meteorologist in the room, jumped up to challenge young Pierce.

Charles Mitchell stepped in again. "Okay everybody, settle down." He made sure they knew it was an order and not a request. He took his already soaked hankie and made a feeble attempt to clean up the perspiration that seemed to be everywhere.

"God damn this heat. Listen Charlie, I appreciate your concern, and it appears you have done your homework, but I think you're wrong. Just before our meeting I checked with our land base stations as well as our marine stations and they reported a slight rise in the barometric pressure, and the sustained wind direction has changed from southeast to east rather rapidly. Thirty-six years in this business tells me that means a turn to the east."

"Charlie, they're wrong. Please, check again."

"I will not put eighteen million people on a hurricane alert based on the hunch of a naïve weatherman with only six months' experience under his belt. There's over sixty years of weather forecasting know-how in this room and we all say you're wrong, Charlie. End of discussion."

64

"I want it on the record that I completely disagreed with this assessment. You better pray that I am not right."

"We will make note of that. And if it makes you feel better, you can issue small craft warnings for the northeast and mid-Atlantic. We will need to notify the mid-Atlantic shipping lanes of the impeding storm. Now, I need some fresh air."

With that, Mitchell and the other two meteorologists stood and left the room, not saying a word to Charlie where he sat, quivering with suppressed rage.

What neither Charlie Pierce nor his superiors knew was that this monster storm was gaining almost unfathomable forward speed. It was later estimated that, at its peak, it was traveling due north at seventy miles per hour. This forward speed meant the winds on the east side of the storm would increase in velocity by that same amount. The worst hurricane in three hundred years, with winds in excess of two hundred miles an hour, was now bearing down on Long Island and southeastern New England, with its real wrath focused on Rhode Island Sound. It was also estimated that this behemoth was indeed pushing a twenty-five-foot wall of water out in front of it. The water temperature recorded at Rhode Island's state beach in Narragansett showed a rise of ten degrees from the day before, and there wasn't even a cloud on the horizon. No one was prepared for such an event. Charlie Mitchell was supposedly quoted as saying, after the hurricane had passed, that "being prepared for this demon would have done little."

Boston radio station WEEI meteorologist E.B. Rideout had also been watching the storm with much concern. He too was unknowingly in agreement with his young counterpart in Washington, D.C. He finally told his listeners to brace for a very powerful hurricane. He was convinced there would be severe damage and a great loss of life. Those listeners that did hear his prediction disregarded it. Only New York and Washington D.C.'s meteorologist forecasts were deemed credible. Those that really needed to heed his warning had already lost power and were beginning to feel the storm's wrath.

Sarah

MARCH, 1875

"Daddy, please don't go to your mill today, something dreadful will happen there today!" Sarah then turned to her mother. "Mother, please, don't let him go, you must listen to me!"

Frederick and Florence Shepard had heard this before from their middle child; she had always been a precocious and different little girl.

She was delivered Sarah Diane at their home in Nottingham, England, on the twenty-seventh of March, 1875. They had named her after her maternal grandmother. Her father had insisted on it. He would always be grateful for how welcomed his mother-in-law had made him feel when he married her daughter. She was a woman of great compassion, and he was genuinely saddened when she passed away just a few short years after their marriage.

"Your father needs to go to work, Sarah. I know you feel strongly about this, but a lot of people depend on your father."

"You know what happened when my brother ignored my warning. He almost drowned."

Her father and mother remembered that day, wished they had understood their daughter's alarming advice at the time; they were still having trouble grasping its extent.

Sarah had pleaded with her older brother Freddie not to go swimming with his friends on that hot day in August. Something would happen to him, she just knew it. Freddie had the brashness of youth and ignored his sister's pleas, heading out to the quarry with his friends. The boys had been horsing around when Freddie and his friend Peter Middleton knocked heads. Both boys went under. The others had seen and heard their heads collide. One of his friends instantly grabbed Freddie and pulled him to shore. Peter was not immediately located and there was panic. If it hadn't been for the heroic actions of a passerby who had heard the boys' screams for help, Peter would probably have drowned and his body never recovered from that deep quarry. Sarah had been frustrated with her brother. He should have listened to her; it could have been a tragedy. There would have been so much pain for the family, and the pain would have been almost unbearable for her. She had sensed this tragedy and had tried to prevent it. Her brother had probably suffered a mild concussion and was still light-headed, but she sought him out in his bedroom. She did not mince her words.

"I told you that this would happen, you damn fool! Why could you not listen to me? You could have died! You will never ignore me again."

Now Frederick and Florence faced the same dilemma once more.

"I have to go work today, it's as simple as that," her father said. "I cannot allow my actions to be dictated by the intuitions of my twelve-year-old daughter, as potentially threatening as they might be."

"I know that, but there are so many far reaching consequences if she is right," Florence told her husband. "I pray that she is wrong."

"For now I will be cynical, I have no other choice." Frederick replied.

Later that day a hoist in the loading bay at Frederick's lace mill snapped and thousands of pounds of raw cotton bails crashed to the floor. Frederick, as well as other workers, happened to be in the immediate area. One man was killed and another man's arm was broken. Frederick's right leg was badly broken and he had internal bruising, requiring that he be hospitalized for the next several weeks.

Her mother approached Sarah several days after the accident.

"Sarah, we need to talk about this ability of yours. It must be so frightening to you. When you tried to tell your brother about the day he went swimming, we all dismissed it as another quirky thing about our special little girl; but now, with what happened to your father, I think we are just as concerned as you are. Maybe more."

"It scares me a little, Mother, but I get angrier when my family ignores my warnings."

"We won't do that again, but tell me about these episodes when you look into the future. I want to understand what is happening to you. Maybe we can help with that heavy responsibility."

Sarah told her mother it was like an invisible bubble that surrounded her family. No matter where the family went this invisible bubble floated along with them. It wasn't a protective bubble. It could not prevent things from happening. It could only warn Sarah when something had penetrated its outer layer. It was up to Sarah to sense the warning and determine who it was for. It was a task that often caused her a lot of anguish.

"But how do you know when something has penetrated this—this—a—a bubble, as you say? What do you feel? Do your hands and feet tingle? Do you see bizarre images?"

"It does come on rather quickly. I can be anywhere, feeling quite content in the moment, and then a wave pours over me. I become very distracted, my hands and lower arms seem to be on fire. My neck and face become quite sweaty."

She did not tell her mother that her heart would speed up and pound in her chest. Strange images of things to come would float in front of her, and although places all over her body were consumed with heat and perspiration, her insides felt icy cold and numb.

"Oh my sweetheart, you need to know you are not alone. We will find what this is all about."

Sarah knew that her family would never understand what she was experiencing. She did not understand it herself.

The Shepard family had seen Sarah take on a different persona. She had become the family caretaker; warning family members and friends of approaching danger or illness became her new role.

* * *

Her family began to accept that Sarah might be more than just a quirky little girl. They knew that a strange dimension had been added to their lives when her father had the serious accident at his factory and her older brother and his friend nearly drowned. Sarah had no idea where her developing ability would take her; she was concerned it was slowly beginning to define who she was. She was a passenger on a train that had an unknown destination every single day, and she was simply along for the ride. It excited and frightened her at the same time.

Her parents often talked about these events and how their daughter had seen them from afar. They became anxious by what was happening to their daughter. She never seemed in danger of any physical harm. It was the potential emotional harm that concerned them. Sarah's gift had two very expressive concerns, knowing and knowing how to tell. Being made aware of impending events was the simple reality of it all, but learning how to share sometimes very disturbing news with someone would be a lifelong experiment.

News of Sarah's gift slowly spread within the family. Her mother's niece, Elizabeth, was having a difficult pregnancy. She had experienced difficulty trying to conceive. She had married young and her husband, Eric, was quite a bit older than her. There had been some family concern over their age difference, but it quickly dissipated, as he proved to be a good husband and provider. They both wanted children. Elizabeth had always been painfully thin, and putting on weight had been difficult for her. She had not always been the healthiest young woman. This pregnancy was proving to be as difficult as the previous ones. They had all ended in miscarriages. Elizabeth was sick a lot during this pregnancy, and there had been some daily bleeding. Keeping her food down had also become a challenge. The pregnancy had progressed and she was in her sixth month, but she was obviously still very concerned. And so was her doctor. Fearing that she might lose the baby, he restricted her to bed rest almost twenty-four hours a day. Her husband had pleaded with Frederick and Florence to let their daughter Sarah visit his wife. Maybe Sarah could offer some insight into what they should do.

"What you really want to know is, could you lose your wife too?" her father said. "What does a thirteen-year-old girl know of such womanly things? I would trust more the advice of your doctor."

But his nephew continued his pleading. "My doctor offers nothing but a pessimistic outlook. He tells me to prepare myself for the possibility of a sad conclusion. It is obvious he does not anticipate a healthy outcome."

"What if Sarah foresees the same outcome as your doctor? Are you prepared for that?"

"Elizabeth need not know that. That is something only I will feel the burden of."

"What about Sarah? Do you think a young girl needs such a heavy burden?"

In the end Frederick and Florence gave in to their nephew's pleading. They approached Sarah with her cousin's request. Sarah quickly agreed to do what she could, but was unsure how she could help. She told her father of her concerns.

"I will try to help. People want me to sense something, and that something is not always there. Most of the time there is just nothing to say or help with. This disappoints them, but it's just as simple as that: either I can help or I can't. It's completely beyond my control. People think it's complicated, but it really isn't." Mr. Shepard was amazed with the wisdom of his young daughter, wisdom beyond her years.

Sarah and her mother visited her cousin Elizabeth and her husband Eric. It had been a blistering hot day in June and the accompanying humidity was oppressive. Sarah's cousin greeted them at the door and it was evident that the six months of a very difficult pregnancy had taken its measure on him. He was unshaven and had dark circles under bloodshot eyes. Sleep had not been the daily indulgence he always thought it should be. The white cotton shirt he wore was wrinkled and stained with perspiration. It was opened wide at the neck and the sleeves were rolled up to his elbows.

"Please come in, Aunt Florence and Sarah," he said in a voice that searched for energy and conviction. "I'm so grateful you could come. We have had a difficult evening. Elizabeth has had painful leg cramps all night long and this heat and mugginess has not helped. The doctor left only a few minutes ago. Elizabeth's condition limits what medication he can administer."

"I am so sorry to hear such a thing. Why does life need to be so hard?" his aunt replied.

"Especially on someone as wonderful as Lizzy," Sarah added.

"My wife is in her bed, of course; it's where she lives her life now." Sarah and her mother followed his slow and saddened gait into Elizabeth's bedroom.

Sarah's cousin was lying on her back looking pale and fragile. The recent heat had only increased her discomfort. She wore little clothing, and their maid stood next to her with a broad fan trying to ease her distress. Sarah's mother leaned over and kissed her niece and then excused herself. She would wait in the living room.

Sarah sat with her cousin and learned what a trying pregnancy it had been, all the time sensing nothing. Her cousin even insisted that she should rest her hands on Elizabeth's swollen abdomen. Sarah's mother would comment later that her cousin was not very big considering how far along she was in her pregnancy. Still Sarah sensed nothing. She waited longer, hoping for something, but there was nothing to try and interpret; her gift would provide no special insight today, and she shared the disappointing news with her cousins.

Her cousin twisted in her bed and began to sob. Her husband grabbed the fan from their maid and tried to cool his now despondent wife while massaging her back. They had been praying against all the pessimism and were hoping that Sarah might bring good news.

"You come to visit with us, and that is all you can offer us? Nothing?" her cousin's husband said, clearly agitated. "You have told us nothing!"

Sarah was becoming uncomfortable with his agitation and his look of despair. Her mother had heard the tension in her nephew's voice and had come back into the bedroom. She brought the visit to an abrupt conclusion. "My little girl has told you everything she can. We shall be on our way."

One last time her cousin challenged her. "Your daughter has told us nothing."

Sarah and her mother stopped at the door and turned to them.

"Maybe, in time, you and Elizabeth will come to see how much Sarah actually did tell you." They left him standing there, sad and alone. Sarah and her mother walked away not as alone but just as dejected.

Three months later, after a difficult delivery, Sarah's cousins became the proud parents of a healthy baby boy. They never acknowledged her visit. It became an uncomfortable and embarrassing event that they wanted to put behind them. It was rarely mentioned at the few family gatherings her cousins attended.

Delilah

SEPTEMBER 21, 1938

Everyone was huddled around the big Philco radio on the kitchen table. Aunt Meg was turning the knobs, trying to find out something about the storm. The wind was beyond gale force at this point. My mother tried to phone my father at the Naval base, but could not get through. A look of concern and fear spread across her face. Claudia suggested that we locate some candles and kerosene lamps just in case we lost power. Aunt Meg thought we should go and secure the carriage house. This storm was no doubt making the horses a little nervous. Aunt Meg and I found some rain slickers and headed out. The rain and wind pushed back at us the whole walk there. Aunt Meg held my hand the entire way. The wind was almost blinding and the rain stung our faces. Once inside the carriage house we could see that the horses were indeed unnerved by what was happening outside. Grace's withers were trembling and she was emitting soft grumblings. Buck was stamping the floor and scratching at his paddock door with his front hooves.

"They don't like this weather around them," said Aunt Meg. "Animals have a special sense when it came to foul weather. Let's hope they don't know more than we do."

She had to raise her voice to be heard over the wind. We gave the horses fresh apples and extra feed, hoping the treats might occupy them for a while and calm their nerves. Aunt Meg and I secured all the windows, double-bolted the carriage house doors, and headed back up to the house. The wind and rain made the walk up the hill to the house almost effortless. We stumbled into the front hallway. Mother, Claudia, Stephanie, and the twins were lighting hurricane lamps in the living room.

"We have lost power, and the phone is dead," my mother said with a long sigh. "I wish Jeffery was here."

We huddled around the kerosene lamps in the living room and committed ourselves to waiting out the storm. Corey and T.J. thought all of this was just pure delight. Claudia went to the kitchen to finish her apple pie. Within two hours the wind was almost deafening. We looked out at the bay to a sea of turmoil. It was hard to imagine how any boat could safely navigate in such waters. The waves had to be at least twelve to fifteen feet high. The windows were beginning to shudder in the house. Suddenly one of the large south-facing windows in the living room gave way. We screamed. My mother was in the path of the flying glass. She was knocked to the floor by the force of the wind and glass. She had been cut deeply on her right arm and shoulder and was bleeding heavily. Aunt Meg and I dragged her away from the wind and rain while Claudia ran to the linen closet in the kitchen and returned with a number of towels. Corey and T.J. were suddenly terrified. My sister and I immediately moved them away from where my mother had fallen. They did not need to see all the blood and their mother in such pain. We tried to comfort them and assure them that mother would be okay. Stephanie brought them back to the kitchen and tried to engage them in a game of Crazy Eights. Claudia and Aunt Meg worked feverishly to dress my mother's wound and stop the bleeding. In about twenty minutes they had the wound dressed and the bleeding under control, but it was just a temporary fix; my mother would need multiple stitches. She was in a great deal of pain and had lost a lot of blood, but she still had her wits about her. My mother demanded we all move to the kitchen and away from the south-facing windows.

As we moved to the kitchen, Aunt Meg looked out the small windows on either side of the front door and screamed, "Oh my God!" We all looked to see that the seawater was almost up to the side of the carriage house. "We have to release Buck and Grace!" she screamed "It is the only way they can survive!"

"I will go with you," I said.

My mother screamed, "NO!" that she would go instead, but we all knew that she wasn't up to it.

"It's okay, Delilah is strong, she can make it" said Aunt Meg.

"Meg is right," said Claudia. "Delilah can do it."

"All right, the two of you go if you must. I would prefer your horses be a little unnerved rather than risk your lives, but I know I can't stop you. We need to get things moved upstairs. We need to prepare for the worst. Be careful and be quick," my mother said.

I looked at the twins. Their eyes were wide with terror. I winked at Stephanie and told her to keep an eye on her brothers. Aunt Meg and I donned our slickers again and were out the front door. We had to walk directly into the wind; making it to the carriage house was a huge accomplishment. The seawater was already several inches deep and rising. The ground the carriage house stood on had turned into a soggy mess that pulled at our feet like we had suddenly stepped onto fly paper. We struggled to get the doors open. I glanced back at the house and was stunned with what I saw.

Corey and T.J. had somehow gotten out of the house and managed to get about two-thirds of the way to the carriage house. They had been knocked to the ground by the punishing winds and had taken shelter behind a small stone landscaping wall. I screamed at Aunt Meg and pointed to them.

"They need our help!" my aunt screamed, and we ran to the twins and scooped them up. They must have made their escape to be with us when Claudia and my mother were preoccupied with the move upstairs. I was furious with them, but this was not the time for a scolding. We struggled back to the barn. The water was rising fast, now over a foot deep. We released the horses and they vanished into the storm. We struggled to close the carriage house doors but the fierce winds would not allow it. We suddenly heard the screams of my sister Stephanie. She must have come after the twins and was now also being consumed by the storm.

My father suddenly appeared out of nowhere. Somehow he had made it home. The effort to get back to us must have been an ordeal. He was drenched and exhausted. His clothing was torn everywhere and he had abrasions on his face, hands, and arms. I immediately hugged him.

Aunt Meg called out loudly, "Oh thank God, Jeffrey, you are here!"

He grabbed T.J. in his arms, took my hand and shouted to Aunt Meg, "You stay here with Corey. Move to the loft if you need to, but I will be back. Delilah, you must try to get to your sister. We need to get to the house. We must move fast. I will be right behind you. Now go!"

The water was up to my knees, but my father was pushing us on and we moved towards the house. I looked up at the house and saw that my mother and Claudia were witnessing the whole scene from the living room bay window. They had backed themselves into the corner of the window. They were away from most of the wind and, like patrons at a theater, they watched the whole terrifying scene play out before them, helpless to change the outcome. I could see my mother was excited to see my father had returned, but was in terror for our safety. We were making desperate progress. I had lost sight of Stephanie and was beginning to fear the worst.

The front yard was already too deep with water to navigate. My father hollered that we must try for the back door as the water was still shallow there. I tried to tell him that I had lost sight of Stephanie, but he was burdened with T.J. and the wind had become deafening. We struggled towards the back of the house. We slowly disappeared from my mother's sight. Suddenly, a huge wall of water consumed us and we were completely submerged; I became separated from my father. I was being dragged along what was once our backyard and had completely lost my bearings. I had panicked and was screaming underwater, grabbing at anything I could. I had swallowed a lot of seawater and felt I was about to drown when my father's hand suddenly found me and dragged me to the surface. In a few seconds we were somehow climbing the back stairs to the house. I looked back and saw that the carriage house had also been consumed by this same wall of water. Only the second floor and roof were visible. My father forcefully dragged T.J. and me up the stairs and in the back door.

We fell onto the kitchen floor exhausted. We were only on the floor for a few seconds when above the roar of the wind we could hear the screams of my mother. We rushed into the living room and witnessed what my mother was seeing. She was looking out the shattered bay window and seemed to be in a trance. She was completely numb to the wind and rain that tore at her. The image before us was overwhelming. Aunt Meg, Stephanie, and Corey were desperately clinging to the cupola on what was left of the carriage house roof. It had been torn away from its structure and was pitching in a turbulent sea. Stephanie had somehow made her way to the carriage house. They were utterly helpless and in complete terror. A huge wave suddenly swallowed them and they were gone. My mother screamed one last time and collapsed.

The aftermath of the hurricane had been catastrophic and widespread. All of Narragansett Bay, as well as most of interior Rhode Island, had been devastated by this violent hurricane. We read of bodies being recovered all up and down the Rhode Island shoreline and learned that an estimated 600 people had perished in the hurricane and 286 homes were destroyed and over twenty-five thousand more were damaged. Downtown Providence, at the peak of the storm, was under eighteen feet of water, and many motorists had perished in their cars. The wind odometer at the Blue Hills observatory in Dedham, Massachusetts, which was fifty miles from the shoreline, had recorded winds up to 180 miles per hour before it snapped. Twenty thousand electrical poles had been blown down, and over two billion trees had been destroyed in New England.

Aunt Meg's swollen and battered corpse was discovered on Poppasquash Point in Bristol; Stephanie's and Corey's bodies washed ashore several miles up the shoreline at the town beach in Warren, Rhode Island. They too were almost unrecognizable. We were fortunate to recover their bodies, as there were so many others that were never found.

Few people could attend the wakes or funerals. Shoreline rail road tracks and thoroughfares had been torn away by the powerful storm surge. Interior roadways were blocked with countless fallen trees, and transportation was totally disrupted for several weeks.

My mother was to be in an almost coma-like state for the next several days. Losing her sister, her youngest daughter, and one of her beautiful twin boys, along with the serious wound to her arm, caused her mind and body to shut down. Father said it was her survival instinct taking over.

Somehow we made it through the funeral and the burials. My father and I tried to comfort my mother and, although she never specifically said it, I think in her now-compromised mental state she blamed my father for our horrible loss. I heard her ask Claudia several times why Jeffrey hadn't been home, if only he had stayed home.

My father told me of the ordeal he went through to return home. The naval base in Newport was receiving conflicting information about the approaching hurricane. The initial forecasts predicted the storm passing south of Rhode Island Sound and then further out to sea. Then the forecast had suddenly turned dire and the weather predictions were alarming. It was to be the worst hurricane the region had seen in many, many years. The Navy was in a full-scale secure and lockdown mode. Reports of thirty- to forty-foot seas were being reported. Battleships and cruisers throughout the northeast were scrambling for safe harbor or open water. He knew he had to get home. Jamestown was in the direct path of this massive storm. He had driven down to the ferry that serviced Jamestown, but they had already secured the ferry for the duration of the storm. There were others that had gathered at the ferry landing. They all wanted to get back to their families. They knew they would be needed. Together they pooled their money and offered the ferry captain a tempting reparation if he made the trip. But no amount of money would be enough to entice such a foolhardy trip and he told them so. He told Captain Miller that he should also know better; such a trip would be futile.

More specifically, he said, and he didn't mince his words, "There might be a slight, very slight chance we could make it across to Jamestown – actually, it would be a fucking miracle. It's blowing hard straight out of the southeast and that would push us right up against the wharf. There is no way we would ever be able to tie off once we got there, and the return trip would surely sink my vessel. I am not that goddamn stupid. I will secure my ferry here in the lee of this little cove. I hope it will be sufficient to save my vessel. I fear it will not."

Captain Miller knew he was right, but he would never acknowledge it. He needed to get home and he was willing to risk anything to that end.

He told the others that he would venture up to Castle Hill. There was a small, sheltered cove there where the Navy shared a sturdy launch with the Coast Guard. He was prepared to commandeer any Navy vessel he needed to. He invited anyone that was willing to make the trip with him. Three men took him up on his offer. He told them to get in his car and they headed for Castle Hill.

The base had suddenly been directed to prepare for the approaching hurricane. Sailors were scrambling to secure anything and everything. One destroyer and two escorts had their crews hastily recalled from shore leave and had quickly departed for open water. If they were lucky they might be able to dodge the real wrath of the storm. Whatever the outcome, their chances of survival were significantly enhanced on open water rather than secured to the pier. There the ships would be subjected to a constant battering of one giant roller after another. The storm surge itself could potentially lift the ships out of their slips, deposit them on the pier, or even push them inland, leaving them high and dry once the waters had retreated. It had happened several times in the two-hundred-year history of the U.S. Navy.

He got to the small pier just as several sailors were getting ready to pull the launch out of the water. He quickly ordered them to stop what they were doing and report to another area of the base. He described a fictitious crisis that required their immediate participation:

"There is a serious fuel spill at B dock. There is diesel fuel everywhere and we're afraid it could contaminate the potable water supply. You men need to get there. The launch will be fine until you get back. I will take these civilians to safe quarters. On your way." No mere sailor was going to challenge a captain's order. They were quickly gone.

The wind had increased significantly in just a short time. The waves were huge. Two of the men that had come with Captain Miller had suddenly decided against the trip. It would be just Jeffrey and Bill Summers. They had briefly made introductions on the way there. Bill lived on the northern and opposite end of Jamestown.

They needed to get the launch turned around. Captain Miller took charge. He secured a line to the front of the launch and shouted to the two other men who decided against the trip.

"Take this line and walk it out to the end of the pier. Bill and I will get in the launch and I will quickly start the engines. I will signal you when I am ready; then you must pull like madmen. We will only have this one chance, and we must do it quickly."

He passed the line to the waiting man. They wished each other good luck. Theirs was a desperate act.

"Now, let's do this!" Captain Miller shouted.

The two new shipmates struggled to get in the launch. It was pitching and rolling violently. The other two men moved towards the end of the pier with their line. They made it about half way down the pier before the wind and the piercing rain knocked them to the ground. The rest of the distance would be on their hands and knees.

Jeffrey got to the starboard-side steering station and started the engines. There was a spare line in one of the seat lockers; he wrapped it around him and the station several times to help keep himself upright.

He shouted to Bill: "Take this knife – be careful, it's very sharp! – and move to the front of the boat. The minute they get us turned around, look to me, I will signal you when to cut the bow line. I don't want to drag those men into the sea, nor do I want to run over my own line and foul the props. Do it quickly."

He signaled the men at the end of the pier to begin their frantic pulling. The launch quickly came around and Jeffrey engaged the engines half-throttle. He reached down and turned the bilge pumps on. They moved along the pier towards open water. Jeffrey and Bill looked briefly ahead and what they saw took their breath away: Massive breakers, many feet higher than the wharf, were thundering by. The powerful winds and driving rain had become a lethal mix.

The two men looked quickly at each other, their eyes met; No words were exchanged, yet they shared a simple, dire observation: We will die in those giant rollers, there is no going back.

Jeffrey screamed to Bill when the time was right. "Cut the line and lie down on the deck!" He pushed the throttle all the way forward and hoped for the best. Bill Summers quickly cut the rope and threw himself on the deck. The boat surged out into open water.

The sea was in turmoil. The first roller nearly capsized them. They took on more water than the pumps could handle. He turned the boat with the wind. It was their only chance.

The boat welcomed the change of course and the following seas. They stabilized and were making quick progress. It was short lived.

The next roller crashed over the stern and swallowed the boat as it moved forward. When they emerged from the back of the breaker Bill Summers was gone. Jeffrey caught a glimpse of Bill about a hundred and fifty feet away, thrashing in the surf. There was nothing that could be done for him. He was on his own.

So was Captain Jeffrey Miller. The wind and the seas were pushing him towards the Jamestown shoreline. Huge waves would engulf the stern of the launch and then move along its whole length, completely submerging the boat and then, miraculously, he would emerge on the back side. He was convinced that each new wave that rolled along his craft would be its last. Whether he lived or died was beyond his control.

The distance across the bay from Newport to Jamestown is about one mile. On a balmy summer's day it is a short ten-minute ferry ride; today it was another world away. He had been driven by his need to be with his family and now he was at the mercy of this angry ocean. He could only hope that he might stay afloat long enough to get close to the Jamestown shoreline, abandon the boat, and hope that the wind and surf would push him ashore. It was then that his craft finally succumbed to the beating it was taking. Its hull had split apart in two locations. The pumps were useless at this point.

He leaped from the boat as it went under. A terrifying surf immediately consumed and pushed him towards the shoreline, only to be returned to those same treacherous breakers by a deadly undertow, all the time being dragged across an ocean floor covered with jagged rocks wrapped with razor-sharp barnacles. Miraculously, he finally staggered on to the beach, his clothes and skin torn and tattered. He knew he needed to get to his home as quickly as possible; the worst of this hurricane was yet to come. He began to run.

Sarah

JUNE, 1890

Frederick Shepard's lace mill in Nottingham seemed to have plateaued over the last few years and he knew why. His stay in the hospital because of the accident at his factory had allowed him the time to reflect on his business dilemma. Product from the United States was just starting to enter the global market. An industrial revolution was taking place in that country of abundant raw material and aspiring entrepreneurs. Frederick wanted to be part of that insurgency.

He had talked at length with his competitors and others in the trade about this new industrial shift to America. Everyone was in agreement; the United States was a player to be reckoned with. He was convinced that the growth and future of his company could only be secured by moving to America and building his new lace plants there. The global demand for silk was staggering. He needed to move swiftly and forcefully.

He sent his trusted young apprentice, Tom Shaw, to New England to research his re-location plan. The logistics would be a real obstacle, as would the task of trying to persuade his wife and family of its value.

Frederick began pitching the idea to his wife the very day he sent his young intern to the states.

"Flo, I have sent Tom Shaw to America. He left this morning from South Hampton. I think you should know that I am thinking about moving my business there, probably somewhere in the New England area, and of course that means moving our whole family there too."

It was Sunday afternoon and Daphne, their housekeeper, had the day off; it was just the two of them. It had been a warm day in early May and they had spent most of it tending to their garden. It was something they enjoyed doing together. Florence took pleasure in her azaleas, irises, daffodils, and tulips, which had peaked in the last few days. Their vibrant blooms swayed in a soft breeze, and bees that seemed to be everywhere were busy with their instinctive burden. Florence could see that their legs were covered with gobs of pollen.

Frederick Sr. took pride in his King Arthur roses; they were his singular botanical passion. He had finished his delicate pruning and had spread bone meal and fish entrails around their base. It was something their retired gardener had always done. They had not yet secured his replacement, and Frederick would never subject his roses to such prolonged neglect. Their gardener had always felt that roses were just not worth the effort.

"My Lord, Frederick, I certainly did not see this coming," Flo responded. "I should take a seat while you explain this to me." They retreated to their white wicker chairs beneath the willow tree.

"I know this is quite sudden, but I have anguished over it for quite some time. I believe the livelihood of our business is at stake."

"Is it that serious?"

"I believe it is. Why, we could make New York City our new home. I have heard only marvelous things about it."

Florence rose from her chair and stood before her husband. She leaned forward and tenderly placed her hands on either side of his face.

"Frederick, I would go with you anywhere. I love you that much. But this involves our children now. Frederick Jr. is engaged and about to marry, and I'm not sure if little Pamela would be pleased. But a change of scenery might be good for Sarah. We have a lot to talk about."

Frederick stood and embraced his wife. "Yes, my love, we do."

In the weeks and months that followed, Florence found herself more accepting of the move to America. Her son was not sure he would travel with his family; it would be too much to ask of his new wife. But her two daughters were excited. They had heard so much about New York, and they were not hesitant in letting their parents know they welcomed the change.

Florence Shepard now embraced the thought of relocating her family to America. Initially she had not been receptive to the idea. Uprooting her family and leaving close friends and family would indeed be difficult. But now, maybe it was the best for Sarah. Mrs. Shepard knew she needed to remove her from an emerging lifestyle that would be too suffocating for her adolescent daughter. Maybe in New York she could shelter her from the prying world and keep her special talent under wraps. Let Sarah mature a bit; give her time to understand her gift. It would be a heavy responsibility, and she would need to learn how – and when – to use it.

Frederick Shepard Sr. was not so sure. The move to America would be difficult for his family. Financially he was convinced it would be a successful relocation. But he knew in time Sarah's secret would follow her to America and the tortured, empty souls of the new world would come calling. He knew his beautiful, caring young daughter could never say no to them.

Sarah

MAY, 1892

The Shepard family arrived in New York in the spring of 1892. They moved into a two-story brownstone on Pineapple Avenue in Brooklyn Heights. Its lofty windows faced out on to the busy thoroughfare. It was a wide, active street, and young elm and maple trees lined the roadway. The people of the neighborhood were friendly and engaged. There was a sense of community.

Frederick Shepard Sr. had actually arrived several weeks ahead of his family. His business plan to set up a lace mill in southeastern New England had been expedited by a fortuitous opportunity. Frederick had sent his young assistant, Thomas Shaw, on ahead of him to America. Tom's goal was to seek out a location for the mill, and within two weeks of his arrival he had hastily telegraphed Frederick Sr. indicating a complete change of plan. He had discovered a lucrative proposal that needed to be addressed as quickly as possible.

Tom Shaw had worked for Shepard Lace Works in Nottingham for many years and had become a trusted confidant. Fred respected his young assistant's insight, and Tom was prepared to move his young family to America if necessary. He and Fred Sr. had discussed the potential move many times. Fred and Tom's relationship had moved well past employer and employee. Fred Sr. was well aware of the long hours and hard work his young apprentice had invested in to the success of his company. He recognized that Tom had sharp business instincts and that he had a strong and progressive vision of how the company needed to grow to maintain a strong position in the industry in the coming years.

Frederick Sr. was also sadly aware that his only son, Fred Jr., would not be moving to the United States. He had recently married, and his young wife would not support the relocation. She was very close to her mother and immediate family. Jeopardizing his new marriage was something Fred Jr. was not prepared to do. Fred Sr. would dearly need the services of Tom, especially now that his son would not be by his side. He had always planned that Fred Jr. would take over his business when the time was right; he had invested a lot of time and knowledge to that end. He did, however, understand his son's dilemma.

Without his son's strong presence, he would now need to secure Tom Shaw's commitment to his company. He offered to make Tom a partner, with a twenty percent share in the company profits. It would take five years for this partnership to become fully finalized, and Tom left for America energized and keenly focused.

* * *

Tom had been prepared to recommend two possible locations in Massachusetts. One was in Fall River and the other in New Bedford. Rail lines had been built to both of these communities and offered access to the major hubs in Boston and Providence. Both locations were located on potent rivers, and there was a burgeoning population of newly arriving immigrants.

The textile industry had a long established presence in Fall River. Its population had invested in generations of its hard-working people to keep their textile plants profitable, and they had become skilled workers. The economical wages that Frederick offered would be more than enough for the English, Irish, and Portuguese pioneers that were arriving in droves. Many had left their homelands where there were no jobs at all.

During his efforts to locate potential plant locations and business opportunities, Tom had stumbled on an existing mill that was for sale. The owner had been forced to put his property up for sale when he discovered that his bookkeeper had embezzled most of his funds. It had all come crashing down when the unpaid invoices quickly began piling up and his bookkeeper had suddenly disappeared. The owner was desperate to sell and to sell quickly. His financial exposure was perilous.

The mill had been recently built in 1879 on the Quequechan River, which provided easy access to Narragansett Bay and the Atlantic. National and international shipping issues were immediately addressed. It was built of luminous gray granite, typical of most mills in Fall River. It was an abundant natural resource. The city itself was built over granite. Young Mr. Shaw was also acutely aware that no one else in this enormous textile metropolis was manufacturing lace. They had no competitor.

Tom's telegram to Fred Sr. had outlined the reason for the change of plans and what was on the line. The mill could be purchased for a song, but they would have to move aggressively. Frederick Sr. immediately saw that opportunity was knocking and was elated that his young protégé had seen this vision. He authorized Tom to take whatever steps necessary to acquire the mill. Purchase and sales agreement papers were drawn up and signed. Tom placed sufficient funds in escrow to secure the deal. They would have sixty days to close.

Frederick Sr. traveled to the states as quickly as he could. There were some logistical issues – after all America was not his home yet. He and Tom made it to their new plant about three weeks after the purchase and sale agreement had been signed. Assessments were made, contractors were lined up, and capital equipment was procured. They were committed to converting this cotton mill into a state of the art lace factory, producing some of the finest lace this region had ever seen. Tom Shaw would remain in Fall River to manage the project. Frederick Sr. would be involved in this effort too, but he would be traveling back and forth to New York via rail or steamship. He needed to get his family settled in New York. New England Lace Company would be an up and running company in just over eighteen months. Frederick would be away from his family for great lengths of time, but he was convinced that his lace mill would become a very successful venture.

The Shepard family settled into their spacious brownstone. Sarah and her siblings attended private schools in the city, and life went forward for the Shepard household. Sarah's gift had remained a guarded secret.

But then fortunes were told, cards were read, and astrological charts were created for her servants, friends, and family. Slowly, Sarah's unique ability began to disseminate to a broader base of people. Sarah's gift didn't allow for secrets. Friends of classmates and relatives of servants soon began asking for her special insight, and there was always a sad tale connected to their plea. Sarah found it difficult to say no, but soon discovered she was being drawn into an uncomfortable dilemma; offering people a glimpse into their future sometimes brought disturbing news. She began to temper what she told people. She simply chose not to share some of the dark premonitions that she saw. It made no sense to bring fear and trepidation into people's lives, especially in these lighthearted settings.

Sarah and her family had adjusted to their new life in New York and they were relishing it. It was a thriving city. The local papers told of over seven thousand immigrants a day being processed through Ellis Island. The city was alive with energy and diversity, and there was opportunity and potential everywhere. New York's natural harbor welcomed the world's goods, and its thriving and quickly expanding rail system distributed these goods to a country with an unappeasable appetite.

Sarah moved through school with ease and went on to higher learning at Pembroke College in Providence, Rhode Island. Majoring in English and minoring in Journalism, she was a member of the first graduating class of young women from the institution in 1898.

Her father had quickly become a prominent member of New York's business world and had developed personal relationships with some of its most powerful men. Money and power seem to gravitate towards each other. Knowing her father's business connections, Sarah began to pester him to help her pursue her journalism career. Her father eventually gave into her pleadings and approached William Randolph Hearst, the new owner of the *New York Journal.* He hoped there might be a position for his daughter, but he wanted it to have some merit. He felt that Sarah could best lobby for herself, and he only asked that Hearst give his daughter the opportunity to make her case. She was given the chance to interview for the position of secretary to the city manager's desk. Frederick hoped his daughter would be content in such a limited role, but he was not sure she would.

A 9:00 a.m. Monday morning interview was scheduled; Sarah arrived precisely on time and was smartly dressed. A young teenaged boy showed Sarah the way to the city editor's desk. They weaved their way through a large open room with hefty wooden desks and tables that seemed to be everywhere, finally arriving at a glass-walled barricade in the middle of chaos. The name etched on the smoked-glass window read "Mitch Atkinson – Editor, City Desk." There were people scurrying in all directions, and it seemed that the only form of communication was accomplished when someone in a position of authority shouted out his instructions. These directives would then be relayed down the appropriate stations with equally as loud directives. The constant ringing of phones also provided the ideal backdrop for this organized mayhem she now found herself in. She found it all energizing and perfectly entertaining.

Mitch Atkinson, the city editor, was at his desk, shouting his own demands into his telephone. He waved Sarah into his office with his left hand and indicated that there would be a brief delay with the index finger of that same hand. Sarah took a seat in the only chair in his office. The editor quickly ended his conversation and turned his attention to her.

"Our delightful Mayor is raising hell with our police union. That's an engagement he'll never win. Now tell me Miss... ahh... ah...." He pulled his watch out of his vest pocket, quickly glanced at it, and returned it to its nest. "Ah... ah... oh boy, where was I?"

"Miss Shepard. My name is Sarah Shepard."

"Right, of course, Miss Shepard. Mr. Hearst has asked me to interview you for a position as secretary to my office. He said you might offer an interesting perspective on some potentially newsworthy elements. I'm all ears, let's hear what you have to say. But please be brief and to the point, my plate is rather full today, is most days, probably why I need a secretary; which is exactly what I have been pleading with Mr. Hearst for, these last several months. Please go ahead."

"Thank you for your time, Mr. Atkinson. I'll get right to the point; during my senior year at Pembroke College, I became aware of a women's movement that is taking root in this country and all over the world."

"I suppose you mean the suffragettes. I know a little about them, and I suppose you're about to tell me I don't know enough."

"They are attempting to bring about change to our country. Change is not always easy, but it's absurd that a woman in this country can campaign for public office but is legally prohibited from voting for herself. I would think that needs to change."

"I suppose we could debate that, although I don't think I would have the gumption to tell my wife and oldest daughter that I chose to deliberate that specific issue. But let's put the debate aside for now. How do you see this new women's movement and your position here all coming together?"

"As I said, this cause is steadily gaining momentum in this country, and this newspaper needs to pay attention. I think it would be difficult for any man to acquire the internal trust of this women's group. I could be the woman that could gain their respect and provide your paper with the insight that will someday soon prove invaluable. But I will never function as a spy. That will never be my role. I have too much respect for these women. Women like Susan B. Anthony, Lucy Stone, and Carrie Chapman Catt, who right now leads this spirited group. The *New York Journal* needs to take a bold step and provide an outlet for their voices."

City editor Mitch Atkinson was impressed with this young woman seated in front of him. She was smart, attractive, and convincing. Uncrossing his legs and pushing himself away from his cluttered desk, he did not dwell on his decision.

"All right, let's give it a try. But know that your primary duties will still be that of a secretary. We will slowly venture out with efforts to report on this organization of women, and I am afraid you are right: their cause is worthy of the fight, and it will become an important issue that will need to be confronted sooner or later. My guess is it will be sooner. If we are a country defined by individual rights, we can't turn our back on half of our citizens and say your rights are limited. It will not stand, and you have beguiled me, Miss Sarah Shepard. Can you start the first Monday of next month?"

"Yes, yes I can." Sarah was elated.

Sarah's hard work, intelligence, and charm began to make inroads into the male-dominated and chaotic atmosphere that existed at the newspaper. There was some pushback from the skeptics that were uncomfortable with women in the workplace—those that believed the fairer sex's station in life was in the home with their children. Nothing could be done to change the minds of such cynics, and Sarah knew so, but the people of true significance at the *Journal* quickly measured her worth and welcomed her contributions. As promised, her editor gradually allowed Sarah to seek out the suffragette's movement and gain their trust, as she had predicted.

Providing them access to her newspaper only increased her sense of self-worth, and she became comfortable with who she was.

She was also to fall madly in love with a tall, handsome reporter who covered local, national, and international news events. She met William Lowe, actually got knocked into a soft snowbank by him one wintry night in February.

Snow and frigid conditions had made leaving work at the end of the work day a little treacherous. It was already quite dark, and workers from the *Journal,* all bundled in heavy coats, woolen scarfs, and hats, were leaving the building and scurrying to trolleys, taxis, and waiting rides. Blowing snow and people's chilled breath, illuminated by city street lights, only magnified the frigid scene. William had been outside for only seconds; he had been in a moment of indecision of whether he should walk home through the snow drifts and bitter temperatures, or seek the warmth of the sure-to-be crowded streetcar. He spun around quickly to make his dash to the waiting trolley and turned directly into Sarah Shepard, knocking her into the nearest snow bank. He quickly recovered and soon had her on her feet.

"I am so very sorry Miss, I hope I did not hurt you. I got a little ahead of myself. I was trying to get to the trolley and didn't look where I was going. Again, my deepest apologies, and to think I knocked you down for a trolley that has already left. Please tell me you're okay."

Removing her scarf and shaking it and her thick blonde hair free of clinging snow, she delayed her response. When she had refolded her head wrap, returned it to the top of her head, and tied it neatly under her frosty chin, she turned to this man who was stumbling over his apology.

"I am fine, Mr. Lowe. A little snow in my shoes and gloves and down my back, but I think it'll melt."

"I suppose I should ask how it is you know my name, and more pointedly, why I don't know yours."

"I started work at the *Journal* just a few weeks ago, and you are a fairly well-known entity there. My name is Sarah Shepard and I work at the city editor's desk."

"It's very nice to meet you, Miss Shepard."

"Sarah is fine. But please excuse me now, I have to catch the trolley, and if I don't hurry I will miss mine too."

"Yes, of course. Sarah, I will make a point of stopping by your office to apologize one more time."

Running towards her conveyance home, she yelled, "you have apologized enough Mr. Lowe, but stop by if you want!"

"William is fine!" he shouted back. He watched as she jumped on to the crowded street car, turned, quickly waved, and softly said his name. Heavy snow, biting cold, and all the spirited people heading home did little to prevent her voice from reaching him. It was as if she stood next to him and whispered in his ear, *William.*

* * *

William Lowe had taken a position with the newspaper after he graduated from Manhattan College in 1898. His father had hoped William would join the family business but was disappointed when his son chose to pursue a career in journalism. Bill Lowe quickly became a competent and respected reporter at the *Journal*. His easy and believing presence allowed him to quickly create lasting bonds with his sources and those he reported on. Trust was a critical building block in reporting. He respected all, and easily commanded the admiration of many; his reporting was deemed fair and impartial.

Bill was also a true patriot. The simple constitutional guarantee of freedom of the press, for obvious reasons, echoed deeply within him. No other country had secured this right and so vehemently protected it. This was something worthy of defending, and Bill Lowe knew to his inner core he would never shrink from that duty. He joined the New York National Guard shortly after taking his position with the *Journal,* and he was soon promoted to the rank of captain in New York's Forty-seventh Infantry.

Sarah was drawn to him on her first day at work; he was tall and lean, with the longest arms she had ever seen. The sleeves on his suits, shirts, and sweaters never seemed to be long enough, which made his gestures appear awkward. He had a long, purposeful stride and an easy, comforting presence. Piercing blue eyes surrounded by a dark Mediterranean complexion and dark, thick, wavy hair could hypnotize her from across the room. She wondered what those same eyes would do to her when they focused on only her. Would she melt or would she tremble? A wish and a fear at the same time.

Bill Lowe never appeared to even notice her, although she made numerous excuses to be in his area or field of vision. He always seemed too preoccupied with the people and events he had been assigned to cover. But now the snowy collision on that winter's day had solved that dilemma. Bill was at her desk the next morning with a drawn out apology, as she hoped he would be. She was drawn to his gentle nature and his capacity to make her feel so very relaxed whenever he sought her company. He was always very cordial, with little indication of intent. He seemed to be the most unassuming man she had ever met. There was always a joke or a comical observation that he wanted to share with only her, and his laugh was infectious. She immediately fell in love with him.

William Lowe, however, was slow to react to Sarah's beauty and charm. Although he felt relaxed in her company, her natural beauty was intimidating and brought about unneeded caution and hesitation. He saw himself as a tall and awkward fellow with his own social inequities. He was a little unsure of what a woman of Sarah's beauty and charm could see in a man like him. She, however, was convinced that William Benjamin Lowe was the man she had waited her whole life for. She had not dated much, but always felt she would know when the right man entered her life. And now he was here. She pursued him and he never once sensed her pursuit. But he slowly fell under Sarah's spell.

William finally found the nerve to ask her to a quick lunch on a Wednesday, after which he found it less intimidating to suggest dinner the following Saturday evening. They began to see each other frequently and soon became inseparable.

* * *

Sarah and William soon announced their engagement, to no one's surprise. Their families thought the match was ideal and could not imagine a happier couple. They were married in a very small and close wedding in October of 1900. They held their small but lively reception at her parents' home in Brooklyn Heights. They had decided to honeymoon on the Outer Banks of North Carolina, in a little seaside village called Buxton. Williams's good college friend Howard Teasdale was from the Cape Hatteras area of North Carolina. William had listened to his good friend talk extensively about his home. It sounded like the most pristine spot in the world. He finally traveled there with Howard in the summer right after college graduation. He had a month before he took his position at the *Journal,* and Buxton was indeed the paradise that Howard had described. William found himself walking the white, sandy beaches just about every day. He swam in the warm, crystal clear Gulf Stream waters that caressed these same beaches. The soft evening breezes would gently rock him to sleep in his seaside hammock. William vowed he would return someday with his future bride to spend their honeymoon there. He had to share this paradise with someone.

* * *

Their honeymoon was dreamlike, and their lovemaking was passionate and seemed endless. William's touch was magical. Sarah could feel the electricity move between her breasts and her thighs. Her loins ached for him, and her wetness welcomed him. They spent the first day of their honeymoon in bed. Their little cottage on the beach offered all the intimacy they needed. During the day they would walk the white sand beaches and hold hands incessantly.

Every day they walked to Buxton's village center and ate lunch at Evelyn's, a small restaurant with a pair of outside tables and chairs. There were ample golden locus trees that offered cool protection from the noon day sun. There was always an onshore breeze, and they took their time savoring the local cuisine. Sarah

96

insisted that they visit at all the gift shops that sold sea shells and trinkets to the tourists. Sarah bought an ornately painted porcelain seahorse with 'Buxton, N.C., 1900' hand-painted on the side. She bought William a tacky tie clip and matching cuff links.

Word travels fast in a small town, and soon everyone knew they were the happy couple here on their honeymoon. One of the owners of a gift shop suggested that they have their portrait painted in front of the honeymoon cottage. His daughter was a talented artist and she had done such portraits many times before.

"If you do not like the portrait then there will be no pressure to buy it. My daughter and I have made this offer several times before and we have yet to have an unsatisfied client. You will be very pleased with her work."

Sarah and William thought it a wonderful idea. They quickly agreed. The owner knew his daughter's schedule and assured them she would be there tomorrow morning at ten o'clock.

Savannah Phillips arrived the next day at a little after ten. She was a short, heavy woman in her middle forties. Sarah thought her curly bright red hair was remarkable, and thought her sallow complexion with freckles that seemed everywhere stood no chance against the overpowering Carolina sunshine. Savannah had trouble carrying all her brushes, oils, and easel through the soft shifting beach sand, and was out of breath and perspiring heavily. She cursed the heat and tropical moisture.

"My God, 10:00 a.m. and this weather already has the best of me. Welcome to our little slice of heaven. My father says I should always make that my opening line with potential customers, but one look at what this tropical heat and humidity does to me and I really think you would doubt the sincerity of such a greeting."

She wiped the perspiration off her face and shoulders with a white wash cloth and was set up and ready to paint in just a few short minutes. She engaged Sarah and William with the history of Buxton and with tales of lost loves, mysterious deaths, and shipwrecks while she blended oils on her canvass. Sarah found herself especially drawn in by Savannah's tales of marine disasters that had occurred just offshore from where they sat. She suddenly saw ethereal images of panicked seamen and petrified travelers, hopeless, all at the mercy of a powerful sea, bodies floating down into the deep and smooth white skeletons resting gently on a sandy ocean floor. She pressed Savannah for whatever stories and details she might have on these sinkings.

"You are certainly taken by my accounts of these seaside calamities," Savannah said.

"For reasons I'm not sure I understand, this is all very mysterious, entertaining, and extremely compelling to me," Sarah responded.

They broke for a quick snack and stretch at lunch. Savannah had brought some fresh fruit with her and shared it with her newlywed clients. Savannah was finished by five o'clock and the honeymoon couple were absolutely thrilled with the finished portrait. It would be something they would cherish the rest of their lives. They paid Savannah and tipped her quite generously.

"Keep this out of the wind and beach sand the next couple of days and you should be okay. If you need to ship this home, just talk to my father and he can arrange it. He's done it many times before. You are a wonderfully happy couple. Thank you, and good luck in your marriage, take care," she said, and was soon waddling off down the beach.

The last night in their honeymoon bungalow, Sarah and William talked and shared their most intimate thoughts. They laughed at the silliest things, and those last little ticks of time became moments they would cherish the rest of their lives. They swam naked in the late evening waters one last time and made love on the beach afterwards. They returned to New York blissfully happy.

* * *

William and Sarah spent the next several years nurturing their love affair. They would fall asleep in each other's arms every night and awake the next morning even more in love. Sarah could not dream of being any happier.

Delilah

NOVEMBER, 1938

My grandfather journeyed from Philadelphia to be with my mother as soon as the rail lines were cleared from all the storm debris and deemed safe to travel. It was a lonely, sad train ride for him. One of his daughters had drowned in a horrific storm, the other, he had been told, was a fragile, empty soul. His heart ached for the grandchildren he would never again bounce on his knee. Now they were little saints in heaven. He was emotionally unprepared for what waited for him. This was when he desperately needed his wife. She could provide the caring comfort that their shattered daughter would need, but he was traveling alone. His wife had suffered a stroke just two years ago. It had taken her speech and most of her mobility. She understood the tragedy that had been visited on her beautiful daughter, but was incapable of helping her, and it tore at her.

When he arrived, it was obvious that his daughter was in a deep depression and had withdrawn into her own private but fragile sanctuary. Comforting his daughter became a task that frustrated and pained him, so he sought out the things that he could do. He located and directed contractors to make repairs to our home and rebuild the carriage house. The carriage house needed extensive work. The southeast corner had taken the brunt of the storm and had been completely torn away. Most of the second floor was destroyed and the entire roof and supporting gables were gone.

I was perplexed by my father's decision to yield this responsibility to my grandfather.

"He needs a sense of purpose. He has tried to soothe your mother, but he is out of his element and shares the same pain we all do. For his own sanity we need to let him do this, he needs this diversion. He is very capable of it. I will keep an eye on the workers. If I witness any shoddy craftsmanship, I will let them know and will likewise tell your grandfather. Besides, it will be good to have the carriage house rebuilt."

My father always seemed to have the most common sense approach to our family quandaries; and he was right, it would be nice to have it rebuilt. I missed my room in the loft. My grandfather and Claudia had located some used furniture much like I had up there. Grace needed a place, too. She had been staying in a neighbor's shed. They had only recovered Grace. Buck was never found. Grace must have found higher ground, and now she was back in her own stall again. The carriage house had retained its musty smell. It was all comforting, and it gave me some diversion from my mother's hell and our own plight.

* * *

Recent developments had saddened my father. Reverend Chard had stopped his Sunday visits and Claudia was now leading my mother in a bizarre and foreign direction. It was around this time that my mother, with Claudia's incessant pleading, sought out alternative spiritual healing. The Sunday afternoon visits with Reverend Chard had done little to help her. Claudia was now trying to steer my mother in a new direction. My mother's loss was so devastating to her that she had become vulnerable and easily manipulated. This new direction had raised concern with Reverend Chard and was what had finally driven him away. My mother wanted to reach beyond the grave.

Claudia had convinced her that, with the right person, she might be able to reach beyond the barrier that separates the living from the dead and contact her deceased loved ones. Claudia hoped this might bring closure to my mother and help her move on. My mother was no longer thinking rationally. She had become desperate, and my father sensed that her grief was beginning to consume her.

I knew my father had taken full responsibility for what had happened to our family. He had talked about it many times with me, and repeatedly questioned his decision to go to the naval base that morning. They had been briefed about the anticipated bad weather, but they had predicted just a glancing blow by the storm.

"I should not have gone to the base that day, it's as simple as that," he would say.

I pleaded with him not to torture himself.

"Dad, it was never as simple as that. I am old enough to know how crystal clear hindsight is, and how pointless it really is. How could you possibly have known how severe that hurricane was to be? Nobody knew. This is not your fault."

"When your mother and I met, we immediately fell in love and couldn't wait to be married. We were even more impatient to have children. I am convinced that you are the result of an absolutely blissful honeymoon. Having the four of you was just another way of expressing how much we loved each other. Lying in bed at the end of a long day, with you between us wrapped in your linens, was like a touch of heaven. We would take turns holding you, or sometimes we'd place you on the bed and examine all your perfect little features. We did it with all of you and we never tired of it, because it energized us. Loving our children only made our own love richer. I loved your mother so much, there were times when I looked deep into her eyes and could see the souls of my children.

"And your children become a responsibility for the rest of your life and so do your grandchildren. You feed, clothe and nurture them, but most of all you are driven to protect them, and as a father it is even more of a charge. Beyond anything, it is your greatest challenge. It is such a raw and basic instinct. It's the same with any parent. You place goals or expectations on how you should shield them, and those parameters are unrealistic, but that never comforts you. You take precautions and hope that they will be sufficient, and then something or someone violates those barriers and you torture yourself with hindsight, as you say. It is the only sight that improves with age. I will always deeply regret that I went to the base that morning. Two beautiful children and a special sister-in-law were taken from us, and now my beautiful wife is a fragile thing, lost in an empty and lifeless world. Things would have been different if I had stayed and protected my family, as I should have. I am sure of that."

"You are not sure of that, Father. I know I will never convince you of that, but every time you doubt your actions on that day, I will defend them, that I am sure of."

"Then I will never question them out loud."

"Please don't do that. Holding everything inside only makes me worry about you. Isn't mother's problem enough?"

He would nod his head and say that he needed to keep his thoughts to himself. But he was concerned about our mother.

"We are losing her and we can't let that happen."

✳ ✳ ✳

My father, T.J., and I had just left my mother's room. It had been another frustrating visit; she was again non-responsive, with the same empty stares. She did mumble her affirmation that she wanted Claudia to help contact her loved ones.

"I must find them. I have to tell them I love them and I will always love them," she said

102

Claudia comforted her: "Katherine, we will reach across and find them."

My mother was on tranquilizers at this time. Her doctor had left it up to Claudia to determine her needs. He prescribed sufficient medication with the instruction to "sedate as needed," and Claudia had begun to distribute them all too freely.

We gathered in my bedroom as we often did after visits with my mother. My father was sitting in his big rocker. He had moved it from their room not long after my mother had left his bed. Claudia had questioned why he had moved it, apparently it had unnerved her. My mother was oblivious to it all.

The vibrations suddenly began. I looked at T.J.; he sensed them too. I looked at my father. He looked puzzled.

"You feel the vibrations, don't you? You do! You do! This is what I have been trying to tell you," I said.

"Yes, I feel something," he said. "Quickly, follow me downstairs."

I took T.J.'s hand and we followed him at a run. The same unpromising shadow as before suddenly appeared in the hallway and seemed to lunge at us. I screamed and pulled T.J. closer to me. It followed us as we ran past my mother's room. Claudia opened the door and shouted at us.

"Must you torment her so? You know how fragile she is!"

T.J. turned to say something to Claudia but I held his hand tight and pulled him along as we followed my father down the stairs, through the foyer, and into the living room. T.J. and I were frightened and out of breath, and we looked at my father for an explanation.

"Daddy, what are we doing?" I asked.

"Try to be quiet," my father said.

We stood there in silence for a while. Finally, my father said, "I wanted to see if it was unique to your room."

"I don't understand," I said.

"I wanted to see if the noise, the vibrations, were just in your room or if they were occurring all over the house.

"I don't feel anything now, do you?" he asked

"No, I don't," I said. "But did you see the shadow? It was in the hallway and it followed us. Do you believe me now?"

"Yes, I saw a shadow if that's what it was, it wasn't anything of this world. I believe you now, I am sorry I did not trust you before, Delilah."

"Why does this happen to us? What is going on?"

"I don't know," he said. "I just don't know."

We stood in the living room facing each other, unnerved by what had just happened, unsure of what lie ahead. The house was quiet, silent for now.

Delilah

MARCH, 1939

My mother and Claudia continued their close relationship and I began to despise their intimacy. I wanted my mother to be a vital part of our family again, not this detached being she had become. A tremendous amount of healing needed to take place, I knew that, but why did she need to lick her wounds in seclusion, like a solitary lioness gored by an impala during a frustrating hunt? She had dragged herself under the nearest acacia tree in the Serengeti and would lick her wound until it was healed. She would be of no value to the pride until then.

But I felt we should be healing together as a family; our wounds were similar. There is a medicinal salve that only a family can apply to its own lesions. I wanted to talk to her about our loss and what it had done to our family, but my mother would always ignore my attempts, pretending not to hear me. Somehow she perceived this as her pain and only hers. Perhaps trying to take on the pain of the rest of her family would have been too much for her.

T.J. wanted his mother to hold and comfort him. The horrifying and sudden disappearance of his sister and little twin brother had left T.J. aimless. He would slowly wander the halls and rooms of our house for hours on end, as if he were searching for a lost toy, but never looking very hard, probably knowing he would never find it. What he was searching for would never be found again. I wanted to explain why he was feeling sad and so alone. Did he understand that part of his identity had been stripped away? Being only ten years old, I wondered if he sensed the real uniqueness of being a twin. I'm sure he sensed that he had a mirror that followed him everywhere, sometimes leading the way; after all, they wore the same clothes, combed their hair alike, played and did their homework together, they liked the same foods, and felt the whole world should be painted royal blue.

T.J. and Corey were the twins, our twins. Whatever we did or wherever we went, it was always the twins, Corey and T.J., they were the special ingredient to our family's recipe for happiness. It made it a little challenging for their teachers and friends at school, but that's who they were and they liked it.

"I just don't know what to do with myself anymore. I wish Mother would be Mother again and not the zombie she is now. What's the point of having her around if she is going to be like this all the time?" Then his frown would deepen and his lips would quiver and the tears would flow.

My father and I did our best to be there for T.J. We took turns tucking him into bed, frequently reading to him. He slept so poorly during the night; often he would wake confused and frightened, sometimes even trembling in fear. I knew what his nightmares must have been like. His world had been turned upside down. I would hold him in my arms and try to make sense of it all. He had his simple, naive little questions that he just wanted someone to answer, and I could not.

My mother seemed to be oblivious to it all. She was now under Claudia's spell. When my mother wasn't sedated and sleeping in her room, she and Claudia would spend hours in the living room trying to reach out to her loved ones. Claudia was embracing her Haitian Voodoo culture and it made no sense to us.

Claudia felt she needed to explain the traditions of her Voodoo practices and what they were meant to do.

"Madame Miller, I am a very proud Haitian woman and you know that."

They were again seated in the living room and had just finished their afternoon tea. Claudia knew that this was when my mother was the most focused: after tea and before her sedatives. But my mother seemed to be distracted.

Claudia grasped my mother's hands and raised her voice. "Madame, you must listen to me, can you do that?"

My mother turned towards Claudia and for the moment was attentive.

"What is it?"

"Madame, I want to talk about my Haitian traditions that I hold very dearly. They are the Voodoo practices that have always seemed so very odd to you, but they are not so strange to me, and I truly believe they will help us contact your family in the other world."

"Oh, how wonderful," my mother said, as if Claudia was giving her tax advice.

Claudia would move the outstretched fingers of one hand in towards my mother's face and then away from it. Sometimes she would do it with both hands, like she was moving them across a warm hearth; the bright red nail polish and the odd collection of bracelets seemed to hypnotize my mother.

Madame Miller, you must not let black magic tell you what Voodoo is all about. Black magic is a part of Voodoo, but only a small part. It does not define us as a people. Do you understand me?"

"I think so," my mother replied, as if she had been asked if she could recite the Ten Commandments.

"Madame, you are so sad now and feel empty. This is what we Haitians call *morin pap refe*, or, 'I will never be well again.' You

107

must not feel this way. You are just possessed by a demon spirit. We will pray to *Bondye* to expel this demon. Bondye is our supreme God."

"If you think this will help," my mother replied again. She was clearly not comprehending Claudia's message.

Claudia continued unfazed. "We will try to reach across to *Iwa*, or the spirits of your loved ones, and to do that we must ask for *Legba's* help. He is the gatekeeper that separates the living from the dead. We will burn special oils and mix only those herbs that are blessed by Bondye. We must seek his blessing."

Claudia began what became a daily ritual. She would light a black and bright red candle at both ends. It was the Voodoo *mort celeste* taper. It was meant to expel the evil from her world. She began to shake her *ason*, or black magic rattle, and recite her chants. Haitian herbs and spices were mixed together and burned in small dishes. Long thin tapers in bright reds and yellows were lit. Special teas were prepared and my mother would sip on them while Claudia would recite some ancient chant that her mother and aunt had taught her many years ago.

The smell of incense, candles, and the different herbs and spices seemed to be everywhere. There seemed to be no rhyme or reason as to how Claudia conducted these spiritual readings. They became a painful ritual for myself and my father. After a month of attempting to reach across this barrier, Claudia became frustrated with her unsuccessful attempts. As much as it disappointed her she knew it was time for a different approach. She decided to seek out a friend that she had known in her psychic circle in Philadelphia. His name was Simon.

Sarah

OCTOBER, 1908

¶n the fall of 1908 William decided to leave the *New York Journal*. His aspirations of being the reporter that broke the story of the decade had faded because the account had never surfaced. He made the decision rather easily and did not anguish over it as he thought he might. The newspaper ethics of his boss, William Hearst, had also begun to disturb him. It seemed that, if there wasn't any front page news to print, Hearst would create it. One of Williams's first assignments in 1898 as a novice reporter was to travel to Cuba with the *Journal's* high profile reporter, Karl Decker. A beautiful young Cuban rebel named Evangelina Cisneros had been imprisoned for refusing the sexual advances of a Spanish officer; But the fact that her father was one of the rebel leaders of the Cuban independence movement had more to do with her captivity. William Randolph

Hearst saw opportunity to sensationalize a rather obscure event. He sent his swashbuckling senior reporter to save the damsel in distress.

In reality he should have removed himself from the politics of the situation, but Hearst never met a story he didn't like to manipulate. There was intense competition between Hearst and Joseph Pulitzer, of the *New York World,* for New York City bragging rights. They did whatever it took to sell newspapers, even if it meant exaggerating or distorting the truth. Their style of reporting was beginning to be called "yellow journalism."

In the end, Karl Decker and his team orchestrated Evangelina's escape from her jail cell and three days later, disguised as a man, she boarded a steamer bound for New York. William Lowe had played only a minor role in this rescue, but he felt like a gallant patriot. Spain was outraged that a New York reporter would have blatantly invaded their sovereignty. It became one of the many incidents that precipitated the Spanish-American war.

William's father was also disappointed in the Hearst style of reporting and how he tried to manipulate his newspaper's readers. In fact, he saw right through these deceptive practices and tried to get his son to see the sham that he was being dragged into. William would have none of it. Evangelina Cisneros and Cuba's struggle for independence was a noble cause. He had the idealism of youth.

Now, years later, he had seen that his father was right in his assessment of William Randolph Hearst. He had become disillusioned and tendered his resignation. Sarah chose to remain with the newspaper for now.

* * *

William had also finally given into his father's pleadings to join the family business. His father had established his wine importing and distribution company in 1878. There had been some lean years in the beginning, but now they were importing French, Italian, and Portuguese wines in prodigious quantities. New York Liquor Importing and Distribution had expanded its dissemination into New Jersey, Pennsylvania, and east into New England. It had become an established and very successful business. William's father's age was beginning to hinder his ability to manage the business. He was now in his early sixties and his energy level had begun to wane the last two years. Memory lapses were becoming more frequent and were lasting longer. The family had become concerned. Several months ago his sister had arrived at his home in complete panic. It was almost ten o'clock in the evening and their father had not returned home after work.

She paced back and forth in his living room and nervously rubbed her hands together. She could barely control her voice and it cracked with tension.

"I was hoping I would find him here. He is always home by seven at the latest. I had Mason drive me to the office and we found it closed, as it should be. There was no sign of father. I am afraid this is another one of his memory lapses."

They called the police and began their search. William remembered his grandmother having the same issues; she would often have flashbacks to events of her youth. He followed a hunch and decided to explore the neighborhood where his father had grown up. Finding him on a park bench in Washington Square, he came upon a frightened and bewildered man conversing with friends from long ago but no longer there. William sat next to his father and gently placed his arm around his shoulders and spoke softly to him.

"Dad, why don't we go home?"

His father startled. He quickly turned and studied his son's face, searching for a way back; and then, in a voice so empty and sad, said, "Oh William, I have had a terrible time. I think I have fallen a few times, my hand is swollen, and my suit is heavily soiled. I want to go home. I am afraid I don't know the way though."

"I am here, Dad. I will take care of everything. Let's go."

He brought his father home and settled him in his room for the night. The next morning his father remembered nothing of his misadventure and wondered why his left hand was so swollen and uncomfortable. But the family dynamics had been changed forever.

William lost his mother during the delivery of his sister, Marjorie, and their father never remarried. His father had frequently told William and his sister that their mother was the only woman he could ever love. His heart simply had no room for anyone else. But that meant there were no other children to help move the family business forward. It all simply defaulted to William. There were no other realistic options.

William knew his father's business had lost its focus. His father's dementia was sabotaging the company's business strategy. William knew his involvement could counter act the bad decisions that his father was making, but if the company was to continue their growth, they would be in need of a young, sharp, and energetic mind.

William wanted someone that could grow with the company and become that second in-command when his father stepped away from the business and he took over. He recruited Samuel Bosworth out of Columbia University in New York City. Sam was young and lacked hands-on corporate skills, but William saw that he was driven and had remarkable business instincts. He knew Sam would rapidly grow into the role expected of him and become the asset William would surely need. His biggest concern would be in trying to retain this talented young man. William knew Sam's family was from England and his father was deeply involved in the emerging oil industry. Sam had enjoyed his years at Columbia and had grown attached to New York, but William was a little concerned that Sam someday might feel the need to return to his roots.

William's sister unexpectedly solved that dilemma. It was only a matter of time before his attractive young sibling and Sam crossed paths. Sarah thought the two would be perfect for each other and went out of her way to make sure their paths intersected. When they both began to inquire about the other it hadn't taken long; Sarah felt the time was right and finally introduced Sam to her sister-in-law.

William, his father, and Sarah were impressed with Sam. He was hardworking and likeable. Blending intelligence with charismatic social skill, Sam would come alive in collective issues or debates and it was intriguing to witness. Friends and relatives had often asked him how he managed such a velvet tongue and his reply was always the same: "I suppose it's like asking me how is it that you walk. It's not complicated, you just put one foot in front of the other. I just put one word after the other, and it's even less complicated."

Marjorie was instantly smitten by the handsome, ambitious young Englishman. They were soon courting, and Sam quickly fell under her spell.

Despite the age difference between the couples, the four became good friends. They began to spend a lot of time together. New York's Central Park was the site of numerous Sunday afternoon picnics, and they enjoyed the abundant night life that New York offered, often securing much desired seating for the New York Philharmonic at Carnegie Hall. The two couples were filling their societal calendar as only their youth could allow.

The summer months became filled with social commitments. There were excursions to the Catskills, trips to the Jersey shoreline, and voyages by steamer to Newport, Rhode Island. Sarah insisted they make as many trips to Newport as possible so they could spend time with her father. She missed him terribly. He was just as delighted to see his daughter and son-in-law and was anxious to share them with his Newport friends; too often he attended social gatherings as the unaccompanied, lonely family man. It seemed so unfair, and so he was always demanding that Sarah and William visit, and often funded their excursions. He was a free spender, almost to a fault.

Every summer he would rent the estate "Tall Oaks" at the intersection of Belleview and Ruggles in Newport. Frederick Sr. would relocate his housing staff from his home in the Heights of Fall River. It was a welcomed relief from the tedium that his lace mill subjected him to. Newport was quickly becoming the mecca for American high society, and Frederick Shepard was in it up to his neck. He relished the extravagant lifestyle that defined Newport. The Vanderbilts, the Asters, the Gatsbys, and others all built their summer mansions there. The Widener family had already set the bar high in 1895 when they built the Breakers, their monument to opulence. Lavish homes were being constructed at a frightening pace all along

Cliff Walk and Belleview Avenue in Newport. Thousands of European craftsmen were brought in to support the demand for skilled labor. New York's own architect, Richard Morris Hunt, designed many of these homes. Newport was simply the place to be. Even Rhode Island rotated its own state legislature to Newport during the summer months. It was the Gilded Age.

The summer trips to Newport became captivating, fun-filled excursions. The select of New York were converging on Newport in the summer and most went by steamship. Sarah and William wanted to participate in that seasonal migration.

There were several side wheel steamer companies that offered the New York-to-Newport service. Sarah, William, and their entourage most often chose the Fall River Line. These coastal steamers were like floating palaces. First class passage always had its benefits. They would board the luxurious *Commonwealth* at Pier 16 on the North River just before 7:00 p.m. on a Friday evening and would be underway by the time they had settled into their state room. The Fall River Line had mastered the science of boarding and receiving their passengers. Ships left their piers at the scheduled time; arriving late for boarding would always have consequences. Sarah, William, and their traveling companions would join other passengers on the open afterdeck for cocktails and conversation. The mood was always festive and the conversations lively. People were dressed in their finest summer attire, and everyone seemed anxious to begin their weekend. People were letting off steam from the kind of work-week that only New York demands of its inhabitants. The lights along the Connecticut shoreline began to turn on like giant fireflies. The setting sun would create long shadows of the passengers as they strolled the open topdeck. Often the shadows would give way to a magnificent sunset behind the huge wake of their steamer. The pinks, yellows, and oranges of the sunset would mix with the spray from the paddlewheels and create an almost magical scene. It heightened the already jovial mood. Sarah knew they would no doubt be seeing many of these same passengers at the lavish parties hosted by Newport's elite.

Dinner was next, and the foursome would journey down to the main dining room. It was a lavish affair, with tables draped in the finest white linen with lace overlay, opulently upholstered Queen Anne chairs, and fancy chandeliers throughout. Black tie stewards and boutonniere-wearing maître d's saw to their every wish. Dinner on the *Commonwealth* had become a science for its kitchen staff and a culinary delight for its passengers.

After dinner, they would then join other revelers in the ship's casino for music, dancing, and games of chance. Stan Hoppe and the Hoppe's Band and Orchestra always provided engaging renditions of recent Irving Berlin and Duke Ellington hits. Casino partygoers would jump to their feet when the band played Will Cobb's "If I Were A Millionaire." They would pack the parquet dance floor, sweating and dancing like they were participating in some ancient and powerful mating ritual. They were all seduced by the moment and 100,000 years of sexual evolution.

After a spirited few hours, Sarah and William would say goodnight to their friends and retire to their stateroom. Many of the young carousers remained in the casino into the wee hours of the morning. It was a thrilling time and place to be young and single.

There were those that had difficulty with the swaying of the boat, but William and Sarah loved to be rocked to sleep by the motion of the waves. When they traveled with Marjorie and Sam, however, they would arrange for the ladies and gentlemen to share separate suites. William insisted on such protocol with his younger sister. They would wake refreshed and eager to begin their weekend in Newport. The steamer would have already tied up at Long Wharf in Newport, and Sarah's father would send his driver and carriage to retrieve his weekend guests and Carson was always there waiting for them to disembark. They would load their luggage into the carriage and make their way along the thoroughfares of Newport: first Thames Street for a short distance, then left and up Touro and then right on to Bellevue. Newport was already awake, the wharves along Thames Street bustling with activity. Coal, lumber, and fish were being offloaded from their respective ships and boats and then reloaded with their outgoing freight. Sometimes they would stop at the Ocean

House Hotel. The hotel's grand dining room was full of guests seeking their morning coffee and hardy breakfasts. The ride on the cobblestone road to their father's house after breakfast gave the foursome a chance to take it all in. It was all so reassuring to be part of the Newport experience.

Sarah, her husband, and their friends were soon mingling with the society of Newport. Because of her father's New York connections, they were guests at many of the lavish parties that defined the social order of Newport. Sarah and Marjorie fell in love with the quaint shops and hotels that seemed to be everywhere. Their trips to Newport were exciting and, sadly, over all too quickly

* * *

On one of their return trips Sarah began to tell her husband more about her gift. It was a huge part of her identity, and Sarah knew he did not fully comprehend its reach. He had already been briefly exposed to her gift. On occasional visits to her home in Brooklyn Heights, before they were married, William would find Sarah in the middle of a light-hearted séance, or reading Tarot cards with a friend or a member of the household staff. He thought very little of it at the time. It seemed as if Sarah was simply trying to amuse or entertain her friends. When he began to question her about these little gatherings, she was careful about what and how much she told him. They were married now and she felt that William deserved to know more. As their marriage grew she began to tell him more. She found their return trips from Newport to be the ideal setting in which to peel away the protective outer layers that she shielded her ability with and apprise him of its depth.

She told him about her experiences back in England, the near drowning of her brother's friend and her father's serious accident at work. She told him about the awkward visit to her cousin's home and how, although her cousin had delivered a healthy baby, the event had forever changed the dynamics of her family.

William was unsure just how to react. He wondered why she had not told him of this before their engagement and wedding. He listened as she nervously shared these experiences with him. He could sense that she was very concerned with what his reaction might be.

But William saw no reason for concern. He was a skeptic by nature when it came to this type of thing and this was why Sarah hesitated in telling him. He came to accept this as just a quirky side of her personality; just another reason to love her even more. Examining her gift with any depth would only increase his skepticism, and any cynicism would only conflict with his deep love for Sarah. He simply could not tolerate such a conflict. In just a few short months William would experience firsthand the depth of Sarah's gift and the devastating sadness and alienation that can sometimes accompany it. It would invade their happy world and dissolve it.

Knowledge of Sarah's gift was now beyond her restricted circle of friends and family; it had worked its way into the masses. People began to seek her out. She was having a difficult time separating her private life from the demands of her new flock. But now her gift had added another dimension: she was now communicating with the dead. She had not shared this new element with anyone, even William, and was unsure if she should.

The first time it happened had frightened her a great deal. Timothy, a close friend of William's family, had approached Sarah. He had lost his twin brother in a street accident and could not move forward with his life. He and his brother had just celebrated their birthday with some friends at a pub on Fifth Avenue. Upon leaving the bar some good-natured horseplay had ensued and his twin brother, Terrence, suddenly stumbled on to the street and into the path of a fast-moving, horse-drawn carriage. He was immediately trampled by the frightened horses. The left side of his skull was severely depressed and his chest was crushed. Terrence took a couple of desperate breaths and then was gone. Within a few short moments Timothy had witnessed the sudden and horrific death of his twin brother and his best friend. Now, years later, the pain was still there and the event was like a ball and chain around his spirit. It was so hard for him to pick up the pieces and move on. He was beginning to drink heavily and was slowly withdrawing from the world. Family and friends were seeing less and less of him, and there was a lot of concern. Timothy happened to be present at a family gathering when Sarah had done one of her readings and shared her previews of things to come. He was drawn to her, but he was not sure why. He knew that people genuinely believed in her and that she was developing a following. Perhaps she could help him find the peace he desperately sought.

So he sat with Sarah on a Saturday afternoon in his living room. She had asked William to go with her, but he had declined. He was still uncomfortable with Sarah's gift and thought his presence would only add to any awkwardness his cousin might have. Timothy's sister and his mother were there to support him. They exchanged pleasantries, and Sarah made sure that they were as comfortable as possible. Sarah then asked Timothy to talk about his brother.

"Also, tell me what your life was like before your brother passed on and what your life is like now. Losing your twin brother must have been tragic injury to your identity. I am sure it has been difficult for you."

Sarah needed him to share his pain with her. It was this human suffering that could sometimes help her connect with the other side, and Sarah again was unsure why this was the link to that next dimension. She had come to simply accept that these were the boundaries of this conveyance she provided to people or spirits who struggled against that barrier that separates the two universes.

As she anticipated, Timothy became uncomfortable with her probing. He attempted small talk. Sarah had no patience for small talk.

"This is about you and the brother that you loved dearly. Unless you open up to me, I am not sure I can be of any help to you. We can't squander our energies talking about the weather and the lack of rain."

Sarah had grown more confident in her efforts to help people. Her years of experience with her gift had helped her understand the depth and impact of its capabilities and had contributed to this new confidence. She held Timothy's hands while he began to talk about his brother. Sarah sensed nothing. They talked more and Timothy was becoming more emotional. He began to relive the events of the night his brother suddenly died.

"It was our birthday and we were at Alexander's. It was where we always celebrated birthdays and other special occasions. We were having such a great time. We had drunk very little. My brother and I were not big drinkers. We often discussed that oddity about ourselves. Most of our peers enjoyed their stout and spirits, but Terrence and I simply did not enjoy the taste or its effect. Our friends thought it odd, but it made perfect sense to us. It certainly did not impact our social lives, especially Terrence's. His personality needed no stimulant. He valued the people he was around, and they simply loved him."

His shoulders slumped; he cocked his head ever so slightly and paused. He stared at Sarah without seeing her. She knew the next words would be difficult.

"It turned so tragic so very quickly. We had just left Alexander's and were engaged in a little pushing and shoving, nothing very aggressive. Something about the birthday boys getting a little too big for their britches. Eddy and Charles made an attempt to push me and my brother together. Terrence stumbled on the edge of the curbstone and simply fell into the street. It was as innocent as that. No one saw the horses that were suddenly on top of my brother. It was horrible. My brother was alive just a few seconds, but in that brief moment he looked at me and smiled. I will never forget that look. He told me that he would be fine and that I would be fine. He had no regrets. But things are not fine and they will never be. I lost the one thing that was the most precious to me, and I will never be whole again."

It was obviously a very painful experience for him, yet still Sarah sensed nothing. Then Timothy broke down. This grief and sorrow that was always at the center of his existence simply boiled over.

"You will never know how much I miss Terrence. It was as if my heart was ripped from my chest that awful day," and he sobbed uncontrollably for several minutes with Sarah and his mother trying to comfort him. Sarah knew that this pain was a critical element to letting go. There would be more of these moments.

Timothy's sobbing gradually subsided, and he just sat at the table with his head resting on his folded arms. He talked more about the sudden and tragic loss of his brother. Everyone in the room was moved with his sadness and emptiness. Sarah again felt the burden of having to share in someone else's deep despair.

"Sarah, thank you for helping me to take this first step. I knew I had to do this, but I could not move forward. I believe some of the burden of my brother's death has lifted. For so long I have I tried to keep it together. I miss him so much. I could feel you caressing my hair when I was crying. It was very comforting and thoughtful of you, but you can stop now. I am indeed feeling better."

Everyone in the room looked at Sarah and then at Timothy. They all knew that Sarah had never touched Timothy head. Then she saw him. It was Terrence, and he was bent over his brother, slowly caressing his hair, trying to comfort him. His clothing was tattered and torn. The left side of his head was still shattered and the interior remnants of it were exposed and protruding ever so slightly from his traumatized skull. There was dried blood still on his face, neck, and on the front of his shirt and jacket. Sarah was witnessing a living being without life; she was frozen with dread and struggled to breath. Her eyes darted around the room to see if the others saw this wretched person from another world, but no one saw a thing.

He spoke softly to his brother. "You will be fine, Tim. This too shall pass." Then he turned to Sarah. His jaw was unhinged and it moved in the most awkward motion. It was painful for Sarah to witness, but his words were smooth and clear. There is no pain in the afterlife. "Please, tell my brother I will always be watching over him, loving him, caring for him, but from a distance. I have moved on, and it is very draining for me to come back like this. I do not know why it is, but it is. Tell him all of this; but most of all, he needs to let go of me. He has so much to give the world. We will shortly have eternity for us to be together." Then he was gone.

Sara's gaze lingered on the spot where the apparition had been a moment longer, then she turned to Timothy.

"Timothy, I never touched you. It was your brother that was caressing you. It will be difficult for you to believe this, but your brother was here. I know this because I saw him and he spoke to me. He wanted me to tell you that he loves you and will always be near you. But he wants you to move on with your life. All the deep sadness and despair that you carry around with you every day is slowly destroying you and your loved ones. It is also pulling him back. It's not good for your brother either, and he told me to tell you that 'this too shall pass.'"

"Oh, but I do believe you," Timothy said, and tears were in his eyes—but there was relief in his voice. "I sensed something too! And I know it sounds strange, but I thought I could smell him. His clothes had that smoky odor from the pipe he always had lit." He turned to those in the room. "I feel better. I think I will be fine." And Sarah knew he would be fine. She knew it would be a long road back, but Timothy had finally experienced some optimism for the first since his brother's passing. It had given him some healthier expectations. He had begun to fill a great void.

Sarah

FEBRUARY, 1912

It was in early September that Marjorie and Sam announced their engagement. April twentieth, 1912, would be the date of the grand affair. Marjorie's family was excited about the engagement, as they all approved of Sam. Sam's family was in England but no doubt would make the trip to New York for the wedding. The potential visit of Sam's family had unnerved Sarah just a little. She did not know why. Sarah had hoped it would slowly fade with time, but it never did. Something was probing her senses and, instead of diminishing with the passing of time, as she had hoped, it was now putting her special gift into a heightened state.

The months leading up to the wedding were full of excitement and anticipation. Sarah and Marjorie became even closer. Marjorie wanted an extravagant affair and would omit no detail. It was certainly more lavish than anything Sarah would have done, but she was happy for Marjorie and enjoyed the trips to the dressmaker, the restaurants, helping with the invitations, and all the other wedding activities. Marjorie's mother had died during her delivery. She had her aunts and cousins that helped fill that void, but Sarah had become her confidant, the big sister she never had.

Sarah was delighted with her new role. She was in love with William, and to have such a close friendship with his younger sister was absolutely blissful.

With all the activity surrounding Marjorie and Sam's wedding, Sarah found herself slowly backing away from those that sought her out. It was difficult for Sarah to turn away from those that needed her help. It went against every fiber of her being, but Marjorie's demand for her time and attention unwittingly denied Sarah the time to spend with those that sought her. Sarah began to feel her spirits lift, and she looked forward to each new day with growing excitement and happiness.

Sarah and William's love for each other had grown deeper and stronger. All this time spent with William, Marjorie, and their family was nurturing their relationship. The Lowe family simply adored Sarah and she adored them.

They got together with Marjorie and Samuel that evening for dinner. They met at Delmonico's on Forty-fourth Street, one of their favorite restaurants for dining. It was the restaurant to be seen at, and New York's upper society frequented it. Sarah and William, through her father-in-law's connections, were invited to and subsequently attended Mark Twain's seventieth birthday there. It was an exclusive event.

The couples had just been served their evening entrees in an intimate setting. William and Sam had opted for Delmonico's unique steak that was suddenly the rage. Sarah loved the Oysters Rockefeller that the restaurant had recently introduced to their patrons. They had toasted the evening, and an easy, comfortable conversation had settled in. Marjorie was all excited about the progress of their wedding plans and was anxious to bring Sarah up to date. She hopped her chair closer to Sarah and bubbled with her latest wedding activities.

"Sarah, I was at Gimbal's today and saw the most wonderful gowns for my wedding party. You must come with me this week and give me your opinion."

"That would be fun! Now, tell me, have you heard from Sam's family regarding their travel plans?" She turned to face Sam, smiled, and placed her hand on his. "I do hope that some of your family will make the trip. How could they not attend such a special occasion?" Sarah knew that multiple invitations had been sent to Sam's family in England, and they were anxiously awaiting their RSVP.

"Actually, I heard from my family just today. My mother and father, my brother and sister, along with my uncle Lewis and aunt Eileen, will be traveling to New York for the wedding."

"Oh, how wonderful!" Sarah said.

"Isn't this marvelous?" said Marjorie. "They have just booked passage on an ocean liner. In fact, it is to be the liner's maiden voyage. A fast and luxurious ship called the *Titanic*. Sam's family is looking forward to the voyage and the wedding."

An immediate sense of dread came over Sarah. Old, all too familiar symptoms were suddenly upon her, the sweaty palms and forehead, and yet the feeling of ice water running through her veins. Ghostly images floated before her, people screaming, running in absolute terror, being chased by some unseen demon. But it was the eerie smiles of terrified, helpless children that shocked her the most. They were dressed in tattered clothing and trapped in a dark, cold space, their innocence stolen from them by this same demon.

The color drained from her face and she became lightheaded. If they had not been seated at their table she might have fainted. William was at her side in an instant, trying to comfort her.

"Are you all right, my love? Maybe you should lie down." He quickly summoned the waiter and demanded cool water and extra linens be brought to the table. Some patrons at nearby tables stopped their dinner conversations and began to stare.

Sarah placed her head in her hands as she leaned on the table and tried to erase the disturbing images.

"I think I will be fine," she told William. She hoped she was right.

Marjorie too had quickly come to her aid and knelt beside her, but in her haste her skirt was caught up in the table linen and some of the table setting was dragged to the floor. Sterling silverware clanged, and fine crystal and china shattered when it hit the floor. Now the whole restaurant suddenly ceased all of its activity to focus on the scene at table twenty-four. It only enhanced Sarah's awkwardness and drove William to protect his wife even more.

"Perhaps we should go to the ladies' room, they have a settee there. William may be right, you should lie down for just a few minutes."

"This is not a feminine issue, I can assure you of that, Marjorie." She once again told everyone that she would be all right and that her dizziness would soon pass. The waiter arrived with the linen and water, and William began placing the cool damp cloth on her forehead, cheeks, and the back of her neck.

Something about Sam's announcement that his family would be traveling to the States had unnerved Sarah. She picked up her head and looked directly at Sam. His eyes were swollen and red and he was crying. His hair was suddenly a mess; he was unshaven and looked unkempt. Sympathy was all Sarah could feel for this man, who appeared sadder than anyone she had ever seen. She could not look at him anymore. Turning away from Sam she spoke to him:

"Sam, please don't cry over this little dizzy spell. I will be just fine."

Sam put his arms out to his sides, looked at Marjorie, then at William, and then shrugged his shoulders in confusion. His puzzled expression saying it all: *what...who, me?*

"I am not crying, Sarah. I am concerned for you, but I am not crying."

Sarah quickly spun around and looked up at him. Sam was not crying. His eyes were no longer red and swollen. His handsome and stylish persona had returned. What was happening? Sarah's eyes moved around the room, searching for someone's affirmation as to what had just happened, but it never worked that way. It was always Sarah's burden, and hers alone. What was happening? The mere mention of the *Titanic* had filled her with terror. She needed to leave, get away from this restaurant.

She asked William to bring her back home. Marjorie suggested that contacting a doctor might be the prudent thing to do. "Doctor Priswell's home is just a few minutes from here. He is a good friend of the family and the hour is still not that late."

Sarah would not have it. "It is much too late to intrude on Dr. Priswell. Besides, I am feeling better now. My lightheadedness has passed. I just need to go home."

Marjorie and Sam backed off their insistence about seeing the doctor. Perhaps it would be best if Sarah got back to the comforts of her home. They excused themselves from the restaurant and the two couples parted outside and went their separate ways.

After a few steps, William stopped and turned to his wife, asking again if she was okay. "You seemed fine and then quickly you were not."

"Everything was fine until Sam said that his family would be traveling to their wedding on that ship," Sarah said.

"You mean the *Titanic*."

"Yes, of course I do. Just hearing that ship's name unnerves me. It troubles me so, and I am not sure why. This night has been very disturbing. I think I should go home and get some sleep." She did not share with him all the ghostly images and the faces of the frightened children she had seen. That would have demanded too much explanation, and she had no reasoning of her own to attach any meaning to it. That would have to come later, if at all.

"I think that would be best. Let's see what tomorrow brings." With his arm securely around her, Sarah's head nestled into the corner of chest and shoulder, they walked home at a slow and deliberate pace. Very little was said between the two. The normally hectic streets seemed empty, and the street lights illuminated a very lonely couple. Sarah's insides trembled with what she had just experienced. She knew this was not the end, only the beginning of something very tragic. William feared the unknown, not as though he did not know

126

what lie ahead, but rather, he knew something was moving toward him and he had no idea what it was.

Sarah got herself to bed rather quickly. She wanted the comfort of her sheets and quilts. William stood above her in her bed. She suddenly seemed small, fragile, and afraid. They searched each other's souls for explanation and assurance—they had always been strong for each other. William leaned over and gave her a kiss that he hoped would tell her that everything would be fine by the new morning.

"Good night sweetheart, get some sleep." He turned to leave the room and she grabbed his hand and squeezed it.

"I have the most awful sense that our world is about to be turned upside down."

"Let's wait for tomorrow before we debate that." He could not share the uneasy feeling he also now felt. It would be of no useful benefit. He softly released her hand, gently patted it, and then left her room.

* * *

The next day and the weeks that followed were the same. Every time she saw Sam and Marjorie the same sense of dread she had experienced at the restaurant would return. The flashes of Sam in a tormented state persisted; images of panicked people and terrified children floated before her. She knew something terrible would happen to Sam's family. It was her gift, and again she cursed it.

William could see her demeanor had changed. A dark cloud had settled over his wife. Their get-togethers with Marjorie and Sam became strained and less frequent. Sarah was not as engaged in their conversations and became distracted whenever their discussions involved Sam's family and their planned excursion on the *Titanic*. It was obvious to all that something very troubling had taken root in Sarah.

"Sarah, what is wrong with you?" They were at La Belle Femme on Fifth Avenue looking at potential wedding gowns. "I asked your opinion on this gown and you seemed to look right through me. You appear to be a hundred miles away. Did you even hear my question?"

"I am so sorry, Marjorie. I think the color is absolutely marvelous."

"My question had nothing to do with color. Sarah, what has come over you? You seem so distracted as of late."

"I am just fine. You are placing too much significance on a momentary lapse."

Marjorie was not convinced; she approached her brother with her concerns. William conceded that Sarah had become a little troubled recently, but felt it was nothing to be concerned with. To share his wife's concerns about Sam and his family's trip on the *Titanic* would serve no purpose. But he began to press his wife for a clearer explanation of her suffocating dark mood.

Finally, she gave in to William's insistent pleadings. They were in bed and had just settled in for the night. Sarah was lying with her back to William's chest. He wrapped his arms around her and delicately inquired again about her odd behavior when they were around Marjorie and Sam.

She could no longer hold it inside. The moment was right, and lying there in William's arms she felt secure. She told him of the almost crippling sense of tragedy that had engulfed her when Sam revealed his family's plans to attend the wedding via the ocean liner *Titanic*. She could not dismiss it. It had consumed her.

"William," she said, "tragedy is a passenger on that ship, of this I am sure. But how do I tell Sam to discourage his family from attending this very special occasion? Sam and Marjorie would certainly dismiss this as quackery, and it would no doubt impact our friendship."

William had reached a crossroad. Sarah's gift had finally brought him to the point that he either had to accept its reality or risk deeply hurting the woman he loved. Her gift had always been something that humored and entertained him, but now it began to frighten him.

"How can you be so certain of this terrible outcome?"

"I have lived my whole life with this. It was thrust upon me when I was just a little girl, without my consent and for reasons I still do not understand. I have told you about some of these experiences, but there are more that I have not shared with you. But from the very first revelation I never doubted the outcomes as revealed to me. They were that real to me, as were their conclusions. But with the reality of it all I have been offered nothing but skepticism. Suspicion when I foretell the days ahead and cynicism when I don't. It has hardened me over the years.

People have asked me, if I am so sure of its outcome, why am I not more forceful to share or warn people of these impending events? My reluctance has been secured by years of people's doubt, scrutiny, and my own personal fear of what I know. Do you understand what I am telling you? We—*I* have to tell Sam and Marjorie not to let his family make that journey on the *Titanic*."

"Oh Sarah, this is all difficult and troubling to me."

Sarah was convinced that something awful was going to occur, and as much as William knew that this was all very real to her, the skepticism that his wife despised began to creep into his own analysis of what she had foreseen. Sarah was sure that a tragic event was going to occur on that maiden voyage, and now she was seeking William's support in sharing this disturbing news with Sam and Marjorie. The repercussions from this would be far reaching. However, whenever William approached or tried to digest it, it brought him right back to the dangerous crossroad he was at. There was no avoiding it, and there would be no winning strategy. William began to reflect on his feelings for Sarah, and it was unsettling. This event was not a cute and entertaining component of Sarah's personality anymore. Was there something emotionally wrong with her? He began to ask himself that awkward question; he knew their marriage hung precariously in how he answered it. He wondered if Sarah also realized they had reached a crossroad. Maybe she did not; she had mentioned the need to tell the happy couple of her dark premonition several times before. It was time to confront this issue.

He released her from his loving embrace and sat up in their bed. She rolled over to face him. He could not face her pleading expression and stared directly at the ceiling.

"No! We will not tell them of these bizarre thoughts of yours."

Now it was out there. William knew there would be no going back.

Sarah was immediately pained. "Oh William, how can you say such a thing? These are not bizarre thoughts. I am not an unstable person. Please tell me you don't think that. You know how much I love you. Please look at me."

William slowly lowered his head and turned it to look at her. "I love you also, and of course I do not think you are mad, but this crazy talk about Sam's family about to die… it's … it's just too much. You must never talk of this again. You must never mention it to anyone, ever! Do you understand?"

"How can I keep this to myself? This is so very real to me, as real as the hand I hold in front of you."

"What will you tell them?" asked William. "Is Sam's entire family in jeopardy, or just one of them? Who? Will there be a storm or a fire? How do you tell this to Sam?"

"I don't know!" Sarah screamed. "All that I know is that Sam's family is surrounded by tragedy. I have to say something!"

"And again, what do you tell them? It's too late to reschedule their trip. Do we tell them to cancel their voyage and miss the wedding completely? And what happens if the ship then makes the trip without an incident? What do you tell Sam and Marjorie then, after his family missed the most important event of their lives? You shall not say anything."

"Something very terrible will happen. I do not know what, but it will happen. As I have told you already, there will be only the outcome that I have predicted. Of this I am confident."

"You will not like their reaction. Do you think they will be at all receptive to what you are trying to tell them? Don't be foolish. Please say nothing, let it go!"

"I hope I can," Sarah replied.

130

"You must," William responded. "I am going to the living room to read. I need to calm myself down. Why don't you try to get some sleep?" And he left without kissing her goodnight. He had never done that before.

* * *

Sarah said nothing and it tore at her. Every time she was with Sam and Marjorie that awful sense of dread was reinforced. She was suddenly tense all the time, and her appetite began to suffer. The littlest things would startle her. As the departure date for Sam's family got closer, she became a bundle of nerves and could no longer contain it. She sought out Sam and Marjorie about three days before the ship was to depart. She said nothing to William of her intent. He would have stopped her. She knew that Marjorie would always stop by Sam's apartment at the end of his work day. They would review their wedding plans and chat about their day.

She waited outside Sam's apartment for Marjorie's arrival. It was a chilly day, and Sarah had worn her heavy woolen coat and hat, should it turn into a longer than expected interval. Marjorie, however, was as punctual as Sarah had anticipated.

"Sarah, what a surprise! What brings you here?"

"I need to talk to you and Sam. Something has happened, and I must share it with you. It has been tearing at my spirit since that night at Delmonico's."

"What in heavens are you talking about? You are making me nervous!"

"Please, just hear me out. But I need to talk to both you and Sam. This is not an easy thing for me; I can only do this once."

"Oh Sarah, this seems so odd," and she fumbled with the keys to Sam's apartment, finally opening the door. Sam was in the living room in his recliner and rose when they entered the room, making a hasty attempt to straighten his tie and button his collar.

"Hello, sweetheart! And this is a surprise, Sarah, but it is good to see you, as always."

"Sam, Sarah has some information that she wants to share with us."

"Let's have a seat and hear what you have to say."

"I cannot sit right now, but please sit down." She began to nervously pace back and forth in the living room, staring only at the floor the whole time. Sarah told them her fears about the voyage that Sam's family was preparing for. Sam and Marjorie became extremely disturbed by what she told them. It seemed so bizarre. Something you'd read in an Edgar Allen Poe poem. How could she be so sure of such a tragedy? But they could not and would not stop the events that were already in play.

"Please do not let them get on that ship," Sarah pleaded. "You must tell them."

"We will say nothing!" Sam finally shouted. "Have you gone mad?"

"You must stop this now!" Marjorie demanded. "I will not have you ruin this special day for us. Please stop this before you damage our friendship. This is insane!"

Years of frustration and anxiety and the certainty of this tragedy suddenly boiled over. Sarah grabbed Marjorie by her shoulders.

"My God, you must listen to me! You need to understand what I am telling you! This will become the saddest day of your lives if you let your family travel on that evil ship!"

Marjorie tore herself away from Sarah and stood spellbound, her fingers held up against her trembling lips. "Sarah, are you well?" she nervously whispered.

"I am fine, just don't do this."

"You are scaring me, Sarah." She turned to Sam. He stepped in between Sarah and his fiancée,

"I think it's time for you to leave our home. In fact, I insist on it. I do not see anything productive coming out of this if you continue on this course."

"But—," and before she could say anymore, he added, "Please, not another word."

Sarah left frustrated and anxious. Every part of her being had pushed her to approach Sam and Marjorie with this disturbing news, and now she had left the couple as anxious and uncertain as they had ever been in their relationship. They were suddenly very tentative about Sarah.

A heavy burden slowed her walk back home. She had delivered upsetting news to Marjorie and Sam; God only knew what damage she had done. And now she must tell William what she had just compromised. Each step she took became more painful; it was a walk she would never forget and yet remember none of. She feared she had forced a crack in her marriage and she was petrified it would lead to a crumbling.

William was not home. He must have had some business issues at work that delayed his return. Waiting for him to get home was torturous for Sarah. She began her nervous pacing again. Just how to tell William what she had done began to consume her. She perseverated over what she would say to him and was not comfortable with any of it. Her thoughts were scattered. She began to cry.

When William finally returned, he saw that his wife was indeed in an unsettled state. She looked sad and lost. His insides told him he would not like the answer when he asked, "What is wrong?"

Sarah stood in front of him and grasped his hands and held them against her bosom. She looked in his eyes and searched for the understanding that she now desperately needed.

"I have been to see Marjorie and Sam, and I told them of my fears of the *Titanic*."

His body stiffened and he turned his gaze away from her. He tried to pull away, but Sarah would not release him. "Please don't be mad with me. Don't you understand I had no choice?"

He gathered himself, thought for a while, and then replied. "I feel you have done more damage than you realize; damage that may never be undone. I'm not sure how we go from here."

They saw even less of the now troubled Marjorie and Sam as the departure date got closer.

Jacob

JUNE, 1921

Sarah and Jacob were at last about to talk about the *Titanic*. Sarah could hardly believe it. It had been an elusive reality for so many years. She made the trip to England as quickly as she could. Fair weather, calm seas, and the ever present Gulf Stream current had made the trip a pleasant one. They arrived on schedule and her brother met her at the pier in South Hampton where her liner had docked. Frederick Jr. had already telegraphed Jacob and arranged their first meeting. There would be a nearly three-hour, bumpy drive to Jacobs's home in West London.

He lived in a small urban cottage located on a narrow lane. There was just enough room to park their motorcar and not obstruct other potential traffic. The bungalow had only a single ground floor and seemed quite small to Sarah. But then Jacob didn't need much, especially since his health had deteriorated so quickly.

He had hired the wife of an old friend from his days at the shipyard. Her name was Ida Hill and her husband Horace had been a good friend of Jacob's; in fact, they had started work at the shipyard on the same day. They were both sixteen-year-old shipfitter's apprentices. The two took separate paths from there, but always remained good friends. Horace had passed away several years ago. Jacobs's wife and Ida had also become good friends over those same years. She had been very supportive of Jacob when his wife passed away and was once again there for Jacob when his own health deteriorated. Ida agreed to temporarily leave her home in Belfast to aid her dear friend in his final few months. Sarah and her brother arrived late in the afternoon, as planned. Ida greeted them at the door and showed them into a small parlor.

She was a petite woman and Sarah thought her to be in her mid-sixties. Ida had been an attractive woman in her younger days, and there was still an element there of the natural beauty that she once possessed. Life had added a few pounds to her middle, but it detracted little from her figure. Her red hair had grayed ever so lightly over the years, but her green eyes still sparkled through the oval, framed glasses she wore. Light brown freckles delicately laced her soft, snowy complexion, and secret admirers were still rewarded when they chose to examine her fleeting beauty. She was still a true Irish princess.

Ida had prepared tea and asked them to please help themselves; cream and sugar were there if they wanted.

"I will leave you for a short while to get Jacob. He is in bed and I will need time to get him up and into his wheelchair. He is not a well man. Jacob has asked me to review some... ground rules, so to say. His energy level is very low and he does not wish to discuss the hows and whys. He will greet you, Mr. Shepard, and exchange pleasantries. But you will not be allowed to remain in the room. You will need to leave this house, as will I. What is to be discussed will be for Sarah and Jacob's ears only." She delivered this stern lecture standing as the two guests sat. She was firm but welcoming, clearly concerned with Jacob's well-being above all.

"Whatever you two are about discuss must weigh heavily on Mr. Sweeney. I have known Jacob many years and I have never seen him this anxious and weary. Not even the passing of his wife was this upsetting. Jacob has asked that today's meeting be limited to about one hour. I will return in precisely one hour. I know you were expecting more time, but believe me, this is all Jacob is capable of. He wants you to return each day at the same time for the same duration until his story is complete. If his condition changes for the worse, we will make adjustments. He tells me that he has a great deal to share with you. Please be patient with him, Sarah. Enjoy your tea, I will return shortly with Mr. Sweeney."

Ida emerged from the back of the cottage with Jacob Sweeney about fifteen minutes later. They had finished their tea. He was indeed a very sick man. His eyes were sunken and his face was gaunt. His skin, wherever it showed, had numerous spots where the natural pigment had disappeared and been replaced with irritated and raw patches of skin abrasions. His speech was soft and clear but his voice was slow and labored.

"Hello Mr. Shepard, this must be your sister Sarah. Sarah, I am so relieved to finally meet you. You and I have your brother here to thank for that, especially with the horrible crime committed against that poor man and how your brother was treated. I am glad that you did not give up on your efforts to contact me. How are you?"

"I am well, Mr. Sweeney. I, too, am relieved to finally meet you."

"Please, call me Jacob, I will not insist on any formality. What we are about to talk of deserves none. I know that my good friend Ida has defined the parameters, so if you will excuse us, Ida and Frederick, Sarah and I have much to talk about. There is a small restaurant not far from here and I have been told they offer the most delicious rhubarb pie. Ida, you can tell Mr. Shepard how to get there. Please excuse us now. We shall see you shortly."

Jacob began. "I would like to learn as much as possible about you, Sarah. You must be a very intelligent and gifted woman, but I

136

am afraid we simply don't have the time. Perhaps, when I have finished my dreadful tale, we can engage in friendly conversation. I also hope that by lifting this burden from my soul it may energize my spirit a little.

"I will spare no detail in what I tell you. Much of what I will tell you will be the truth. The rest will be what I assume to be the truth. I will explain as we go along. Let's start at the very beginning."

Sarah nodded her head in acceptance. She hoped she was prepared for the truth, as tragic as it might be.

"I was in my office in the shipyard. It was late in the afternoon on a Thursday. I will not give you dates. Dates are of no consequence. Only people's names and the actions they took are relevant. The Harland & Wolff shipyard was in turmoil. We had been pushing hard to bring *Titanic* to the finish line. The yard had already missed her scheduled completion date. We had been forced on three separate occasions to redirect our yard activities in order to deal with emergency repairs on the *Olympic*. Our own Captain Smith's ineptness at the helm of the *Olympic* was not making him any friends in the upper echelon of the shipyard, nor at White Star Lines.

"David Gurney, who was Mr. J. Bruce Ismay's personal secretary, walked in to my office. He told me that I should report immediately to the director's office and no explanation as to why was given.

"'This seems to be of some significance and I would not hesitate in your efforts to get Ismay's office.' He made that quite clear.

"I had met with Mr. Ismay on many occasions, but never in his office. I had been employed at the Harland & Wolff shipyard for twenty-eight years, starting as a ship fitter and rising through the ranks to where I was now, the senior general foreman and director of shipyard activities. Mr. Ismay and I had developed a good working relationship over the last seven years. I had followed through on some of his aggressive rescheduling demands. I became a trusted man of J. Bruce Ismay's inner circle. J. Bruce was not a man that I admired, as I had often witnessed the results of his ruthless and heartless decisions too many times, all in the name of his precious bottom line. These decisions often affected every corner of the shipyard. The men in the yard were family to me and I knew many of them personally. I respected Mr. Ismay's position, but was weary of his authority. I also knew my station and understood my role.

"I entered his office. He was alone and standing in front of his desk. Because of his exclusive and very profitable relationship with the shipyard, he had been given a large, impressive office, with broad windows that looked out over the shipyard and the river Lagan. He had occupied this office for the last thirteen years. There wasn't any area of the shipyard that was not visible from his office. The shipyard now employed 15,000 workers and anyone that had ever worked in the shipyard at some time had looked up to see these big windows facing the yard. The view was assumed to be panoramic. Now, up in Ismay's office, the view was even more spectacular and I told him that. He seemed unaware of my observation. He did not see these views as humbling; they just reinforced his position and his power. He chose only to look down on his minions so that he might witness their sweat and toil from his ivory tower.

"He greeted me. 'Jacob, thank you for coming. I don't think you have ever been to my office. I know you are probably quite curious or concerned as to why I suddenly asked you to my office. Before I explain why you are here let's have a glass of some fine Irish whiskey.'

"He opened the bottom right-hand drawer of his desk and retrieved a fresh bottle of Tullamore Dew. It was the only whiskey he would drink. He poured hearty portions into three separate brandy snifters. Before I could guess who the third snifter was for, he gestured with his left arm and opened hand and announced, 'Jacob, this is Lord William James Pirrie. Lord Pirrie has been very instrumental in securing American investment for your shipyard.'

"I had been so preoccupied with the view that I had not seen him. Lord Pirrie stepped out from the shadows behind me.

"'Lord Pirrie, this is Jacob Sweeney. He is the senior general foreman for all shipyard activities. Jacob has been of valuable assistance to me over the years. He is a man I truly respect and trust.'

"I extended my hand to Lord Pirrie and we shook. He was a large, impressive man. I was quite amazed that I had not seen him when I entered Ismay's office.

"'Please sit down Jacob, and please accept this drink. When Lord Pirrie and I are done telling you about the task that lies ahead of you, you will surely need it.' He gestured with his right hand towards one of the two big leather Chesterfields that were in his office. I sat down in one and Lord Pirrie reclined in the other. J. Bruce settled in behind his desk.

"I knew that J. Bruce took over White Star Lines leadership role in 1899 when his father passed away. He had strong business skills and had steadily grown the company. Now, three additional vessels were on the docket at the shipyard.

"My instincts told me that something of tremendous importance was about to transpire. Meeting with J. Bruce Ismay in his private office with Lord Pirrie in attendance told me I was being drawn into something of dramatic significance. I had never met Lord Pirrie, but I knew a great deal about him. Besides his peerage, he was director of International Mercantile Marine and was a large shareholder in White Star Lines. I also sensed that I would not be given the option to decline my participation. I took a long pull of the whiskey. It was smooth, warm and comforting.

"'Jacob', he said, 'I will try to keep this simple. This weekend we will close the shipyard to all but a small crew of men. Who these men are and how many there will be is to be determined by you.' I was getting an uneasy feeling.

"He continued. 'Currently the *Titanic* and the *Olympic* are berthed next to each other in their slips. The *Titanic* is about completed with her finish work. Punch lists are to be concluded next week and her sea trials are to commence two days after that.'

"I was more than aware of the *Titanic's* schedule and nodded my head in agreement.

"'Jacob, this weekend you and your hand-picked crew will change the identity of these vessels.'"

Titanic

APRIL, 1912

The Bosworth family booked six round trip passages on the most luxurious ocean liner in the world, the RMS *Titanic*. They had assembled themselves on the promenade deck as if they had gathered to watch a parade. There was pomp and ceremony everywhere, and the air tickled with energy and anticipation. Strangers introduced themselves, shook hands, and lively pleasantries were exchanged. People of all ages dressed in their finest were pressed against the rails and were waving to the crowd below on the pier. Thousands of people had turned out to see this splendid liner off and were waving and shouting envious bon voyages to the fortunate travelers. Bands were playing, streamers and confetti filled the air like an early spring dusting of snow. Thousands of handkerchiefs seemed to be bidding goodbye in unison. Doves and homing pigeons that had

140

been released still circled the majestic liner. All the pomp and circumstance animated the Bosworth family and heightened the anticipation of their voyage and Sam's wedding in New York.

"Oh, can you believe this?" squealed Cynthia Christine, their only daughter. She had squirmed and squeezed herself to the viewing rail like a young hatchling struggling for the best spot for her mother's return. She was anxious to absorb as much of the festivities around her and on the wharf below and her head pivoted like a meerkat on the Kalahari. The waterfront breeze teased her long brown locks and she struggled to keep them out of her eyes.

Titanic's massive horn suddenly bellowed its departure, and passengers and people on the wharf below erupted in cheer. Cynthia twisted around and called back to her older brother. "Can you believe all this pageantry? This is just marvelous!" Her brother Colin was packed into the crowd behind her, the rest of her family gathered around him. He brought his palms to either side of his mouth and shouted back, teasing her.

"Don't fall overboard, there is still a lot of this trip ahead of us!"

Sam's aunt and uncle were also making the trip. They had been quick to accept their nephew's invitation and were excited about being part of the festive outing. The six Bosworths would provide the sense of family that Sam needed at his wedding.

"Please go easy on the beautiful young women that seem to be everywhere." His uncle playfully nudged his young nephew's rib cage.

"I'm sure he'll be a gentleman," his aunt added.

"He'd better be," his mother demanded. And they all laughed.

* * *

Sam was so much like his father. He had the same sense of adventure and was likewise as driven. He had grown up in East London with a younger sister and brother. He remembered his father being away quite often when he was very young and knew it had caused some lonely and difficult times for his mother. Then it seemed like his father was home all the time and there was harmony in their home again, but it was so long ago and his memories of the time had faded like a brightly colored window drape with a southern exposure.

His parents had him attend Westminster School in London, and he excelled in his studies and was captain of the school's rugby team. Sam had the charisma of a leader, loved the game, and had inherited his father's wide frame and athleticism.

In his last two years at the academy, Sam became aware of places and events far removed from his life in London. America suddenly beckoned him, and he began to read as much as he could about this new and vast country. It all intrigued him, especially New York City. He pleaded with his parents to let him apply for admission to Columbia University, a very prestigious school in that same city. Sam's mother did not like the idea; such a city would simply devour her naïve, adolescent son. However, his father understood completely what his son was experiencing. This would have been just the type of escapade he would have entertained at Sam's age. The apple had not fallen far from the tree. He convinced his wife that she need not fear New York, but rather New York should be wary of their ambitious young son. Ernie Bosworth's perception had proved accurate: their son thrived in New York City.

The Bosworths had received numerous letters from their son since his arrival in New York. They could trace the development of Sam's love affair with Marjorie by his correspondences. The letters before he met Marjorie had been infrequent and common. He had enjoyed his years at Columbia, and living in the Morningside section of upper Manhattan had allowed Sam to participate in campus activities and experience the night life of New York. But Sam was also committed to his studies. His knew his scholastic responsibilities came first; there would be plenty of time for social commitments later on.

Now, graduating near the top of his class, Sam was anxious to fully explore the opportunities that New York City offered a determined graduate of a prestigious college.

There was still something missing from his life. Then Sarah introduced her beautiful sister-in-law to Sam and his letters became more numerous. He challenged his correspondence skills in describing Marjorie and their love affair to his parents. He was in love and never doubted that he would someday marry this woman that had fit so comfortably into his life. Both of his parents would approve and be happy for him; he was anxious to share Marjorie with his family.

* * *

Sam was excited about seeing his family, especially his father. He knew his father would be thrilled about the trip aboard the *Titanic*. He had always had a passion for the open water. His father had been following the construction of the *Titanic* since its keel had been laid in March of 1909. Ernest M. Bosworth, as a young boy, had been intrigued by these steel giants that navigated the globe, and the oceans of the world had beckoned him. Ernie's father was a business associate of Marcus Samuel, the founder of Shell Transport and Trading Company. Through his father's connections Ernie secured a position on a commercial freighter. He was elated; at just seventeen he was about to travel the world and visit ports he had read about as a child.

There was something about being at sea that connected with Ernie's soul: the smell of the open ocean, the colors of the sky in the morning and at sunset. The ocean could be potent and frightening at times and Ernie accepted that, but there was also something special about standing watch on the open quarterdeck of a vast ship at two in the morning, the crystal clear skies filled with the lights of a million stars. He was alone in a vast ocean that was alone in an immense universe. It could make you feel small and insignificant, but it made Ernie feel like the luckiest man on the planet.

Ernie Bosworth served on several commercial tankers. He worked his way through most of the important positions on a commercial vessel: navigation mate, first assistant engineer, deck mate, and chief steward. He was a quick learner and took his duties and responsibilities quite seriously. At the young age of twenty-one he was made chief officer of the oil tanker *Lumen*. He was a hardworking and respected merchantman in the Shell Company's maritime fleet.

The company that employed him was moving more and more refined oil and crude. They were importing from Burma and the Middle East. Their ships were traveling great distances around the southern tip of Africa, even though the Suez Canal had been open to commercial vessels for a number of years. The Suez Canal Company was not allowing oil-carrying barges or ships to navigate their waterway. There was just too much liability.

Ernie had been on too many trips around the treacherous Cape of Good Hope. Not being able to move crude oil through the Suez was pure stupidity. The Suez Canal Company was simply saying no to any proposal presented to them. Young Ernie Bosworth approached his father with a novel idea: why not let the Suez Canal Company design their own oil-carrying vessel? It would then be built to their own specifications and requirements. Shell Transport & Trading could also pay for all the design work as well as the building cost. It would be an offer that they could not possibly say no to.

Ernie's father thought the idea was brilliant and passed it up the line. Unfortunately, it passed through too many layers at the top for Ernie to be given the full credit he deserved. But it was immediately blessed by those at the top and quickly presented to the Suez people. As anticipated, they overwhelmingly supported the idea. Safe, secure oil tankers passing through their locks really meant more revenue for them. On March sixteenth of 1892, the newly constructed bulk tanker *Murex* passed through the Suez Canal. Ship's master Ernest W. Bosworth was invited to be present on the bridge in an honorary capacity. He had orchestrated the important occasion and was proud to be part of this historic event. He was just twenty-eight.

* * *

Sam had become close to his father in his later years. His father seemed to be away at sea most of the time when he was quite young. His mother was very unhappy during these times. When his father did return from his long voyages, he and his mother were elated, but the elation was short lived and his father was always returning to the sea all too quickly. His mother and father seemed to grow angrier with each other as his departure day grew closer. Sam's house became a very sad place to live. He hoped his father knew what an unhappy and lonely home he was leaving.

Then suddenly his father seemed to be home all the time. His father told him he loved him dearly and was home to stay. Their house became a happy place again and then Sam had a little brother and sister to share his life with. His father grew close to his family again.

Sam's father had lobbied for a senior position in the newly founded Anglo-Persian Oil Company. It was a burgeoning supplier of petroleum products to the United Kingdom and all of Europe. As much as he loved his life at sea, he loved his wife and son more. Ernest knew his marriage was in trouble and that his young son worshiped him, although he wondered why. He was so infrequently home and despised what he was doing to his family. Things had to change if he ever wanted to be worthy of his family's love. He spoke with his father and the board of directors. He sought a position with the company that allowed him more time with his family. Ernie had more than paid his dues and was hoping they would acknowledge those efforts. The company was gratefully indebted to Ernie Bosworth for what he had accomplished with the Suez Canal Company. His request was quickly expedited, and they offered him the position of senior vice president responsible for all company oil exploration and drilling efforts. Currently all those energies were focused in the Napatha valley in southern Iran. There still would be some required travel, but it would be limited to just several trips per year. He was also offered an advisory position to the board of directors for the Burma Oil Company, the parent company of Anglo-Persian Oil.

Several months into his new title Ernie received a telegram from his lead engineer, Roger Zaluski, at the Masjid-i-Suleiman drilling site. The site had reeked of sulfur for the last two days and everyone at the location was elated by the overpowering smell because it meant that crude would be discovered at any moment. They were drilling at 1,180 feet on May twenty-sixth, 1908, when oil exploded into the Persian sky. Preliminary tests indicated the strike was massive. Ernie Bosworth advised the board of directors to expand drilling in the oil fields of the Napatha valley where the Masijid-i-Suleiman site was located and to accelerate the completion date of the Abadan refinery 230 kilometers away on the Persian Gulf. Within one year the Anglo-Persian Oil Company was in business. Oil in vast quantities was now being discovered all over Persia. Ernie had more than secured his new position with the company.

The petroleum producers of the world knew that the internal combustion engine was about to power the globe. The global demand for crude oil would be growing exponentially. England had already decreed that all of its commercial and military fleets were to be converted from coal fired to oil fired in 1910. The United Kingdom had made its intention clear about securing drilling rights in Persia, but the Russian government was also forcefully injecting itself into these discussions. There was sure to be an issue.

There was also growing friction between Germany and the rest of Western Europe not at all related to the demand for crude oil. There was concern that it could escalate into armed conflict on a global scale, which would only create an even bigger demand for oil. Ernie Bosworth knew better than anyone what the potential for crude oil was.

Ernie also knew that the Americans had been ahead of the curve. The first oil well in the United States was drilled in Oil Creek near Titusville, Pennsylvania, in 1859. At start-up, it was producing thirty barrels a day. Two years later it was delivering 4,000 barrels a day. Oil had also been discovered in abundance in western Pennsylvania in 1885.

Crude oil's commercial value for many years had been limited to that of a raw lubricant and the production of kerosene as a byproduct through the distillation, but then the horseless carriages of the world came calling for a more economical and more efficient fuel.

John D. Rockefeller and the engineers at the Standard Oil Company answered the call. They discovered that by adding pressure to the heating process required for distilling kerosene, they could produce gasoline at a highly proficient rate. This process became known as thermal cracking. Ernie Bosworth had often jokingly posed the question to others in the oil business: which came first, the internal combustion engine or gasoline? It made little difference. It was an engineering marriage that was to create an industrial offspring of unbelievable diversity, opportunity, and incredible wealth.

* * *

In 1909 Henry Ford produced 11,000 units of the affordable Model T. By 1912 there were over 148,000 "Tin Lizzies" prowling the back roads of America. Crude oil production was barely staying ahead of the demand. Automobile growth was nearly as robust in England and Europe, and they would soon be on par with the Americans. Henry Ford projected that by 1922, global demand for his automobiles would surpass six million. There were other car manufacturers in the U.S. and Europe that had just as ambitious goals. Demand for crude oil would become insatiable.

Rockefeller and Standard Oil had seen this explosion developing. Existing oil fields were being expanded in western Pennsylvania and successful oil drilling had spread as far west as Indiana. Vast crude oil fields were also being discovered all over Oklahoma and Texas. Rockefeller had become ruthless in his business ethics to develop and control the crude oil industry. The Standard Oil Company in 1909 employed over 60,000 people worldwide. Finally, in 1911, the United States Supreme Court intervened and ruled that Rockefeller had illegally secured a monopoly within the crude oil industry. Congress legislated anti-trust rulings against Standard Oil and took actions to break up the company. Rockefeller's stranglehold on crude oil was broken. Ernie Bosworth now saw opportunities that he could only have dreamed of.

There would now be intense competition within the industry. Ernie loved competition.

Now, twenty years later, they weren't just constructing freighters and tankers, they were building these floating grand hotels like the *Titanic*, with the sole purpose of moving passengers in the most luxurious style that money could buy. Ernie's business connections in the U.S. had shared with him that American industrialist J.P. Morgan was the owner of White Star shipping. It was his company that was constructing the *Titanic,* and Morgan was sparing no detail to make this ship the most well-appointed ocean liner the world had ever seen. There were to be some very influential people aboard its maiden voyage.

* * *

Ernie had decided to pursue a different career path; more than that, he wanted to start his own company. It was something he had anguished over the last two years. He had developed a unique but sound business plan and was looking for outside investment. Aboard the *Titanic* he would have J.P. Morgan and some of America's most wealthy and influential business men as a captive audience for five uninterrupted days. They were not all associated with the oil industry – in fact, very few were – but they were men who had all built their livelihood on wise investment. Befriending these powerful men could only lead to future opportunities.

Titanic

APRIL, 1912

First class passage on the *Titanic* was costly. Large family or parlor suites were £870 one way, about $110,000 by today's standards. First class cabins were significantly cheaper. The Bosworth family, with the aid of White Star customer service, decided to book three first class cabins next to each other. The cabins all had large interconnecting doors. Travelers could open these doors and achieve the feel of the more spacious luxury suites at about one-tenth the cost. This also allowed the convenience of sharing a private bathroom and tub. Only the first class suites were provided with this luxury. In fact, personal hygiene was a perplexing practice, not really embraced or understood by the masses. The European lower class believed that frequent baths would contribute to respiratory diseases.

That is why the *Titanic* had only two bathtubs for 710 third class passengers, and they saw little reason to be offended.

The Bosworth family dined daily with John Jacob Aster IV and his young, pregnant wife, Madeleine. Ernest Bosworth's daughter, Cynthia Christine, quickly bonded with Madeleine. They often walked the promenade deck together during the day and would spend many hours in the reading room.

Benjamin Guggenheim, the patriarch of America's largest mining company in Colorado and member of the U.S. House of Representatives, was often part of the evening sitting, as well as presidential advisor Major Archibald Butt. Major Butt had been an adviser to President Teddy Roosevelt. He had served with him during the Spanish-American War and had become a close friend and confidant. He went on to become an adviser to the current president, William Howard Taft. Mr. Guggenheim and Majors Butt's political connections were obvious.

J. Bruce Ismay, White Star Line's managing director, and Harland & Wolff's chief designer, Thomas Andrews, were also passengers, as required by company policy.

George and Eleanor Widener, the owners of "Miramar," a lavish 30,000 square foot summer estate in Newport, Rhode Island, were also participants in the daily activities. George and Eleanor were close friends of the Asters, who also summered in Newport at their "Beachwood" estate. They were families that spent many summer days together. Ernie Bosworth put all of these people on his networking list.

Isador Straus and his wife Ida were first class passengers. Isador and his brother Nathan were co-owners of Macy's. It was a large department store, with five different locations in the New York area. They purchased the large department store from the Macy family in 1895. Ironically they began their business relationship with the Macys after securing a license to sell china in all of the Macy's stores.

Ernie Bosworth also introduced himself to George Dennick Wick, founder and president of Youngstown Sheet and Tube Steel Company, and also to Charles Hays, president of Canada's Grand

Trunk Railway. No doubt this christening voyage of the *Titanic* would be that common bond that Ernest Bosworth would always have to springboard him into many future business opportunities.

The list of important and influential passengers went on and on. It read like the who's who of Wall Street. However, the real focus of his efforts were two very powerful men, J.P. Morgan and Milton S. Hershey.

Milton Snavely Hershey was a wealthy confectioner or, as he once said: "Chocolate is my business and my only business and I do it exceptionally well." Milk chocolate was considered a luxury that only the wealthy could afford. Milton was determined to develop a formula that would lead to an inexpensive but delicious chocolate for the masses. He produced the Hershey Bar in 1900. Mr. Hershey finished his huge factory that implemented mass production techniques in 1905. He introduced the Hershey Kiss in 1907 and the almond bar in 1908. His chocolate products were the first food products to ever be nationally marketed. Milton S. Hershey was worth tens of millions by 1912. He was also a close business associate of John D. Rockefeller and J.P. Morgan. Men with that kind of wealth and influence always gravitate towards each other. They saw themselves as the Knights Templar of America.

John Pierpont Morgan was a giant in the industrial and financial world. He had founded, owned, or directed forty-two major corporations, including AT&T, General Electric, U.S. Steel, and International Harvester. He also owned and operated twenty-four regional railroad companies. J.P. was a large, impressive man. He had wide shoulders and piercing blue eyes. He used his size and wealth to intimidate his competitors. He did, however, have a physical feature that would affect his self-confidence for all of his life. He suffered from rhinophyma, an affliction of the nose that progresses from a skin disease called rosacea. The nose begins to swell and deform, changing to an unsightly purple color. Morgan tried desperately to avoid being photographed. When he did allow himself to be photographed he would often have the pictures retouched. Sidewalks and walls of vacant buildings all over New York City were often scrawled with the expression, "Johnny Morgan's nasal organ has a purple hue." It was a challenging task for city workers to keep ahead of the graffiti.

During the economic panic of 1893, the United States treasury was nearly drained of its gold. The United States gold standard was in peril. J.P. Morgan approached sitting president Grover Cleveland with a possible solution. J.P. Morgan offered to join with the wealthy Rothschild family and supply the U.S. Treasury with 3.5 million ounces of gold to restore the federally mandated amount and stabilize the country's economy. The President quickly accepted his proposal. It would take the country several years to repay Morgan and the Rothschilds. The deal had been negotiated with a healthy interest factored in, but it had saved the country from economic chaos. J.P. Morgan was a man of incredible wealth with deep connections and influence. His participation was critical to Ernie Bosworth's business plan.

Ernie knew he would have to leave his position with Shell Oil. His father would be questioning his decision and his wife would be unnerved by the whole affair. She would no doubt be concerned that they would be returning to the time when Ernie was never home and she was lonely and her days were empty. However, he knew it was the right decision. His business plan was well defined and he had done his homework.

Ernie knew the next big hurdle for the young oil industry would be the conveyance of crude oil. The need for oil would be increasing globally. The company he worked for had struggled with its own product distribution. Shell Oil had its own small fleet of barges and tankers and was already falling radically behind in their efforts to meet their customers' demands. John Rockefeller's Standard Oil employed thousands all over the world and yet they only had four case oil steamers and sixteen sailing tankers. Ernie was amazed that Standard Oil would have such a weak link in its supply and distribution network. The crude oil tankers that currently existed were small, poorly designed, and underpowered. Longevity had also become a concern. Most tankers had issues with internal corrosion, and the unstable, heavy loads they carried frequently caused premature structural failures.

Ernie Bosworth had envisioned a new breed of oil tankers. He proposed a tanker that was twice the size of present carriers. They would have multiple interconnecting storage tanks with a reinforced center line bulkhead the entire length. There would also be powerful transfer pumps that would give the ship's crew the ability to redistribute their load after partial off-loading or in foul weather. Ernie also addressed the undersized engine rooms and lack of power. He had researched a new, powerful type of internal combustion engine. It was being called the diesel engine. Requiring a slightly different type of refined fuel, it had been used in limited applications, but the feedback up to this point had been very good. He even envisioned oil tankers with a double hull construction, something completely unheard of at that time.

Most oil tankers were privately owned and contracted by individual oil companies. Ernest Bosworth wanted to design and build his own new breed of supertankers and contract them to oil companies all over the world. They could carry twice the crude oil as existing tankers at about one-tenth the cost. Ernie knew his sales pitch was finely tuned, but his biggest selling points were the numbers— they simply spoke for themselves.

He had a trusted friend who was an accomplished marine architect put together some preliminary drawings that he knew would illustrate his oil tanker of the future. He had reached out to Morgan with some very preliminary written correspondence and a brief outline of his business plan. Ernie would be careful in just how much he shared with Morgan; J.P. would never be reviewing these drawings until the moment was right. He hoped that future discussions with J.P. Morgan would lead to the super tanker the industry needed. He wanted J.P.'s investment, but most of all he wanted Morgan's shipyards. He knew Morgan would ensure that this new breed of tankers would be well built and on budget. Ernie was convinced his design would revolutionize the oil shipping business. J.P. Morgan's shipyards and his American corporate connections were critical. Mr. Morgan's business coordinator had cabled him back and expressed keen interest in his proposal. He proposed getting together with Mr. Morgan at "Mr. Bosworth's earliest convenience." Ernie would do better than that; he would dine daily with J.P. Morgan in a luxurious setting aboard the RMS *Titanic*. He hoped it would be an absolutely painless but effective ambush.

It was only after the *Titanic's* final boarding in Deerbrook, Ireland, that Ernie Bosworth learned that Milton Hershey, due to some last minute business demands, had canceled his trip on the *Titanic,* and that J.P. Morgan also canceled his voyage shortly before departure due to illness. These were two huge lost opportunities, but there were still investment and business prospects everywhere on this voyage. Ernie was full of confidence. That would all change dramatically at 11:40 p.m. on the evening of April 14, 1912, when the RMS *Titanic* struck an iceberg.

Titanic
APRIL, 1912

Ernie Bosworth introduced himself and his family to a number of the first class travelers their first night at sea at the captain's dinner reception. He could not have anticipated a better setting to engage perspective investors. Each of the privileged diners had their own tale to tell of their position and their lineage, and each one thought theirs was the more impressive narrative.

A gentleman at the opposite end of their dining table called across to Ernie. "Mr. Bosworth, I understand you are in the oil business. I've been told it is a fascinating new business with tremendous potential."

"I'm not sure fascinating would be the best word. I think challenging would be more appropriate. But I suppose there are some redeeming moments. But you have me at a disadvantage, sir! I am afraid I don't know you."

"My apologies. My name is Tom Andrews, I am *Titanic's* chief architect. Welcome aboard!"

"How did you know I am involved in the oil business?"

"I work for Harland & Wolff, the company that built this ship, and they are both owned by J.P. Morgan. Apparently the two of you have had some discussions; he is very impressed with you. He made a point of cabling me, asking me to introduce myself and to extend a hearty 'welcome aboard.' I know Mr. Ismay, the director of our shipyard, will drop by later to introduce himself and also welcome you aboard. He is committed to the Captain's Dinner and other related social engagements. He hopes you understand."

Everyone at the table immediately turned their attention to Ernie Bosworth. Who was this man of mystery? The mere mention of J.P. Morgan's name had that kind of impact.

Archibald Butt was seated at the table and had been listening to the dinner conversation. It was a gathering of strangers and had all the potential for social awkwardness, but Ernie Bosworth seemed to be in his element—he was engaging from the moment he introduced himself. Archibald immediately liked him.

"Mr. Bosworth, I am Archibald Butt. So good to meet you. Tell me, Mr. Bosworth, what has brought you and your family aboard this splendid ship on her maiden voyage?"

"It is indeed a pleasure to meet you also," Ernie replied. "We will be attending my oldest son's wedding in New York City. We expect it to be an entertaining and memorable event."

"I sincerely hope that it will be. You must have been disappointed when Mr. Morgan canceled his trip on the *Titanic* shortly before we left South Hampton."

"Yes, I was. You see, I am seeking outside investment in a business I expect to begin within the next eighteen months, and Mr. Morgan had expressed keen interest." So there it was, Ernie had dropped his baited hook into the gaping mouths of this school of big fat tunas.

"I would like to hear more about this start-up company of yours. If it can spike J.P.'s interest, it only makes it that much more interesting to me," offered Archibald.

156

A thin-mustached gentlemen entered the conversation. "I would also be interested in hearing the same. We introduced ourselves earlier, but again, I am John Jacob Aster."

Ernie told them of his years at sea as a young man and his later success in the oil fields of Persia. He shared with them his ambitious business plan and how he expected a healthy return on any outside investment. He was astonished at the interest it generated. These wealthy travelers knew an investment opportunity when it was placed in their trough. Word travels fast among those with capital to invest. He was approached during the day by potential financiers, and dinner that night was spent reiterating his business plan to these same people. Each night Ernie went to bed knowing he had secured more financial commitment from his fellow travelers. He would have to delay his return trip to England to follow up with these committed investors.

J. Bruce Isamy approached Ernie later that evening in the gentlemen's smoking lounge. It was just Ernie and his brother-in-law at that point; the rest of the family had long since retired to their suites.

"Mr. Bosworth, I am sorry I did not greet you earlier. Welcome aboard. Do you think we could sit and converse privately for the next few minutes? I hope your friend will not object."

Ernie's brother-in-law made no objection, saying it was getting late, and politely excused himself.

Ernie knew that Ismay and J.P. Morgan were connected at the hip; he was sure that Morgan had sent Ismay to evaluate him and his business plan. His brief discussions with Ismay were focused and with purpose. Ernie was confident that he had impressed Ismay with his insight into the oil industry. He expected Ismay would contact Morgan and encourage his participation. Ismay did exactly that. The next day Ernie Bosworth received a telegram from Morgan expressing his regrets for missing the excursion and their lost opportunity to further discuss Ernie's plan. He suggested they get together at the first opportunity. He would travel to any location Ernie chose. He apologized once more and then, peculiarly, wished him a safe journey. Ernie quickly cabled Morgan:

Mr. Morgan—return date to England has changed—will advise when schedule clarified—looking forward to meeting—E. Bosworth.

Ernie's cup was overflowing.

* * *

Now here he was, just two days later, in the first class lounge and Thomas Andrews, the ship's chief designer, had just told him to return to his family and do his best to secure their safety. The *Titanic* was indeed in serious jeopardy. There was fear in his eyes and terror in his voice.

How could this be? He, Archibald Butt, John Jacob, and Thomas Andrews had been enjoying a nightcap and a late night conversation before retiring for the evening. A weary waiter in a loosened collar had just set his tray of spirits on their table when there was a slight shuddering of the ship. Everyone starred as the collection of fine crystal shook and pinged with every delicate collision. The chandeliers throughout the lounge also shook ever so slightly and the crystal and china on other tables vibrated. It was just before midnight and no one in the dining area paid much attention to it. Tom Andrews, however, seemed concerned.

"That somehow unnerves me."

Conversation at the table abruptly stopped. Short minutes ticked by. Everyone waited on Andrews' next thought. Then the ship's normal hum suddenly stopped and it became quiet and disturbingly still.

Andrews was suddenly on his feet. "They've stopped the engines. I must get to the bridge. I will return as soon as I can. This may not be good."

They waited in the lounge. Ship's personnel seemed to be scurrying everywhere. John Jacob left the table after his wife sent one of her attendants to fetch him. Archibald Butts quickly decided it was best that he return to his cabin where his wife was probably sleeping.

"The woman could sleep through a typhoon," he joked. It was the last time Ernie would see him.

He waited for what seemed like eternity. The activity on the ship had begun to escalate. *Titanic* personnel were directing passengers to return to their cabins and put on their life jackets. Ernie wanted so much to return to his family, but he also wanted to return with an accurate assessment of what had happened. Finally, Tom Andrews returned. The look on his face said it all.

"Mr. Bosworth, get to your family quickly and get them to their lifeboat station even quicker. This ship will be at the bottom of the ocean in three to four hours."

Ernie briefly thought it all a prank, but Tom Andrews' look of complete panic and despair needed no further clarification.

Andrews quickly turned away and disappeared into the throngs of hurried passengers and crew. Ernie stood there briefly frozen in disbelief. He immediately thought of his young son. Sam was in New York, anticipating the arrival of his family for a festive and memorable wedding. Would this happy occasion be supplanted with tragedy? He sent Sam a little prayer, asking God's help for his family on this sinking ship.

Ernie hurried to his cabin and rousted his family. They quickly put on their warmest coats with life jackets over them and arrived at their life station in minutes. They had been assigned lifeboat #8 on the port side of the boat deck. There was a lot of confusion but little panic. Passengers weren't sure if they had the right lifeboat. Crew members were of little help. They seemed to be unsure on how to prepare the lifeboats and it heightened everyone's sense of urgency. Travelers were becoming anxious from the crew's ineptness and edginess. Ernie could sense that panic was only moments away.

They seemed to wait forever for the crew to prepare the lifeboats for launching. They finally began to board women and children. Ernie and his son had to forcibly place his daughter in her lifeboat. Emily decided to stay with husband Ernie and his sister with his brother-in-law. It was a very emotional separation. Officers of the

Titanic were promising that they would soon be boarding adult male passengers. Ernie was not so sure.

Theirs and others' lifeboats were filled with woman and children in an orderly fashion and were lowered into the water, even though most of the boats were not filled to capacity. The ship had begun to develop list to starboard and she was losing her bow to the water line. People were panicking, pushing each other towards the stern of the vessel. Woman and children waiting to board the remaining lifeboats were being dragged away by the crushing mobs. Frightened children began to scream when they were separated from their mothers. Some male passengers were trying to force their way onto the few remaining lifeboats. *Titanic's* officers were quickly losing control; the situation was about to give way to a mob mentality. Ernie and his family witnessed one of *Titanic's* officers remove a pistol from inside his jacket and fire several warning shots into the air. It seemed to briefly restore order.

Thomas Andrews was suddenly standing next to Ernie and shouting at him through all the mayhem.

"You need to get to the starboard side, there still may be some lifeboats there and I think they are boarding men, too. You must go now, hurry! And good luck!"

Ernie quickly hugged Thomas and thanked him. His family had all heard what Andrews had said to the him. There was little need for discussion—they all instantly moved together with purpose.

There was now chaos everywhere. They worked their way across the promenade deck and into the first class dining room. *Titanic* had nosed deeper into the sea and movement had become difficult. Passengers were turning on each other. Several fights had broken out. Violent pushing and shoving was everywhere. People were screaming and struggling for their lives. There was no longer any moral compass aboard the ship. Human compassion had vanished in seconds.

The first class dining area was in shambles, already difficult to cross. Table, chairs, tableware, and crystal were cascading towards the bow. Others were trying to make it across the banquet area.

Everyone knew they were on their own and so made their desperate dash. Suddenly a large buffet broke free and slammed into Ernie and his wife. They were violently swept off their feet and driven across the length of the dining area, smashing into tables and chairs along the way like tumbleweeds at the mercy of an evil wind. They finally came to rest at the far wall. Both of Ernie's legs were broken and he was sure his jaw was fractured as well. The taste of his own blood was overwhelming and it gurgled in his throat as he struggled for air. The pain was crippling, and it took a short while to get his bearings. He quickly scanned for his wife. Emily was a short distance off to his left, slumped against the wall. Her arms were contorted in an unnatural position behind her back, as was her life jacket. There was a deep gash above her left eye and blood had streamed down the side of face and stained her tattered nightgown. Unmoving, lifeless eyes searched for things not of this world. Ernie knew instantly his bride was dead. In tremendous agony, he dragged himself over to where she lie and cradled her in his arms, vowing to never let her go. His son was soon by his side. His brother and sister-in-law must not have witnessed their calamity. They were nowhere to be seen—and with all the noise and chaos, it was not surprising. They were all at the clemency of fate. His son was crying and clutching at his mother. Her blood was all over his hands and face.

Ernie grabbed his son forcefully by the shoulders and shouted through his pain and tears, his own blood splattering on Colin's face and hair, "You need to get to a lifeboat, and fast! Your sister will need you. I will stay here with your mother. It's what I must do. I loved her so very much. I love you. Now go!" He forcefully pushed his son away.

His son briefly stared at him and then understood his father's urgency. He told his father he loved him, kissed him and then his mother, and scrambled away on his hands and knees.

Ernie knew that it had all fallen apart. Those nights at sea as a young lad, alone on bow watch, had shown him the insignificance of it all. Now the fragile irony of his last few days became crystal clear. He had attacked every day of his life with purpose, with an evolving destination at the heart of it all. He had built a life for his

161

family and was content with what he accomplished. His son in New York, and whatever family survived this night of terror, would grieve for a time, but their character and values that he and his wife had tried to instill in them would see them through these dark days ahead.

In the end you only really have the love of your family and dear friends to measure your life's worth. All the plotting and scheming and pursuit of material worth was not why they loved him. His family was not that shallow. Ernie suddenly loved them all so very much, and he drew his wife of twenty-eight years to his side and softly kissed her lips. He knew how it would end and he was as calm as he had ever been in his life.

Sarah

APRIL, 1912

Titanic's departure day had come and gone without incident. Two days after the departure, Sam received a cable from his family aboard the *Titanic* that had been relayed on from Cape Race in Nova Scotia. Everyone was having a lovely time and couldn't wait to arrive in New York for the wedding. Sam was anxious to see his family. He hadn't seen his parents in several years, and Margie was just as eager to meet her new in-laws. The couple was overflowing with anticipation and excitement.

William shared this news with Sarah. She was confused and said very little.

The next morning William left for his office at the usual time but returned shortly after. He held the morning paper in his hands. The look on his face said it all.

163

"The *Titanic* has hit an iceberg and sunk. There are at least a thousand people dead, maybe more. No one knows. A ship has come to their aid and has the remaining survivors on it. We must pray that Sam's family is on that rescue ship."

"Yes, we must," said Sarah, but she knew they would not be on it.

The rescue ship RMS *Carpathia* arrived in New York two days later, and it brought devastating news with it. Sam's sister Cynthia Christine was the only one to survive the horrible ordeal. She was emotionally devastated. She told her brother and Marjorie of the terror of boarding the life boats late in the night.

They had retired for the night. Her father had remained in the lounge to talk with his new found friends. Then he was suddenly in their rooms demanding they get out of bed and dress as quickly as possible. He required they put on their life jackets, telling them that the ship had struck an iceberg. They hadn't felt a thing. How could this be? But her father had become friendly with *Titanic's* chief designer, Thomas Andrews, who had just informed her father that the *Titanic* was indeed in trouble. Crew members were hastily rousing all passengers. They were pounding on cabin doors, directing all to put their life jackets on and report to their lifeboat station. There was a lot of confusion. Passengers had never participated in any lifeboat drill; in fact, the only scheduled lifeboat drill of the voyage was mysteriously canceled the day that *Titanic* hit the iceberg. Also disturbing was the fact that only two officers and eight crewmen had actually practiced a lifeboat drill, and that was with the *Titanic* secured to her pier in South Hampton. Passengers were unsure where their lifeboat stations were, and *Titanic's* officers and crew were ill-prepared in instructing them when they did arrive.

The *Titanic's* officers were allowing only women and children to board the boats first. Passengers were told that once that had been accomplished, then all others would be allowed on. Cynthia's mother and aunt's decision to remain with their husbands was based on this assumption. What the officers did not share with those terrified passengers was that there were simply not enough lifeboats. Sadly, *Titanic's* original design had called for forty-eight additional life boats, but company officials were concerned those extra lifeboats would obstruct passenger views and detract from *Titanic's* pleasing profile. Those left behind would surely perish in the frigid waters of the North Atlantic. The water temperature was twenty-eight degrees and most of those entering the freezing waters were dead in two to three minutes.

Cynthia Christine told of having to be forcibly placed on a lifeboat by her father and brother. She had not wanted to leave her family. She sat next to Isadora Astor, the young bride of John Jacob. They had become good friends during the trip and that had helped. But she was angry and frustrated because, when their lifeboat finally slipped from its tethers, many of the seats were empty. Most of the lifeboats left the *Titanic* barely half full. Watching the huge ship go down and hearing all the screams of people in the water was horrible. All Cynthia Christine could envision was that her mother, aunt and brother's voices were among those screams. They had begged the oarsmen to return to those in need, but they refused. They were convinced that returning to those people struggling in the freezing water would surely overturn their boat and seal their fate as well. The screams of those drowning people would haunt her for the rest of her life. Waiting for a rescue ship to arrive had also been traumatic, if there was to even be a rescue ship.

Finally, the ship RMS *Carpathia* arrived at about 4:00 a.m. Those in the lifeboats could see its signal flares as it approached. The *Carpathia* retrieved all the survivors by 8:30 a.m. and left directly for New York. Other ships, including the *California,* had arrived on the scene and would be tasked with recovering what bodies they could. Cynthia Christine could not locate any of her family on board the *Carpathia,* nor did Mrs. Astor reunite with husband, John Jacob. Cynthia Christine was puzzled; many adult men were among the survivors on the *Carpathia.* Had they changed the evacuation procedures? She would learn later that most of these men had survived simply by seeking out available lifeboats on the starboard side of *Titanic.* Most passengers had panicked and moved to the port side of the ship, away from the side that had collided with the iceberg. *Titanic's* crew on the starboard side had simply started to board adult

165

men on the lifeboats when there were no longer any women or children left. First class passenger Dr. Washington Dodge had testified at the hearings that he had witnessed this odd behavior and that crew members had pleaded with him to board the lifeboat. There simply were no women and children left to board. *Titanic's* crew made no effort to redistribute the passengers.

"I was actually approached by one of the crew," the Doctor asserted, "and politely asked if I would like to join other passengers on lifeboat #14. My wife and I joined the already seated people. There was lot of confusion, but we bordered rather easily. There were still many empty seats on our lifeboat when we finally dropped into the water. As we rowed away from the *Titanic,* we could see that panic was quickly escalating all over the ship."

Sam, Marjorie and Cynthia Christine could only anticipate the worst. Sam's brother and his aunt's bodies were recovered. The bodies of his mother, father, and uncle would never be found. There were many other bodies that were never recovered. All of the deceased that were located were brought to the city morgue, and the grim task of identifying the corpses began. Relatives and friends almost as insensible as the corpses themselves began to filter through the assembly of lifeless victims. Hundreds of bodies of people that just a few days ago were celebrating a unique journey or the start of a new beginning in a new land were identified, claimed, and funeral arrangements were made. Many of the bodies had been in the water for several days and were unrecognizable. They were grouped in a separate area of the morgue and were numbered. Sex and approximate age were established, and a description of their clothing and the contents of the pockets were detailed:

Body #124
Male approx. 50 years

Clothing – *Blue serge suit; blue handkerchief embroidered w/"A.V.," belt with gold buckle; brown boots with red rubber soles; brown flannel shirt w/ "J.J.A." on back of collar.*

Effects – *Gold watch; cuff links, gold with diamond; diamond ring with three stones; £225 English notes; $2,440 U.S.*

currency; £5 English pounds in gold; 7 shillings in silver; 5 ten-franc pieces; gold pencil; pocketbook.

Later identified as John Jacob Astor

✳ ✳ ✳

Friends and family had begun to gather at Sam's apartment. Shock and disbelief permeated the room. Marjorie and Sam suddenly found it difficult to be around Sarah. The horrible, ghostly image of Sam that Sarah had seen several weeks ago at Delmonico's was now in front of her, alive but numbly greeting people and accepting their sympathy. He was sadder and emptier than the eerie preview she had witnessed. William and, especially, Sarah's presence among all the mourners became too overwhelming. Marjorie and Sam soon asked everyone to leave. It was the only way to remove Sarah from the gathering without specifically singling her out. It was becoming just too awkward with her in the room, and they needed time alone.

The next few days required that some sad and difficult decisions be made quickly. Sam and Marjorie's wedding was hastily postponed and funeral arrangements had to be made, the deceased returned to England. It was what the immediate families in England wanted, and Sam and Marjorie made the sad journey across the Atlantic. The whole ordeal left them feeling empty, physically and emotionally exhausted When they returned to the States they announced the new date for their wedding. They privately asked William to convey their wish that Sarah not attend. Sarah was devastated. William was also deeply hurt, but he instantly sensed the weight of Sarah's gift and knew that the burden would be too much for him. He felt like he had suddenly found Sarah with another man. As much as he loved Sarah, he knew he could not continue their marriage. It quickly fell apart.

Within a few short months he asked Sarah for a divorce. She was devastated. They were back at their flat when William told Sarah of his disturbing decision. She immediately felt her legs weaken and fell on to their living room sofa. Everything suddenly had no relevance and she struggled to find her breath. She could not imagine an emptier or more crippling feeling. Her voice was choked with tears. "Oh William, this cannot be happening! You are killing us! Oh my God, is this what you really want?" Tears that were always near the surface now began to flow.

"I will always love you, Sarah, and I have tortured myself so much over this. This whole *Titanic* event has been too much for all of us. My own sister has told me I am not welcome at her wedding and I completely understand why. I might do the same if the positions were reversed. I have tried to look past it and I just can't. I wanted to think our love for each other would be enough, but my instinct tells me to run. It will never work and you know it, too."

"I know no such thing!"

"I cannot do it, Sarah."

They would have many tearful talks over the next several weeks, with no reconciliation. To participate in a slow and painful process that would ultimately destroy their marriage was something William would not do. William had all of his possessions removed from their apartment when he knew Sarah would be away all day. He left a note that he hoped would explain and comfort Sarah. He knew he was being naive, as his owns words had done little to comfort himself. There would only be pain for the both of them, but he was leaving.

Sarah's world had suddenly collapsed. William had been her rock and now he was gone. Not through death, but through withdrawal and abandonment. She was suddenly without purpose and experienced a complete loss of identity. The tragedy of the *Titanic* was being played out on the world's stage and it was suffocating her. New York was no longer her home. There was no comfort or sanctuary for her, and within a few months, in an act of pure self-preservation, she moved to Rhode Island to be near her father.

* * *

Frederick Shepard could only imagine the pain his beautiful daughter was going through. Her gift had finally exposed its ugly side and turned itself on Sarah. It was destroying her on the inside. It was something he had always feared. He welcomed her move to Newport and hoped that the full social calendar he could offer would help heal her wounds.

"You can't shut yourself off from the world, but I also know you will need time to yourself. I will see that you have all of what you need. You did nothing to deserve this. Curse those fools in New York," he said. "You know your mother will be worried sick about you. You must keep in touch with her."

But seclusion was all that Sarah desperately wanted. She and her father found a little two-bedroom cottage in the Island Park section of Portsmouth, Rhode Island. It set was on a small isthmus and the windows in her tiny living room gave a picturesque view of the surrounding bay. She looked forward to summer's soft breezes and quiet walks on the beach in front of her cottage. Sarah hoped this would be the fresh start that she desperately needed.

Not long after she settled into her cottage, her father brought a little Standard Poodle puppy. He was a ball of curly, chocolate-brown hair.

"His name is Soleil, it's French for 'sunshine.' I am hoping that is what he will bring into your life. Poodles are very smart dogs and they are fiercely loyal. He should become your close companion. I believe you will not be ready for close human companionship for some time. Living by yourself does little to ease my concerns, but knowing Soleil will soon grow into those large paws he currently has will comfort me and hopefully protect you. Give him some time. Soleil will help you heal."

Her father was right. Soleil was the companion she needed, the kind that makes no demands and only offers boundless love in return. They quickly bonded. A puppy fills up your day rather quickly. Sarah made no objection when Soleil found his way to the foot of her bed every night; it was comforting to have him there, and on frigid winter nights he became a warm haven for her chilly feet.

* * *

Sarah changed her name, although not legally. She now called herself Alice. It was her mother's middle name and she had always liked it. Sarah from New York was gone—maybe gone forever. It was an identity change that she quickly realized was necessary and welcomed. The pain of losing the man that she loved so very deeply and the tragedy that had engulfed Samuel and Marjorie were just too much. She desperately wanted to put it all behind her. It was time to move on. However, *Titanic's* demise still pulled at her.

How had such a tragedy occurred? The months following the catastrophe had been painful. There was so much human suffering. Over 1,500 people had suddenly perished at sea. A dark cloud stretched from New York to London. Sarah had shared the pain in all that loss of life and the even greater pain when her William suddenly left. She knew there was a darker element to the tragedy of the *Titanic,* but for now her grief pushed it to the far corners of her mind. Sarah knew when she was ready she would re-visit this disaster.

Sarah

JANUARY, 1918

She lived in Portsmouth for the next six years, content in her solitary existence. She tried to accept her new identity as Alice. If she could convince herself that she was someone else, then all the pain that had overwhelmed her in New York belonged to someone else. It was a way to heal some very deep wounds. She had ignored her emotional needs, and she wondered if she would ever be whole again. But eventually she slowly began to realize she was ready for structure and purpose in her life again. Developing a clientele and allowing her clairvoyance to once again be a part of her life was a bold step forward. She slowly began to tell people about her gift.

Hank Pimental and wife Louise, owners of the local grocery store, had allowed her to put a small index card on their community bulletin board. Over the years, with every visit to their store, she slowly told them her sad tale. It was just enough exposure, as her gift has its own way of connecting with people. They began to reach out to her, and the days began to have the little events that validates living. The money it generated also helped her feelings of self-worth. The healing process had finally begun.

She was ready to revisit the uneasy feelings the *Titanic* had stirred up. The pain of losing William and the agony and mystery attached to the *Titanic* no longer crippled her. Her inner feelings were now pushing her in a strange new direction.

Sarah was driven to collect every possible document, every newspaper clipping, magazine article, and any available public record that was linked to the *Titanic*. The maritime hearings in New York and in London were of compelling interest. The events leading up to and after the collision with the iceberg were analyzed and reviewed at these hearings. *Titanic's* surviving officers and crew were questioned, and some passengers were brought into the hearings. Records were shown that iceberg warnings had been sent out by several ships in the area, and that Captain Smith and *Titanic's* bridge had received and noted the warnings. That time of year icebergs were common in the North Atlantic. Sarah later learned that the iceberg that had struck the *Titanic* had been migrating in the North Atlantic for over 1,500 years. The SS *California* had contacted the *Titanic* directly and gave its exact location, sharing that it was mired in a thick ice flow as well. Other large icebergs were also in the area. Then why, she wondered, was the *Titanic* steaming at a powerful twenty-two knots? All twenty-nine of her boilers were being stoked for maximum speed. Here was a sixty-thousand-ton ship speeding through areas reported to contain multiple icebergs. It all appeared to be a recipe for disaster. Even more egregious was that this luxury liner only had enough lifeboats for about one-third of the passengers and crew.

Sarah was livid that such a miscarriage of maritime responsibility was tolerated. The public on both sides of the Atlantic were outraged as well. It was hoped that the maritime hearings in New York and London would explain this disaster and punish those that had caused it. However, it was revealed that such speeds, as unwise as they might appear, were actually quite typical for those types of conditions. Information on ice conditions and icebergs in the North Atlantic were openly exchanged between all vessels in the area. Dangerous icebergs were given exact navigational locations, and these locations were frequently updated, as these were very busy shipping lanes. It was felt that with navigational aids as well as posted look outs, any vessel would have ample time to alter course and avoid any potential hazard. There had never been a fatal collision with an iceberg in the north Atlantic prior to this. The system had been working flawlessly for many years; why would any vessel anticipate such an event?

The *Titanic* was making maximum speed for two other reasons. First, because she was trying to establish a new trans-Atlantic record. The existing record was established by the RMS *Mauretania* in 1907. Captain Smith was also trying to secure an optimum docking time in New York. She had been scheduled to arrive mid-morning at Pier #60 in New York harbor on the seventeenth of April. There was a lot of fanfare about the *Titanic* and its maiden voyage. New York society and the press wanted as much of this as possible. Arriving in New York at three o'clock in the morning would serve no good purpose. Captain Smith was under strict orders to dock his vessel at the scheduled arrival time.

Sarah also discovered, to her astonishment that, though the *Titanic* did not have adequate lifeboats, irresponsible as that may be, it was not illegal. Maritime law at the time dictated that lifeboat capacity was determined by tonnage and not by the number of passengers. However, the real disturbing fact uncovered at the hearings was that the British Board of Trade, upon reviewing *Titanic's* innovative, water-tight compartment design, judged that the likelihood of a catastrophic event would be extremely slim. Here was a luxury liner the likes the world had never seen. Passengers were pampered like royalty, wanting for nothing except their lives. The *Titanic* cost over ten million dollars to build, and yet passenger welfare was of little concern in its design and construction. Again, the public was outraged. They wanted someone to be held accountable.

173

In the end both the American and British boards of inquiry seemed to whitewash the whole tragedy. No one could fault Captain Smith; he had gone down with his vessel. They did, however, find their scapegoat. With no living person of sufficient rank to level charges against, both boards ruled that Captain Stanley Lord of the *California* was solely responsible for the loss of life. He had not responded to *Titanic's* calls for assistance in a timely manner, though his ship had been within a few short miles of the collision. It seemed ironic and of no consequence to the maritime boards that it had been the *California* that had reached out directly to the *Titanic* and warned her of the danger that lie in her path.

They quickly implemented new lifeboat requirements. All commercial steamers were required to have sufficient lifeboat seating for all passengers and crew. Ships were to be stationed in the North Atlantic on a permanent basis to monitor sea conditions and take appropriate action. Something still pulled at Sarah. Everything she felt inside told her there was much more to this tragedy. Everything she read about the tragedy only reinforced that. In time, most of the world had dismissed it as an act of God. Sarah could not.

It was like the *Titanic* had reached out and made her another one of its victims. Her marriage had been destroyed by that ship. When William had asked her for the divorce she immediately sensed the feeling of complete helplessness those remaining passengers must have felt when the *Titanic* slipped into the deep. She hadn't drowned in the icy waters of the North Atlantic as those 1,500 passengers had, but it was as if her spirit had been torn away and pulled down with those other poor souls.

Sarah

JANUARY, 1919

It was January of 1919, the start of a new year, and Sarah knew she must look deeper into the tragedy of the *Titanic*. It pulled at her and she could no longer avoid it. Going back to *Titanic's* very conception was where she would begin her examination. She had gathered even more newspaper articles over the last six years from both countries, and whatever documentation she could find. Her father's connections provided a lot of avenues to pursue a search of privileged people and guarded information. He had pleaded with her not to follow this course. It would only prolong her sadness and would offer nothing at its conclusion, if there was even to be one. Sarah would hear nothing of it, and in the end her father knew he would not sway her. Sarah had her father's determination and focus.

She was prepared to dig as far as she had to. She was not prepared for what she unearthed.

Titanic's keel was laid at the Harland & Wolff shipyard in Belfast, Ireland, on March thirty-first, 1909. White Star Shipping was the company of record. Trans-Atlantic shipping of passengers and freight was booming. The great immigration to America and Canada had begun. Thousands and thousands of people were looking for new opportunities and a better life. There were not enough ships to meet the demand.

Sarah learned that American industrialist J.P. Morgan had seen this potential and had stepped in to purchase the struggling White Star Lines. It was being poorly managed in its upper echelon. Morgan saw that his timing was perfect. He merged White Star with his other trans-Atlantic shipping companies to provide the method of escape that millions of Europeans sought. America had become the land of opportunity. When Morgan's consolidation was complete there were over one hundred and twenty vessels operating under his most recent company, International Mercantile Marine. Morgan and White Star Lines then contracted the Harland & Wolff shipyard in Belfast, Ireland, to build three luxury ocean liners. They were the *Olympic*, the *Titanic,* and the *Britannic*.

The *Olympic* and *Titanic* were sister ships, almost identical in their design and construction. The RMS *Olympic's* keel was laid in December of 1908. It was scheduled for completion and the start of sea trials in May of 1911. As a publicity stunt Harland & Wolff arranged that the *Olympic* begin its maiden voyage on the same day that *Titanic's* hull was launched for final fit out at her berth. *Olympic* was completed on schedule and was ready for sea trials. She was to be commanded by Captain Edward T. Smith, the same Captain Smith that was to be at the helm of the RMS *Titanic* on her fateful voyage.

Rigorous sea trials were successfully completed in about three days. She left on her maiden voyage with Captain Smith in command on June eleventh, 1911. It was uneventful. At the start of her return trip, the *Olympic* had a collision in New York harbor with a tending tug. Her starboard aft section and rudder were badly damaged. She was towed back to New York, where emergency repairs were completed. Construction on her sister ship the *Titanic* continued at an accelerated pace.

The RMS *Olympic* made the return trip to England, where final repairs were completed, and resumed her task of moving passengers across the Atlantic. On September twentieth, 1911, the *Olympic* was involved in another collision, this time with the British frigate HMS *Hawke*. The collision occurred just off the coast of South Hampton, England. The two vessels were navigating the channel in the Isle of Wight when the *Olympic* suddenly turned hard to port. The *Hawke* simply did not have enough space or time to react. The *Olympic's* huge propellers sucked in the helpless *Hawke*. Captain Edward Smith was once again at the helm. This time the damage was severe. The British frigate was nearly sunk and six seamen were injured. There was extensive damaged to *Olympic's* rear starboard side, the same area that was hit by the tug several months earlier. She barely made it to the closest shipyard.

A naval inquiry was convened. It would take months before the results of the inquiry would be shared with the public. In the meantime, *Olympic* spent two weeks in south Hampton and then limped home to Belfast. Work on the *Titanic* was halted and all efforts were focused on the *Olympic*. Repairs took seven weeks to complete, much more time than originally estimated. In October of 1911 a meeting at Harland & Wolff was convened to review the extent of her damage. There were conflicting opinions as to whether the *Olympic* could be repaired sufficiently enough to pass the upcoming yearly marine trade inspection.

The RMS *Olympic* resumed her trans-Atlantic voyages and on February twenty-forth, 1912, after leaving New York harbor, she struck an underwater wreck. She was once again under the command of Captain Smith. The *Olympic* threw her starboard propeller and severely damaged her shaft. She limped home to Belfast on just her port engine. She had a noticeable list to port. She was dry docked in Belfast, and the assessment of her damage was not good. The propeller that was to be installed on the *Titanic* was used on the *Olympic*. The severe collision with the frigate and the subsequent collisions had apparently caused more damage than they had realized.

177

It was determined that her keel had been bent. To facilitate repair and make her seaworthy again would require an almost complete tear down. It would be cheaper to scrap her and build a new *Olympic*. What severely compounded this effort is that Whites Star Line's insurance claim was denied by their carrier, Lloyd's of London. The naval inquiry determined that Captain Smith was one hundred percent at fault for the collision with the HMS *Hawke*. Sarah sensed the beginning of something evil taking root.

The *Titanic* was just a few weeks away from her maiden voyage. Speculation was that White Star was not solvent enough to absorb the loss of the *Olympic*. It was rumored that J.P. Morgan was furious with White Star chairman and director J. Bruce Ismay. He wanted this financial catastrophe resolved. He also wanted Captain Smith reprimanded and dismissed. Smith had made a total of nine trans-Atlantic crossings in the RMS *Olympic* and three of them had resulted in serious collisions. Morgan must have been furious with Smith's seamanship. This must have presented a huge dilemma for White Star. Again, this was all speculation, nothing concrete, and it frustrated Sarah.

Chairman and director J. Bruce Ismay quickly scheduled a very exclusive meeting behind closed doors with a select few of the board members. Lord Pirrie, a major shareholder in White Star Lines, was rumored to be in attendance.

Sarah's intuition told her that some very fateful decisions were made at that board meeting, decisions that had sealed *Titanic's* fate. She knew that she had uncovered something very disturbing, but the pieces of the puzzle had to be put together. What decisions were made and how far reaching were they? Sarah struggled for months trying to move forward with her disturbing theory; then the Diamond twins had entered her world. They had stimulated the clarity she had desperately sought.

She knew she had arrived at the final truth. *Titanic* and *Olympic* were identical ships. White Star executives had switched vessels. *Titanic* had not gone down in the North Atlantic. It was the RMS *Olympic* that rested 14,000 feet down on the ocean floor. They had simply changed the names.

Changing the names, however, would have been the farthest thing from being simple. It would have required a lot of people's coordination and efforts. The decision to exchange the identities of the *Olympic* and *Titanic* must have been difficult. Something had forced their hand.

Sarah approached her father with her theory. He had a sharp business mind and was not convinced of his daughter's terrifying theory. A deception of this scale would be difficult, with potential for huge repercussions. It seemed a path that no sane man would take. But he was willing to concede that if her hypothesis was correct, there would only be one condition that would force that kind of decision: the potential loss of money, and a great deal of it.

"The owners of the White Star Lines," he told Sarah, "would have arrived at their decision because it was the only option they had, twisted as it might sound. The survival of their company must have been on the line. Men in those positions do not take the loss of millions of dollars and their livelihood very lightly."

Jacob

JUNE 1921

I was speechless. I rose from my chair with my empty snifter and
walked to the large windows overlooking the shipyard. I gazed
down at the thousands of laborers as they pursued their craft like
busy ants on a crowded ant hill; suddenly I was a thousand miles away
on a foreign shore, abruptly engulfed in a thick blanket of haze and
fog. Change the identities of these two mammoth ocean liners. What
in God's name for? Why am I being asked to do such a thing? With
a numbing and complete disbelief, I turned to face Mr. Ismay.

"What new names do you wish me to use?" I asked.

"You seem quite perplexed, Jacob. Relax, let me refresh your
brandy glass. I know more explanation is required here. First of all,
there will be no new names. You will simply interchange their
identities. The *Titanic* will become the *Olympic* and the *Olympic* will
become the *Titanic*." My expression must have begged for more
clarity.

Ismay continued. "I cannot tell you why this is being asked of you. You may form your own suspicions and arrive at your own conclusions. I will confirm nothing, nor will I deny anything. I strongly advise you keep any suspicions to yourself. As you already know, the *Olympic* was involved in three serious collisions. What you don't know is that these incidents have left her in a much compromised state. Our own engineering review has concluded that she would not pass her upcoming yearly maritime inspection. What has also compounded this is that Lloyd's of London, our insurance carrier, has denied all compensation for damages that occurred when she collided with the HMS *Hawke*. The Royal Naval review board has ruled that our own inept Captain Smith was one hundred percent at fault for this collision. Captain Smith has yet to learn of the heavy price he will pay for his incompetence. This shipyard is not solvent enough to absorb such a financial loss. Some difficult decisions have been made.

"We will need to exchange the names on the bow and stern of each ship. Lifeboats and life rings will need to be switched. Deck and ship furniture are all marked with standard White Star Lines identification, as well as all china, crystal, tableware, linens, and related goods. Those items will not be an issue. You will take all steps necessary to accomplish this. Spare no expense; secure whatever manpower you will need. But focus on quality first, then quantity, when choosing your crew. Make sure these are all skilled men you can trust. This will become a well-guarded secret. The men you pick will need to know this. They will all be well compensated for their work, as will you. I will privately speak to all of them, after their tasks are completed. See to it that your job is thorough. If you need to remove tile that is scuffed or carpeting that is stained or worn, then do so. The *Olympic* is now the *Titanic,* and she must have the shine of a luxury liner on her maiden cruise. You know the trades, you know the people, and you know the material that you will need. I have personally reviewed our ship's stores inventory and I am confident you will have whatever you need to support these efforts. You will have the next few days to prepare for this. Just be ready to go this Saturday morning.

"I am sorry I cannot tell you more. But it is just as well that you don't know more."

Lord Pirrie had not said a word; he had listened intently, sipped his whiskey, and occasionally nodded with affirmation at what Ismay was telling me.

Lord Pirrie finally stood and walked directly to where I was seated.

"Mr. Sweeney, you have the heavy responsibility of a difficult task. You cannot shrink from it. It will require your full commitment. You will need to do your best." That was all he said.

J. Bruce then added, "There will be other tasks that we will require of you, but they will come later. For now, you will need to focus on this task only. You should probably leave now and begin to organize your actions. Let's plan on meeting here Friday at two o'clock to review where you are in this process. Do you have any questions? Do you completely understand your charge?"

I had been assigned other significant and clandestine duties in the yard before and had followed through on them. Mr. Ismay was right though, I knew the shipyard like the back of my hand. This time with unlimited resources and with people I knew well. I saw no issues.

"No, Mr. Ismay, I have no concerns. I completely understand what is being asked of me. I should leave now. I have a lot to do." I shook his hand and left.

Lord Pirrie made no effort to participate in my departure. I walked back to my office in the shipyard completely bewildered. What in God's name had I become involved in?

I met with Mr. Ismay on Friday as we had planned. I had slept very little the last few nights. I don't ever remember being in such a dilemma. I either focused on the task at hand or tormented myself as to why I was involved in it. I had time to walk through the *Olympic* with key members of the team I had already assembled. I informed J. Bruce that we should carpet the first class dining area and re-paint the boat deck. They were the two areas that had seen the most wear. I also recommended we perform a general touch up wherever needed. I scheduled a special crew to clean and square away the engine and boiler rooms. But other than that I saw no real issues. The *Olympic* was only four months old and much of that time had been in our yard repairing damage from her three separate collisions. There was little wear to her condition.

Swapping the names on eighteen lifeboats and forty eight life rings would be done easily. Moving the liners in their slips could be done with little effort. I told him that we would drop canvass over the bow and stern of each vessel. This would shield our name-changing efforts from any prying eyes. I never asked for his approval or authorization. It was not required. It simply became a matter of, *if this is what you want, then this is how it must be done.* Mr. Ismay listened intently, and in the end he felt I had an adequate understanding of what needed to be done. He reiterated that my work had to be completed well before first shift activities began on Monday morning. He again highlighted how much I and my team would be compensated for our weekend of work. He hoped this very generous amount would guarantee everyone's silence; if not, they needed to know the company would go to any length to guard this secret. He was very clear on that.

The weekend went off without a hitch. Everything was completed. Fifteen thousand shipyard workers returned to their duties on Monday morning. Few people, if any, took notice of what had occurred over the weekend. The crew was given the next week off with pay, plus handsome compensation for their two days of work. J. Bruce was pleased. I found out later that he had met with my crew first thing Monday at a location away from the shipyard. He paid them and made it painfully clear that what they had just done was to remain a very guarded secret. The health and well-being of themselves and possibly their families were at stake. It was a point lost on no one.

I was still perplexed by all our efforts. I had just directed and coordinated the most clandestine project that had ever been undertaken in our shipyard. Why? Workers and their families had been threatened to maintain this secret. Why?

Simon

MARCH, 1939

His name is Simon; Francis Simon Bouchard, to be exact. He had received numerous phone calls and letters from his old friend Claudia St. Louis, pleading with him to help her. He finally agreed to make the trip to Jamestown, Rhode Island. Simon was hopeful that he could help his close friend. If what Claudia was describing in her many correspondences was accurate, they described a very troubled woman, existing now in a lonely world brought on by a horrible event. He trusted Claudia. He had no reason not to.

He had met Claudia twelve years ago. He had been approached to conduct Tarot readings at a home in the Chestnut Hill section of Philadelphia. Some of the finest homes in the city were located in this area. Seven ladies and two gentlemen of Philadelphia's finest had requested readings. He remembered these numbers because he was always compensated by individual readings. It was standard practice. He had completed the readings and remained for wine, appetizers, and conversation. Claudia had been one of the people that had requested a private reading. It had revealed a great deal about her: he sensed that she had traveled a great distance at a very young age to be there. America was not her native country. Her mother had been a strong figure in her early childhood, and he sensed that her father had passed away as a young man and that his death remained a mystery. She was impressed with what Simon knew about her life. It was obvious that they had made a strong connection and formed a lasting bond.

"What you know about my family is really remarkable. I am shaking on the inside. I think we are destined to become good friends," she told Simon.

They talked for quite some time, and Simon shared much of his life's story with her. They talked freely and honestly.

Simon shared with Claudia that he had suffered from scarlet fever as a child and that his mother felt that it was what contributed to his diminutive stature. Simon's mother was a beautiful, tall woman with attractive proportions, and his father a commanding man of six-foot-four. There had to be a reason why Simon never grew beyond five-foot-four, and had always been noticeably thin. His father was an imposing, aggressive man. He was foreman at a brewery for many years before becoming part of management. He often used his size to intimidate and control the men that worked for him.

Simon was the oldest of three children. He had two younger sisters, Rebecca and Sandra. He knew his father was disappointed in his diminutive stature. He never openly displayed his embarrassment or overtly persecuted Simon for it, but there were subtle comments: *Can you get that by yourself?* or *You'd better get your sisters to help you with that, it may be too much for you.*

They became little pinpricks that pained very deeply. Simon became nervous around his father and would sometimes go to great lengths to avoid him. This uneasiness began to spill over into his life outside his family and negatively affect his overall demeanor.

He began to stutter in moments of stress, his heart feeling as if it was about to leap from his chest. It was so unnerving, and he developed a habit of feeling his pulse at the wrist during these flashes of anxiety. He wasn't sure how this habit had developed and most of time he was completely unaware of it. School became a setting where his classmates made the most of his idiosyncrasies, torturing him at length.

Mrs. Edna Garrison had been gracious in hosting the event, but now she was politely attempting to conclude the activities. Some of the guests had already left and early evening was drawing near; it was time to leave.

Claudia said that she would like to participate in a more in-depth reading and that she knew of others that wanted the same. She also told Simon that she had heard through friends that he had conducted séances and that some of them had been successful. She felt that Simon had a gift. She wanted to further pursue this.

"I have been told that you have contacted souls in the afterlife. If this is true, then you do have a unique gift, and I know people you could help. Would you like to help them?"

"I do have a given ability," Simon told her. "And I would like to help in whatever way I can."

Simon gave her his address, sure that he would hear from her again.

* * *

His interest in the afterlife and the paranormal had taken on a new passion after the death of his wife. Simon loved her deeply and missed her desperately. She had passed away several years earlier and they never had any children. They had been trying since their marriage four years earlier, but were never fortunate enough to conceive, possibly another consequence of his scarlet fever. Children would have been very special for them, but not having any had no impact on how much they loved each other. They were very happy until she was suddenly taken from him in July of 1919.

186

They had decided to take in a long Fourth of July weekend at the Boardwalk in New Jersey and had rented a cottage near the shoreline. Olivia had thought of everything they could possibly need for their getaway and had made a list. They would review it every night to make sure they hadn't forgotten anything; Simon would tease her about it. She was excited and anxious to begin their little vacation. When it was time to leave, Olivia had their old Buick busting at the seams, and he took a picture of her standing next to the car. She had on the most attractive skirts and summer blouse, her hair pulled back in a ponytail. Olivia was wearing her most stylish sunglasses and Simon was struck by her beauty. He would treasure the picture for the rest of his life, as it would be the last time he would see her so healthy and so beautiful.

They spent the first day on the beach enjoying the sun and the ocean. That night, Olivia complained of some common cold symptoms. It seemed harmless at first – slight fever, stuffy sinuses, and achiness – but it became quite serious in just a short time.

They left the Jersey shoreline early Sunday morning. She had become too sick, and it made no sense to remain there any longer. Wrapped in a woolen blanket, she slept in the back seat the entire ride home. When they arrived home she was burning with fever; Simon carried her to bed and immediately called the doctor.

There was little he could do. He had just recently started to see many patients with these same symptoms, and an unsettling number of them had suddenly and quite unexpectedly passed away. He gave her something for the fever and hoped it would pass in a couple of days, but his demeanor suggested a shallow conviction in that. Neither their doctor nor any other physician was prepared for what was to come.

His beautiful wife passed away less than twenty-four hours later. Struggling for every breath she took, she lie in his arms for the final six hours of her life. Olivia looked into his eyes in those final moments and softly, slowly, blinked *I love you,* and he saw the smallest flash of light streak away from her brown eyes that had always mesmerized him. A stunning woman of abundant energy and rich optimism had been ripped from his life in less than two days. She had always been his rock. Simon was numb and without purpose.

He found out later that his beautiful Olivia had become one of the early victims of the Spanish influenza, and would learn that, from 1918 to 1919, forty-five million people worldwide died from this aggressive virus. More people died from the Spanish Flu in one year than in four years of the Bubonic Plague in Europe during the twelfth century.

The Great War had just ended and history would come to define it by the horrible trench conditions that men on both sides were forced to endure. Few battles were ever won by either side, and it became a war of attrition. The constant bombardment by both sides had stripped the area of any living tree, shrubs, or foliage. There was nothing to absorb the frequent rain and dampness. Trenches and underground shelters became thick with mud contaminated with urine, feces, bloodied bandages, and decaying body parts. It provided a fertile environment for infection and disease. Large rats fed by the acres of carnage were everywhere and spread disease rapidly. These same infected rats also became the one of the main food staples soldiers could depend on. Hunger and malnutrition were rampant in the trenches. Soldiers would go months without bathing and body lice flourished. Simon wondered how these men could have survived in such inhumane and deplorable conditions. Trench fever and trench foot were widespread. The medical community theorized that these horrible environments, along with the use of mustard and chlorine gas, had created a unique and purely evil virus.

Men returned to their homes in droves with the war's end, and then in pockets all over the world something wicked erupted. These unknowing survivors of a barbaric campaign had carried the virus home with them. It started as a common cold and progressed very rapidly into something quite deadly. It appeared to be especially lethal to young adults, twenty to forty years old. In two years it affected over one-fifth of the world's population.

It infected twenty-eight percent of all Americans. 675,000 people died from the flu, more than ten times the amount of American service men killed in the Great War. More American soldiers died in

Europe during the war from influenza than perished on the battle field.

The effects from this venomous influenza were severe; it reduced life expectancy by ten years. It had a death rate of three out of every one hundred. The city of Philadelphia, with a population of 360,000, could anticipate over 12,000 fatalities; certainly a strain on any city's health system.

The medical community was simply overwhelmed. There was a dire shortage of doctors and nurses to combat the virus. People heard stories of medical students with only two or three years of schooling being sent out to treat the sick. The Red Cross would plead with employers to give workers that volunteered for evening shifts at local hospitals the following day off.

The country's president, Woodrow Wilson, was battling this same flu while trying to negotiate the treaty of Versailles. The world never knew until much later how terribly sick he really was.

Federal and local governments were enacting bizarre policies in the hopes of containing the lethal virus. Health departments issued gauze masks to be worn in public. Stores were not allowed to have sales. Funerals were limited to fifteen minutes.

Simon could remember children at that time skipping rope to a rhyme.

> *I had a little bird*
> *Its name was Enza*
> *I opened the window*
> *And in-flu-Enza*

So many people infected with the influenza, much like his wife, would die within hours. Physicians told stories of people struggling to clear their airways of a blood-tinged froth that would sometimes gush from their nose and mouth. Then they would simply choke to death.

Doctors had never seen such an aggressive type of influenza before. They were completely helpless against this deadly virus. The flu then suddenly vanished. Health officials were baffled.

His wife's death had left him feeling empty and incapable of any true happiness. He tried to attack each new day with fresh new confidence, but it was difficult to refill a great emotional void with a teaspoon of optimism every day. His grandmother used to say that happiness demands a twin. A beautiful sunset means nothing if you can't share it with someone else.

* * *

Claudia was true to her words and organized and scheduled more readings. She was considered a trusted and respected housekeeper and governess. She worked for and had contacts with some of the wealthiest families in the Chestnut Hill area of Philadelphia. Most of the people attending these gatherings considered them a novelty event, fun and entertaining. They were usually held on a Saturday evening or a Sunday afternoon. It was something they could talk about after, more so if the things that Simon foretold actually came to fruition. But there were those who wanted much more than his readings were ever meant to offer. Those who had lost loved ones, those whose daily existence was so empty and void of any real happiness. People like Simon.

He began to counsel people outside these gatherings, those that wanted him to reach beyond. This new challenge unsettled him, and he wondered if he could really be that conduit between those two separate dimensions. The deep love and raw emotion that we have for those that have passed on is, he believed, the vital instrument we must use to break through the barrier that separates the living from the dead. He knew he had a gift, but had never contacted his wife, Olivia, though, he had tried many times. Wanting to contact her had consumed Simon, and he became desperate in his increasingly futile attempts to reach out to her. Perhaps he had not loved her enough, or possibly she did not want that communication to take place. If Simon could not contact his Olivia, how could he help others in search of that same connection? It may be that solutions to such mysteries are never meant to be.

Simon began his séances with just himself and a single client. All were unsuccessful, and he began to feel that his first few clients were not as emotionally tortured as they said they were. He began to sense this lack of connection and started to screen his clients to see if they were as emotionally void as they claimed. Some wanted to know if their loved ones were all right and had found peace. Others wanted to know where lost money or family jewels might be hidden.

All of these séances were frustrating and fruitless. They all lacked the true ingredients that Simon needed to build an emotional bridge, as he began to call it.

Then he was introduced to Oliver Campbell. He had been an old friend of Claudia's and had lost his wife of fifteen years in a terrible automobile accident. Claudia would often talk about his plight. Her friend had been left to raise three young daughters on his own. Family and friends had come together over this sudden loss. The calling hours and funeral had been difficult. Claudia painted a picture of a broken man who had suddenly and tragically aged twenty years overnight, supported on either side by his teenage daughters as they numbly plodded behind their mother's casket. Oliver and his daughters had cried for days, their swollen faces and broken spirits all that they could muster that day in their church. They were emotionally devastated, but held each other up and stood together as a family that morning. It was the saddest funeral she could ever remember. Claudia always worried about her friend.

Now Claudia was at Simon's front door asking him if he might help Oliver. She had stopped by on her way home from her trip to the market. Simon had invited her in, but she had declined.

"I can't stay for very long, I have some fresh meat and fish that I need to get home with rather quickly. I spoke with Oliver Campbell this morning, and he asked me again if you have decided to help him contact his wife. I have pestered you for the last several months on this, and you have not really said yes or no. I think we owe him an answer."

"I suppose we do," Simon replied. "I didn't mean to be evasive. I am very sorry. I guess I didn't know how serious or committed he was about this. I know now."

"Simon, you must help this poor man. Once you understand his plight, you won't hesitate."

He agreed to help, but was nervous when Mr. Campbell insisted that his three daughters participate in the séance as well. Too many people meant too many distractions, and that would make it difficult to channel or focus all of these emotions. But they were insistent, and he could truly sense a deep loss among them all. They agreed to meet at Simon's home.

Mr. Campbell and his three daughters, Maureen, Meredith and Marylou, arrived several weeks later on a Saturday afternoon in late November. It was a bitter cold day and it had snowed the night before. Simon greeted them at the door and welcomed them to his home. They were all bundled up, and he took their heavy coats and wraps. They stamped their shoes on the scuff mat to be rid of the snow they had carried in, and he steered them into his living room where he had built a strong fire in the Franklin stove, making the room warm and comfortable. Mr. Campbell's daughters were attractive young women; they were cordial, but you could see they were unsure of what was about to happen. They chatted for a while, and Simon soon learned more about their family dynamics. They had brought pictures of their mother and a recent family portrait of when they were a happy family. Maureen was the oldest, and Simon was told she looked the most like her mother; the pictures confirmed that. Marylou was the youngest of the three and was the closest to her mother. She had her father's likeness. Simon suggested they sit around a table that he had brought into the living room in order to be near the fire.

After explaining what he would be doing and how he hoped things might progress, they began the séance. They tried for more than an hour, but nothing appeared to be imminent, and he was beginning to feel the afternoon would be a frustrating experience. Simon's anxiety was beginning to escalate and he began his cursed stuttering. Simon sputtered out his concerns and doubts about the progress of the séance. Marylou, the youngest daughter, began to cry.

192

She wanted so much to contact her mother. Mr. Campbell and one of his other daughters also began to cry. Simon very much touched by this family. Their loss and their pain were profound.

Blinding light suddenly pierced his eyes and then Simon's mind saw violent images of being dragged through a thick and wooded forest; tree branches were being thrown at him, but never striking him. He instinctively brought his arms up to protect himself from the wooden projectiles and to shield his eyes from the blinding light, and then bright light and the disturbing images abruptly vanished.

Oliver and his daughters were confused by Simon's actions and probably wondered if this might be part of the unique process.

"Are you all right, Mr. Bouchard?" asked Mr. Campbell.

Simon's reply was there, ready, on the edge of his tongue, when a voice, soft and quiet, spoke to him:

"Don't cry, Peaches."

He looked at the family. It was clear that they had heard nothing. Then again, the same piercing light and more images of tree limbs and brush being pitched at him, and the feeling of a sudden jolt. Simon knew immediately that again his guests had experienced none of this. He needed to stay focused.

"Who is Peaches?" Simon asked. They all focused on him immediately, but said nothing.

"Who is Peaches?" he repeated.

"That is what my mother would sometimes call me," said the youngest. "It was her special name for me."

"I think your mother is here with us. I heard her say, 'Don't cry, Peaches.'" The penetrating flash of light was there again and Simon saw more quick images of two women in a car, screaming, out of control, crashing through thick woods. Then suddenly back in the warmth of his living room with a family now more than ever seeking answers.

"What do you mean 'you heard her say'? Did she talk to you? We did not hear a thing," said Meredith, the middle child. "Did we?" She searched her family for an answer.

193

"I'm not sure if she's talking to me directly," said Simon. I can only tell you what I am sensing." He was not sure how long he could maintain any balance in this paradox that had now surrounded him.

"Is she okay? Does she miss us? Tell her we love her!" they all said through their tears.

But there would be no more communication, and the piercing light and disturbing images were gone too. Simon began to collect himself. Some outer direction told him not to share these images with the Campbell family. After about an hour of tearful pleading, the Campbell family left. They were frustrated and emotionally drained. Simon was now intensely aware of just how physically and emotionally demanding his special gift could be. He was also left trying to make sense of the powerful and traumatic images he had experienced.

Over the next several weeks the Campbell family visited Simon two more times. No communication took place, but more images of what must have been the fatal car crash that killed Mrs. Miller were shared with him. She had experienced a long and painful death. She had been a passenger in a car driven by her sister when her sibling lost control on an ice-slicked road. They had veered off the road and penetrated deeply into the woods before striking a large oak tree. Her sister was killed instantly. Simon could visualize the penetrating tree limbs and could hear the sounds of breaking glass and crumbling steel, as well as the screams of both terror and pain. He felt the sudden jolt when their car struck the rugged oak, and saw the violent snap of her sister's neck and her instant and painless passing.

Mrs. Campbell had suffered internal injuries and numerous broken bones. She was trapped alive in the car for many hours in tremendous pain before she finally passed on. It snowed briefly sometime after the accident and it had covered their skid marks. He could feel the coldness of that night and the sensation of snow that must have fallen through smashed windows and settled softly onto her face and hands. It was almost two days before authorities found

194

the wreckage and the sisters' bodies. He now knew why he hadn't shared these details with them.

Someone from the other side, probably Mrs. Campbell, had shared these images with Simon, but he could offer this family nothing. He was given this glimpse into a very tragic passing of a loving friend, mother, and wife, and saw no need to compromise that image. What they wanted most was a connection with their mother and Simon was failing miserably.

* * *

He reluctantly agreed to meet with them on Christmas Eve. It had been a special time of year for the Campbell family. The weather had turned a little milder and most of the snow had disappeared. He had stocked the Franklin stove as before, and the room was again warm and inviting. They sat around the same table in his living room and it felt like a Christmas morning, when you sit with your loved ones dressed in plain pajamas and robes, unpretentious, relaxed, and anticipating only good things. Today would be likewise as worthy. Simon began trying to reach out to Mrs. Campbell. He began again to feel their pain and their loss. Then Mrs. Campbell spoke to him.

"Please tell my family I love them; I will always love them."

"Your mother is here," Simon said to the family.

The Campbell's sat and waited. Several minutes passed and there was nothing. Simon was hoping for more. He could sense their trepidation. With still nothing, he finally told them what she had said.

"She says she loves you and will always love you."

The tears and sadness were slowly returning again.

"Did she say anything more?" Mr. Campbell asked.

"No, that is all she said to me," Simon replied.

"Oh please, please don't let that be all there is," said Marylou, the youngest. She was becoming desperate and wanted something more this time. She had wrapped her arms around her chest and was slowly rocking back and forth in her fixed chair.

"Please let us know that you are all right," said another anxious daughter.

"Don't you love us? Don't you miss us?" pleaded Maureen, the oldest.

Simon heard the response immediately: "Oh, I love you all and I miss you all dearly." He quickly relayed this to them. Then, as this woman suddenly realized that the communication was fragile and would be brief, her words poured into Simon's consciousness.

"I am fine. I have moved on to a beautiful world. You must move on, too. You keep pulling me back. Our worlds are meant to be separate for a reason. You will understand when we are all together again. But I can't keep coming back. It takes me out of my element and puts me under great stress. I have to struggle back to my peace. Please let me go, when you let me go you will find that you can move on. Do you remember that pendant that you all gave to me on Christmas Eve? It had all your birthstones. Know that, before I passed on, I held it tightly and sent each one of you a little prayer. It was such a special gift, and I will cherish it for eternity. Now I must go. I love you all." Then, only to Simon she said, "Simon, thank you for not telling my family how painful my passing was. Those images were meant for you only, so that you would understand the circumstances of my passing. They did not need to know that. God bless you!" And with that she was gone.

Simon had relayed her words as quickly as they had come. When he finished they looked at him bewildered. He knew that they wanted more, but he also knew there would be no more. He told this family that he would hear nothing else from this beautiful woman that had passed on. "She is happy and she wishes you nothing but happiness, too. You need to move on."

The family left his home early Christmas morning. They were saddened, but relieved. There were lasting embraces and deeply sincere thank yous, and they left with life and optimism in their stride. Other than a generous check Simon received in the mail a few days later, he would never hear from this family again. That was as it should be. He had finally helped someone, in this case a whole family. It felt so incredibly good.

Simon

MARCH, 1939

His train trip from Philadelphia to Rhode Island had been a long one, and there had been frequent stops along the route. This was the railroad line that serviced the northeast corridor from Washington D.C. to Boston. Claudia had pleaded with Simon to help, her letters and phone calls from Jamestown described a woman completely used up by grief. She had worked for this woman and her family for many years and had become a close member of their extended family. Helping this woman had become Claudia's focus.

He arrived just after six o'clock on a Sunday evening, and Claudia was there to meet him at the train station in West Kingston, Rhode Island. It was a busy stop; a lot of students bound for the University of Rhode Island had exited the train. It was an established agricultural and engineering school. He had a little trouble locating

Claudia in the throngs of passengers, but they soon found each other—old friends have that ability.

"Claudia, it is so good to see you! It's been so long, you look well."

"You look good too, Simon. It has been too long. Having you here is so good. I hope you can help."

Claudia filled Simon in on the more intimate details of Mrs. Miller's condition on the ride back to Jamestown. Her health had continued its decline, and Claudia now told him of a woman that was sedated much of the time and was sleeping a great deal. Claudia told him that she helped Katherine with her hygiene and prepared all of her meals. Katherine's most lucid time was early afternoon, right after her tea in the living room. The tea seemed to perk her up.

"We should wait until then. Tomorrow will be soon enough," Claudia said.

They arrived just after seven. The sun had set and the sky was alive with color. There was a hint of spring in the air. All along the bricked walkway forsythia and crocuses were in bloom. Claudia helped Simon with his bags and showed him to the guest room.

"This is where Margret would stay when she visited. She was the last one to stay in this room. I hope that is okay with you."

"I am fine with that. If anything, it may help me connect with her spirit. I am famished. Could I get something to eat?"

They sat in the kitchen as Claudia prepared sandwiches and tea for the both of them.

She told Simon more about the day of the hurricane and how the pain had been unbearable for Mrs. Miller. She told him about the visits by Reverend Chard and his attempts to comfort Katherine and guide her back to the church. She also told him that these attempts were frustrating and only added to Katherine's stress level. They seem to be pushing Mrs. Miller deeper into her despair and isolation.

"I think Katherine's faith, or perhaps the Reverend's, was just not enough," Claudia reflected.

"Experience has taught me that faith sometimes has little to do with connecting with our loved ones. In fact, I am not sure at all how I am able to reach beyond. It is simply a gift I have, and I often wonder if it is a gift or a curse."

"But surely it is a gift," Claudia said. "Think of the people you have helped. You have brought closure for them. These people have been able to pick up their shattered lives and move on."

"This may be so in some cases, but there were those that I could not help and their pain often became my pain. Then, when I am fortunate enough to contact someone's loved one, what I bring back from beyond is not always comforting. I remember a very loving woman who met with me to reach beyond to her husband. They had been married for twelve years and had two wonderful children. He had suddenly died in a horrific automobile accident. His car had crashed through a guard rail and plunged into an icy river nearly fifty feet below, where he drowned. This woman had this sudden and horrible loss to deal with for the rest of her life. She wanted answers, or closure. The first time we attempted to reach beyond, there was a very fragile connection. I sensed something was wrong. There was a very cool emptiness to the room. I did not share this with her. The second time we met, I managed to reach her husband, and what he conveyed to me explained why I had sensed a disconnect. He had killed himself by driving his car at a very high speed through the protective barrier and into the chilly waters below. He died instantly. He had suffered from depression for quite some time and was severely depressed that day. This desperate man just could not go on. He was fine now and hoped that in time things would be better for his wife and two children. He wanted me to tell them it was not a selfish act. In time his depression would have pained the family. He did not want to be at the root of so much misery. And that was it; the connection was gone. I told her what he had said and could offer nothing beyond that. This poor woman was almost lifeless. It was just too much for her. 'Oh my God, my poor Michael, I had no idea,' she mumbled, and she left barely saying anything more. I received a letter from her several months later. She had discovered that her husband's family had a history of depression. Her husband had managed to keep this and his own depression a secret from her. She thanked me, but it was obvious that I had created more questions than I had resolved.

Her deep love for her husband would cause her to focus on the depression and anxiety that led to her husband's suicide. The rest of her life would be an endless search for reasons why she had not seen her Michael's sadness and what she could have done differently. This caring woman did not deserve this and I had been the terrible messenger."

Claudia nodded her head in sad acceptance of this darker side of Simon's gift. She seemed to dwell on this for a while and then whispered, "They are here with us now."

"Who is here?" he asked.

"One of them, or all of them, I am not sure. I believe that those that perished in the hurricane have not moved on. I do not know which of them continue to dwell here. But I sense their presence and I am sure of this. You have to help, Simon. This grief and emptiness is consuming us all."

Simon felt her urgency. "I will do my best," he said, "and you are correct, there is indeed a presence here. I sensed it the second we drove onto the property. There is also something troubling and confusing that is occurring here. It will take time to put it all together, but I sense this is not all about Katherine."

"How could it not be about Katherine? She has been deeply wounded. They were an extremely close and loving family."

"It's still a little early to be speculating. We will have ample opportunity to examine all the events and to speak with Katherine. I am tired from my long trip. Let's talk more in the morning."

Delilah

MARCH, 1939

Now there was a new visitor to our home. Would he be someone we could trust? He was an old friend of Claudia's from her early days in Philadelphia. Claudia felt he truly had the gift to reach across. My father had his misgivings and no doubt would approach this new visitor to express his concerns.

My father was also troubled with the type of care Claudia was giving my mother. He felt that Claudia was over-sedating her. He was convinced that it was contributing to her poor eating habits and her deepening depression. He knew that Claudia believed she had my mother's best interests at heart, but he worried that her fierce loyalty might be clouding her judgment. Claudia was also allowing her Haitian black magic roots to become part of these attempts to reach across. We had all witnessed the strange mix of herbs and spices and the cryptic chants.

He wanted my mother to heal at her own stride. She was fragile. My father had pleaded with everyone to give his wife the time and space she needed, and yet everyone thought they had the most effective way to help my mother. Reverend Chard tried to bring the church back into her life. That had not worked. Claudia had tried to reach across and contact my deceased family. That too had not worked. Now Simon Bouchard, this new visitor to our house, was about to attempt the same thing.

My father approached Claudia and my mother in the front living room. They had just taken their afternoon tea. Claudia had brought in some laundry from the outside clothesline and was busy folding it while she sipped her tea. My father wanted to discuss and hopefully stop the excessive medication Claudia was giving my mother. It brought too many risky side effects with it, including an escalating dependence and a warped sense of reality. It was all contributing to her withdrawal from the outside world.

He pleaded with my mother. "You have lost your loved ones, but we suffered the same loss as you, don't you think we miss them too? Delilah, T.J., and I need you. Please stop this withdrawal from us. Let us help you. We need to become a family again, what's left of us." My mother only stared back, void of any feeling. Claudia pretended to be busy folding laundry, trying to stay away from their intimate conversation. My father's frustration had been building for some time now. He suddenly turned, forcefully slapped his open hand on the near wall, and abruptly left the room. My mother screamed. He headed for the stairway and up to my bedroom. Claudia quickly followed my father to the open foyer and shouted at him.

"Why must you startle her like that? Damn you!"

My father ignored her and continued up the stairs and down the hallway into my bedroom, where I was playing cards with T.J. He slammed the bedroom door behind him. Claudia followed him up the stairs and into my room, shouting again at us, that we needed to be more understanding of our mother's condition.

"You obviously can see the pain the she is enduring. I am doing the best that I can. I love your mother just as much as you do. But you are not helping her with these tantrums. This will take time; a long time, I am fearful. But time is all we have." She turned and left the room.

My father was drained from the yelling and slamming of doors. He began to regret his impulsive behavior. "It was wrong of me to behave like that. I think Claudia truly believes that she is doing the right thing for you mother. Your mother is like a ship without a compass. I suppose she needs Claudia. I think we should support Claudia and her attempts to help your mother. They will settle into their own pace."

I forced myself to trust Claudia a little more after that. My jealously of Claudia and my mother's relationship slowly began to fade. I began to understand that Claudia was performing a role that neither I nor my father could provide. She was not as emotionally connected as we were. She was better prepared to make the hard, objective decisions when the time came. I knew I should be grateful for that. We rarely interfered after that.

Simon

MARCH, 1939

Simon met with Claudia in the kitchen the next morning. She had a fresh pot of coffee perking. "Help yourself to the coffee. I have fried up some bacon. How do like your eggs?

"Scrambled, if you don't mind."

"Certainly. How did you sleep? A strange bed in a strange setting is not the best recipe for a restful night."

"I did not sleep well, it's true. This coffee is just what I need right now. I experienced so much last night. My senses have been heightened with my first step into this house."

Trying to understand the incursions his senses had been barraged with had kept him awake most of the night. His temples and forehead had tingled with an energy not of his own, and the air in the room would momentarily turn frigid, his breath hovering like thick

204

cigar smoke. He thought he sometimes heard a soft murmuring sound like that of a purring kitten. It had been a long, bizarre night, but oddly he never once felt threatened. He had never experienced anything that intense.

Claudia had been up most of the night too, but for a different reason. She was enthusiastic at Simon's arrival and hoped that with him there they could start the healing process for Katherine. She was on edge and anxious to begin.

They drank their coffee and talked more about Katherine's condition and her deep desire for closure. Claudia expressed her frustration in the way the rest of the household was hindering these attempts.

"I think they are jealous of the closeness that exists between us," she said. "If they could just understand that this poor woman's daily existence is a living hell. She sleeps most of the day and eats very little. Granted, the medication has a lot to do with this, but I am convinced that the medication is the only thing that keeps her emotionally stable.

"She is slowly wasting away, and if we don't do something soon we will lose her. I know she wants and needs closure, and until we secure that, the healing process will never begin. I am not even confident that will be enough, but it's the only chance she has in reclaiming even the smallest part of her life. Simon, you must do something."

"I will try, but I cannot promise anything; and as we both know, sometimes the results we get are not what these poor souls wanted. But I will tell you that her family is very much aware of what she is going through. To expect anything less is doing them a big disservice. They love her just as much as you do, probably more.

"Now tell me, who is Mrs. Miller's doctor? Obviously he must be the one prescribing her medication? What are his observations?"

Delilah

MARCH, 1939

There was a lot of outpouring immediately after the hurricane; doctors and nurses were brought in from all over to help with the thousands of people injured, both physically and emotionally. My grandfather had traveled up from Philadelphia to be with my mother, his daughter. My mother's severe laceration on her arm had to be treated. My father's connection to the Navy and the war college allowed my mother easy access to a doctor; the Navy was very supportive. Numerous stitches were required to treat the deep lacerations on her arm and shoulder. She continued to see the doctor until the stitches were removed and the wound had healed. Her emotional wounds, however, were beyond anything he could do and he said as much at our last visit.

"I wish I could do more, but sadly I cannot. I wonder how any physician could treat the deep wounds she now endures," was how he ended the conversation.

He suggested we seek out a doctor who was better prepared to deal with her psychological issues. He recommended a Naval psychiatrist, but Claudia wanted someone that might be closer to home. The ferry rides to Newport were extremely draining on Katherine. She was now terrified of the open water, and the rocking of the ferry only pushed her closer to the edge. My father was not a big supporter of Navy doctors or psychiatrists and he offered no dissent.

We located Dr. Lawrence Palmer, a psychiatrist, right here in Jamestown. He was treating a lot of people that had been affected by this devastating storm and he was simply overwhelmed. My father and Claudia brought my mother to Dr. Palmer for her first visit. His office was on North Main Road, near the Jamestown Inn. It was in an area that was nearer the center of the island and had provided more protection from the damaging winds of the hurricane. It was small Cape with clear, weathered shingles and white trim, very New England looking. It had been a small general store that catered to the seasonal influx of tourists and summer rentals in the early 1900s.

Dr. Palmer had purchased the small cottage eleven years ago. He did some minor renovation to prepare it for his future clientele. He divided the first floor into two rooms, a small waiting area with a powder room, and a larger and more comfortable office area. The small upstairs area served as storage for his casework files, his medical references, and his artwork. When things were slow he would retreat upstairs to his little sanctuary and allow himself the peace of mind that his oils offered him. He painted much of the wildlife that wandered into his ample backyard. There were numerous apple and peach trees that had been planted by the previous owner. They provided a sweet alternative to the bland and sometimes scarce diet they existed on. Dr. Palmer also installed several bird feeders and kept them well supplied. After several years it became the place to see most of the wildlife that Jamestown offered. He displayed many of his paintings in the waiting room and office area. He also displayed his Ph.D. in psychiatry from Brown University and his license to practice from the state of Rhode Island and Providence Plantation. He opened his doors to those in need in May of 1927. His practice had steadily grown over the years, but it suddenly exploded after the devastating hurricane of 1938. There was no time for his oils.

Dr. Palmer and his family were also members of the same church as us. We were both families that Reverend Chard looked forward to seeing on Sundays. Our families knew each other and we were always cordial after Sunday services and other church activities. However, there simply had not been enough time to nurture or develop any relationship, and it was a little unsettling to me and my father when we discovered that my mother's potential psychiatrist was also a member of our congregation. My father was uncomfortable sharing intimate details about his family.

Dr. Palmer was originally from Providence. His grandparents on his mother's side owned and operated a small farm on the north end of Jamestown. His father had been a lawyer and operated a small practice in the upscale east side of Providence. He had met his wife from Jamestown while representing her family in the execution of a family trust. They married and raised their family near his law practice on Thayer Street in Providence. Mrs. Palmer would return to Jamestown every summer with Larry and his three sisters. There was always plenty to do on a working farm. Larry loved the work that the farm required of him. His dirty hands and achy muscles fueled his deep connection with his environment. He also loved the people of Jamestown. They were a warm, unassuming, and hardworking community. It's where he met JoAnne Denise Mathews, who would later become his wife and the mother of his four children.

Claudia and my father quickly discovered that Dr. Palmer was a caring and dedicated man who was simply overwhelmed. His small waiting room was full of lost souls searching for answers or escape from the tragic reality that the hurricane had brought to them. He met privately with Katherine for about twenty minutes. His brief interaction with her had been very revealing. Her loss was deep and devastating. She had withdrawn so completely from the world around her. The healing process would be long and difficult, and he told this to my father and Claudia.

"You must accept that Katherine will be an empty soul for quite some time. Please do not make any demands of her nor expect too much. She is barely holding on to what's left of her world. I will see her in about a month, but let's keep her sufficiently medicated in the meantime."

My father and Claudia were taken back by this approach.

"Keep her medicated and see you in a month," Claudia blurted out. "Can't you see that she is in need of a more a focused and timely approach than that?"

"I am very aware that more is required of me, but I simply do not have the time. Did you see the people in my waiting room? It's like that just about every day and that does not speak to those that I visit in their homes or in hospitals. I wish I could do more, but I just can't."

"Doesn't her level of emotional suffering account for anything? Doesn't that allow her some priority?" Claudia demanded.

"Of course it does. But as worthy as she might be, I am just overwhelmed with this sudden surge of people that have suffered very real emotional trauma. Have you thought about seeing another psychiatrist? I could recommend several in the Newport area as well as the Providence area."

Claudia shook her head. "Any trip off Jamestown would require boarding the ferry. It is something that Katherine cannot deal with. The rolling and pitching of the ferry, just being in the same area of the bay where her loved ones perished, simply pushes her closer to the edge. I don't understand why you are so overcome with patients. Jamestown is not that big of an island, and at this time of year most of the seasonal visitors have long since left."

"You obviously are not aware of the magnitude of the suffering brought to this whole area. There are many that have suffered the same, and not just those from this island. I am seeing people from all over Rhode Island. But I will tell you of a local man that I think you are aware of. Do you know Morgan Gustafson?"

My father and Claudia both knew him. He was a man that had done some handy work, landscaping, and odd jobs for us and others in the neighborhood. He was from a good family, and it was rumored that he had experienced firsthand the horrors of The Great War. It left him mentally fragile. He is a timid and honest soul.

"Morgan began his day much like the rest of us. One of his part time jobs was driving the school bus for grammar school kids at Martin Elementary. He dropped the children off in the morning without a hint of what was to come. We were all unprepared for what lie ahead.

"By early afternoon it was quite evident that the weather had turned terribly bad. School officials decided to get all the kids back to the safety of their homes and family. Roger boarded his fourteen young passengers on to his Wayne Company school bus. He began his trip in near hurricane force winds and driving rain. He had dropped off six of his young travelers along his route and was heading towards Beaver Tail with the rest of his charge. He had traveled along Hamilton Ave and was about turn on to Beavertail Road, a narrow stretch of land with Sheffield Cove on the north side and open ocean to its south. It is the lowest point on the island. There was already too much seawater there, and any crossing would be very difficult, if not impossible. Morgan stopped his bus at what he thought was a safe difference from the water's edge. He got out to get a better look of what he was up against. The wind had become almost lethal. He climbed some nearby rocks to gauge the wind and tide. The wind and rain tore at his clothing. Maybe they should wait the storm out from where they were – the kids were warm and dry in the bus – or should he return the kids back to the safety of their school? He knew he must decide quickly.

"Then the storm surge came. It nearly swallowed Morgan. He was older and stronger and he managed to crawl to higher ground. The children were not so lucky. The bus was quickly engulfed by the ocean. Morgan watched in horror as the bus bobbed on the water like a bright yellow cork. He could hear the screams of the children. The bus quickly disappeared in the turbulent waters. Morgan stayed where he was, huddled among the boulders, until the storm had passed. Then he began his search.

"No one really knows how long he looked for them. The search parties found him two days later. He had found his bus and his passengers. The bus had finally washed up on the very northwest tip of the island and all the windows had been smashed. It was a crumbled hulk. All eight of its precious cargo were still in the bus and they were all dead. Morgan had removed all of the bodies and gently laid them on the ground away from the bus and the water. He had straightened their clothes, smoothed their hair, and folded their hands on their chests. He sat by them and simply waited for help to come. He was conscious when they found them, but was unresponsive. He had not eaten or drunk anything in the two days that he had sat with them.

"I have counseled Morgan for many hours, and it took a lot just to get that much from him. There is so much guilt and self-loathing impeding my attempts to help him. I am not sure how – or even if – I can ever help him. I wake in the night with the fear that this poor man has or will commit suicide. I am not sure if I could continue with such a tragedy hanging over me, and he is just one of many. Do you see what I am up against?"

Claudia and my father were moved by this heartbreaking story and understood Dr. Palmer's dilemma. "Then how do we get her the help she needs?" Claudia asked.

"Continue to see me whenever I can squeeze her into my schedule. But I also know that Reverend Chard at our church has begun to visit her. I would support that and just be as nurturing as possible. I will keep her prescriptions on an 'as needed' basis for now. As I said, you will need to keep her medicated throughout this difficult time. I'm afraid it could be a long time."

Simon

MARCH 1939

Simon said to Claudia, "I must speak with Mrs. Miller and I must speak to her without the medication fogging her mind. Do you think that would be possible?"

Claudia wasn't sure if that was something they should attempt. "We can try, but I am afraid that without it, all the emotion and pain will come rushing back to her," she said. "We will also need to worry about her withdrawal from the medication. It may be just too much for her."

"We have to try. How can I help this woman if she is in this medicated fog all of the time? As I have told you, I have this gift. I am not sure how it works or when it will work. But I can assure you that it will only work if Mrs. Miller is in touch with her feelings, as painful as they might be. Let's take her off the medication. We can't just suddenly stop all of them, but we will need to wean her off with some haste. We will talk with her several times each day. I will recognize rather quickly when she is ready to contact her loved ones. Mrs. Miller may not know that she has reached that point, but I will."

My father and I had listened to Simon and Claudia's conversation from the other room and realized that Simon was here to help my mother. My father felt we needed to be more trusting and accepting of Simon. "He is here to help your mother and we must support him in whatever way we can." We encouraged my mother to be more accepting of Simon.

* * *

Without the sedatives, it did not take long for my mother's condition to deteriorate. Her nights became sleepless and she ate even less. She cried and sobbed a great deal. But she also quickly became aware of who Simon was and why he was in her home.

Simon and my mother met in the living room at random times over the next two days, and he tried to engage my mother in small talk. She would respond with agitated nods or short responses. Father and I tried to encourage her. Most of the time, she ignored us or just gave us that empty stare we had become all too familiar with.

On the third day we once again gathered in the living room. Simon began his simple dialogue with my mother. She turned to face Simon, looked at him without seeing him, and then her eyes seemed to be moving all around the room, as if trying to find someone or something. The vibration entered our world and put us on edge again. My mother turned to Simon.

"I think my family is here. Can you help me talk with them? Maybe this is the breakthrough that you have talked about."

"You may be right, Katherine," Simon said. "He too had sensed something. There was a presence in the room, but it was difficult for him to channel. Someone was trying to communicate with us; I detected a foreign dialogue and understood none of it."

Claudia was suddenly excited. "This is good, Katherine. Your loved ones are here. They must be trying to reach out to you. Perhaps something good will come of this."

My mother brightened just a bit. "Maybe it will. Is my family making the floors move?" she asked, and then began to cry. It was just too much for her.

The vibrations stopped, and then Simon announced that the fragile connection was gone.

"This may be all there is today. It may not seem like we accomplished much, but I assure you, we did. Katherine, you sensed your family was near and you were right. This is indeed a very good start. We shall try again tomorrow." We all left the room with the most hope we had experienced in a long time.

We tried again the next day, but nothing occurred. There was no presence. My mother had been without her medication for some time now and she was becoming more unstable. Her nights continued to be mixed with intermittent sleep and nightmares. She sustained her poor eating habits. Claudia felt that they were at a crossroad. She approached Simon the next morning.

"Katherine cannot continue on like this any longer. She is physically and emotionally fragile. We must make a decision in the best interest of Katherine, and we need to make it quickly."

"I am afraid you are right, Claudia. Let us try one more time this afternoon. I want to attempt a different approach. If it doesn't work, then we need to get Katherine stable again. If that means we return to her medication, then so be it. It will indeed be a tragedy. I can sense that closure is being sought by so many souls. But as you and I know, quite often that is simply how it resolves itself. No resolution is sometimes the only conclusion."

That afternoon we once again sat in the living room. It was an early spring day, cold and overcast. There was the threat of snow and several lights were on. The fireplace was built up and warmth had permeated the room. My mother was reclined in her favorite stuffed chair. It was where she sat most days. Simon brought a small end table up next to my mother. He lit a candle and placed it in the middle of the table. Claudia and Simon joined my mother. We would try one more time to reach beyond. Without her medication my mother was unstable, always close to the edge.

"Kathrine, can we talk about the day of that terrible storm?" Simon began.

"I will try," she replied. "You know they are gone. Drowning is such a horrific thing for my babies, for my sister, and I saw the whole thing. There was nothing I could do. I should not have let them go to the carriage house. Jeffrey should have been home." My mother was staring intensely at the candle. Its flame flickered ever so slightly. It seemed to capture my mother for a moment. Simon let the moment linger. Finally, my mother turned to Claudia.

"Claudia, you saw them swept away too. Oh my God. Why? I do not want to live like this. It just hurts too much. Why does life offer so much pain?"

Claudia began to cry. Her grief and loss was almost as severe as my mother's. Simon was once again in the all too familiar sea of grief and sorrow.

"You can't let this destroy you. Your family is here. We should try to reach out to them. They love you and you love them very much. All that love and emotion can be the connection we can use to reach across."

"Oh I love them very much. I miss them even more. I want to hold them in my arms." My mother was in deep despair. Simon grasped both her hands and Claudia stood next to her and stroked her hair.

"They can never come back," Simon said. "But you can tell them you love them and miss them. You can also let them know that they need to move on, release their grip on your world. It is not their world anymore and it will help them. And it will help you."

My mother turned her face directly into Simon's. "How?" she said. "What do I do? Can't you see that I want to talk to them?"

"You must think it to yourself, or even express your thoughts out loud. They will hear you."

"Don't you think I've done that a thousand times?" My mother was becoming agitated. "Every day since that goddamn hurricane ripped them from my life, I have said a million prayers and asked God everyday why this happened. I try to talk to them every single day. What more can I do? Go back to your home in Philadelphia and leave me alone."

"I am telling you that your family is here and they are trying to reach out to you. Of this I am sure. There is something that is confusing and complicating this process, but your loved ones are here. We need to find a way to channel this. You must not give up. I will help you, and so will your good friend Claudia." Claudia nodded in affirmation.

My mother's anxiety was growing and my father and I were becoming concerned.

"I think we need to give her a break," my father said.

But Simon continued. "Katherine, you need to release this grief that is crushing you. Your love has created a bond. Use this bond to reach out to them and allow them to move on."

My father and I had heard this before, about Aunt Meg, Stephanie, and Corey's spirits being here and not moving on. It had come from Claudia. Now Simon was saying the same thing. We had just accepted and trusted Simon for what we thought were his sincere efforts to help my mother and now he and Claudia were tearing this trust apart.

We had witnessed the death of Aunt Meg, Stephanie, and Corey. We had shared this terrible loss with my mother. It was very painful for all of us, but my father and I had accepted the finality of their deaths.

Simon was sure that he was about to break through. He needed to push Katherine a little bit more. "Katherine, talk to them, as painful as this must be. You have to try. Do not turn away. We are very close, I can sense it."

My mother was crying. Her emotions were raw. "I am so empty. I don't know if I can do this."

My father yelled, "Simon, that is enough!"

But Simon continued. "You cannot give up now. They need you. I can sense you telling them to move on. Stay with that. They are close."

Suddenly my mother stood and grabbed Simon by the shoulders, screaming, "I am not telling them anything! I do not sense their presence! If they are here like you say, then I do not want them to move on! Leave me alone!" Then she fell back onto the table with her head in her hands, sobbing uncontrollably.

I had seen the anger building in my father. He could not allow my mother to be tortured like this anymore. He instantly despised Simon and was going to end this insanity. He went to the table and pounded his fist several times and screamed "THIS HAS TO STOP!" Simon and Claudia suddenly looked at my father, not saying a word.

The vibrations erupted. The table and the objects on it began to shake. The candle flame was suddenly extinguished. The pictures on the wall began to quiver and suddenly fell to the floor. Objects on the fireplace mantel flew across the room. The tremors had us all unsteady on our feet. Unnerved by the shaking and the objects being tossed about the room, my mother put her head and shoulders on the table and grasped it in absolute panic. Claudia ran to her side and pulled her to the floor, trying to shield my mother and herself from these now deadly projectiles. My father and I took cover on the floor behind the large living room couch, and Simon protected himself behind my mother's armchair, likewise cradling his head with hands and arms. Then came the mumbling voices; this time they seemed human, but nothing that anyone understood. Then the vibrations and mumbling suddenly stopped. Candle sticks, books, and knickknacks that had been moving in the air precipitously fell as if they too were seeking security in the floor.

We all lie on the floor for brief moments and then emerged from our cocoons, trying to understand what had just happened. Claudia had my mother quickly settled into her chair and was trying to console her. She turned to Simon. "Oh, my Holy Mother. Simon, what has just happened to us?"

"I am not sure. I believe there was a link or an attempt to break through from another dimension, or maybe it was more than one spirit trying to reach across. I just don't have any answer."

My father's forceful and vocal interruption at the séance had been triggered by his instinct to protect my mother. But the shaking and trembling that had quickly followed had convinced everyone that other forces were at work. Once the shaking had stopped my father reached out to Simon.

"Simon, I am sorry for my temper tantrum and I am sorry for not believing that you had my wife's best interests at heart. If you can help ease her suffering, then please do so; but remember, she has suffered a great deal and is very fragile." Tears ran down my father's face. He turned to Claudia and also apologized to her for not trusting her. The whole room was silent. I think everyone was still shocked by my father's forceful interruption. Finally, Simon stood, said that the séance was completed, and he needed time to reflect.

His stuttering suddenly resurfaced. "I think we ah-ah-are done here. I-I need time to think," and with that Simon got up and left the room.

My father and I stood at my mother's side trying to comfort her. I was petrified; I had never seen my father so frightened. He wrapped his arms around me and hugged me as I searched his face for an explanation.

"Try not to be afraid, sweetheart. I think we will soon make sense of all this insanity."

Simon

MARCH 1939

The next morning Simon was sitting at the kitchen table. He was dressed, and his travel bag was next to him on the floor. Claudia walked in and quickly understood what was happening.

"Simon, you cannot be leaving."

"I'm afraid so," he replied. "This is beyond me."

"Oh please, do not leave, especially after last night. It was a real breakthrough."

"Just the opposite, I'm sorry to say. Last night was anything but a breakthrough. In fact, we ran straight into a brick wall, a spiritual barrier. I have said many times, and you know I have, that this so-called gift I have is a complete mystery to me. I do not know why I have it, I do not know who it will work with, and I do not know

219

when it will work. But I can say with total confidence that this gift or curse of mine will not help this poor woman. It is beyond me."

"Katherine needs you," Claudia begged.

"Katherine does not need me, nor does she want me. The damage that was done last night may never be repaired. Last night, one or more of her loved ones reached out to me, to her, or to all of us there. I don't know, but it was clear that whoever it was, they were not comfortable with the direction we were trying to go. I am sure of this. It is not my intent, however, to leave you with no options. This woman and her family have lost so much. Cries for closure come from everywhere. There is a woman who used to live not far from here. I do not know if she still even lives there. I haven't heard from her in over twenty-five years. My God, I am not even sure if she is still alive. She is probably close to seventy years old. If anyone can help us, it is she. I don't know if she will want to help. I will try to find her and tell her Katherine's story. If she is willing to help I will return with her. Pray that she returns with me. Her name is Madame Alice."

✳ ✳ ✳

Simon knew he had to get back to New York. The trail would start there. The train ride to New York was torturous for Simon. His gift had surely become a curse. There were all these people with their tortured lives, their worlds all torn apart; most of the time he could not help them, and when he did help there was often little closure. This visit with the Millers had drained and saddened him. His last night with Katherine had only added to the confusion and frustration. There clearly was a presence there. The vibrations, shaking, and the flying objects had frightened everyone, even Simon himself, but it was a clear communication from beyond. Last night's episode just reinforced what he had sensed from the moment he set foot in the house: there was strong communication happening, and it was coming from many directions. It was all very hard to understand. It was as if questions were being asked in English and being answered in French. It was beyond him. He hoped it was not beyond his old friend Madame Alice.

Delilah

APRIL 1939

The next morning Simon announced that he would be leaving for a few days to locate a woman named Madame Alice. He seemed to feel that she was the only person that could help.

The next few days were quiet. The return to her medication and Claudia's nurturing helped my mother collect herself. We were sitting in the living room on an early spring's day and a soft, breeze filtered through the open windows. My mother was sedated and relaxing in her big chair. T.J. was playing jacks on floor and began to annoy Claudia. Finally, she snapped at him.

"Must you? Can't you see she is sleeping?"

T.J. was hurt and I tried to comfort him. Overstepping her boundaries was becoming easier for Claudia, but she was right: my mother needed her rest. The vibrations suddenly started again, and I knew that they would intensify. Items on the fireplace mantle and on the end tables began to tremble. We all just sat there, again frozen in fear. Suddenly my mother was awake; something had roused from her deep slumber. With unsteady legs, her hands pushing on the arms of her chair, she slowly raised herself up. With her right hand on the back of her chair she steadied herself and looked intently out into the foyer. Raising her left arm, she pointed out towards the vestibule with a left index finger that hung loose and quivered ever so slightly.

"Oh my lord, please tell me this is real. Stephanie… and my precious little Corey... and Margret. Are you really here? Am I losing my grip on things?" My mother pleaded through her sudden tears and distress. "They have come back to me," she said, and carefully short stepped her way into the front entry way as if she were walking on a layer of thin ice.

Claudia was immediately on her feet and quickly followed my mother, but suddenly stopped and brought her hands to her mouth and inhaled quickly.

Father and I watched from where we were and saw no one. My mother paced around the foyer and was conversing to an empty room.

"I have missed you so much. You look so tired. Why are you here? Let me hold you. Please talk to me."

The vibrations suddenly faded away and the living room and hallway were still. My mother stopped her pacing and turned her head in all directions, searching for those that were never there. My father and I had seen nothing. We looked at each other and knew that my mother was starting to break down. It was something we had feared for some time but hoped would never happen.

Claudia had followed her into the hallway and was now trying to comfort her. She began to guide my mother back into the living room and her chair. My mother was shaking and wobbly on her feet. In a tearful voice she said, "They have come back to me. Oh God, help me."

Claudia got my mother seated in her chair and leaned down and looked directly into my mother's eyes. "Madame, I saw them too!"

My mother grasped Claudia's face in her hands; it shook with my mother's trembling. "Please tell me you did. You know the hell I am living. If you truly did see them, who did you see?

"I think I saw Margret, Stephanie and Corey. They were blurry images, and they seemed to be floating, I think. I don't really know how describe it. I couldn't even tell you what they were wearing. But it was the three of them."

"Oh, my God," was all my mother could say, and she fell back into her chair.

"And Madame, I don't think they wanted to be here. They were pointing their fingers at us and shaking their heads, 'no.' Did you see that?"

Only settling deeper into her chair, my mother did not respond. She was clearly overwhelmed with what had just happened.

Father and I were at a loss. We had seen nothing. We felt a complete sadness for my mother. She was so empty and so desperate – or perhaps it was the medication – but it was obvious that her mind was playing tricks on her. Claudia was not helping with her patronizing support. My jealousy and resentment of Claudia was beginning to resurface again. Claudia brought her a cup of tea with her medication and in a short while my mother was asleep.

* * *

The next few days continued the same way. The vibrations would occur and develop in intensity. My father and I would always feel them, and sometimes Claudia and my mother would see Aunt Meg and my siblings. But as before, my father and I saw nothing. It was always draining for my mother. We kept thinking that each event would put my mother over the edge, but she somehow persevered. Claudia's devotion and the medication no doubt had a lot to do with that.

My father was completely mystified by the vibrations and the mumbling noises. He was also troubled but not surprised by the visions that my mother was having, considering the medication she was on and what she had gone through. But now Claudia was also having these same visions. Maybe it was part of Claudia's fierce loyalty to my mother?

That afternoon Simon returned with Madame Alice.

Simon

JUNE 1911

He was an old colleague from New York, though Sarah knew him as Francis – Francis Simon Bouchard. Simon was a very young man when he first witnessed Sarah's gift. He had participated in some of the séances that she had organized with her co-workers at the *Journal*. He had just completed his sophomore year at a Manhattan college where he was a journalism major and had taken a part time position at the *New York Journal*, working nights and weekends in the print room. During the summers he worked full time in the advertising department. Sometimes, at the end of the work week, a number of co-workers would talk Sarah into reading cards or conducting séances. They would gather in the conference room after their day was over. It was an entertaining diversion for the staff, but Simon saw immediately that Sarah took it very seriously.

224

Simon had experienced strange sensations in his youth. He would often finish his mother's sentences or have a sense of what his father was about to say before a single word had left his lips. There were times when Simon answered his mother's questions before they were asked. His father was perplexed by these events, but his mother seemed to be more accepting of them; apparently she had had a great aunt with these same abilities. They were, however, very unnerving to Simon. He did not understand why these things happened to him. There was no one to talk too, no one that could understand what he was experiencing. It was only when he spent time with Sarah at these Friday afternoon gatherings did he realize that he had the same special gift as her.

They began to talk more after these friendly meetings. Sarah soon realized that Simon had been given this gift too. The next two years saw their friendship grow, and they began to see each other as colleagues in the same craft.

It was near the end of his final summer at the paper. He had graduated from college that May and chosen to remain at the newspaper for this one last summer. He had taken a position at a small publishing company in Philadelphia and would be leaving New York City in August. He would be saying goodbye to a lot of good friends. His internship at the newspaper had taught him the value of diplomacy and had helped him grow as a person. Sarah felt it was time to talk to Simon about their gift and prepare him for the potential repercussions that it could have on his life.

They were in the conference room, as they typically were for their mystic assemblies. It was the usual Friday gathering of Sarah and Simon's co-workers. It would be the last time Simon would be part of this lively, selective crowd. They had prepared a small send off for Simon, snacks and a good luck chocolate cake to see him on his way. Everyone took their turn embracing Simon and wishing him well. Most of the participants had already left to start their weekend. Sarah suggested they should have their own private conversation. They had the room to themselves.

"Simon, people will tease you about your gift and think of it as a novelty and that it is very entertaining. But when a very lost soul comes to you and pleads with you to help them with the terrible burden of a lost loved one, and you reach beyond and make contact with that person, it frightens them and it will frighten you. These people that come to see you have no idea how far reaching your gift can be. Sometimes you can help; most of the time you cannot. But when you do help, they feel they are indebted to you for life. But both parties want to put as much distance between them as quickly as possible. It helps people, but it also frightens them. Be careful with your gift, Simon. It can be a terrible burden. Someday you will understand its impact. As we speak, I have this terrible sensation that I will have to share some extremely disturbing news with a very dear friend, and it frightens me terribly."

Simon thought this must be a dreadful burden for Sarah. "What will you do?" he asked. "This has to be very troubling for you."

"I am not sure what to do. I can sense this tragedy approaching. I am not sure who it will affect or when. I am sure as it gets closer I will know. I also know that I will have no choice but to share this awful news with my close friend. It will not go well—it rarely does. As difficult as it might be, it is our responsibility to share these premonitions with the people they affect. What else is the purpose of this gift?"

The following spring, the tragic news of the *Titanic* reached New York.

Without understanding why, Simon sensed immediately that this was the tragedy that Sarah had foreseen. He knew that she would be devastated and emotionally drained. He made many attempts to contact her, all unsuccessful. He finally decided to give her the time and space she seemed to want.

Several months later, Simon learned through a mutual friend that Sarah's marriage had quickly fallen apart and that she had moved to Rhode Island to be near her father. He knew little about the reasons why she left New York in such haste, but understood that his dear friend must have been traumatized by her divorce. He knew how much Sarah loved her William.

He received a letter from Sarah several years later. She apologized for not reaching out to him much earlier, but she needed time to heal a deep wound. She told Simon about the tragic events surrounding the sinking of the *Titanic* and how Williams's sudden desertion had been devastating, causing her to flee to Rhode Island in a simple act of survival. She could no longer live in New York. Sarah said that she had assumed a new identity, now calling herself Alice; her new clientele had begun to call her Madame Alice. Sarah seemed to like her new name and title. This told Simon that Sarah was allowing her gift back into her life despite its sometimes unhappy consequences. She reminded him of the conversation they had about their gift and its significances. *Please, be careful with it*, she wrote. *It sometimes carries a terrible burden.*

She wished him well, but made it clear that she had moved on and wanted no ties to her past life in New York. Simon understood that meant him also. He would never hear from her again. But he understood why Sarah had suddenly moved away. He might have done the same thing, but he would surely miss his friend and confidant. Sarah was the only one that understood the burden of his gift. It was a gloomy day for him.

* * *

Simon settled into Philadelphia. His decision to take a job at Medallion House Publishing turned out to be a prudent one and he learned to enjoy his craft. He would also meet his future wife in this new city. Olivia Minnelli was the cousin of Anthony Minnelli, one of Simon's coworkers and also his roommate. Olivia's parents owned a small Italian restaurant in South Philly. Italian cuisine was something that Simon had only recently been exposed to, his diversified circle of friends providing the outlet for him to break away from the uninteresting French Canadian diet that he was raised on. Simon found the Mediterranean food a little too spicy, but was willing to make an effort to acquire the taste; after all, it wasn't a difficult task.

His roommate was always trying to persuade Simon of its worth. "I am quite sure my cousin Olivia could refine your dreary French pallet," he said. One conversation with her and she will have you craving veal parmigiana and lasagna on a daily basis. She is a very attractive Sicilian."

"You seem quite sure of your cousin's charms. I think I would like to meet her. But what would a woman of such beauty, as you say, see in a man like me?"

"Simon, enough of that. My cousin Olivia is quite capable of seeing the quality of your soul. She is a special person, and so are my aunt and uncle. They would welcome you to their restaurant. I am careful about who I share my family with."

The two roommates ate at Minelli's Fine Italian Dining later that evening. The restaurant was alive with activity, like a beehive on a hot summer's day, and they skillfully worked their way into a waiting area already buzzing with patrons anticipating their accustomed culinary experience.

Anthony leaned into Simon's ear. "Just follow me," he said, and they weaved their way through a maze of tables filled with patrons seduced by their own senses and waiters that moved among the chaos like performers in a circus, delicately balancing their large trays heaped with steaming entrées. The maître d' doted upon and entertained the clientele, seeing to their every wish, like a master of ceremony at a Hollywood event. Simon instantly sensed a feeling of familiarity and comfort, like being at his grandparents' home on a Christmas day many years ago. The whole experience welcomed him.

As they neared the back of the restaurant they heard a young woman's voice squeal "Anthony!" and Olivia was suddenly upon them.

"Mother, Daddy, come see who is here!" she yelled back into the kitchen and then threw her arms around Anthony. Olivia's mother and father soon joined them. They both wore broad white aprons that were covered with the evidence of a busy Saturday evening and an involved ownership. Mrs. Minnelli quickly reached back, untied and removed her soiled apron, and softly patted the thick brown curls of her hair, hoping that would be enough to make herself presentable on

228

such short notice. Mr. Minnelli stood with his closed fists resting on his large middle and offered a broad, ear-to-ear smile that said "welcome" and demonstrated his pride in his family and his restaurant.

Anthony introduced Simon to his cousin Olivia and his aunt and uncle. "Simon, this is my beautiful cousin Olivia. And this is my Aunt Francesca and my Uncle Louis. This is my good friend and roommate, Simon Bouchard." His uncle shook Simon's hand forcefully, slapped him on the back, and welcomed him to his restaurant. Aunt Francesca and Olivia hugged and kissed him on the cheek and also welcomed Simon to their cucina.

"Olivia, show your cousin and his friend to the best table we have left and bring them a fine bottle of Chianti on the house. Things are quite hectic now. Take your time with your meal, and when things slow down a bit we will join these two handsome young men. Anthony, try the shrimp scampi or the three-cheese ravioli. Delicious!" Uncle Louis excused himself and disappeared into a bustling and noisy kitchen.

Olivia was as striking as Anthony had promised. She was a petite woman with a creamy olive complexion and hypnotizing big brown eyes. Her thick dark auburn hair was pulled back and tied with a yellow ribbon. She carried a little extra weight around her middle, probably a hazard of sampling so many of the rich Italian entrees, but her beauty had stunned him.

Simon and Anthony enjoyed their meal and waited for the patronage to thin out. The diners at Minelli's seemed to be in a talkative mood and the tables remained full. Coffee and dessert had become a popular choice this evening; few people were leaving. Olivia suggested Anthony come back another time and that he bring his handsome roommate with him. "My mother and father are sorry they never made it to your table. Sometimes things get just too hectic."

There was no keeping Simon away. He and Anthony returned several days later and many times after that. Olivia was always engaging and mothering with her approach to customers, especially with Simon. She was attracted to Simon's quiet and shy demeanor and would tease him that he needed to make his visits more regular. "You need to fill out that handsome frame of yours, your face is too thin. You should have some of my father's homemade pasta and my mother's tasty lasagna and special sauce." She would call in Italian to her mother in the kitchen, "Non ti pare, Mama?" *Don't you think so?*

Her mother would step out from the kitchen and smile, shaking her finger at Olivia and responding boisterously in her native dialect. Olivia would listen to her mother, shake her own finger back at her, and smile coyly. "My mother says you should try the eggplant parmesan. That would help more than the spaghetti and meatballs."

"I will do that," Simon replied. He turned to his friend Anthony and whispered, "why do I feel they are talking about more than just food?"

"Oh, they are indeed talking about things that have nothing to do with the kitchen. Be careful, my friend. You are about to have a spell cast upon you. You are no match for my cousin's big brown eyes and my aunt's home cooking."

They both had a good laugh. But Simon had been smitten.

Before too much time had passed Simon asked Olivia out. They went to the Metropolitan Opera House to hear the fine Italian tenor Enrico Caruso perform as Rudolphe in *La Boheme*, and after that returned to her parents' restaurant for coffee and conversation. Simon felt welcomed and knew he had found his soul mate. One year later they exchange their vows at the altar of St. Mary's. Simon felt incredibly blessed to have such a giving and beautiful woman to journey through life with.

Sarah

MAY 1922

Sarah had not struggled with her name change; in fact, the transition to Alice had been a lot easier than she had anticipated. No one knew her as Sarah, so no one called out that name whenever she walked the neighborhood streets or when she visited the local shops or the post office. When she stole a glance in the mirror she saw a strong and confident Alice; the fragile and withdrawn Sarah rarely visited. Her new identity had helped heal the wounds and brought her comfort.

As she approached her middle years, her growing flock had begun to call her Madame Alice. Apparently she had provided some favorable insight to one of her patrons, advice that had helped her client make some pro-active decisions regarding her health. Decisions that had probably saved her life. "You told me of an

231

ailment that I had no idea existed," her patron had said as she sat at the mahogany reading table, reaching across to hold Sarah's hand. Her words were deliberate and intermittent with tears. "Despite his hesitation, I pressured my family doctor to follow through on your advice and I will be forever grateful for that. You saved my life."

"It is simply a gift that I have. I am glad to think how wonderful this outcome has been for the both of us."

"You're making light of what you did for me. There was nothing simple about it." Her client held her hand even tighter, pausing and pressing her lips together in a soft smile as she searched for her next words. "You have helped other people; I know because I have talked to them, and we are all grateful. We pay you what we can afford and that is not much, but we feel that is not enough. You have earned some recognition among us. I have learned that women with your gift, especially those with your profound ability, often have the term Madame used before their name. Please allow us that privilege."

Sarah could find no reason to object, and honestly she enjoyed the subtle title. Madame Alice fit quite well.

* * *

In the spring of 1922 she met Milton. Milton Post had visited her several times, always on a Saturday afternoon. He had lost both of his parents in a freak boating accident and was looking for answers. Sarah – or Madame Alice – could sense nothing during these visits and she finally told Milton there was nothing she could do to help him.

"I think your parents have moved on. They must be content where they are. I know you miss them very much. They must have been an important part of your life. But I believe you should think about letting them go and moving on yourself." He was taken aback by what she said.

She could see he was disappointed. "I am sorry I could not help you."

He put his hands in his pants pocket and the coins there clinked as he fiddled with them. "Thank you, perhaps you are right," he said and moved towards the door, then nervously turned and timidly asked if she would like to join him for dinner that evening, or some other evening.

Sarah was stunned by his invitation. Milton was fourteen years younger than her, and she was puzzled by his offer. They had talked a lot about his life in their attempts to contact his parents, and she knew he was mature beyond his years. He was a quirky but very practical man, and she sensed that he would make few demands of her. Something told her she would be safe with him. She accepted his offer and they went to dinner that night. Their relationship grew. Sarah became very comfortable in her friendship with Milton, and he seemed completely at ease with her. Their bond was growing and expectations were developing. Sarah knew a great deal about Milton, but he knew little about her. She felt it was time to share her past with him. She told him about her experiences in England, moving to America with her family, college, her marriage to William, and of course her own personal connection with the tragedy of the *Titanic*.

She also told Milton about her hurried trip to London and the emotional visits with Jacob Sweeney. Jacob had confirmed the very dark feelings she had sensed about *Titanic's* fateful voyage—feelings and experiences that she no longer wanted in her life. Sarah was relieved that Jacob had sought her out and shared his terrible story with her. Now she wanted to put the tragedy of the *Titanic* behind her. The deep wounds that William had caused had finally healed, too, and she no longer wanted the burden of that either. This process had unknowingly allowed her to bring Milton into her life. Milton was her therapy and had become her happiness.

Sarah felt it was also time to approach the issue of their age difference—she was too old for children. Milton was amazed how full and varied her life had been before she had settled in Portsmouth. He saw no issue with their age difference and did not see himself as a nurturing father figure. Children were never in his long term goals. He had come to love Sarah very deeply. He understood why she might want to share her concerns, but she did not need to worry about such insignificant matters.

Eighteen months later, in the fall of 1923, they were married at St. Michael's church in Bristol, Rhode Island. It was a small and intimate service. Shortly after their marriage they moved to an island in Narragansett Bay called Prudence. It was a thirty-minute ferry ride from Bristol. Milton had grown up on the island and had cherished his time there. It did not have the limitations and restrictions that other large towns seem to have, and it gave him the personal space that he needed. Milton built a small inn there that catered to the summer crowds. Most of Madame Alice's clientele found the logistics of the trip to Prudence Island a little too intimidating and they stopped their visits. Those that felt a true connection with Sarah cared little about the extra thirty-minute ferry ride and the possible extended stay on the island. Sarah was content to live out the rest of her life on this inimitable little island. Her gift had been very demanding over the years and it had almost consumed her at times. Now it was time to back away from her gift's unwanted responsibility. Sarah had given enough of herself—Prudence Island would be the place where she could hide and be at peace with herself. Her inner spirit reinforced that it was the right thing to do.

That all dramatically changed when her old friend Simon Bouchard came to see her sixteen years later.

Sarah

1933

Sarah's father was not prepared for the economic collapse of 1929. Few were. He had made some aggressive business decisions and had over extended himself. He lost everything.

They seemed to be sound decisions at the time. His business in Fall River was doing quite well; in fact, it had reached its maximum output, and Frederick believed he was missing opportunities to increase his market share. It was time to expand. He had located a rundown mill in the Fall River area. Its owner was asking much more than it was worth, but Frederick knew he had to act quickly and aggressively on it. There were others that wanted the potential that even this rundown factory offered. It would need to be retro-fitted and would require extensive work to bring it up to efficient factory standards. A lot of expensive lace weaving machines would need to be purchased. Her father felt the time was right. The economy was doing well and his business was healthy. He would, however, need to heavily leverage both his business and personal wealth and his financial exposure would be precarious.

Frederick overpaid for the neglected factory and its upgrade. No one saw the crash of 1929 coming, least of all Frederick Shepard Sr.

Now the creditors were calling. He knew that survival for his wife and daughters hinged on them returning to England as quickly as possible. He knew his family had to leave before they liquidated whatever remaining assets he had. His son, Frederick Jr., had purchased his father's business in Nottingham from him when the family had moved to America. He had managed it well and had made it profitable. The global economic calamity of 1929 had created financial chaos everywhere and no doubt would have a significant impact on his business, but he believed he was solvent enough to survive. He had not over-extended himself as his father and many other businessmen had done. It would be difficult, but he was confident he could provide for his mother and sister.

Sarah had her new life with Milton and was secure in that. She saw no reason to return to England. She would no doubt miss her mother and sister, but life had taken them and her in different directions. It was sad that her once proud family had been reduced to such a level. Her mother had written to her shortly after their hasty departure from New York. She wrote of feeling like a vagrant on the run from an economic demon that was destroying everything in its path. They could barely afford third class passage on a small steamer out of New York and were forced to share a small cabin with six other travelers. She and her daughter had no choice but to share a single size bed. She was concerned for Sarah's father and pressed her oldest daughter to be vigilant with him. "I do not think he is well," she said." He has had a mild cough for some time now, but has insisted it's nothing to be concerned with. I think his cough is more than it appears."

Her father's plan was to return to England once the fallout from this economic disaster had settled. Frederick Sr. fought for his own economic survival on a daily basis. When the money vanished, the realities of economics simply forced some very hard decisions.

236

Properties were repossessed by the banks and servants had to be dismissed.

The stress became too much and his health became compromised. He became quite ill and was shortly diagnosed with an aggressive type of consumption. His health swiftly spiraled downward.

There was no one to care for him. Sarah stepped in to fill that role and had her father moved into her small cottage in Portsmouth. She and Milton had decided to keep the cottage, as it provided rental income for them in the summer and also gave them an off-island retreat when the need arose. Caring for her father would be easier in Portsmouth, and there would be unhampered access for her father's doctor and any medication he might prescribe. Prudence Island would always have a very restricted ferry schedule limiting any medical treatment.

She had always adored her father. He had been a good provider, a strong role model, and a loving figure for her. It was very difficult to watch him slowly waste away. Medical theory at the time recommended that cool, fresh air, especially dry air, was the best way to combat consumption and the damage the disease did to its victim's lungs. Sarah had a carpenter install a breathing box in the bedroom of her small cottage. It had been prescribed by her father's doctor. This was done by simply cutting a hole in the exterior wall of his bedroom, which allowed her father to extend his head out beyond the wall. It was essential that her father be exposed to as much outside air as possible. This hole would then be boxed in and screened to keep insects and the elements away from him. Their doctor also informed them that many patients would often relocate to the drier climates of the world, as it often lessened their discomfort and extended their life expectancy. But he was also confident that it was much too late for Frederick Sr. He would not survive the move. Sarah did not share with her father's physician they could not afford the move anyway.

The last six weeks were quite painful for the both of them. She made his tiny bedroom as comfortable and homey as possible with old family pictures and paintings that she hung on the ship-lap walls. Milton moved two vintage stuffed chairs into the room and would often lift his father-in-law from his bed to the chair. It made conversation a little easier and it helped his wife stay connected with her father; they always took pleasure with each other's council.

Sarah had now witnessed the slow, agonizing death of two remarkable men—remarkable for very opposing reasons. One man had been forced into a despicable act and had the burden of 1,500 souls crushing and stifling any desire to live. The other had raised a loving family and built a successful business. Yet tortuous death would come to them both.

Near the end his doctor had sought to treat her father with injections of gold and arsenic solutions. These were the last, desperate attempts to stave off the inevitable. They seemed only to increase her father's discomfort. Sarah would learn years later these medical theories were completely unfounded and were actually determined to be highly toxic to the patient. When her father finally passed away, it was only after days of desperate, painful retching. His blood-filled lungs finally succumbed and he died on March twelfth, 1931.

Sarah would also later learn that consumption could be passed on to others through airborne bacteria and that it was highly contagious. Her father had employed a lot of newly arrived immigrants at his factories. Many of these immigrants came from countries that had little to no healthcare system in place. It was one of the many reasons they sought a new life in America. The crash of 1929 had certainly severely impacted his health, but Frederick Shepard Sr. was probably infected with the virus long before his economic demise. He no doubt took steps to hide his affliction from the family.

Her father died penniless. There was no money to even provide a proper funeral and burial. He left Sarah and her family with nothing. Frederick Jr. in England cabled his sister some money for their father's last rites. She and Milton provided the remaining required funds. They held a service at St. Michael's in Bristol where they were married and had him buried at Island Cemetery in Newport, Rhode Island.

Her father was gone and the rest of her family had returned to England. The sad reality of it all was that Sarah would probably never see any of her family again. Life brings you down a strange path. But now she had Milton and he would be the only family she would need. Milton loved her and would stand by her and they would stand together.

Simon

APRIL 1939

Simon had some difficulty tracking down his old friend. He discovered through his old connections that Sarah's family had returned to England after the crash of 1929. Apparently her father had been financially ruined in its wake. Sarah, however, had remained in the U.S. No one was really sure where she was. Most of her old friends knew, as did Simon, that Sarah left the city in 1912. That was twenty-seven years ago. She could be anywhere, so he sought out the only person that might know.

* * *

William Lowe was still living in the New York area. Simon pored through the city phone directory. There were a few William Lowes, but only one William Irving Lowe. He called and explained his predicament and hoped that William might help. William remembered him from his early days at the *Journal* and offered to assist in any way he could. Simon had been a good friend to Sarah and they had shared a common ground.

"I believe I have some information that might help you find Sarah." He paused and then softly, almost as if was thinking to himself, said "My, I haven't spoken that name aloud in so many years." Simon sensed that William was suddenly struggling with some long suppressed feelings.

They made plans to meet later that afternoon at a small Italian restaurant on the east side. Some very tender feelings, a lot closer to the surface than William realized, were about to be stirred up. Simon wondered how William would deal with the past and present suddenly colliding. He hoped Will's feelings would survive the impact.

Simon arrived a few minutes ahead of William and asked for a table that would offer some privacy. He ordered a bottle of wine and enjoyed its bouquet while waiting for William. The wine and the smells of this cozy Italian restaurant stimulated some very bittersweet memories of his own. Simon and Olivia were always dining at Italian restaurants, investigating their entrees and sampling their wine lists. Olivia always felt obligated to see what their competitors were serving and pouring. "And if you haven't noticed, I do enjoy my Italian food," she would say. More than just Will's recollections and feelings were about to be tormented, and Simon tenderly sensed the irony of it all.

Simon took in the sights and sounds of the busy little diner. Most of the tables were full, and mustached waiters with combed-backed dark hair were scurrying all about in their white aprons. The red sauce stains that seemed to be on most of the aprons told Simon that this bistro was more about the food than the presentation. He wondered if an Italian eatery had ever failed in New York City; the cuisine itself seemed to guarantee its own success.

240

Simon saw Will when he walked into the café; there was no mistaking him. His tall frame gave him away and Simon was sure he still wore the same fedora of his younger years. Will removed his hat when the maître d' greeted him, and Simon saw that most of his hair was gone. The little that remained was now gray. Time pulls us along, caring little about our reluctance and ignoring our protests. The maître d' pointed in Simon's direction. He stood and gestured so Will would see him and his head and the hand that still held his hat rose together in recognition. Will's walk to the table was steady and his steps measured. A loose-fitting herringbone suit gave away the slender frame underneath, and though his plain collared shirt was securely buttoned at the neckline, it revealed a thin and hanging gullet. His face had lost some of its roundness, replaced with heavy wrinkles on his forehead and cheeks. Time had left its evidence.

His face lit up when he got to Simon's table, and a smile spread across his face. He extended his hand. "It's very good to see you again, Simon. It's been a long time."

Simon rose from his seat and firmly grasped his hand. "It is good to see you, too. Please have a seat. I have taken the liberty of ordering some Chianti for us. I hope that is okay.'

William sat at the table and they began to catch up on their lives. William had remarried and had two daughters. He had taken over the family business after his father passed away in 1920. Simon suddenly noticed he was missing his left arm from the elbow down. Before he could say anything, William spoke. "I lost my arm in the War. You look surprised. You probably forgot that I was in the army reserves. My unit, the New York Forty-seventh Infantry, was activated and we were part of the first wave of American troops sent to Europe." Simon had indeed forgotten that.

General "Black Jack" Pershing had led the American incursion into the Great War. It was hoped that America's long-awaited arrival would be enough to turn the tide against the Huns. The sinking of the U.S.S. *Lusitania* by a German U-boat had ultimately secured that entry.

Major William Lowe had witnessed the horror of the war first hand. He had seen the senseless waste of life for just a few meters of

241

landscape. The years of this conflict had turned into a military stalemate. His unit had been brought in for the spring offensive of 1918. It was to be the costliest engagement of the war. Almost 2000,000 casualties were inflicted on the two opposing forces. He was to participate in the Second Battle of Somme. He had been ordered to coordinate and direct his division's assault from his position in the trenches. The allies' bombardment began at exactly 6:00 a.m. and lasted four hours. At 10:00 a.m. on the morning of June eleventh, 1918, whistles up and down the allies' trenches screeched in unison. Major Lowe and 6,000 Americans, along with the tens of thousands of allies, leapt from their trenches. On the opposite side, German infantry that had taken cover from the bombardment in their underground fortification now scrambled to their machine gun and mortar placements. It had become a sad and deadly ritual along the front: each side would begin their offensive with a large and sustained artillery and mortar assault. When it ended, the real bloodbath would begin. Thousands of men would advance across "no man's land," a wide open area between the opposing forces. There was no place to hide from enemy machine gun positions and artillery batteries. Thousands of men were to die in this acreage of carnage, obliterated like insects and with little, if any, attached feeling.

A German artillery shell stopped Major Lowe barely fifty feet from his trench. He was severely wounded. There would be no saving his arm. It had been completely severed from his elbow. Major Lowe spent the rest of the war in an army field hospital.

Now, sitting with Simon at their table in the little café, he gazed at his stump with a faraway look. "Losing my arm is the price I paid for my treatment of Sarah. You will be quite surprised to learn that I kept in touch with Sarah's father after she left for Rhode Island, although it would take many years of reaching out to him. Initially he was very angry with me for the pain I had inflicted on his daughter. I wrote several letters to him over the years and tried to explained how difficult it had been for me to leave Sarah.

"Can you imagine what it would have been like to carry on my relationship with my sister and her husband after the tragedy of the *Titanic*? Every time we would have been together, there would have been deep soul searching by them; why had we not listened to Sarah, not trusted her more? And for us, there would be the pain of knowing and not doing enough. Everywhere we turned there would have been an abundance of painful hindsight. To this day my sister and I share a very fragile and difficult relationship. She and her husband moved to Houston many years ago. He is involved in the oil industry and is doing quite well. But we rarely talk, and haven't seen each other in years. Never doubt that I loved Sarah, or that leaving her was the most difficult thing that I have ever done."

Simon believed him.

"I finally heard from Sarah's father in 1923. He told me that Sarah had remarried and was happy. I believe this is what finally allowed Frederick Sr. to reach out to me. His daughter's happiness was his first and only concern. I told him that I was very happy for her. She deserved it. I believe he began to trust me more after that and our correspondences became a little more frequent. We exchanged cards at Christmas for several years and would always include little updates on our lives. We decided to keep these correspondences between the two of us a secret. I am sure my wife knows nothing of this and I am convinced Sarah's father has said nothing to her. I stopped receiving cards and letters from Mr. Shepard late in 1929. I have no idea why.

"I was not heartless and I will say it again: leaving Sarah was the most difficult thing I have ever done. It is a pain that still lingers."

Simon told him he knew about what had happened to Sarah. How she had sensed the approaching disaster that turned out to be the *Titanic* and was so frustrated by it. It must have been a terrible burden. "I have the same gift as Sarah," said Simon, "but it is not as profound as hers. It can be very disturbing." Simon told William that he had received a letter from Sarah years after she left New York for Rhode Island. She told him that she had been deeply hurt by the divorce and by the tragedy of the *Titanic*. She could no longer stay in New York.

William told Simon that he had learned from Frederick Sr. that his daughter was now living on a small island in Narragansett Bay called Prudence and that she and her husband operated a small inn there. "As I said, I have not heard from Sarah's father since 1929,

243

so we will have to hope she is still living there. Her father seemed convinced that she was very comfortable in her new marriage and new home. I cannot see Sarah jeopardizing any of that. I believe she still lives there."

"I am also confident I will find her there; in fact, I am convinced," Simon responded. Simon knew he would have to visit her there. He thanked William for his valuable assistance.

"But Simon, before you leave, you must tell me why you have gone to such lengths to find her. I will conjecture it has something to do with her gift."

Simon told him that it had everything to do with Sarah's gift. "I hope she can help an old friend of mine, and also a poor woman who lost everything in that terrible hurricane that ravaged the North East last fall."

"I believe Sarah will do everything she can to help. That is who she is. You may tell Sarah whatever you like, but please tell her that I did love her and only wish her the best. I hope these years have healed her wounds and that you find her healthy and in good spirits. Have a safe trip, and take care."

They shook hands, and Simon left directly for Grand Central Station. He boarded the first available train to Union Station in Providence. It would arrive late that night and he would have to rent a room at the Biltmore Hotel. The next morning, he walked the short distance to the city plaza where he boarded a bus to Bristol, Rhode Island. The bus dropped him off in the center of town on Hope Street. It was brief walk down Church Street to Thames Street, where the ferry was docked.

He boarded the ferry that serviced Prudence Island with just a few minutes to spare and entered a small, U-shaped cabin near the stern of the boat. There was contoured seating around the three interior walls and the seats were worn but glossy, with a recent layer of marine varnish covering them. The windows that rimmed the upper cabin walls were weather-beaten and coated with saltwater spray. The cabin was bustling with people and children, and they were all talking like old friends. There were numerous canvas bags filled with groceries and clothing. They stopped their chatter when he entered.

A couple with two young children rearranged their belongings so he would have a place to sit. Most of the riders nodded or said hello. Once Simon was seated they all went back to their chatter. He asked the couple next to him where he might find the Prudence Inn and how he might get there. He was told that the ferry made two stops on the Island: Homestead and Sandy Point. He should get off at Sandy Point. The Inn was a short walk from the dock. He was told by a young teenage girl with dark hair done up in pigtails and banana curls that "you can see the inn when you get off the ferry, just walk up the hill and turn right, only a fool could miss it."

The inn was indeed just a short walk from the ferry landing at Sandy Point. The entrance was just a few feet off the main thoroughfare, which was just a well-traveled, hard-packed dirt road. Simon took the few short steps to the door and knocked. He hoped that his unannounced visit would not upset his old friend.

For just a brief moment he was back in New York. He was that young man just out of college, his whole world ahead of him, and he was sitting at the conference table at the *Journal*. Sarah was there with him; young, beautiful, so in love with her man. Neither of them knew it at the time, but it was probably the happiest point in their lives.

An elderly woman opened the door and greeted him. "Hello, Simon. I have been expecting you." It was Sarah, his old friend from a different time and place.

Madame Alice

APRIL 1939

Sarah was now close to seventy years old. The passing years had peeled away her youth and splendor. Her nose, cheekbones, and jawline had sharpened a little, and the creases at the corners of her eyes and mouth had kept a favorable measure of the years, but her blue eyes still sparkled, and the broad smile she now shared with Simon softened those same wrinkles and almost made them disappear. Her smile still welcomed and energized him. Her hair was thick and wavy, as he had remembered it, but was pulled back with a bright red ribbon and bow. It had turned a soft gray. An erect and committed posture told him that, with all that had happened, life had taken little from her. She wore a simple house dress with a blue and red floral print from the waist down and a plain white cotton top. An apron spotted with flour and other ingredients was being quickly untied and removed. Simon had arrived on a baking day. She took a baking towel from her shoulders and hastily wiped her hands and arms and ardently embraced her old friend.

"Oh Simon, it is so very good to see you again." She held him tightly. Life is about sharing and loving. Simon and Sarah knew this even if some did not.

* * *

The next ferry leaving the island wasn't until late that afternoon. It was a beautiful late spring day, crisp and clear, too early yet for the seasonal crowds to make their way to the island. They would have several uninterrupted hours to catch up on their lives. Sarah suggested that they sit among all the dandelions on the inn's expansive front lawn. It overlooked the east passage of Narragansett Bay and the late spring sun was already casting its warmth. Sarah said her husband Milton was at work, but would be home for lunch. They would have until then to talk. Lunch was something Sarah and Milton always did together, but Simon would be welcomed at their table. They could continue their reminiscing after that. They began to recall their early years.

Sarah told Simon more about her premonitions connected to the *Titanic* many years ago and how they became painfully real, quickly destroying her marriage to a man she absolutely worshipped. "I was hurt so deeply by it all," she said. "I didn't think that I would ever recover from it. I ran away to Rhode Island to be with my father. He was very good to me. I will always be indebted to him for that. Unfortunately, my father died in 1931. He lost everything in the crash of '29. He died penniless. I am not the debutant daughter you used to know."

"I am so sorry," Simon said.

"Don't by sorry for me. I found Milton and I am secure in that. I will probably never love him as I did William—that type of love happens only once in a lifetime. But Milton loves me, makes no demands of me, and accepts me for who I am. He brought me to this wonderful little island and its quaint people. Here I can hide away with my gift and spare the world from its despair."

Simon was stunned by Sarah's comment. "Do my words puzzle you?" she asked Simon.

He paused for a moment and reflected.

"No, I suppose not. I would have been troubled by such a statement years ago, but I too have come to personally experience the power of this gift and its sometimes tragic consequences." Simon told her of his experiences over the last thirty years and Sarah saw that they had walked a similar path. They spent the rest of the morning catching up.

Milton returned at noon and they moved back to the inn's kitchen for lunch. Sarah introduced the two men. Milton was wearing his long-billed fisherman's cap and sunglasses. He wore khaki pants with brown Red Wing work boots and the sleeves of his green work shirt were rolled up to his elbows. His face, neck, and forearms were already tanned from his days in the sun. He was a slight and wiry man.

"Milton, this is Simon Bouchard. He is an old friend of mine from my years in New York. I believe I have spoken of him."

Milton extended his hand. "Hello, Simon. It's good meeting you. I do recall Sarah mentioning you. Will you be joining us for lunch?" He seemed unfazed by Simon's unannounced visit. They sat in the kitchen at the sturdy oak table that looked out over the bay. Sarah made sandwiches and heated some homemade split pea soup. Conversation was limited, and Milton contributed very little to it. Simon could see that Milton was a quiet man, but he could also see that Sarah and Milton had a strong and loving relationship; they were always touching each other or briefly holding hands like young lovers. He could remember the days when he and his wife used to do the same. He envied Sarah and Milton.

Milton announced that it was time to return to work. Normally they would have shared a cup of tea together, but he sensed that Sarah and Simon had much to talk about. He was soon on his way.

They cleaned up after their lunch, and Simon helped with drying the dishes and putting them away. Finally, Sarah asked, "Simon, why are you here? I feel your visit is connected to that destructive hurricane we had last year, isn't it?"

"Your perceptions, as always, are amazing, and how you knew I was coming is something you will need to explain to me at another time. But for now I will get to the reason for my visit.

"I have been trying to help a very troubled woman. She lives on Jamestown Island, not too far from here. That storm completely tore her life apart. She actually witnessed the death of some of her family as they were swept away in one massive wave. Her last vision of her younger sister, her daughter, and her son was of them desperately clinging to the small roof of an out building they had taken shelter in, and then the seas of that terrible hurricane swallowed them.

"I have been visiting with her for the last several weeks, trying to help her to get closure by reaching out to her loved ones."

Simon told her how Claudia had contacted him and pleaded with him for help. He told her about his talks with Katherine Miller; tearful discussions that were permeated with deep sighs and empty stares.

"I will tell you this, Sarah: There is a very deep sadness that fills this home, but it is more than that. I am convinced that those family members that perished in that storm did not move on. At first I thought they were there in need of closure, but I now sense something different is happening. It's almost like they are there to comfort and protect their mother. I do not think they want closure. They do not want to move on."

"You might be right," Sarah offered. "Spirits sometimes do not want to move on, especially when the bonds are as strong as you say they are. There was a sudden and tragic destruction of a very close family. This sounds all very possible, considering all that has happened to them."

"But there is something else going on." Simon told Sarah about the séance they attempted his last night at the Miller home. "It was confusing and frightening at the same time."

"You cannot allow yourself to be frightened," Madame Alice said. "Fear only shuts down our fragile connection with the other side. You know that."

"Oh, I do. But this was something I had never experienced before. I told Mrs. Miller and her close friend that these confusing communications from beyond are very troubling. It is very difficult to explain, but it almost like there are different languages being spoken, but there is no understanding of what is being communicated. I need your help."

"What can I do? I came to this island to shelter myself from other people's pain. You of all people know how draining it can be."

"I believe you know what you can do. You know more than you are telling me. When you met me at the door you said that were expecting me. There is something you are not sharing with me."

Sarah sighed heavily. "Yes Simon, I knew you were coming. Shortly after the hurricane you began to enter my dreams. It was puzzling, but I knew you were somehow connected to the tragedies that terrible storm had brought to this area. You see, I personally witnessed the fury and the pain that the storm brought with it." She stood and pointed out the window to where they were siting earlier this morning. "Look down towards the dock where the ferry dropped you off this morning. Do you see that concrete foundation? That is all that is left of a very rugged lighthouse. Milton and I watched as a huge wall of water swept it away in seconds. It took the lives of the lighthouse keeper, his wife, and their two children. Only their oldest son George survived the onslaught and that was only because his closest friend risked his own life to pull him back to shore. It was a miracle that he saved him and as I said Milton and I witnessed the whole spectacle. The poor boy that survived is now a withdrawn, confused and lonely lad. It was probably the same wall of water that brought tragedy to your friend's family.

"That lighthouse was sturdily engineered and constructed, and it was thought to be indestructible. The poor family that lived there believed they were safe from the storm's fury. Yet as I said, they were gone in seconds. Their bodies were recovered several days later more than ten miles up the bay. I knew then that there was to be a great deal of human suffering connected to that storm and that I would be drawn into it. That is when you started to enter my dreams, and I knew it was just a matter of time before you showed up.

"But now there is something you are not sharing with me either, Simon. How did you find me? What trail led you here?"

Simon told Sarah of reaching out to her ex-husband in New York. "I knew that he might be the only one who knew where you lived. I went back to New York and sought him out. He had taken over the family business when his father passed away and has done well. Tragically, he lost his left arm while serving in Europe. As you know, he was in the Army Reserves. His unit was called up when we entered the Great War. He was severely wounded in an engagement in France. But he remarried and has two daughters. He seems to be content with his life, but I am convinced his happiest days were with you. Sharing the potential consequences of your terrible gift for the rest of your lives was more than he could bare. His relationship with his sister and her husband was severely compromised by what had happened. It is still a very strained relationship." He told Sarah that William had written to her father for several years and heard nothing. "He finally heard from your father when you had remarried and seemed happy with your new life with Milton on Prudence Island. He repeatedly told me that he truly loved you and that leaving you was the most difficult thing he had ever done. I am grateful he persisted in his efforts to find you. I'm not sure I would have been able to by myself."

"I think you would have found me," said Sarah. "It might have taken a little longer, but you would have found me. The gift we share would have guaranteed that. I am so sorry to hear about Williams's injury in the war. It pains me deeply to hear that. I loved him so much so very long ago. Losing an arm does much more than just physical harm. I am sure he and his family have lived with the pain of that injury for quite some time now. He was a good man. But I believe he gave up too easily on our marriage. With time we could have put things back together. We loved each other very much. That should have made us secure. I suppose it was not sufficient for William. I believed he was stronger than that, but I wish him well." With that Sarah turned away from Simon and seemed lost in her thoughts.

"What are you thinking?" Simon finally asked.

She turned to look at him. "If I am to help this woman, we will need to leave on the first ferry in the morning. I will need to explain this to Milton and I will need to pack. I have a lot to do. Oh and one more thing, please do not call me or refer to me as Sarah anymore. Sarah was a long time ago. My name is Alice now, and to all my clients I am Madame Alice. Please call me Madame Alice."

"Yes, of course," Simon said.

That night, Sarah reflected on how William had again entered her life. Time, Milton, and her quiet new life on Prudence had helped her repair the damage done to her identity. She wished that Simon had never reached out to William. She was not prepared to open old wounds, especially when the healing layer on this lesion was still very thin. Hearing that William had lost his arm in that horrible war had not helped; it only made the reconnection with her traumatic past more painful. The horrible things he must have seen in that terrible war. How could any man not be permanently changed by such experiences? Sarah's instinct to protect and soothe became too much for her, and her tears flowed.

Simon had settled into his room for the night and it was just Sarah and Milton sitting in front of the fireplace. Milton was poking at the dying embers. Shortly they would be making their way to the bedroom. Milton looked over to see his wife quietly weeping. He moved softly to her side, settled to one knee, and tenderly stroked her hair.

"I think some very tender memories have been stirred up with Simon's visit. I am not the best talker, but I am a good listener. If talking about these tears will stop them, I am here for you. I know you had another life before we met and you have memories that are dear to you. Just know you are not alone. I love you."

"Milton, you are so special to me. You have become my rock. There were some fond memories that were rekindled. But they are only memories of a time long ago. This too shall pass. Our love for each other will see to that."

"Will you be okay on this trip to Jamestown?"

"I will be fine; you need not worry. Let's go to bed."

Jacob

JUNE 1921

Jacob and Sarah had been meeting for eight days and their get-togethers had become very draining for him. He tried to be very specific in what he told Sarah. He wanted there to be no misunderstanding. There were things that he knew to be true and there were things that he could only speculate on. He sought to make that delineation quite distinct.

Jacob was becoming very weak, and they had moved to his bedroom. He had become too sick to leave his bed. He now allowed his good friend Ida to be with them in the room. Ida and Sarah carried two of the stuffed loungers from the living room into his bedroom. He was now allowing someone else to share in his terrible secret. It was obvious he had reached the point where he did not care anymore. Sometimes he would become very sick and Sarah would have to leave

253

the room while Ida attended to him. What color he had would leave his face, and he would turn a lifeless pale pigment; he would vomit, gag and struggle for his air. Twice she had to leave his home and return the next day to continue.

Sarah sensed that Jacob was close to his death and it made little sense to continue on.

"Mr. Sweeney, you have told me more than enough about the *Titanic*. You need your rest. There is no need to torture yourself like this anymore. It is difficult for me to participate in your discomfort."

He eyes instantly flushed wide open, his jaw clenched and his face became red. He was angry. His words were slow and labored: "We will finish this to the end. The torture is indeed mine. It is a small price to pay for what I did and for what I know. Do not make any more attempts to end this. You sought me out for what I know, and in the end I am glad you did, but have the courtesy to hear me out."

Ida kept a basin of cool water next to his bed and she dabbed a white cloth in it and began to wipe Jacob's forehead and neck. "Please, Jacob, Sarah had only good intentions."

He would not have any of it and pushed her hand and the wash cloth away. "This type of digression must never happen again. I don't have the energy for it. I will finish this story or I will die."

"I am sorry Jacob; it won't happen again."

"Good. Let's continue," and he carried on his narrative.

"The *Titanic* was made ready for sea trials in April of 1912. Normally they are very strenuous exercises. *Olympic's* sea trials were completed in two and half days and were quite rigorous. *Titanic's* sea trials began after breakfast on the second of April and were completed before lunch. There were no efforts at all to challenge her seaworthiness. It was just a façade for the public's curiosity. The *Titanic* was never opened to public inspection like the *Olympic*. White Star had scheduled a gala event when they presented the *Olympic* for public inspection. There were bands and plentiful food and refreshments were served to the visitors. Thousands of people attended the event.

"There was no such fanfare for *Titanic*. There was not even any newspaper coverage of her completed sea trials. I knew why, but the public did not. There were some polite inquiries, but there was never any official reason why and no one really seemed to mind.

"Six days before *Titanic's* maiden voyage I was approached by Mr. Ismay, this time in my office behind closed doors. I was told that the SS *California*, an American vessel that was operated by The Leyland Line (which was part of J.P. Morgan's International Mercantile Marine Company) would be docking at our shipyard for a short stay. I should expect her arrival early the following day. I was told to prepare her for a trans-Atlantic voyage. She was primarily designed to transport cotton, but was also capable of carrying up to fifty passengers. It was rare that she disembarked without being close to capacity with passengers. This time she was scheduled to leave Liverpool with no passengers and with nothing in her holds except a small load of woolen sweaters. I stocked her coal rooms with sufficient fuel and made sure all other ocean-going needs had been addressed. She departed from Liverpool on April fifth, 1912, just six days before *Titanic* began her voyage.

"I remarked to Jay Bruce that it seemed hardly worth the trip with a cargo of such little value.

"'Just be sure the *California* is prepared to leave Liverpool on the fifth. That is all you need to know,'" Ismay answered. Again I knew I was asking too much. The less I knew, the better off I was.

"Now I will begin to mix speculation with fact. There were a number of puzzling activities that transpired shortly before the ersatz *Titanic's* departure from South Hampton that now demand closer scrutiny. For the most part the general public is unaware of these activities.

"Fifty first class passengers canceled their trips within two days of *Titanic's* departure. Most of them were friends or business associates of J.P. Morgan. Morgan himself also canceled his trip shortly before departure. He also had rare and expensive bronze statues removed from the *Titanic* only hours before her exodus.

"One week before sailing, White Star Lines increased *Titanic's* insurance coverage by fifty percent. Five days after the sinking, J.P. Morgan and White Star Lines aggressively sought compensation from Lloyd's of London and subsequently collected 12.5 million dollars.

"Florence Ismay, wife of J. Bruce, suddenly announced that she would not be joining her husband on this excursion of a lifetime. No excuse was offered. People close to the Ismays were astonished. This was the prized vessel of the Ismay fleet, the largest and most luxurious liner in the world, and Ismay's wife was absent from its christening voyage. She had never missed a ceremonial voyage on any of her husband's vessels.

"There are so many of these probing incidents that, if taken individually, meant little, but collected and examined as a whole demanded clarity. Mr. Ismay told me several times to keep my suspicions to myself. I believe he told me that because he knew my inquiries would easily lead to a conclusion that was too dark to even talk about. He knew what we were about to do and why we were doing it, and he knew I knew. It was the big elephant in the room that no one wanted to talk about."

"Jacob," said Sarah, "as you know I followed the hearings in both the U.S. and the U.K. Much of what I read also led to my own speculation. Now what you have told me only strengthens that speculation. I can remember the testimony of Winston Dodge, a high school math teacher traveling second class on the *Titanic*. Shortly after putting out to sea, he noticed that she had a pronounced list to port and he shared this observation with others traveling with him. At the time I simply deemed it a curious observation and struggled to understand its significance. Now I learn that the *Olympic* had developed a list to port after her collision with the HMS *Hawke*. I wonder how Mr. Dodge would now view his astute observation." She asked Jacob, "Do you think that the SS *California* was a willing participant in this plot that went terribly wrong?"

Jacob paused for a while, started to say something, then paused again. He seemed confused. He was struggling to find his words, and then he started again

"I believe the *California* was indeed involved in this ill-conceived conspiracy, but I'm not sure 'willing participant' is the right way to phrase it. No more willing than I was. It was simply something we were told to do. I believe very few people were told specifically what their roles were. Captain Smith and second officer Lightholler of the *Titanic* were probably the only ones onboard that were brought into the fold, as was Captain Lord of the *California*.

"I believe Captain Smith was ordered to deliberately strike an iceberg in the north Atlantic. Captain Lord of the *California* was to be waiting in the immediate area, which he was, and he was to facilitate the rescue of all of *Titanic's* passengers. However, something went terribly wrong, terribly wrong. I can never prove this, but I am absolutely convinced this is what was supposed to happen. I have more theory and speculation to share with you. But I am too weak to continue right now. I need to rest. Let's continue our speculations tomorrow."

Sarah left overwhelmed with what these men had done. They had caused the death of thousands in the most horrific tragedy in maritime history and now they had successfully hidden their involvement. God damn their greed!

She wondered how far the cover up had escalated. She knew Jacob had his own theory and would surely share it with her. He was intent on cleansing his soul, and every piece of evidence, every morsel of conjecture or theory, would be handed over to her. His burden would become Sarah's.

Madame Alice

APRIL 1939

Simon and Madame Alice arrived the next morning. Father and I were sitting in the front living room with my mother when they pulled into the drive away. Here was another person promising closure and unknowingly contributing to her agony. We were skeptical. Closure was now being defined as just more disruption and pain for my mother and for us. How many more attempts at closure could my mother survive? My God, does this make any sense?

Claudia met Simon and Madame Alice as they pulled into the driveway. "Simon, I am so glad to see you back so soon," Claudia said.

"Claudia, this is Madame Alice, the woman that I told you about."

"Simon did not tell us much about you," Claudia said. "But if he believes you can help, Madame Alice, then I also believe you can aid Katherine."

"Let's not get ahead of ourselves," said Madame Alice. "Simon told me about the tragedies that have occurred at this home and what a fragile, spiraling state Mrs. Miller is in. I cannot make any promises, but I will try."

Claudia then turned to Simon. "I met you out here so Katherine could not hear us. Things have changed a great deal since you left. There are the same vibrations as before, but now Mrs. Miller's sister and her children have appeared to her." Claudia hesitated.

"What is it?" Simon asked.

"I saw them too," Claudia said.

Madame Alice interrupted. "There is so much emotional suffering and anguish in this home. It completely engulfed me the very moment we arrived. But it is too much to be all connected to Mrs. Miller. This whole family is suffering terribly; those that have passed on and those that have not."

"I am not sure what you mean," said Claudia. "But does that mean you believe me? Meg, Stephanie, and Corey were right there in front of me. You do believe me, don't you?"

"Yes, of course I do," replied Madame Alice. "We will need to talk more about this; but first I would like to meet Mrs. Miller."

"She is in the living room. It's where she spends most of her afternoons. I just gave her medication with her tea. She will be a little sleepy. Please come this way."

My mother was staring out the big living room window. She had begun to remain in her nightgown long into the day, sometimes not even changing at all. Claudia would try to get her to dress, but it was always a challenge. Bathing and personal hygiene had become a daily struggle.

She turned to them. "Oh Claudia, we have company. Why didn't you tell me earlier?"

"They have just now arrived, Katherine. You remember Simon, don't you? And this is an old friend of his. This is Madame Alice."

"It is good to meet you, Madame Alice. I believe you are here to help me bring my loved one's home again. You know they left me in such a horrible way." She started to cry, but then checked herself. "You know they have visited several times now, haven't they Claudia?"

"Yes Katherine," Claudia said. "I think they want to come home too."

"What do you think, Madame Alice?" asked Katherine. Her medication was making her a little drowsy.

"This is always so unpredictable. I believe that your loved ones have reached out to you. I sense a presence in this room right now. I am not sure what their intent is. We shall try to help everyone here. My goal is to help you put your life back together. I am sure that your loved ones want the same thing. You have to believe that." Madame Alice looked around the room and said "Isn't that right?" She seemed to look at my father and me. We immediately liked her.

"I can see that you were a very close family. There was a strong bond. Simon told me how that horrible hurricane destroyed your family. There needs to be closure. You, your family in this room with you, and your loved ones, all need to move on. If you hold on to the past no one will ever move forward. Some people do not want to move on. Some people or spirits cannot. There is a very big difference.

"You need to get some rest now. Simon and I will be staying with you for the next few days if that is acceptable to you. We will talk a great deal and I will try very hard to ease your pain."

"Yes of course, you are welcomed in my home. Claudia can help you get settled. I think I shall nap now."

Delilah

APRIL 1939

That evening, Father, T.J., and I sat in the living room with my mother, Claudia, Simon and Madame Alice. They talked for a while and then Madame Alice lit her large rose-colored candle and placed it on the end table next to Mother. It immediately secured her attention. She stared at it intensely, as if looking for answers within its flickering flame.

Madame Alice began. "I need to hear from you, and only you, about the day of the hurricane and what you have experienced or sensed since that time, especially these recent visions. These events tell me that things are beginning to peak or are culminating. But it is your pain and your loss that is at the center of all of this. It is what's pulling your loved ones back. It has been my experience that when spirits have moved on, they do not want to be called back to our

261

world. It is very draining on them. As difficult as it might be, you must talk about your family and, by doing so, it will allow you to let go. This in turn will allow your loved ones to move on."

My mother answered but never took her eyes of the candle. "But I have let them go, all of them. The pain of their loss has been unbearable. I have been changed. But I have not been selfish. I loved them all very deeply and I desperately miss them, but I want their spirits to be at peace." My mother was crying. "They can move on; I will be with them all soon enough."

My father and I were crying too and we immediately went to my mother's side. Madame Alice was startled by our rush to my mother. "You are so fortunate that your loved ones are here to support you." She whispered to Simon. "This loss, this sadness, is suffocating," and then the vibrations began again. Everyone in the room stood frozen in place. No one said a word. Madame Alice attempted to take it in, make sense of it. Finally, she said, "this too shall pass. There is nothing to fear. It is only loved ones reaching out to you."

Katherine pointed towards the fireplace and gasped. "Meg, Corey, and Stephanie have come to visit again. Do you see them Simon? Madame Alice?"

"Yes! Yes we do," Madame Alice replied. "They were indeed there; blurry, floating images of them. Their mouths are moving but no sound can be heard. They are motioning for us to come with them, to follow them."

But my father and I saw nothing. We sensed the vibrations like everyone else. But the ghostly images were not visible to us. My father would not allow us to be part of this charade. We left the living room and went to our rooms. I waited a few moments until the sounds from my father's room had ceased, then crept silently to the landing on the staircase to observe.

"We can't go with you," Madame Alice said. "Our worlds are separate now."

I could still see nothing, but Madame Alice spoke of the ethereal images moving closer to Mother and then stopping. They no longer continued to beckon to her. She was choked with tears and told them she loved them dearly and missed them so. "But I can't go with you now. You must move on. I will be with you sooner than you think."

Madame Alice described Aunt Meg, Stephanie, and Corey shaking their heads, and seeming to be say no. They began to move back from my mother and then they quickly faded away. The vibration and shaking stopped with their disappearance and the room went silent.

No one spoke a word. Finally my mother spoke. "This is more than I can bear. Oh, my poor family!" She slumped in her chair, almost lifeless, certainly lifeless on the inside.

Claudia intervened. "We need to get you to bed, Katherine; let's get you some tea and something to help you relax."

"Yes, of course," was all my mother could mumble, and she and Claudia slowly made their way to the stairs and up to her bedroom.

Later that night, I found my father in his study, vainly attempting to distract himself with one of his many books. It was no use.

His opinion of Madame Alice had changed instantly. She had bought into Claudia's charade, he said, pretending she saw these visions of Aunt Meg, Stephanie, and Corey. It was too much for my father. He was saddened and agitated by all of this pretense. "I can understand Claudia telling your mother that she saw these visions. I have said before, this is just Claudia's devotion to your mother. But now this Madame Alice and Simon becoming part of this charade is just despicable. They are just charlatans. It has been a long day and I am drained. Why don't we call it a day? I will retire shortly, but first I will need to have a talk with this Madame Alice. I will see you in the morning."

He stood up from his chair and walked determinedly out of the room. He was no doubt certain I would head straight to my bedroom. But I was too concerned, for him and my mother both, to worry about violating rules of etiquette; my eavesdropping would continue. I waited several beats and then crept silently after the sound of my father's footsteps.

* * *

What I found was Simon and Madame Alice alone in the living room. My father was nowhere in sight. He must have doubled back or slipped into another room to collect himself. His anger was great, but he was not a man prone to violent outburst, and he understood that could only further hurt the situation.

Simone and Madame Alice were talking. "These were the vibrations and shaking that I told you of," said Simon. "But this is the first time that I have seen the spirits of her family. This is extraordinary. Do you think they are connected?"

"Oh, they are most certainly connected. I also agree with you, Simon, that there is something else going on. There are mixed signals. It appeared as if her family was beckoning her, almost asking her to cross over to be with them. That does not make sense. This whole thing we do does not make sense. People are skeptical of what we do. I would be skeptical, too, but we and others like us are granted this special gift to reach across an unknown barrier. We communicate with the deceased. We sense impending doom or things that will come to pass. We are then left with the burden of trying to filter what we have learned and figuring out how to pass it on to those who will probably not appreciate what we have offered them, and who often regret ever contacting us. I rarely ever hear from people that I have helped, even though I have often given them the closure that they desperately needed but could not accept."

Simon offered, "I think people's emotional pain is so very deep that they sometimes slowly drown in it. Katherine is steadily slipping away. This depression, along with the medication, will have her dead within a year, and when her time comes she will welcome it. This is no life for her. How could it be? If you were this woman would you even want to wake up in the morning?"

"I am not sure that I would, and I am also not sure just how much we can really help her. But I think there are others in this home whose pain is just as severe. Maybe we are here to help them, too."

"What or whom do you mean by 'there are others'? Others besides Meg, Stephanie, and Corey?" Simon asked.

"I am not sure," she replied. "There is also Jeffrey, Delilah, T.J., and even Claudia, whose pain and loss must have been just as severe. However, I agree with you, there are some very mixed signals. This is not at all what we think it is. We will have to keep trying to work with her. I can assure you though, that in the end it will be something so very simple and so obvious that we will feel quite foolish for not seeing it sooner."

Jacob

JUNE 1921

Sarah was not allowed to visit the next day. Jacob had been very ill the night before and needed more time to rebuild his strength. She was astonished by Jacobs's determination to finish his account. She had told him that there was no need to continue. His failing health was difficult to witness on a daily basis. Sarah told Jacob that she had heard enough, but that wasn't completely true. There was a little selfish intent in their conversations: Sarah knew there was much more to Jacobs's saga and she wanted to hear as much as he could tolerate.

* * *

It had been several months since the murder of Shepard's driver and the dust had settled. His people had told him that Frederick Shepard disappeared back into his world in Nottingham and returned to his daily grind at his lace mill. He had given his information to the local police department in Belfast and was very upset with the murder and his own beating. He also became quite angry and frustrated when the investigation kept hitting dead ends, but in the end he returned to his home in England. Nothing of any significance was reported after that. Cheswick had done his job and driven Shepard off the scent. His superiors were pleased.

It was time to check in on Jacob. He had pulled his people away from the crime scene immediately after the hit, no sense in providing any potential leads to Scotland Yard. Now Dudley stood at Jacob's door waiting for someone to answer. He had begun to pound on the door with the side of his closed right hand. Polite knocking had not achieved anything.

He began to look closer at the home: the drapes had been closed, mail from several days had not been brought in, and the shrubbery along the pathway seemed neglected. Jacob was away. Dudley walked around back and found an older man tending to the garden.

"Can you tell me where Jacob Sweeney might be?" he called out. The old man was on his hands and knees, weeding the garden. He looked up and acknowledged Dudley's presence with a slight wave of his hand and then on stiff knees and with vindicated grunts and groans he righted himself.

"Mr. Sweeney is quite ill, lung cancer I think, left for some hospital in London several weeks ago. Are you a friend of his, or family?"

"I'm an old friend of his from long ago. Do you know what hospital he went to?"

"No, no I don't, I'm just a part time gardener, mostly just a lot of weeding. I don't get to know about stuff like that."

Cheswick was mad with himself. How did he let such an important target slip through his web and leave Belfast? And now too much time had passed. He cursed softly to himself several times and pounded his fist into his upper leg.

"Pretty upset you missed Jacob, it looks like," said the old man.

"Yes, I am. Do you know anybody that could tell me where he is? I really want to see my old friend, especially after hearing he is in poor health."

"I don't think so. Jacob did not have a lot of friends, kind of odd he was a good guy, real likeable. The woman who took care of him went to London with him. I think her name was Ida, that's all I know."

"Thanks so much for all your help," Cheswick told him.

He was in deep trouble. How would he explain this to his superiors? He knew he had to remove his people from Jacob's neighborhood after he had Frederick's driver killed. It was the prudent thing to do, but he had taken too long to engage his people again and now Jacob had simply closed up his home and left for London and he was clueless as to why and when.

Dudley knew he had to keep this blunder under wraps; none of his people would know anything about it. If it found its way to those he worked for, he would pay a heavy price for such ineptness. How could he not know about Jacob's poor health?

He would have to resolve this by himself; this would be his own clandestine mission. He prepared to leave for London.

Cheswick finally located Jacob, A few well-placed schillings at St. Stephen's hospital and confidential medical records were soon revealed. Jacob was listed as a patient under the care of a Dr. Henry Washburn and was being treated at the client's residence in west London.

Dudley had watched the cottage the previous day but had seen nothing suspicious; actually there had not been a single visitor the entire day. He had seen an older woman venture out to the yard a few times. She didn't seem to accomplish anything in the yard, she would just stand with her hands on her hips, arch herself backwards, take in some deep breaths, and then quickly return to the bungalow.

"She's taking a quick break from something," Cheswick whispered to himself.

It was time for Dudley to surprise Jacob and his caregiver. Cheswick loved ambushes, he loved to see people squirm—squirming told Cheswick a lot. He would pay his elusive friend an untimely visit tomorrow afternoon.

Sitting in his carriage, Dudley Cheswick was about to make his move towards Jacob's cottage when a car pulled up to the front of the house and a young woman stepped out and approached the front door. She knocked and was quickly given entrance. The vehicle moved off and Dudley never got a good look at the driver. It seemed like a well-rehearsed action. He watched the cottage for the next hour without incident; the house seemed lifeless. It raised his level of suspicion. *Time for the ambush,* he thought.

* * *

Sarah returned the next day at the usual time. Jacob had regained some of his grit, but he was still very frail. He struggled with his words.

"I am sorry we could not get together yesterday…I will try to make up for the lost time…I am having trouble organizing my thoughts…and finding the right words. I believe…the pain medication is…also handicapping me. I must ask you…to help me in this effort…please be patient with me."

"I will be very patient, Jacob," Sarah replied. "And I will help in any way I can. Maybe we should try a different approach. Perhaps I could share what I learned in my research into the *Titanic* tragedy and what I believed happened leading up to the disaster and what ensued after it?"

Jacob seemed to understand where she was heading, but needed more clarity.

"I am hoping that my theories and insights might help you organize and express your thoughts. Together we can do this."

"You are indeed an angel sent to me, Sarah. I think you are right. Let's start again."

"Jacob, when I read about the ineptness of your Captain Smith, I wondered how such a fool would be allowed to pilot such a grand ship as the *Titanic*. He had just been involved in three separate collisions, all quite serious, with her sister ship, the *Olympic*. Now I learn that these collisions may have caused a fatal blow to the financial viability of White Star Lines. Typically, companies do not reward such incompetence, especially ineptitude on this scale. How did this happen?"

"Sarah, that is a good question, and it's one that I have asked myself a hundred times. Let me tell what I know about Captain Smith. First and foremost, he was a showoff. He was always trying to impress friends and passengers with daring and aggressive maneuvers, sometimes steering too close to landmarks to obtain more spectacular views. I also know that he reportedly had a drinking problem."

"Do you think that contributed to his history of bad judgment?" asked Sarah.

"I'm not sure. I do know that there were several design review meetings that he and I participated in. Those meetings addressed all issues, including how the vessel would respond from the wheelhouse, something any captain worth his mettle would deem invaluable. The design team had concerns that they may have undersized the rudder on both the *Olympic* and *Titanic*. This meant that the vessels would not respond well to sudden course changes, especially at high speeds."

"I find this all fascinating, to be privy to all this inside information; so were the concerns about the rudder founded? Did *Olympic* have trouble answering the helm?"

"Yes, *Olympic's* sea trials bore that out. *Olympic* did not respond as well as they had hoped in tight turns, but it was well within maritime guidelines. Captain Smith was well aware of *Olympic's* and *Titanic's* steering limitations."

Jacob had still not answered her initial question. "But Jacob," she said, "how did Smith come to skipper the *Titanic?* He did nothing to deserve that assignment."

"This is where I must speculate again. I know that Smith met privately with J. Bruce Ismay several weeks before *Titanic's* departure. I theorize that he was given a chance to redeem himself with Whites Star Lines. Captain Smith's reputation and credibility had been severely compromised. It was doubtful he would ever skipper his own vessel again. J.P. Morgan would also see to that. I believe Smith was given an ultimatum: participate in the sinking of the fraudulent *Titanic* as laid out by White Star Directors or disappear into a life of poverty and obscurity. I believe Smith's ego would not allow that. He must have been under tremendous pressure. I would not be surprised if J.P. Morgan himself spoke with Smith."

"I can't imagine that Smith could have pulled this off by himself," said Sarah. "There had to be others involved."

"I'm not sure who else had been involved. If I had to guess, and I am quite confident in this conjecture, I would say that *Titanic's* first officer, Lightoller, was involved with staging the calamity and its cover up. If you remember, he was very uncooperative at the hearings."

"I do remember that being an issue at the maritime hearings," Sarah said. "He actually went so far as to claim that while he was on the bridge he never received any warnings about icebergs or ice flows in the immediate area. That completely contradicted the testimony of other officers and crew."

Jacob was suddenly overcome with grief. Tears appeared in his gaunt, almost lifeless eyes. He shook his head from side to side. Sarah knew that it was not because of anything she had said or done. Jacob had simply arrived at the point where his and other's deeds caught up with his conscience and he could no longer live with the guilt. Sarah saw a tortured soul on his deathbed.

"Jacob, you have done your best. You are letting the sins of other despicable men define your life. Don't let them do that to you. You had no idea that your participation in White Star Line's

271

conspiracy would have such tragic consequences. You could not have possibly foreseen that."

Suddenly there was someone pounding on the front door. It startled everyone; whoever it was, they hadn't bothered to use the cast iron knocker. Ida hurried to the front door and was quickly back in the room with a name that brought fear to Jacob's face.

"Jacob, there is a Mr. Dudley Cheswick at the door, and he is very insistent upon seeing you."

He was suddenly alert and focused. "Sarah, this is an evil man, he must not know your real name or why you are here. Your life depends on it. Listen to me carefully, we only have a few moments. You are my cousin on my father's side and you are here for obvious reasons. I will conclude our meeting as quickly as possible. Get to your brother at the restaurant and go directly to the hotel you are staying at. Ida will send a note when it's safe to return. You must trust me on this."

Sarah appeared stricken. "I know he is evil, I sensed his presence this morning and it only grew more intense the closer I got to your home and I—"

Dudley Cheswick was suddenly in the bedroom.

"Jacob, I am sorry to see you are so ill," he said loudly. "You should have let me know in Belfast, perhaps I could have been of some assistance." He paced around the room, picking up various medicines, reading their labels, and then pulled the curtain aside and looked out the solitary window. No one said a word. Finally, he turned to face Sarah and Ida.

"I will assume you are Jacob's nurse; I saw you earlier in the day. Thank you for taking care of Jacob," and then to Sarah he said, "I am sure you and I have never met, my name is Dudley Cheswick and I have the pleasure of meeting…"

"My name is Beverly Brown. I am Jacob's cousin."

"Very nice meeting you, Miss Brown," he said with an obligatory, half-hearted nod of his head and turned to Jacob in his bed. "Jacob, I do not recall the Brown name in your family's lineage. How did I overlook that? I will have to re-examine your records. I do keep accurate chronicles, you know."

"My cousin was just about to leave, Dudley. I am becoming quite tired; I need to rest."

"Well, I will see her to the door, you know I saw your driver drop you off here, Miss Brown. How will you get to your auto?"

Jacob interjected quickly. He was becoming very weak and nauseous; the surprise visit and Cheswick's forceful entry into his bedroom had put him over the edge. "My cousin's driver is parked just around the corner at the local ale house. Beverly can make it there, right Bev?"

"Oh of course. You take care of yourself, Jacob," and she leaned over and kissed him on his forehead. "I will return in few days to check in on you. Goodbye Jacob, Ida, and to you Mr. Cheswick."

"No, I insist that I bring you to your auto. No gentlemen worth his salt would allow a fine lady to travel the back allies of this neighborhood unescorted." And he stood in the doorway of the bedroom and blocked her exit.

"Dudley," Jacob struggled with a weak and gurgling voice, "I must speak with you of some very important issues that I have just become aware off. Please remain here with me now while my thoughts are organized."

Cheswick's attention had been secured, but his suspicions had also been raised. He stood there frozen in indecision. He suspected this visiting woman was not Jacob's cousin, but perhaps Jacob was not at liberty to say who she really was, or maybe there was other information for him to separate and analyze. He stepped aside and let the woman pass.

"Good day, Miss Brown. I'm sure we will meet again." He turned to Jacob. "I think I'll get comfortable and hear what you have to say," and sat in the chair that Sarah had just been sitting in.

"Ida, could you prepare tea for Mr. Cheswick and myself? I will need it to continue any conversation." Jacob hoped he could maintain his consciousness long enough for Sarah to complete her escape. It was only a short walk to the restaurant where her brother waited.

Ida left the room to prepare tea and wondered if she had ever met a more revolting, twisted man in her life. Dudley Cheswick instilled fear in her as if he were the bearer of a lethal plague. Just being near him seemed deadly. The water had just come to boil when Cheswick called in from the bedroom.

"Miss Hill, you need to come in here, Jacob is quite ill."

She hurried into the room and saw Cheswick standing over him. Jacob seemed to be asleep.

"Of course, he is quite ill," she said tersely. "The poor man is on his deathbed. This is all very draining on him." She felt his forehead and turned his pillow for him. "He needs to rest. Perhaps you could return tomorrow, if that fits into your critical schedule."

"No need to be so rude, Miss Hill."

"It's Mrs. Hill. You barge into our home and torment a good man on his deathbed. All of your actions have been rude. I do not like you, Mr. Cheswick."

"Very well, I will return tomorrow morning to visit with Jacob."

"And what time should we expect you?" she said sarcastically.

"In the morning sometime; my schedule is critical, you know," and he tipped his cap and walked briskly and forcefully from the bedroom and out the front door, not bothering to close it on his way out.

* * *

Sarah hurried to the restaurant where her brother waited for her, but she also hurried away from evil; Dudley Cheswick was purely that, and she knew it instantly. She hurried into the restaurant to the table where her brother sat with his tea and rhubarb pie. He had a spot near the fireplace and was sitting comfortably reading the *Times*. He immediately knew that something had upset his sister.

"You look like you have seen a spirit, although that has become a common experience with you. What's wrong?"

"I believe I have just seen the Devil. His name is Dudley Cheswick and he visited with Jacob while I was there. But it was hardly a visit. Jacob had but a few seconds to tell me that he was dangerously malignant and that I should leave as quickly as possible. I had to pretend that I was his cousin. He walked about liked he owned the place. We need to leave here as quickly as possible and return to our hotel. Jacob will send word when it is okay to return." They hurriedly paid the bill and were soon traveling the back roads to their hotel.

Delilah

APRIL 1939

The next morning we walked downstairs to find the house empty. My mother, Claudia, Simon and Madame Alice were gone. My father and I were struck with sudden panic and we rushed from room to room looking for my mother. She was nowhere to be found.

"Maybe they went for a walk," I said.

He just shook his head. "No, I don't think your mother would be up for that."

We ran out the front door and saw that the car was gone. We stood in the front yard trying to make sense of it all. Fear had begun to cripple our thinking. Not having my mother in the house was suddenly terrifying. More agonizing than I could have ever imagined. My father and I had become her protector. How could we have allowed her to be removed from our home? She had been kidnapped right from under our watch. My father could only stand there, bewildered. He looked in every direction. "Where is your mother? Why do we have these rumblings and dark shadows that follow us around? Why do these strangers come to our home and torment your mother with their so called noble intentions? Why did that storm destroy my beautiful family? It is all so meaningless. Have we stumbled into a nightmare?"

"Oh Daddy, I am so frightened." I held T.J. tightly in my arms. My father's uncertainty was scaring us.

My father took T.J. from me in one arm and put the other around me. "Let's go back to the house," he said. We slowly walked back and sat in the living room. We tried to make sense of what had just happened. Where were my mother and Claudia? We became anxious for my mother and for ourselves.

"Your mother and Claudia are gone, but so are Madame Alice and Simon. I went to Madame Alice's room last night and told her of my mistrust and concerns. It doesn't take much to understand that she and Simon are connected to your mother and Claudia's departure."

Madame Alice
1939

"We must take Katherine away from this home as quickly as possible," Madame Alice told Simon and Claudia early the next morning. The sky had just the faintest light of an approaching day. They had gathered around one end of the kitchen table. Claudia had made fresh coffee and offered some English muffins that dripped with butter.

"What has brought this on?" Simon asked. "Where shall we go?"

"Katherine will be very unsettled by this sudden move," Claudia added.

Madame Alice got up from her seat and began to nervously pace around the kitchen. She stopped at the window above the sink basin and examined some of the sea shells that had been placed on the sill, then turned to Simon and Claudia.

"Last night Mr. Miller came to my room. He made it clear in his own way that he is very opposed to what we are trying to accomplish. He is very protective of his wife."

"No wonder you seem to be on edge," Simon said.

"That does not surprise me. I believe he has always been an obstacle to his wife's recovery," Claudia said. "I have let him know my feelings, but it hasn't stopped him from intervening."

"It was a little unsettling," said Madame Alice, "but there is too much opposition in this home for anything to move forward. I think we should go to where I was living when I met my husband. It's a small cottage in Portsmouth. Milton and I decided to keep the cottage after we were married and we rent it out during the summer months so there is no one there right now. We should have peace and quiet there, but we need to get Katherine away from this house and her family. I am convinced that there is a division within her family. There are those that have moved on and there are others, like her husband and daughter, who instinctively try to shield her from any perceived threat. They will always be there trying to shield her. If only they could understand that they are actually doing more harm than good.

"I also sense that Katherine's sister Margret has a strong spiritual presence here and is trying to move this all in the right direction. My inner spirit tells me that her presence is what this fragmented family truly needs. Somehow we need to support that."

They quickly packed the car with food, their suitcases, and additional bedding. With Simon at the wheel, they pulled out of the driveway just as the sun was cresting over the horizon. They boarded the first ferry off of Jamestown and made the trip north on Route 114 to Portsmouth. They settled into the cottage and spent the next few days trying to reach beyond to Katharine's loved ones, but no connection took place. They were warm and comfortable in the cozy little cottage. It was Madame Alice's theory that those who had moved on would try to reach back, break through the barrier, and offer some insight into Mrs. Miller's quandary. They were convinced that Katherine was the focal point and the she needed to be involved in all their efforts. They tried as a group. They tried with just Madame Alice and Katherine, or Simon and Katherine, but nothing happened.

This was all taking its toll on Mrs. Miller. Being away from her home was a strain on her, but now she had the added stress of trying to reach out to her loved ones in a different environment. She was in fragile state, and now these sessions with Madame Alice and Simon were pushing her closer to the edge. Claudia finally stepped in and demanded an end to all of these efforts.

Simon tried to protest. "We need to give this a few more days. I think we are close to something. Can you increase her medication?"

"How sedated do you want her? I thought you said medication would only complicate things. Which is it?" Claudia replied angrily. "She is already medicated too much. This sudden departure from her home and staying in this tiny cottage is just too much for her. This has to end. She needs and wants to go home."

"Simon, Claudia is right," Madame Alice offered. "We have done a disservice to this woman. In our passion to bring closure to her, we have almost abused her. She does not deserve this. We need to bring her back home."

"You're not giving up," pleaded Simon.

"We shall to do no such thing. I have no intention of abandoning this poor woman. I have only misjudged things. Mr. Miller's visit to my room several nights ago had convinced me that his opposition to us being there was the one real obstacle to helping his wife move on. Now I know that I was wrong. There are conflicting forces at play. There are, as you said Simon, two different dialects being used, and obviously no real communication is taking place. We need to return to Katherine's home. The real solution is there. I believe we are close to a resolution; we must return immediately."

Jacob
JUNE 1921

S everal hours later Jacob woke to find Ida sitting by his side, as he
often had these past few days. He looked at her familiar face with
its warm smile as he gathered his thoughts. After a while he spoke:
"Ida, you must help me with a task that might be very upsetting for
you." Jacob told her more about the tragedy of the *Titanic*, his
participation in it, and how it had haunted him his entire life. Powerful
men, from the very day the tragedy took place, had taken precautions
to hide their conspiring actions and had secured the services of a rat
of a man to guard and protect their evil deed. "Ida, I have despised
this man from the day I met him. He has threatened my life, my
family's lives, and has tormented so many other people. He has his
own pack of rats that does his bidding. I need to put an end to the
persecution he dispenses. If he finds out who Sarah is and why she is
here, she will simply disappear some day in the near future, that's

how it always happens. When someone gets too close or they begin to talk too much, they vanish, and the follow up police investigation never goes anywhere. Please, help me with this devil."

"He is a bastard of a human being and I despise the man," said Ida fervently. "What do you want to do with him?

"We must kill him, although 'we' is probably the wrong word. There is little I can do. This grim task must fall on your shoulders and it must be done when he returns tomorrow."

Ida's eyes dropped to the floor and wandered along its cracks; she suddenly became consumed with the fate of Dudley Cheswick and knew immediately that Jacob was right, but was surprised how easily she accepted her role. Ida had always been a caring and giving woman. She and her husband had raised three wonderful children. Two of them immigrated to America and the other had moved to Wales. Her husband of forty-seven years had passed away and she had cared for him until the end. Now she was caring for their old friend Jacob. Ida had an abundance of compassion for those that had filled up her life, but Dudley Cheswick was a snake, a low life, he made her skin crawl. He took pleasure in tormenting very good people's lives because some bigger, more venomous snakes had told him to do so. To Ida, it was like killing a rabid dog: it had to be done for the safety of all.

"Jacob, it's a deed that has to be done. I don't know how you have the strength for this."

"The fact is I do not. My time to meet my God is very close and I welcome it. This whole event will be my final act, and a noble one it will be. We must plan quickly, and again most of what we plan will be done by you. I hope I can be of some help. God bless you, Ida."

"It seems odd that we ask God's blessing on such an act, but I think he would indeed bless it. Tell me about your scheme."

Delilah

1939

The sudden departure of my mother and not knowing where she had gone was almost unbearable. Our home had suddenly become a morgue. Even with their limited activities, my mother and Claudia had filled the house with life.

We spent most of the next two days in our large front living room, nervously awaiting her return. My father would constantly pace around the room, often pausing in front of family canvases.

The high-ceilinged room, with its ornate crown molding, had become the home to many family portraits and photographs of previous generations of Millers and Parkers. The oldest portrait was of Colonel Hiram B. Miller, a respected officer in Washington's colonial army. Union officer Major Atherton G. Miller and his wife Priscilla hung prominently above the fireplace mantel. My great- great grandfather was

283

mortally wounded at the Battle of First Manassas. It was the very first engagement of the Civil War and the Miller family had already made the ultimate sacrifice. My father placed a great deal of value on patriotism, especially when a heavy price was laid upon the field of battle.

My father would continue his anxious pacing and then pause in front of a past relative for several minutes, pleading with his past lineage. "Please help her find her way home!" All of the faces with their collective likenesses stared back at my father but offered no response.

It was difficult to witness my father's incessant marching; it only seemed to slow down the passage of time. I began to measure the day not by the steady swing of the pendulum on our grandfather clock in the hallway, but instead by counting his laps around the living room and his conversations with past family members. I tried to pass the time by looking through a family photo album that my mother kept by her chair. I would try to engage him to look at the pictures with me.

"Daddy, this picture of Aunt Milly looks so much like Mother. You should have a look."

He would stop his pacing just long enough to glance at the picture and offer, "I suppose so," and then return to his wandering. The faces hanging on the walls seemed to cynically stare at me, as if telling me, "Don't try to distract him with your childlike interruptions. We have longed for his conversation."

The silence and desolation of our home made the vibrations and tremors that much more alarming. They would occur erratically, without warning, and became more intense. They were like small earthquakes, and though they had quickly become an anticipated event, the suddenness of them always gripped us with fear. I have heard stories of people in southern California becoming used to the numerous earth tremors they experienced, but I could not comprehend ever getting accustomed to and accepting of such violent shaking. We did discover that the tremors and objects being propelled about the room centered around me. They would occur if I was in room by myself or if my father was with me, but never with just my father by himself. It became chilling for me, and my father became very protective and would not leave my side. He slept the last two nights in the spare trundle bed in my room.

That afternoon, my father thought we should seek council with past relatives and decide what our next move should be. We once again sat in our expansive living room with all our departed kin looking down from their lofty locations. My father felt their presence might help our thought processes. I was not so sure.

"I think we should call the police. I believe Mother has been kidnapped, or at least taken against her will," I told him.

He did not think that was a good idea. "Your mother has been gone only a few days, and she left with her trusted friend. Claudia will make sure that your mother is safe at all times. I am sure of that. And I don't think Simon and Madame Alice are criminals. Do you?"

Ever since the day of the hurricane our need to protect and comfort my mother had been powerful. Something had driven us, especially my father, to be vigilant in that responsibility. I was not sure why; even with Claudia there to provide everything my mother could want, there seemed to be this unwritten pledge for us to honor. This had been the first and only chance to see if we could rise to the standards of our new code, and we had failed miserably. The whole house had packed their bags, including my mother's, and had simply left. Unbelievably, we had slept through the whole thing.

My father was disgusted with himself. I tried to comfort him by telling him that they would return shortly. "That's the only thing that comforts me now, and be sure I will be holding people accountable for their shameful and heartless actions," he said.

"But why would Mother leave without saying anything to us? She has never done such a thing."

"I do not know. Maybe she was not given that opportunity," was all my father could offer.

Suddenly the violent shaking began again. Windows rattled, end tables began to creep across the floor, objects placed on them were sent flying, and past Millers and Parkers began to quiver within their frames. There was also the sound of one or more people mumbling or humming, we could not be sure. Then the ghostly image of Aunt Meg floated in front of us. I screamed and ran to my father's side, hugging him in a death grip. Aunt Meg's image seemed to fade and then restored itself. She seemed to be motioning for us to come to her or to follow her. I was shaking with fear. My father was frightened, but quickly became angry.

"What is this, why do you plague us like this?" he demanded.

My aunt Meg seemed to be speaking to us, but there was only the same mumbling noise we had heard many times before. Then she was gone and so were the terrifying vibrations.

"Oh my God, Daddy, they have been telling the truth all this time! Why were we the last to see these eerie images? What does this mean? Why has Aunt Meg not moved on?"

"I have no explanations. This is very disturbing to me, too. I feel we may have misjudged Simon and Madame Alice. We need to be more supportive of them. I think they really want to help your mother and I suppose us, too. Their talk of trying to bring closure and peace to our family is very sincere."

"How will they do that," I asked?

"I don't know. But we must trust them."

Later that day my mother and Claudia returned to the house. Simon and Madame Alice were with them. We heard the car pull into the yard and we rushed to meet them in the driveway. We were so relieved to see my mother again. Claudia was helping her out of the car and up the walkway. She looked fine and her expression said she was happy to be home. She released herself from Claudia's guiding hand and quickly climbed the stairs and entered the front door with a smile that none of us had seen in such a long time. My father and I were just so relieved and happy to see her.

We followed my mother through the foyer and into the living room. Claudia soon had her settled in her chair and she began to look around the room as if searching for someone. Her smile disappeared and the familiar look of being lost and confused returned.

"Where is my family?" she asked Claudia. "Why aren't they here? Jeffrey, Delilah, Stephanie, the boys, and my sister Meg, where are they?" The stress of being away from her home had been too much. My mother was breaking down. My father and I were immediately at her side. She was now very confused, asking where her family was and we were right there with her. There was concern on everyone's face.

Jacob

JUNE 1921

Cheswick arrived at 7:00 a.m. the next morning. He hadn't slept much the night before and he was damned if Jacob and Ida were to enjoy a leisurely morning, although he was confident there had not been many restful nights in that house. Jacob was indeed a very sick man, and Dudley knew he had little time left. He once again pounded on their front door, a second ambush repeated.

Ida answered. She looked tired and worn out.

287

"I was hoping you would not come back. Jacob is so terribly sick; he does not need you torturing his last moments. You are despicable and vile."

"I will ignore your compliments. I assume Jacob is in his room?" He quickly moved passed her and into the bedroom, his heels pounding the floor as he went.

Jacob was startled by the hammering on his front door. He bolted awake. He saw Cheswick's blurry image as he entered his bedroom. Things were becoming dreamlike and reality was sometimes difficult to separate from hallucination.

"Is that you, Cheswick? Are you back so soon, or did you never leave?"

"It is me, Jacob. Let's just get things over with quickly. I checked your records. You do not have a cousin named Beverly Brown on your father's side. Or your mother's side, for that matter. So who is she and why is she here?"

"Dudley, I'm not sure I heard what you said. Allow me my morning tea, it perks me up and helps me organize my thoughts. I believe a cup of tea might help you, too. Ida, could you bring us both one?" He struggled with speaking.

"Perhaps some tea would help me," agreed Cheswick. "I was awake most of the night trying to see through your sham, and a sham it was. It is time for some honest conversation."

"I'm not sure you are worthy of it, I have had many visitors this day: my mother, my great uncle, and even my dear wife. And they all speak ill of you." His breath was slow and shallow and his speech was mumbled. "My thoughts are all mixed up and I am so tired."

Ida came into the room with tea for the both of them and handed a cup and saucer to Dudley. "It's the way you prefer it, cream and sugar. I don't know why Jacob feels he must speak with you. He owes you nothing."

Cheswick waved her away and sipped his tea. "Try to get some tea into Jacob," he said. "I need to finish our conversation."

Ida sat Jacob up and gently fed him some tea. He could barely swallow what was being offered him, but he slowly began to perk up and after awhile found his voice.

"Thank you, Ida." He winked at her and she winked back.

"Perhaps Jacob can speak with you now, although in his state I'm not sure what he can offer you. Do you want another cup of tea? It seems you have already finished your first."

"Bring me another tea, I will be the judge of what Jacob can share with me," he snapped. "Jacob, tell me now who this fictitious Beverly Brown really is."

Jacob slumped in his bed and his eyes wandered around the room until he found Cheswick. "Why, Beverly is my sister, you know that."

"Damn you Sweeney, yesterday she was your cousin." Ida returned with Dudley's tea and he took a long drink of it, clearly frustrated. "Miss Hill, you need to serve tea when it is hot, this is lukewarm and it is almost unfit, but it is what I need. My last night and this conversation with Sweeney is beginning to tire me."

"You tire me and you tire Jacob, you fool."

Dudley Cheswick stood quickly to deal with the insolence of this old woman. He reached for the stiletto in the vest pocket of his blazer; slitting the throat of this mouthy old bitch would be a pleasure.

But suddenly his vision was blurry. The old woman seemed to be floating everywhere, and then his legs lost all feeling and he fell to the floor. He stared up at the ceiling and then Jacob was over him with the mouthy old woman at his side. Jacob was pointing at him, shaking his finger, smiling and saying something about this being the end. His stomach began to contort in painful spasms and his eyes bulged from his head. It finally dawned on him: he'd been drugged and poisoned. Sleep and intense pain were battling for possession of his body. He reached out his hand for Jacob, but it floated lifeless in front of him. His lungs burned and he could no longer breathe. Jacob continued to smile at him and then Ida leaned over and spat in his face. Death came painfully and not quick enough for Dudley Cheswick, and no one cared or would ever care.

Ida had gotten Jacob back in bed; the effort to get him up and standing over Cheswick's dying body to spill his wrath had taken most of his energy. His speech had left him, but his eyes held onto what little, precarious life remained. He looked up at Ida and smiled; they had worked things out the night before, his pain medication and arsenic mixed with tea was the perfect combination and Dudley had unknowingly played perfectly into their scheme. Years of dealing with Dudley had prepared Jacob for the final deadly act in this play. He knew no one was aware of Cheswick's visit to his home; he would have sent his minions to do his dirty work. There was a good reason why Cheswick was here by himself—probably the fact that Jacob had slipped out of Belfast undetected. Such a lapse would have jeopardized Cheswick's job and credibility in his torture-for-hire line of work. Dudley Cheswick would suddenly go missing and there would be little to piece together. Jacob would be dead shortly, even if they ever did find their way back to him.

"Jacob, we have done it. This vile rat will never torture another person. I am amazed how happy this makes me, and I know it brings you peace."

Jacob slowly blinked his eyes, and then his beautiful bride was there with him and his two little girls, all bubbly to see their father again. Jacob was young again, so happy to have his family there. Then a soft light illuminated a path to a new world and he said goodbye to his old world.

"Oh Jacob, you did not deserve this fate," said Ida. "You were dragged into a deed that other greedy bastards perpetrated. God damn their souls! May you rest in peace, Jacob."

Ida immediately contacted Jacob's physician and the local funeral home. She pleaded with Dr. Peterson to hurry and he was there in about two hours, but there was nothing for him to do. Jacob was already dead. Dr. Peterson signed the death certificate and allowed Ida to proceed with whatever funeral or burial arrangements she wanted. Jacob had told him a while ago that he and Ida had worked out the logistics. The funeral home came and retrieved Jacob's body and quickly prepared it for the long journey back to Belfast. Ida had been to Bellow's Funeral Home several times before

Jacob's passing and had outlined his wishes. This time she asked them to expedite the process; she was anxious to begin their journey home. She asked that the casket be returned to their cottage that afternoon with its cover lightly secured; there were some personal items that she felt belonged by Jacob's side and that was a moment for only her and Jacob. She was quite capable of re-securing the coffin lid.

The funeral home was compensated quite well for their hurried efforts. The coffin and Jacob were returned just before three and she had them place it on the bedroom floor while she waited for the freight company to arrive. They too had been notified well in advance of the potentially sudden and hasty use of their services.

She gently pried open the cover and looked down at Jacob ever so briefly, then began her task. Ida reached under the bed and latched on to Dudley Cheswick's body and dragged it from its brief hiding place. Cheswick was a pitifully small man and moving him was difficult but not impossible. She struggled with his body but finally moved it into the coffin, next to Jacob. It was what Jacob had insisted on. He wanted to torment Dudley Cheswick through eternity. Already a slight man, Jacob had lost so much of his weight during his illness. No one would suspect a thing. Ida smiled at Jacob and thought he smiled back at her. She placed the cover back on the coffin and began to nail it in place. There was a gentle knock at the door.

Sarah

JUNE 1921

Sarah had not heard from Ida and was anxious to know how Jacob was doing so she returned the next day late in the afternoon. Ida greeted her at the door. She had been crying and she looked exhausted. Sarah immediately sensed something was terribly wrong.

"Sarah, I am so sorry, but Jacob passed away last night. I know you wanted more from him. He knew that more than anyone. He just had nothing left."

"Oh Ida, I am so sorry for you. I hope Jacob passed peacefully."

"I believe he did not. His condition worsened quite rapidly after you left. You did not know it, but he hadn't eaten anything these last two days. He would have a cup of tea every now and then. He would insist on his tea right before your visit. It was a struggle for him to keep it down. He did not want you to know. Jacob was afraid

292

you might conclude things if you knew how dire his condition was. He was in a lot of pain. I called his doctor immediately. By the time he arrived there was little to be done. He increased his medication to make him as comfortable as possible. He slipped in and out of consciousness. One moment he mumbled about being so sorry and the next he was cursing and lashing out. He did not deserve to die such a lonely and conflicted man. I stayed with him to the end. He passed away just after four o'clock this morning."

Sarah immediately hugged Ida. "Oh, I am so sorry for the night you must have had.

Jacob was right, if I had known how terrible his condition was, I would have indeed brought this to an end. Is there anything I can do? Can I help you with any of the funeral arrangements?"

"No, Sarah, but thank you. Jacob wanted no funeral. He wanted to be buried in a small cemetery close to where he grew up in Belfast. I will see to that."

"I have completely forgotten about that obnoxious man that came to see Jacob. I had to pretend to be some cousin from his father's side. What was that all about?"

"Oh, he was someone from Lloyd's of London, the insurance company connected with the shipyard. There was a serious matter regarding one of their vessels and the shipyard was seeking further payment in court. They were always pressuring Jacob for what he knew, especially since he retired. The fact that Jacob was close to death had little meaning to the fool that was here yesterday. Anyway, he never returned. I had some harsh words for him; maybe I chased him away."

"He didn't seem like a man that could be chased away very easily. Was he inquiring about the *Titanic*?"

"No, it was a completely different ship, I forget the name; but anyway, he's gone and should he return it will matter little, Jacob is at peace now."

They stared at each other for a few brief seconds, then it was time to leave and they both knew it would be awkward. They had both traveled together on a very emotional journey and were about to part, never to see each other again. "You are such a special woman,

Ida. I am sure you were of great comfort to Jacob these last few months. You were a good friend to him and to me. God Bless you. I will miss you."

Sarah's time with Jacob had been special, and she was saddened that she had lost her new friend. There was so much more she wanted to know. Jacob had not told her all of his tragic tale. She thanked Ida one last time and turned to leave.

Ida stopped her. "I have something for you. It is something Jacob wanted you to have." It was an envelope addressed to her. She took the envelope and looked at Ida.

"What is this?" she asked.

"I'm not sure. Jacob gave it to me several days ago and made me promise to give it to you should he pass away before the two of you completed your talks. He said you would want it."

Sarah thanked her again and left Jacob's cottage. She felt sad, but was intrigued by the letter she had just received.

Sarah walked down to the little restaurant where her brother waited when she visited with Jacob. He was once again seated near the open hearth with his rhubarb pie and tea.

Frederick was surprised by her early arrival. "Things are not good?" he asked.

"Jacob passed away early this morning," she said, and began to cry. "He did not deserve such a fate."

"No, he did not," her brother replied, hugging her.

"There was so much more he wanted to tell me. He wanted to cleanse his spirit. I wondered how much he actually purified his soul."

"I believe he did more than you realize. He was allowed that purging solely because of you, Sarah."

"I have a letter from Jacob. Ida gave it to me just now. I am afraid to open it."

"You know you must read it. You owe that to Jacob and to yourself. This restaurant is quiet now and we will have our privacy. Let's order some tea and some pie for you. I haven't yet finished my own slice."

"What if the letter is quite long? We could be here awhile."

"Then we shall order another slice of pie."
She opened the letter.

* * *

Dear Sarah,

I have prepared this letter for you because I know my time with you is growing short and I must write while my mind is still sharp and my thoughts are clear. I knew several days ago that we would never finish our tale. I am sorry for that. If you are reading this, then I have gone to meet my Maker. Only He can determine my fate now, but I know that I will face Him with a clearer conscious and I shall thank you for that. I am indebted to you for seeking the truth. You helped me with a burden that had almost destroyed me.

Forgive me, but I must move quickly through fact and conjecture. As you know, I have defined most of the fact and I have begun some of the speculation. Now the whole heartbreaking event begs for final clarity. I am the one man who can offer that lucidity. This is no longer a burden for me. In fact, it lifts my spirits with every word I write.

White Star Lines was on the brink of financial ruin. J.P. Morgan, J. Bruce Ismay, Lord Pirrie, and others wanted a way out. They switched the identities of the Olympic *and the* Titanic *and began their twisted scheme. But their ill-conceived plot tragically fell apart on them. I believe these are the events that occurred and led to that horrible disaster.*

The SS California *departed just a few days ahead of the* Titanic *(really the* Olympic*). Her role was to locate the iceberg that would serve their purpose. That was not a difficult task; shipping in that area had already identified and located these monsters. The* California *did that and remained at that location until* Titanic's *arrival. Captain Lord of the* California *had been directed to act on his own. As the* Titanic *approached, the* California *reached out by wireless and informed them of their exact position and the positions* *of various icebergs in the area, any one of which would have secured Titanic's demise. I believe that Captain Lord of the SS California and Captain Smith, along with first officer Lightoller, of the RMS Titanic were the only ones aware of the plans to scuttle the Titanic and put her at the bottom of the Atlantic Ocean.*

Captain Lord did his best to keep his end of the bargain. He secured his position close to the general vicinity of a number of huge icebergs and made Smith aware that he was in place through the guise of iceberg updates. Upon retiring for the night, Captain Lord left explicit instructions that his wireless operator send out constant iceberg warnings to the Titanic and other vessels in the area and that the California's boilers remain in a ready state.

Titanic's radio operators had been working at a feverish pitch the last two days of the voyage. Passengers wanted to share their journey with the world. Wireless messages by the hundreds were being sent to friends, family, business associates, and to the media as well. Titanic was also receiving hundreds of returning messages. She was in constant contact with the Cape Race station in Nova Scotia. The messages were being relayed from there.

Wireless operators from the Titanic had been working long into the night the two previous evenings. They were under a lot of pressure to process as many telegrams as possible. They were tired and their nerves were frazzled. Now the nearby California, with its persistent iceberg warnings, was complicating their efforts. Because it was so close, its transmission signal was interfering with that of the Titanic, almost overpowering them at times. They simply could not transmit with the California so nearby.

At 10:50 p.m. the Titanic's wireless operator lashed out at the California. "Shut up, shut up; we cannot transmit with your interfering signal." Annoyed by the Titanic, California's radio operator, Cyril Evans, shut down his wireless and retired for the evening. This simple act, born out of frustration, sealed Titanic's fate and foiled White Star Line's desperate and selfish plot. In less than one hour the Titanic struck an iceberg. Its desperate calls for help went unanswered by a ship that was only about eight miles away and could have easily rescued every living soul.

There were other smaller actions that contributed to the Titanic's demise. The fact that her navigation officer gave incorrect location coordinates did not help rescue efforts.

I was also troubled by the way the British inquiry was handled. Lord Pirrie was the presiding official. Think about that: in essence, White Star was both the plaintiff and the defendant. How could there ever be any justice? Witnesses were not allowed to be cross examined. Yet no one seemed to mind.

If you remember, Lord Pirrie also presided over the hearings surrounding the sinking of the Lusitania. *It was the same business relationship. He was a master of deception and manipulation. England and the United States had stubbornly maintained that the* Lusitania *was a passenger vessel on its normal, scheduled return trip to England. However, Germany had maintained that it was a true military target and their actions were justified. Germany had its spies in New York. Lord Pirrie's limited testimony and altered company documentation to get the outcome he desired. We would learn years later that the* Lusitania *was covertly loaded down with military wares.*

My dear Sarah, I will shortly die. But when I pass on I will be born again. I cannot say as much for J. Bruce Ismay. His remaining life will be a daily struggle. His greedy and selfish plot backfired on him and he deserves nothing less. He should have died with so many of those other brave souls, but he schemed and orchestrated his own escape. He is now referred to as "the Coward of the Titanic.*" The public has demanded that the colors of White Star Line be changed to liver yellow. He has brought shame to his name and his company. When he was recovered by the* Carpathia, *he insisted that he be brought directly to the ship's doctor's office. From there he issued his famous telegram to the world: "Deeply regret advise you, Titanic sank this morning after collision with iceberg, resulting in serious loss of life. Full particulars later."*

The fact that he did not have the courage to go to the radio room on his own illustrates the shallowness of the man. His whole life has been a series of cowardly acts. I will not say that they were easy decisions that had to be made, but he always made them from a distance and always had someone else do his dirty work. That someone was often me. This was the one time in his whole life where he really needed to show his mettle, and he failed miserably. He should have done his best to begin the healing process by being White Star Line's spokesman for the global mourning that was to come. In fact, the very minute he settled into the ship's doctor's quarters on the Carpathia *he began to heavily opiate himself, and remained in that cabin for the rest of the trip to New York. It was rumored that he was again deeply medicated for both the American and British maritime hearings.*

I was relieved to witness his resignation as president of International Mercantile Marine and chairman of White Star Lines. He has finally begun to pay a price for his inhumanity.

I have made my peace and will be judged accordingly. When Ismay's day of reckoning comes and he meets his Lord, I am convinced he will not be warmly received.

And now, finally, to the one question that was never asked at the inquiries and that has plagued me all these years.

On a clear, calm night, with lookouts posted and numerous warnings about icebergs and their specific locations already provided for safe navigation, how could they not see an object that was over one and a half times the size of the Titanic *herself? I will take that and so many other questions to my grave.*

Do what you want with this information. You vowed that you would take it to your grave as well. I will not hold you to that oath, but I also know your own integrity will not allow you otherwise. God bless you, Sarah. Go back to your Milton, be happy, and be at peace with yourself. You deserve that and much more.

Sarah was crying. Jacobs's letter finally confirmed what she had suspected. This tragedy had destroyed her marriage, had drowned so many people, and had consumed her with its dark side. Now she held Jacob's letter in her hand, yet it did not create the sense of peace that she thought it would. The letter immediately became a burden she no longer wanted. Sarah instinctively knew she should flee from any remnants of this tragedy. They still carried emotional pain with them. The *Titanic* was still searching for victims. Sarah rose from her chair, walked directly to the open hearth, and dropped the letter into the flames. Its pages were engulfed in seconds. She turned to her brother and smiled.

"Let's go home."

Madame Alice, Delilah, Simon

DECEMBER 1939

My father was again furious with Claudia and the people she had brought into our lives. He began to yell at Claudia and these other unwanted guests. He told her she had no right to bring such people into our home, she never asked permission nor sought any guidance from him. He was angry and very disappointed in her treatment of Mother.

"Claudia, you, of all people, were the one we trusted so completely. You have been a trusted and loyal member of our family for many years, but this last year your actions have been quite cruel and selfish. You have pushed me into a position I do not enjoy. I am not sure what we will do, but for now your friends must go. Madame Alice and Simon, I am telling you to leave my home immediately."

Madame seemed startled by my father's outburst and turned to face his verbal assault. When he was finished voicing his displeasure, Madame Alice took a step towards him and was about to reply when the vibrations began and the living room exploded with bizarre, uncontrolled energy. Portraits once again swung wildly on the wall and paintings crashed to the floor. Books and keepsakes became projectiles that flew across the room only to smash into opposite walls. Some objects from the mantel shattered the same windows that had been blown out from the hurricane just over a year ago. Then the rampaging airborne objects abruptly fell to the floor and the room was silent. Shadows of eerie human forms suddenly appeared on the wall opposite the broad living room windows with the same twisting movement as before. They quickly transformed into blurry, floating, ghostly images of Aunt Margret, my sister, and little Corey. They then began to take shape, becoming more defined. We recognized the clothes they wore, their expressions, the color of the eyes; and the weight of the burden they carried was clearly visible. For the first time they seemed to be of our world and no longer restricted by laws and limitations of another universe.

My mother again was the first to become aware of their presence. "My little ones are back again!" she exclaimed. "Has your aunt taken good care of you? I miss you all so very much, my darlings, and I love you all. I want you all back in my life. We were such a happy family. I curse that horrible day you were taken from me."

I was at my mother's side. Aunt Meg floated towards her and spoke. "We are all at peace, but you keep calling us back. It is not easy for us to come back. Our worlds are different now. But I did promise you that I would always be there for you. It's time for you to come with us, time for you to come home."

We were all speechless. Could this really be happening? My mother seemed to go numb. She turned to Claudia with a look of bewilderment. Claudia was speechless.

Madame Alice spoke. "Katherine, this is such a special moment. You are so fortunate. We are all very privileged to experience something like this."

My mother interrupted. She was in tears. "How can I go with you? There is only one way for me to go with you. Do you really want me to do that?" We were all so emotionally torn by her words.

Aunt Meg replied, "We are not here for you Katherine. Your time will come."

I loved my Aunt Meg so very much, but what was she saying? She wasn't making sense. I could not control myself any longer.

"Who are you here for then?" I demanded.

"We are here for you, Delilah, and for T.J. and Jeffrey."

"Are they here also?" My mother searched the room as if she did not see us there, and then her eyes found us again. "Oh my God! Jeffery, Delilah, and my precious Thomas James, you are here too! I have been heartsick over never knowing where you were."

"What are you talking about? We have always been here!" my father shouted.

Aunt Meg stepped in. "No, you have not. Not in the way you think. You need to let go, Jeffery, and when you do it will allow Delilah and T.J. to let go, too."

"Let go? Let go of what?" my father demanded.

"Daddy, I don't understand," I said. "Aunt Meg, please, explain all of this to me."

"Delilah, I have been trying to reach out to you for so long. Have you not sensed this since the day of that terrible storm?"

"Aunt Meg, you are just confusing me more!" I was becoming very anxious.

"Delilah, you are not among the living. You perished the day of the storm. We all died that day, the whole family, everyone except Katherine."

I was suddenly nauseous and I could say nothing. I stared at Aunt Meg in disbelief.

"You are insane!" my father challenged. "Why have you come back to torture all of those that loved you and who have missed you so much?"

Finally, my mother spoke. "My family is all together again. I have dreamed of this so many times. Am I in a dream now?" And then Madame Alice said, "Katherine, this is not a dream. We are at

302

some bizarre but very special crossroad. I am beginning to make sense of it. Two, maybe three worlds are converging. You lost all of your family the day of the hurricane. Some of your family moved on and some did not."

I turned to my father. "Please, help me understand what she's saying!" I was beginning to feel weak and was having trouble breathing.

My father turned to Madame Alice. "You are an evil woman! Why do you speak of such bizarre things? Only Meg, Stephanie, and Corey were taken from us that terrible day. Delilah and I have never left my wife's side. We have always been there for her!"

"I know you have," Madame Alice replied. "I have sensed your presence from the moment I arrived. Claudia has also felt your presence." Claudia nodded her agreement. "But you have not accepted your own death and you have not allowed Delilah and T.J. to accept their deaths either. You need to understand what happened that dreadful day in September. Your wife agonizingly watched as Margret, Stephanie, and Corey were snuffed out by that wall of water. You, too, drowned in that same wall of water, but your deaths were not witnessed by Katherine and your bodies were never found. Your wife laid to rest the only family she could. That fragment of uncertainty was enough for you, Delilah, and T.J. to remain in your mother's life, though not in the reality that you perceived. Your own individual loyalty and your desire to protect your wife prevented you all from moving on."

Confusion and fear had now consumed my father. "Oh my beautiful Katherine, I do not want to leave you," he cried. Some force was pulling us away from my mother. I could sense Aunt Meg and the special bond that only she and I used to have. Aunt Meg moved towards me. "Delilah," she said, "you have been reaching out to me all along."

Suddenly I realized that Aunt Meg was always right there in the middle of my thoughts. I was always missing her and wanting her back.

"You have come back for me, Aunt Meg! You promised that you would find me and always be there for me no matter where I was, and now you have found me! I did not know that I was lost, but I know that now."

Everything was rapidly falling into place; all the interactions that had occurred between myself and my mother and Claudia had never really happened, or certainly had not happened in the way I had perceived. They had only been one-sided, desperate attempts by my father and I to reach out to my mother. We could only be grateful that Claudia, Simon, and Madame Alice had the ability to sense our presence and had not panicked with our outbursts. I knew instantly that all the empty stares and frightened looks that we had received were only just that. There was no real mutual recognition in them.

I now shared the loss that my father was experiencing. I desperately wanted to hold my mother. Things were changing rapidly. All my senses were being turned off. The light in the room was painful to my eyes. My father and T.J. and I were having difficulty moving. We reached out for my mother.

"This is as it should be," my mother said. "Go, my loved ones; you will always be in my heart. It is time to go. Take them home, Margret. Bring them comfort, and this will bring peace to all of us. We will all be together in a very short time."

Aunt Meg smiled and opened her arms in a loving gesture. There was instant peace and serenity for me and my father, and then we were floating away on a soft and gentle breeze.

There was an instant calming silence to the room. After a brief few seconds Madame Alice spoke. "They are gone, they are all gone. They are all at peace now. This I am certain of."

EPILOGUE

Prudence Island

OCTOBER 1941

It was early fall and the red maples and white oaks that were settled
to either side of Sarah and Milton's diminutive sea side inn were
displaying their celebrant colors of another completed New
England summer and marking their preparation for the difficult
days of winter that lie ahead.

Sarah walked out on to the inn's roomy veranda, it offered
familiar and soothing views of the bay's east passage. A solitary
freighter with its tatty white hull, chugged it's way north towards
Providence. Long fading shadows were all that remained of a
splendid autumn day.

She searched the yard below for Milton and as expected
found him just entering his large shed, it served as his work shop and
storage area. She shouted down to him.

"Milton, you have fussed enough with that shed's roof for
today, it will still be there tomorrow. It's well after six o'clock, come
in to supper, don't know how can you work with so little light."

Sarah was just so much more appreciative of the simple life
she had on Prudence. Chasing Milton in to dinner was her biggest
challenge and it was all very calming, besides Milton needed to be

305

pestered. She had always said he was like a butterfly in a stiff breeze, too easily distracted.

She shuffled back into the inn's living room and settled into her rocker. She would wait for Milton to make his way up for dinner. Her thoughts began to reflect backwards in time, almost two years ago her old friend Simon had re-entered her life and had drawn her off to a tragic household in Jamestown where Katherine Miller struggled daily to maintain her sanity. Her loyal servant Claudia had stood by her side the whole while. Sarah wondered how Katherine had persevered through all the madness, but she had.

Her complete family had been killed in an almost biblical catastrophe and those spirits that sought only to protect and sooth her had remained in her life, only confusing and jeopardizing Katherine's own healing process.

She, Simon and Claudia had finally brought resolution and peace back into Katherine's life, yet daily she questioned how that was ever accomplished. It had been a terrifying ordeal for all of them. In the end Sarah believed it was her gift and her strong conviction in it that allowed the spirits of Katherine's family to finally reconnect. It was why her clients called her Madame Alice.

She heard from Simon several weeks ago. He had become quite dependable with his correspondences. He had returned to Philadelphia and was trying to move forward with his life. The whole experience in Jamestown had shown him how fragile and terribly brief life is. He had met another woman and they were beginning to see a lot of each other.

He wrote Sarah; "I'm not sure I will love her as I did Olivia, but she has filled a great void for me. Deeply inside of me, I know it is what Olivia would have wanted for me, I truly believe that."

Simon also said that he had kept in touch with Claudia. Katherine put the home on Jamestown up for sale and they too had returned to Philadelphia to be near her father. The stroke that had paralyzed his wife had finally taken her from him. They would need each other.

The house had still not sold, apparently there was too much tragedy and sorrow attached to the home. It intimidated potential buyers. Katherine understood the quandary. She had told Claudia, "There are no longer any ghosts or lost spirits there, only invisible shadows of lives once lived there. In time a family will buy the home and they will love it as we once did."

Just today Sarah had received two letters, one from Simon and a long anticipated one from Katherine Miller. Sarah senses were heightened by the arrival of the two letters that Milton had placed on the end table next to her rocker. She quickly opened Katherine's and began to read;

My dear Madame Alice,

This letter is long overdue. My apologies for its tardiness. I will forever be indebted to you for bringing me back from the world of madness that I lived in. For reasons, I will never fathom my husband, children and sister were all taken from me by an act of God, as they call it. What rational god would ever align himself with such an appalling event; the horrific irony of it all.

I was slowly drowning in a sea of tremendous grief and despair and was completely unknowing. I never thought I would be sane again. I began to think this was all normal and that everyone lived like this. I now know you understood where I was. I did not.

I have returned to Philadelphia to live with my father. I know Claudia told Simon of my mother's passing. Perhaps he told you. My father needs me, actually we need each other.

Simon also shared with us your tragic past and your dreadful connection with the Titanic. You too have had your own burden to carry. I can only imagine the pain you must have endured. Only a fortunate few people go through life without going through hell first, maybe their hell comes after death. I wonder if any of us really escape it.

I was told, however you did find peace later in life, your Milton and your peaceful little island have made you whole again. Stay there, never venture away from those things that bring you peace and happiness. You and I know how great that risk is now.

I will struggle daily with my own loss, but it is a struggle that I know I can endure because of the closure and comfort you offered me. I will always be your servant. God bless you and may he hold you in his arms.

Sincerely
Katherine Miller

Sarah gently returned the letter to the end table, she sighed deeply; people tell her that her gift is special, maybe so. But Sarah was far more impressed with this woman's ability to survive in such a lonely and empty world. Katherine's letter for now had consumed her. Simon's letter would have to wait for another time.

This was the second heart-rending letter Sarah had received in her life time, the first nearly twenty years ago. This one she would not burn.

SPECIAL THANKS

Evan Dardano –editor

Johan Bjurman – art work

Alanna Mehrtens – graphic design

ABOUT THE AUTHOR

Born in Providence, Rhode Island, and a lifelong summer resident of Prudence Island, K.W. Garlick is the beneficiary of a rich and varied professional background, from marine tradesman to educator to commercial contractor.

Ken has finally realized his enduring passion for writing and has published his first book, with his second novel, *George's Hurricanes* due out next year.

He, his wife, and two sons currently live in Massachusetts.

Made in the USA
Middletown, DE
20 January 2017